DRAGONS, MONSTERS,
- AND -
IMAGINARY FRIENDS

Other Titles by
CLIFTON SAVOY

Shades of Color
Baseball, Blue Jeans, Struggling Moms . . .
I Was Blind, But Now I See
Fred & Sally

DRAGONS, MONSTERS, - AND - IMAGINARY FRIENDS

CLIFTON SAVOY

Campfire Press

TALLAHASSEE, FLORIDA

This literary creation was published by:
Campfire Press,
Tallahassee, Florida
CliftonSavoy.com

Acknowledgements:
Unequaled gratitude is extended to the Lord for giving Clifton the endurance, wisdom, creative thoughts, and connections to complete the project. On the human side, much appreciation is extended to Dr. Bruce Bickley, Professor Emeritus of Florida State University, and well known for his professional editing, consulting, and his books on Joel Chandler Harris and others. Professor Bickley inspired Clifton to polish and complete this story. There are numerous others, but the patience and encouragement of my wife, Judith, was monumental. Lastly, thanks to the characters of *Dragons...* for sharing a bit of their lives with me and now you.

Mr. Charles Butler, of Leeds, United Kingdom, sketched the marvelous ink sketches throughout this book: charlesebutler66@yahoo.co.uk

Campfire Press logo by Dr. Paul Reed of Guymon

Book cover and interior design were done by the professional talents of:
The Book Cover Whisperer | OpenBookDesign.biz

978-1-7376498-3-0 Paperback
978-1-7376498-5-4 Hardcover
978-1-7376498-4-7 eBook

FIRST EDITION

In Memory of

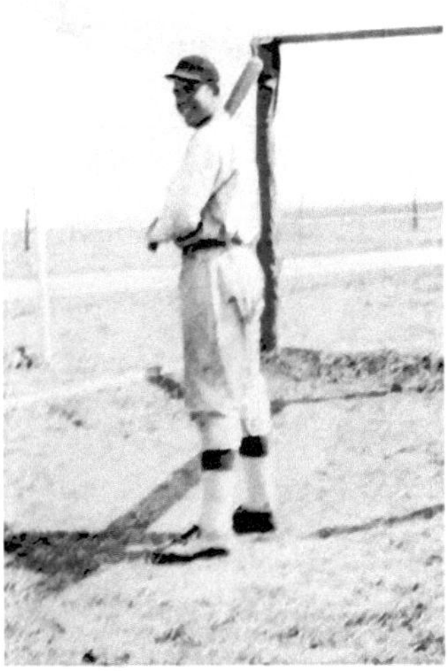

Fred W. Savoy

1935

CONTENTS

FOREWORD

DRAGONS… IS A WORK OF FICTION AND ADVENTURE. It's underdog Peter Marshall's southern *Field of Dreams* with hilarious antics like in *The Bad News Bears*, magical moments as in *Angels in the Outfield*, and heart-tugging, puppy in the rain scenes like in *Blind Side*.

The author, Clifton Savoy, had three sons who played baseball. During their youth league play over a period of seven years, Clifton witnessed the interactions among players and coaches on the field and among adults and youngsters on and off the field. Clifton's experience began as a baseball-ignorant parent, but who was enthusiastically supportive of his sons. Soon, he was recruited by his oldest son's coach to be the team statistician and the same for the league all-star team. Over the years, he served as assistant and head coach, game announcer, and statistician for the league, and five years as President of the Myers Park league. After announcing over sixteen thousand pitches in one season and seeing how play of young boys and girls was influenced by home life and adult agendas, Savoy was convinced this story must be written for every underdog and determined achiever in life. The awesome encounters with nature and wildlife which ventured onto the field at different times make the overall story truly unique.

Learn more on Clifton's author website:
CliftonSavoy.com

[CHAPTER 1]

*Peter Plays with Imaginary Friends in the
Historic Woods; Battles Dragons and
Monsters, and Dreams of Base Hits*

Dragons and monsters roamed the historic woods of Tallahassee, and young, floppy-haired Peter Marshall and his imaginary friends often battled them. His passionate dream, though, was to be a ball player and get base hits. But youth teams and coaches avoided him because his throwing, catching, and hitting skills were pitiful. In his words, "A girl was even better!" There was no one to help. His dad was killed when Peter was a toddler, his mom was exhausted trying to keep from losing their house and provide for the family, and two older sisters had no experience or interest. Peter was alone as he chased his dream, but he had his dogged determination and imaginary friends, as if they could help, battle other dragons and monsters.

"Maaauumm," Peter yelled as he pulled his tennis shoes on and hurried toward the back door. His voice faded as he stepped outside. "Finished my jobs. Going to the ball field if okay."

"Hold on!" Vicki called out quickly, "Not to-daaaaay."

"But Mom," Peter whined and stopped in his tracks. "Baseball tryouts are over Christmas break. Remember? Maybe someone's there who'll know what day." He paused to see if she responded. Didn't hear one so he added, "I'll be back in a jiffy."

Mom appeared in the kitchen doorway with an apron around her slim waist. She wiped her brow, grimaced and said reluctantly, "Well, okay, but be back by noon. We're going Christmas shopping this afternoon, and I signed us up to ring the kettle bell this evening. You and I will be at one door of the department store and, your sisters, Beth and Jane, at the other."

She barely finished speaking and Peter was down the steps. By the time she glanced out the kitchen window, he was already pedaling fast down the street. *Hope his heart isn't broken again. ... He's dreamed about being on a baseball team and getting base hits for a long time.*

Peter took a shortcut trail through the woods to the Myers Park ball field, tennis courts, and playgrounds. During his young years, he came to know many imaginary friends. "Can't catch me!" he yelled as they chased him up and down the rolling hills, over a bridge, and across the stream. He made believe *they're about to get me. I'll jump the stream to escape!*

Only a few playmates lived close by, so Peter developed a great imagination. Also, family financial difficulties reduced the opportunities to go where playmates might be.

He competed with imaginary friends in outdoor games. They rode through the hills and woods together. They challenged each other to see who could bike through the woods the fastest. He matched skills with them in just about everything he did. One delight was jumping contests across the streams. Of course, his mom scolded him, "How do you get so wet and muddy?"

Peter and his imaginary friends dug worms and fished at nearby ponds. They jumped with excitement when "crackers" snapped the bobber below the water surface. He brought the largest fish home for a family meal. He spoke of his friends often.

As Peter grew older, he spent more time on the basketball courts playing against his imaginary friends in one-on-one competition. He counted down from ten, dribble to the left then right, and launch the ball just before the imaginary buzzer sounded. An imaginary crowd roared when the ball swished through the net. Peter would jump, and triumphantly raise both arms in the air like  he saw players do sometimes on TV. He loved being a hero.

Sometimes Peter and his imaginary friends joined forces, and battle the pretend monsters and dragons who roamed the historic Tallahassee woods.

Peter's dream, though, was about playing baseball like his dad. His mom told him stories of how good his dad was. Young Peter would give anything to be on a team and get base hits. He watched so many practices and games that he knew most of the rules. He imagined catching fly balls, throwing out runners, pitching and striking out batters, and hitting a winning home run.

Today, in his mind and journey, Peter would take one step closer to this dream. As he approached the ball field, he heard players yelling, "Hey, batter. Hey, batter. Swing the bat."

Other players in a dugout beside the field yelled, "Pitcher has a rubber arm. Pitcher has a rubber arm."

Peter breathed heavily as he stopped under an old majestic live oak tree just outside the corner of right field. "Hi Big Fella. Save a place for me?" This was his special refuge from his imaginary foes. Big Fella's low branches with lots of Spanish moss hanging down and massive roots made an ideal play area for Peter and his imaginary friends. The tree was so large that some of its branches extended high over the fence and part of right field.

"Strike three!" the umpire yelled.

Players ran on the field, and began throwing to each other. One caught Peter's eye. He couldn't believe what he saw. "It's a girl!" he grumbled. "A GIRL," he said loudly in disbelief, "gets to play and not me?" He grumbled again. "That's not fair."

Peter briefly thought back to a year ago when a coach answered his question about playing, "Son, you have to be eleven before you can play." Soon afterwards, Peter recognized a couple of players on a team who were younger than he was. *They're from my school, and in a lower class. They're younger than me, so how did they get on a team?*

He didn't know the reason was because the coach had been told about Peter's poor playing skills. Some boys who knew Peter at school told the coach, "Peter's really clumsy when hitting, throwing, and catching a ball. At school, he's usually chosen near the last for a team."

Peter's face flushed red in anger as he remembered school playground recreation, *standing in a group as it got smaller and smaller in size, waiting to be chosen to be on a team.* Often he would give up, and go play with others who had also been "pushed aside."

Unknown to Peter, a school counselor had discussed the problem with his mother, Vicki. "Peter's behind the playing skill level of most boys his age, even a few girls," the counselor said. "What he needed was someone to help him develop physical skills like playing ball."

His mom sadly confessed, "I know little about baseball. Peter's two sisters are thirteen and fifteen, and time's a luxury I don't have. I am a single mom, widow, three kids, and few resources." She paused for a moment before responding further in a sad confessional tone, "I've avoided sports and especially baseball since we lost my husband in that car wreck."

"Well, not today!" Peter exclaimed as he leaned his bike against Big Fella. "I'm old enough now to play! And I'm going to get on a team," he said with determination.

The teams on the ball field were from the previous season, and they were in a practice game against each other. One of the coaches soon blew a whistle and yelled, "Everybody bring it in." The players ran to the coach of their team. Some skipped, giggled, hollered, and pushed each other along the way to be there first.

Peter watched the action intensely and tried to hear what the coach was saying. Suddenly, a deep voice from behind startled him, "Better run over there and listen up."

Peter looked around the tree and area to see who was nearby. *Who's that?* He didn't see anyone. Quickly, his mind was back to what the coach was saying, and he moved along the fence to a place where he could hear.

Big Fella's real name was Clarence. He chuckled and gently shook his branches as he watched Peter. *Humans are so strange, but funny sometimes. Wonder what my grandpappy'd think?*

Youngsters swinging a stick at a little ball? Running around a field? Throwing that ball?

The coach told the young players, "Tryouts and drafts will be Saturday after Christmas. It will start at 9:00 in the morning. Come and check out the new players on our team."

Peter was thrilled. *I'll be here.* Christmas was in a couple of days, but he was more excited about the tryouts. *Finally! I will be on a team!*

His good feelings were temporarily deflated, though, with the next comment by the coach, "If you know of any good nine and ten year old players, bring them to see me. We can sign them without going through the tryouts. Now go and have a good Christmas."

"I wasn't told the truth! Why?"

A huge dose of truth hit Peter about the adult statement he heard several times the previous two years. "A player had to be eleven before getting on a team." *I wasn't told the truth*, Peter agonized. *Why would those adults do that?*

Peter, like many youngsters, was resilient, and the question didn't linger long in his mind. He now had the information he came to get. *Need to get home. Mom will be ready to go.* He trotted to his bike and rode away. He never gave a second thought to the voice he heard earlier. His mind was on his dream: *At last, I will be on a team. I will be here early and ready. I can hardly wait. I will be on a team, and get base hits!*

At that moment, Clarence whispered to Peter, "Hope you have a good Christmas."

This time, the voice sound, if Peter even heard it, would have blended in with other sounds of a forest—branches and leaves moving in the breeze.

Hmmmmm, what's up with that boy? Clarence wondered. *Peter usually says "See ya, Big Fella," when he leaves. Didn't today. Oh, well,* he sighed deeply, *probably excited about finally getting on a team.*

Fortunately, Peter didn't hear the last comments of the players to the coach. "That's the one we told you about," they said as they pointed towards Peter pedaling out of sight. "Don't draft him. He is clumsy and not very good." ... Peter now faced one of the dragons of life.

"Why those little..." Clarence bellowed angrily. "Humans of all ages also are downright mean and cruel sometimes!"

CHAPTER 2

Their Plan to Help Peter

"What is the matter, Big Fella?" Charley hooted curiously as he and Caroline glided towards Clarence. He hooted again as they spread their wings to land, "Heard you a couple blocks away."

They settled softly on their favorite branch of Clarence's, fluffed their feathers, and gazed arountd. "Thought we'd stop for a while for a snooze 'fore we went to hunt this evening."

Charley and Caroline were owls who lived in the dense woods near a small water stream of the nearby golf course. They were long-time friends of Clarence, and often came to visit.

"Yes, deaah Cla'ence," Caroline added softly. She shuffled around a bit, fluttered her big brown eyes, and kept a focus on the surrounding area to spie any yummy morsel.

Her southern drawl came from some cousins who lived in an old shade-tobacco barn, located just across the state line in South Georgia. Hurricane Kate had blown her North and Charley finally found her after several months searching. She noticed the Georgia cousins said her name with distinct emphasis on the first and last parts, "Caro-line," and her sweety as, "Cha'lee"

(Chaw'lee). She liked the sounds and, from that time on, talked like them, too.

Clarence shared with them how badly Peter wanted to play on a baseball team. "He was so excited he didn't even say, 'See ya, Big Fella' like always when he left."

"That splains it," Charley hooted.

"Splains wat, Cha'lee?" Caroline inquired, but before he replied, her head began to nod. "Time for ma afa'noon beauty nap," she mumbled.

Charley responded quickly, "Why Peter didn't holler when we sailed over him, Dear." *Too late*, he observed. *One of her eyes is shut and the other has a glazed look.*

Charley continued as if she was listening, "It was here that we came to know Peter. Remember how he'd see us perched in Big Fella and greet us with, 'Hi, Mr. Owl,' and 'Hi, Mrs. Owl,' as he played games?"

Clarence cleared his voice with a rumble, "Is that why you call me Big Fella?"

"You got it," Charley paused and then added teasingly with a ya-found-me-out grin, "Big Fella." He paused again and then added, "It's because Peter calls you that."

Clarence coughed, but before he spoke, Charley thought, *Better change the subject.* "What are we going to do about it?"

"Do what?" Clarence asked, still thinking how he came to be called Big Fella.

"Peter," Charley hooted with a curious, but impatient look in his eyes. "Who've we been talking about?" Before Clarence responded, Charley pointed a wing towards the creek below. He'd caught sight of Maggie, the grey fox who also lived in the golf course woods.

Maggie crept through the brush almost unseen. She'd eventually work her way up the hill and hide behind one of Clarence's massive roots. They protruded partially above ground ten-fifteen feet away from his trunk.

"Hello, Maggie," Charley hooted to her, "What brings you here this early in the day?"

Clarence butted in with a tease to their four-legged friend, "Maggie has a weakness." He paused to let the suspense build but didn't have the patience to wait. "She has a fondness for human food and snacks," he chuckled. "She knows some human will drop a hotdog or hamburger. Her keen smell helps her find them when the humans leave. Right, Maggie?"

The jabbering startled Caroline, and her eyes popped so wide open they seemed double size. "I d'clah," she hooted softly and stretched her wings. "Doncha knoze a zleppin gal when ya see one?" Then she eyed Maggie and said with a big yawn, "Hellooo, Maggeee deaah."

Maggie returned Caroline's greeting, "Howdy, Caroline." Then she confessed that she did like human food. "But I hafta be careful. Dogs around and many aren't on leashes." Then the look on her face changed. Her lips parted to show her teeth, and she teased Clarence in return. "My buddy, Big Fella, usually lets me know when it's safe to come around."

Charley recognized it was "tease Clarence time," and he hooted, "Yeah, Big Fella's roots are really giant worms that are trying to crawl back into the ground."

"Wo'ms?" Caroline popped her eyes open again and asked, "Time to eat, Cha'lee?"

Maggie howled inwardly with laughter, "Big Fella could pull his roots out of the ground and walk around the park when no one's there to see."

"Yeah, and I'd chase you," Clarence bellowed. "Enough already with the jokes. What're we going to do about Peter?"

"Something happen to Peter?"

"What's wrong with Peter?" Maggie howled.

"Not again!" Clarence exclaimed as he sighed deeply, "Not saying this again so listen up," he stated with a threatening tone. Then he told them about Peter's great desire to be on a baseball team and what happened earlier that day. "And Peter didn't say 'See ya, Big Fella' like always before."

Charley added, "And he didn't call out to Caroline and me like he always does when he sees us fly over him or perched somewhere."

Maggie sat her behind down on the ground, frowned inwardly and asked to make sure she understood correctly, "And Peter doesn't know what those boys said about him to their coach?"

"Nope, nodda word," Clarence replied in an angry tone.

"Whada we doing about it?" Maggie asked as a puzzled look appeared on her face. She cocked her head slightly and then asked the real question, "Can we do anything about it?"

"Dono," Clarence answered. "Mind's blank. Let's give it some thought for a while."

The four friends no sooner paused to think, when suddenly Charley's head shot up and his eyes popped wide open. He squawked trying to speak, jumped down to a lower branch, and finally hooted excitedly, "Big Fella, ... er ... uh ... Clarence. You're the oldest living thing near the ball field." He paused for a moment and asked for a confirmation, "Right?"

"Well, yeah in these woods, but there's an older Live Oak tree over the hill in the Cascades area. It's by the Meridian benchmark that's the starting point for all property surveys in Florida. He's lonely, because humans pay attention mostly to the marker and ignore him."

Charley continued, "And you were here before this ball field was built. Right?"

"Yes, I was a seedling in the stable fence of Territorial Governor William Duval in the 1820s." Clarence answered as he reflected back to that time. *Lucky those mules didn't eat me. So many things and changes have taken place around these parts. And...*

Maggie noticed Clarence seemed stuck somewhere back in time. "Earth to Clarence! Earth to Clarence!" she howled to jog him out of his trance and back into the present.

"Oh, sorry," Clarence confessed. "Lost in time for a moment. Interesting days."

"Yeah, we know," Charley hooted impatiently, referring to the "lost" part.

Clarence asked, "What you getting to with these questions?" *Getting impatient myself.*

"Fair enough," Charley eagerly replied. "Any of those players have problems like Peter and were you able to help any of them? … If yes, how?"

Clarence thought and thought, and soon moved his branches excitedly. "Well, I remember one player. I was friends with some owls and a fox. … Probably your ancestors. We did help a youngster. … Might work with Peter because it seemed he heard my voice today. Tryouts are this Saturday and we will know soon if we can help. Let us keep our branches … er … uh … wings and paws crossed."

[CHAPTER 3]

*Youth League Baseball Tryout Day and Peter's
Lucky Jersey; Peter Throws with a Girl -
Importance of Discipline; Peter
Heard Clarence's Voice*

"Creeeaakk, creeeaakk." The sounds broke the early-morning silence in the Marshall house. Vicki half opened her eyes and slightly raised her head. "It is Peter tiptoeing down the stairs," she mumbled and then blinked her eyes to clear the fog. "Going to the baseball tryouts." The creaky sounds reminded her of another time, and she smiled. *How many times did big Peter say he was going to fix those boards? Glad he didn't.* She stretched and considered for a moment staying in the warmth of her bed, but that thought was fleeting. *It's a special day for Peter. Need to see him off.* She dragged herself from the bed, slipped on a robe, and headed to the kitchen.

"Hi, Mom," Peter mumbled excitedly, mouth stuffed with cereal and milk. The big grin revealed his anticipation something good was taking place today.

"Hi, Hun," she said as she bent over and kissed his cheek. Hun was the name she used most of the time instead of Peter as it brought back tearful memories to say, "Peter."

"Big day, huh?" she asked with a yawn and stretched arms for a morning hug.

"Yeah, gotta run," he replied as he grabbed the remains of his raisin muffin, gave her a quick one-arm hug and hurried towards the back door.

She followed him, "Sorry you have to wear blue jeans and tennis shoes today." In the same breath, she reminded him of her promise. "Don't forget. I get paid next week, and we will buy those baseball pants and cleats."

46

"At least I have my lucky jersey," Peter replied with a big grin as he lifted his dad's old jersey outward from his chest. "Baggy, but I'm wearing it!"

Tears popped up in the corners of Vicki's eyes, and she struggled to keep her composure. "Your dad would be proud of your wearing it," she said softly. Her mind drifted back to Hun's comments when he first tried it on.

"When I found it, I'd move my fingers along the silk numbers. Number 46. I'd think of dad dressing for a game and putting on the jersey. Dad touched these numbers, too! Made me feel he was close by; like I could reach out, touch him, and get a warm hug. It was my treasure."

Peter picked up his mitt and bat and opened the door to leave. He called it his "Savoy bat" like the kid did in the movie *The Natural*. He often thought, *Maybe one day I can hit a home run like that to win a game. The bat and mitt were old, but they're his.* They belonged to a neighbor, and Peter worked out an agreement to mow his lawn several times in exchange for them. He strapped them to his bike handlebars and pushed off to the ball field.

"Good luck," Vicki yelled as she watched him ride down the drive and out of sight. A worried look appeared on her face. *Hope he's this happy when he returns.*

"Here he comes," Clarence whispered to Charley and Caroline. "Remember," he cautioned, "act like yourselves so he won't suspect something."

Peter leaned his old bike against Big Fella, unstrapped his bat and mitt, and turned to walk off when the cackling in the tree caused him to look up. *It is my owl friends,* he thought and waved. *Maybe wishing me good luck.* "Morning Mr. and Mrs. Owl."

Charley and Caroline hooted at that moment, but Peter didn't know it was their greeting in return.

On another day, Peter would stay and enjoy their company. *Not today*, he thought as he trotted towards the announcer booth where tryout registration would take place. A few players were there already, and others were coming towards them.

Peter was on cloud nine, but his emotions hit rock bottom immediately when he observed, *Everyone has baseball pants, shirts, and cleats, and most are new.* He felt out of place, but he was determined. *I'm getting on a team today.*

Soon a man blew a whistle and motioned everyone to gather around him out on the field. "This is the tryout day for this baseball league. Your name will be called in the order of signing up. After you are through, you'll be given a form to take home and complete. Don't leave the field without it. Understand?"

Before players replied, he continued, "The form has a place for your parent or guardian to sign. Complete it and bring it back with a copy of your birth certificate to prove your age. The registration and playing fee is $35. Give these to your coach at your first practice. Remember, you can't practice until these are returned. Also, you can't play in this league if you're thirteen before August 1st. Everyone understand?" This time he looked around for a response.

"No questions? … Good. Now everyone get in line."

Immediately Peter and the players moved to get in line. Unfortunately, more bodies tried to squeeze in ahead of him than the space would hold. Peter found himself behind a girl, and she was being pushed further and further back from the registration table as players kept crowding in ahead of her.

Peter mumbled angrily under his breath. "She is not saying anything to stop them from pushing her backward." He didn't like players crowding in line ahead, but he didn't want to be mean and shove her out of the way, either

Fortunately, registration was quick, and Peter was soon back on the field. He stretched for a bit like the players ahead of him were instructed to do. Now he was ready to throw. He looked around. *Everyone is throwing with somebody.*

Then a tryout coach called out the number on Peter's jersey, "Number 46, number 46." Peter looked his way, and the coach pointed to a player for him to throw with.

Peter jogged in that direction, and then he saw the player. "Oh, no!" he grumbled under his breath. "It is *that* girl from the registration line!" *What am I going to do?* he wondered as he trotted towards them. *Just my luck to get a dumb girl. Probably can't throw or catch. She will make me look terrible.*

As he approached the coach, Peter had a look like he was begging to be rescued. *Maybe the coach will understand and match me with another boy.* No help came as the coach turned his attention to another player trotting on to the field.

"My name's Sakine," a voice came from behind Peter. The girl walked towards him. "Sakine Davis. It sounds like, 'Sa-kine.'" … "What's yours?"

She caught Peter off guard for a moment. Then he sized her up and down. He was stunned. *She looks like a ball player, and dressed like the boys except her long blond hair is in a ponytail stuck through the back of the ball cap.*

"Peter," he answered quietly almost under his breath and with his head tilted downward. His eyes darted back and forth to see if other players were watching and listening.

He expected to hear snickers and teasing comments. Something like, "Hey, look at Peter and his girlie friend."

Before he could say or do anything else, a coach tossed Peter a ball, and immediately, the girl put out her mitt for him to throw it. He thought, *Don't want to be seen with a player who can't catch or throw, so I'll throw a gentle toss with an arc to make it easier to catch.* "Please catch it," he begged under his breath.

Sakine easily caught it, and shot him a "What are you doing?" stare. She threw the ball back quickly with more zip than Peter's throw, and without any arc.

The ball hit Peter's mitt with a thud, but it plopped out on the ground before he could secure it with his hand. He was embarrassed and red faced. He quickly picked it up, and snuck a peek. *Were any players watching? Didn't seem to be, as they were busy catching and throwing.* He threw with more force this time, but it didn't matter as Sakine easily caught them.

Peter quickly realized, *She's pretty good at throwing and catching. Can't let a girl out do me,* so he tried to match how hard she threw to him. This didn't turn out good as the harder he threw, the wilder his throws became. Some were over her head, or wide to her side, or bounced off the dirt at her feet.

"Hey," Sakine yelled at Peter as she chased the balls. "Can't you do better?"

Meanwhile, Clarence, Caroline, and Charley talked about their observations of the tryouts. "Peter's not getting off to a very good start," Clarence said in his deep voice.

"Yeah," Charley hooted agreement as he nervously moved back and forth on the branch to see the field, "and don't think he knows the coaches are watching the players."

Caroline asked, "Whadda ya mean, Cha'lee, coaches wa'chin'?"

Charley's eyes opened to about double size and they had a look of "How do I answer this question?" Then he responded, "They want to know how each player performs, Dear. Evaluate and grade them to help draft players for their teams." Charley knew she'd have other questions and he wouldn't have the patience to answer without seeming short with her. So he added, "You will understand more Dear as you watch."

Clarence intentionally interrupted, "Some players are pretty good at throwing, but some aren't. Peter's not good, but I believe he could improve with patience and good coaching."

Sakine caught every throw from Peter that wasn't in the dirt or over her head. She even ran or dove to catch some of his wild throws. In return, she threw hard each time. Peter caught only a few throws.

After time to warm up arms, a coach blew a whistle and yelled out, "Everyone in."

Sakine ran towards the coach. *Yea, no more Peter!*

Peter was relieved. *Hope my tryout will be better than warming up.* Some players ran. Some jogged, and others walked.

"Stop everyone!" The coach yelled as he held up both arms in a

"Halt" signal. He continued after everyone came to a halt. "When a coach blows a whistle, all players are to run to him. No jogging or walking. Understand?"

A few players replied, "Yes."

"What?" shouted the coach. "I only heard a few of you."

"Yes," replied the players.

"What? … Didn't hear you!"

"Y-E-E-S!" yelled the players at the top of their voices. The sound echoed several blocks into the woods and hills around the field.

"That's better, but one more time with 'sir.'

"Y-E-E-S S-I-R" yelled the players again.

"Now everyone go back to the place where you were throwing and catching. When I blow the whistle come running."

When the coach blew his whistle and yelled, "Everyone in here," all ran as fast as they could and gathered around the coach. They didn't know it, but this was their first lesson in learning discipline, which is essential to good teamwork and winning in any sport.

This time about ten coaches were standing near the one with the whistle. Motioning towards the other coaches, he continued, "These men are coaches of the different teams in the league. You will learn their names when they call you to be on a team. Today, each of you'll go through different drills so we can get an idea how well you might be able to play. Do your best!"

He looked down at his clipboard for a moment and continued. "We'll now put you through the tryout where your baseball skills will be evaluated. Do your best. After you finish, pick up your registration form. The coach who drafts you will call you for his team practices."

The coach gazed around momentarily at the youngsters to let

the information sink in. "First, let's see how fast you can run." With that, the players were divided into three groups.

> *Tryout: Catch fly balls, throw from outfield, field grounders & throw. Hitting. Pitching. Speed.*

When Peter saw that Sakine was in his group, he grumbled under his breath, "Oh, no. I'm with that girl again."

Players in each group stood along the base line from home plate down past 1st base. They were to run past the line from 3rd base to 2nd base. "When I blow my whistle, run as fast as you can. Understand?"

"I think Peter will do well in running," Charley commented to Caroline and Clarence. "He's always running through the woods and hills and jumping streams. Seems fast to me."

"Hope so," Clarence replied, "he needs a picker-upper."

At that moment the whistle sounded, and the group took off. Peter finished a few steps behind the lead players, and barely in front of Sakine.

"Oh, no," Clarence moaned. "His tennis shoes slipped in getting started and his jeans slowed him down."

I can do better, Peter thought as the group lined up to run back. "Knew I could," he said to himself when only two players finished just ahead of him. He didn't notice that Sakine did better too, and finished a few feet behind him.

The rest of the tryout went downhill for Peter. He missed most of the fly balls and grounders that were hit to him. One fly ball bounced off his mitt and then off his head. The players in his group laughed when they saw it. He had difficulty judging the flight of the ball and several balls went over his head. His throws from the outfield and to a base weren't very good either. Most were in the dirt, or lobs, wide or over the head of the player he was throwing to.

Hitting didn't go well, either. His Savoy bat didn't come through for him like he thought it would. He hit only two of ten pitches. One was a slow grounder back to the pitcher and the other was a pop up. He missed the other pitches by a mile. *I stink! No one will want me.*

Pitching was next, and any player could tryout. *I can't throw hard enough or with control to get the ball over home plate*, he concluded sadly, *so I'll skip that.* "My tryout's over," he mumbled sadly. "Didn't do very good."

He slowly walked to the dugout with his not-so-special Savoy bat over his shoulder, retrieved his mitt, and picked up a registration form to take home. Peter's day ended just the opposite of the happy expectation he started out with. Unfortunately, it was about to get worse.

Some coaches were standing near the registration booth, making plans to hold the draft. A woman named Priscilla Smart was among

them. Her son, Billy, was returning from the year before. He was one of the best players in the league, and he had two years left to play.

Peter asked for his registration form, and the coach in the booth asked, "What's your name, son?"

"Peter," he replied, "Peter Marshall."

The coach thumbed through the forms, found Peter's, and handed it to him. As Peter walked away, he overheard the woman ask the coaches standing there, "Is 46 any good?"

Peter kept walking, but turned his head enough to see the coaches out of the corner of his eye. Several moved their heads back and forth in a "No" motion.

He could see the woman and coaches still talking, but he was now out of hearing range. Peter didn't know they were talking about holding the player draft right after the tryouts. He imagined, *They're talking about how poorly I did, and my blue jeans and tennis shoes. ...* The dragons and monsters continued to stalk Peter in his pursuit to be on a ball team and get base hits.

His eyes watered, and lips puckered. Head down, he stumbled slowly around the fence to his bike propped against the oak tree. His heart pounded harder and harder with each step. When he reached the tree, he leaned against the huge trunk. Lots of tears were flowing now. He had looked forward to this day for so long. Had such high hopes this morning when he left his bike and ran to the tryouts. "Not even going to get on a team," he mumbled through tears.

Suddenly, a deep voice said, "It is okay, son. Things will work out. Wait and see."

The voice startled Peter, and he raised his head quickly. Looked around. He didn't see anyone. "Who is there?" he asked as he cautiously walked around the tree.

Clarence, Caroline, and Charley did all they could to avoid making a sound.

Peter didn't see anyone, and no one was nearby either. A frightened look replaced the curious one on his face. "Who is there?" he asked again. No one answered. "Did I imagine this?" he wondered out loud while looking about again in all directions. *I see coaches at the registration booth, and a few players and parents loading up in their vehicles. No one else. Musta been my imagination,* he concluded.

Peter's tears were now dry. Yes, he was still upset at the comments of the coaches at the booth. "I know I didn't do very well," he mumbled angrily, "but they didn't have to say so when I could hear." With that, he tied his bat and mitt to the handlebars and pedaled towards home.

"Before you ask," Clarence said to Caroline and Charley, "I wasn't sure he could hear me before I answered him. The time needs to be right, and we need to know if he can hear you, too."

"Okay; we did wonder," Charley replied.

"Good. Now go tell Maggie what happened today."

"Sure thing," Charley hooted and paused before adding, "Big Fella."

"Get outta here," Clarence chuckled, "you feathery critters!"

As Peter pedaled towards home, he kept asking over and over, "What am I going to tell mom? What am I going to tell mom? What am I going to tell mom?"

[CHAPTER 4]

Drafting Players; Oppulence of the Smart's
Business Conference Room; Their Historical
Indian and Spanish Treasures; New Coach,
David Tyree and Son, John William; Talent, A
Major Reason Why a Team Constantly Wins

The league officials and coaches discussed the player draft, and Priscilla Smart said, "You can use our business conference room if you want."

Jerry Cramer, a league official and assistant coach of the defending league champions, the Tiger team, replied after others nodded approval, "Sounds good."

Pricilla handed him a key and added, "If you want, I will pick up some sandwiches so you all can start."

"All for it!" everyone blurted out happily.

Jay Anderson, another coach with the defending champions, chaired the meeting. "You all met two of our new coaches. David Tyree is another." He looked his direction and said, "Welcome to the league, Coach Tyree."

Mumbles of "Welcome" sounded across the room, and Coach Tyree waved in return.

Coach Anderson continued, "Coach Tyree moved up to the league with his nine-year-old son, John William. His team has three players returning, and John William makes four." He paused again and said, "Good luck with your team, Coach."

Jerry then commented about the status of the league, "There

are eight teams, and rosters have to be turned in with the players returning along with the new nine-year-old players." He looked around and said, "For you new coaches, three nine-year-old players can sign each year without going through tryouts." Then, to everyone, "Forty players participated in tryouts today, and there is room for all forty if thirteen players can be on a team."

"Motion so made," a coach said, another seconded it, and all voted "Yes."

Coach Anderson took over again, "Next is the draft order. The team finishing in last place last season will have first choice of all forty players. Same with that finishing order, and the champions from last season will have the eighth choice. The draft order then will be reversed with the champions picking again, or the ninth choice. The draft will continue like these first two rounds until each team fills its roster with thirteen players. When a team has thirteen players, the team will stop drafting players."

Hmmmm, Coach Tyree pondered. *I have the first pick since my team finished at the bottom last year.* He studied his notes. *Only about ten decent players. Since pitchers are key to holding down runs, I better pick one, and maybe he will be good at other positions.*

Prissy Smart arrived at that moment with sandwiches, and the coaches stopped immediately to eat. One coach walked around with sandwich in hand, and looked at the items on display in the glass cases built into the walls on all sides of the conference room. After a few minutes, he looked at Prissy and said, "These things look old. Are they from around here?"

Prissy smiled proudly. "Yes, most of them. My husband, Terry and I are avid collectors of rare artifacts from the Indian and Spanish history of North Florida." She unlocked a display, and withdrew two small items. "These are extremely rare quartz artifacts made by the Apalachee Indians. Clear quartz crystal is extremely rare and prized by them."

The other coaches, except Coach Tyree who was studying his notes, gathered around her. "Quartz crystal was highly prized by Native Americans because it was believed to hold special properties for them."

She placed the crystals back in the case, locked its door, and continued, "Anyway, the answer is yes, and they are all local finds and have been authenticated by archeologists of the State and of the university. These have some flaws, but the State has tried to buy these because they are so rare. Only a few good ones have been found, and they are priceless because of their history and rarity."

Soon, everyone was waived back to the draft. "Coach Tyree, you have the first pick."

He glanced around cautiously at the other coaches like some gambler in a western movie trying to keep his cards hidden from the other cowpokes. He looked back at his notes again and thought, *Rick Taylor looked pretty good at pitching. Also ran, caught, and batted good so if he can't pitch at least he'll be a good all-around player.* "Rick Taylor's my first pick," he said.

Finally the league champions made their pick, and the first round was over. Then immediately the champions made their second choice, and promptly announced, "We have thirteen players. Our roster's full. We had eight returning, and signed three nine-year-olds in the off-season. We needed only two players."

A shocked look was on Coach Tyree's face. *They are full and I still have seven players to draft?* All of a sudden he realized, *their two players came from the top nine of the forty. No wonder they win!* He sat quietly and stewed, *They find good nine-year-old players and draft only a few of the best players in the tryouts. They've set it up where they don't have any of the "not so good ones" from the bottom half of the draft pool.*

Coach Tyree's brow wrinkled and he slumped in his seat. *How can my team compete against that?*

Perhaps if Coach Tyree had known that the three top hitters and two top pitchers from the last year also were on this championship team, he might've resigned from coaching right on the spot. Soon he'd find out about the challenges of trying to coach a bunch of inexperienced players

More teams filled their roster and stopped. Only Coach Tyree's team and one other continued to draft after the fifth round. *Oh, my gosh,* he concluded, *at least six of my players, half the team, would come from the last ten players. This isn't good.* He agonized as the brow wrinkles deepened. *How can we beat anyone?*

When the draft ended, Coach Tyree looked over his list. *Seven boys, two of them identical twins, and two girls.* He thought back to the tryouts on the field, *those twins were the smallest players there.* He thought about the upside: *One good player who hopefully can pitch, and maybe three or four others decent. Downside? Not sure last four or five can chew bubble gum and catch a ball at the same time. Not fair one team's stuck with the last four players of the draft.* Then he read their names: *Phillip Edwards, Angelique Turner, David Petri, and Peter Marshall.* A discouraged look appeared on his face as he acknowledged reality. *Didn't see much positive about them. Inexperienced. They'll probably get discouraged and drop out.*

A smile, a consolation of sorts, came to Coach Tyree's face as he thought about the unusual occurrence of two girls on the team. *At least one, Sakine Davis, seemed to be a ball player.* She was his third pick, seventeenth out of forty. *Wonder if she uses that catcher's equipment I noticed in her bag? Hope so. We'll need several catchers.*

"Here's the practice and season schedule," Jerry Cramer said. "Anything else?"

A coach asked, "Anything worked out to improve the field and facilities?"

"Agree," another added. "Been needed for years and the trees around the field need trimming. After a storm, pine cones and Spanish moss are scattered all over the field. And that oak tree outside the corner of right field has limbs that extend over the playing area. Fly balls hit the branches all the time. Thought we agreed to trim them."

Cramer responded to the latter issue, "We don't have approval to cut those limbs." Then he paused and said, "For you new coaches, when a fair fly ball hits a branch of that large oak tree outside right field, we have a special rule that an automatic homerun is awarded."

Another coach spoke up, "Don't forget about that rusty outfield fence. It's been there thirty or forty years, since I played here. It's too short and dangerous. I've had players fall over it trying to catch a fly ball."

Another mentioned the poor condition of the dugouts. "Those dugouts have dirt floors, the benches are splintery, paint's peeling off walls, and rain leaks through the roofs. There's a lot of wood rot underneath."

Another coach spoke his piece. "I agree with what's been said, but let's not forget the scoreboard. It's a throwback to metal ones of the 1950s. Someone has to hang numbers each inning. Paint's gone, and the numbers are rusty. Let us get a new one, or get this one painted. Maybe we can work out a deal to get one of those new ones with electric bulbs."

Cramer added, "Put spectator seating on the list. It's falling apart. The boards are full of splinters and are hazardous for sitting." Everyone laughed when he said, "I got a splinter in my behind today watching the tryouts."

Laughing continued as a coach jokingly said, "Have a knife. Bend over. We'll dig it out."

"No thanks," Cramer replied. "Spectators don't use the bleachers much. They either stand along the fences or bring their lawn chairs. And don't forget the announcer and scorekeeper platform. The backstop fence keeps it from falling onto the home plate."

He continued, "The only thing new is the concession stand, but..." he paused and looked Prissy's direction, "we wouldn't have been able to get it approved if not for some extra influence. Needs rebuilding."

Another coach spoke up, "Don't overlook the outfield. Little grass grows on it because there's no irrigation, and the wear and tear from junior football played in the fall wears away what grass is left. The only water is from rain or when some dedicated person drags sprinkler hoses around the field. Takes lots of hoses from the water connections by the dugouts. I've done that a few months, but no more because the football teams tear out chunks of grass."

A coach expressed to Cramer, "How about putting these requests to your bosses at public lands and recreation?"

"I'm not the one to do it," Cramer replied. He turned toward Prissy and said, "Others can pull their chains enough to get a response."

Prissy understood and responded, "I'm sure the city and county will do what they can." She added a positive reply, "I will see what we can do to help. Maybe we can get them to do at least something, like put in the irrigation."

This satisfied the coaches, and they departed talking excitedly about their new players, expectations for the season, and making calls to their draft picks. Each hoped there'd be a diamond in the rough among them.

Coach Tyree heard the comments and thought, *I need a miracle—a bunch of those diamonds. Maybe one of those last six players will be my miracle diamond.*

[CHAPTER 5]

*Peter's Tryout Performance; A Girl was Even
Better, and Some Adults Made Fun of Me*

Peter pedaled fast and wildly down the street from the tryouts to his house. He jumped the curb without slowing down and zipped around to the back yard. He leaped off and running before the bike hit the ground. The family dog, barked excitedly expecting to play their usual game of tag and ran towards him. She nipped playfully at his legs as he jumped over her.

"Not today, Pokey. Not playing today," he yelled sadly over his shoulder.

Vicki was making one of Peter's favorite treats, oatmeal raisin cookies. It was a surprise for his special day. She was taking some out of the oven when she heard the back door open and slam closed. She glanced up as Peter flashed by the doorway. A puzzled look appeared on her face. Quickly she called out to him, "How was the tryout, Hun?"

He mumbled over his shoulder, "Uh ... okay," as he bounded up the stairs to his bedroom. He flung himself on the bed and buried his face deep into his pillow. He could no longer hold the tears back, and they flooded his face. Big sobs and chest upheavals, the signs of a distraught youngster, came with each breath.

"Strange," Vicki said as a motherly concern look came on her face. *He always asks for a warm cookie before it cools. I thought he would be bubbly today and bounce around with excitement telling me about the tryout.* Her memory briefly flashed back over the last couple of years. *He often said how much he looked forward to the tryout and getting on a ball team.* "Something must be wrong," she mumbled as she took off her apron and turned off the stove.

I'll take him a few cookies and a glass of juice. Maybe I can find out if anything is wrong.

Peter's door was closed. *Hmmmm, Why? He seldom closes his door. The girls, yes, all the time, but not Peter unless ... unless he's upset about something.*

She knocked gently, but didn't hear anything. After a few moments, she leaned her head against the door and knocked again. *Still nothing,* she concluded. She waited for a few moments and spoke softly, "Hun, it's mom. I baked your favorite cookies: oatmeal-raisin. I brought you a few and some juice." She paused and listened for a response. *Still nothing.*

Her alarm juices began to flow as she mumbled, "My baby's hurt! I have to help him!"

She pressed her ear to the door to see if she could hear anything. There was a faint sobbing sound. *I've got to find out what's wrong.* Slowly she turned the handle and opened the door a crack. Peter was lying with face in a pillow, and his chest heaved with big sobs.

Tears came to her eyes, as they would for any protective mother. She hurried to his bedside, set the cookies and juice on the nightstand, and sat down next to him. She leaned over, and touched her face to his. Their tears flowed together as she asked, "Hun, what's wrong?"

Peter rolled to face her quickly, reached up with both arms and hugged her so tight it almost choked the breath out of her. He buried his wet face into her neck, and they sobbed together. After a few minutes, he mumbled through thick lips and between deep sobbing gasps, "I was really bad, Mom. I couldn't catch a ball, throw, or hit."

Vicki was disturbed, but wanted to be positive for him. She gently stroked his brow and tried to console him, "Hun, everyone can't be the best. Many times, someone will be better."

"I know," he moaned, "but even a girl trying out was better." He stopped to catch his breath between sobs and then continued.

"*...and the coaches made fun of me!*"

The words stunned her, and anger flushed over her face as she pictured grown-ups acting that way. She didn't know what to say. Her first impulse was to rush downstairs and call the league officials and give them a piece of her mind. *Treating a young boy like this is just not right. Someone'll answer for doing it to my baby.* Her thoughts quickly returned to Peter. *Important thing now is to help him get through this day.*

She went on, "Hun, you can be a good player. All you need is a little practice. You will get on a team I am sure, and you'll get better when it practices. It'll happen. You will see." She repeated the words...

Neither said anything more for a long time, but his hug became more intense like he was afraid to let her go, as if he'd lose her forever. She hugged him the same way. Truth was, hugs and caresses with her children were precious moments, and comforted her deeply.

Peter raised his head, still teary-eyed, looked in her eyes, and expressed a truth, "If Dad was here he could help me learn to play ball, to catch, hit, and throw. Do all those things. It's not fair he had that accident! The other boys have a dad to help them. Even that girl. Why, Mom?"

The question didn't surprise Vicki, but the timing stunned her. She looked back into Peter's face and thought, *I can't explain. I've agonized "Why?" out loud many times in the quiet moments of the day and long into the night. What do I say?* Before she could answer, Peter buried his head back into her neck again and sobbed.

Vicki hugged him back, as she had no answer to help with this moment. They hugged and cried together for a long, long time. Their wet cheeks against each other. The sobs slowly subsided, and Vicki could feel Peter's body relax. The tension was passing, and he was going to sleep in her arms like he did many times as a baby and little boy.

She slowly lowered him onto the pillow, pulled the bed cover on him, kissed him on the cheek, and whispered, "I love you, Hun. You are precious, and something special will happen."

"Me too, Mom," he mumbled half asleep.

At the door, she turned and looked warmly at her little boy. *He breathed okay now.* She bowed her head and said a little prayer, "Dear Lord, please help things to get better for Peter. There will be better days for him and our family." She paused a moment, "... and me, too."

She closed the bedroom door, stopped, and leaned against the wall. Fresh tears appeared. "I miss your dad, too, Hun. Almost ten years, June 6th. Miss him in so many ways."

[CHAPTER 6]

*Mom Remembers the Devastating News About
Peter, Sr.; Coach Tyree Calls Peter; "I'm
on a team; Rosies' Café!"*

As Vicki walked slowly down the stairs, Hun's comments were still on her mind. *"I did really poorly, Mom. … The coaches laughed at me. … Why did dad die? … It's not fair. … I won't even get on a team."* He was so devastated by his baseball tryout. *How can I convince him he did poorly only because he had no experience?*

She glanced at the clock. *Mid afternoon. What a day!* She entered the kitchen, and busied herself by cleaning the floor. To do it right, she had to be on her knees. … Guilt set in as her thoughts returned to Hun's tryout. *Could I have done more to help him? … How? No time with three young children,* she reasoned as she scrubbed harder. *Had to work a second job this last year to make ends meet.* Her face puckered and she cried softly as she moved the sponge in circles on the floor. *Just couldn't provide all the attention that each of my babies needed.* She leaned back on her heels, wiped her brow, blew her nose. *How do single parents raise their children—even if money is no problem?* She repeated the thought…

She leaned against the wall as tears turned into sobs. The clothes dryer buzzer suddenly sounded, and she hurried to fold the towels. Hun was still on her mind, though. *I hope he gets on a team. Not fair if he doesn't. He's looked forward so long to playing and getting a base hit. Now, after today, not sure what will happen.*

She finished folding and started to dust the window shades and pictures. Kept thinking, *Hun's day started off so good today. So excited. Now, what will happen?* The question stopped her, and a puzzled look appeared on her face.

She took a break, sat at the kitchen table, sipped on now cold coffee, and thought about the question. After a few moments, another difficult thought entered her mind, *What if he doesn't get on a team? How will I help him feel good about himself again?*

Her mind was blank. She discovered long ago that prayers were often the only way she could make it through some nights and days. This was one of those moments, and she pleaded, "Oh, Lord, I hope you'll help. Maybe a little extra attention since Peter doesn't have a dad to teach him these things. I hope you understand. I can't be at all their activities."

At moments like this, Vicki's thoughts often turned back to *a late-night knock on her door. A highway patrolman stood nervously, trooper's hat in hand. She didn't remember much of what he said, "Peter was in a car accident, and didn't...."* It was *like a dream.*

The struggles to survive kept Vicki and her children going, and emotions were held in check most of the time except when one of the girls asked, "Where is dad? Why doesn't he come home?" ... Now Hun's question, "Why did dad die?"

Vicki took another sip of the cold coffee and turned her attention momentarily to some mail on the table.

She studied one piece she had opened earlier and sighed agonizingly. *Property taxes due.* She wondered, *How are we going to pay this? Will we lose the house? ... Everything's wearing out and breaking, insurance money's gone, and family support's out, too. Don't even know how to pay the utilities or mortgage, let alone pay the property tax or insurance.* She stared out the window in hopeless thought. ... *We need a miracle. ... Do they really happen?*

Suddenly the cackling hoot of some owls startled Vicki, "Whooo, whoo-kooos-fo-uooouuuuuuu." It was Caroline and Charley, and it wasn't unusual for them to perch high in trees late in the evening, overlooking the backyards of humans. They'd watch for a squirrel or other type of meal to come out into the open. Today, though, they were also checking on Peter.

Those owls, Vicki thought. Then her mind returned to her to-do list. *Better prepare the lasagna for the Sunday meal.* After a few recipe measurements, her thoughts were back on Peter.

"Should I wake him up?" she asked out loud. "Don't want him to sleep now and be awake all night upset about his tryout."

"I better go wake him," she concluded. "No, I'll let him sleep."

This went on a while. She finally decided, "Better wake him if he's not down soon."

Suddenly, the phone rang and startled her. *Who can it be? Don't expect any calls. No mood to talk. I will let it ring.*

A person started leaving a message. "Hi, my name is David Tyree. I'm one of the coaches in the league where Peter Marshall had tryouts today. The coaches finished the player draft, and Peter is on my team if he wants to play. I'm leaving my number. I want to have a short practice and parent meeting tomorrow afternoon. My number is..."

She grabbed the phone and interjected, "Hello, this is Vicki Marshall—Peter's mother."

Silence occurred for a moment, then David Tyree spoke, "Hi, I'm glad you answered. I'm calling to speak with Peter about being on my team." He paused for a response, but Vicki was so excited she couldn't speak. Hearing nothing he continued, "Let me tell you a few things about it. To be on the team, he must turn in the signed registration form along with a copy of his birth certificate to prove his age. The registration fee is $35.00. We must order jerseys right away so we can get them by the first game. They cost $15.00. What number would Peter like to have?"

Vicki was stunned and silent for a moment but finally responded, "I'm positive Peter wants to play, but he will have to tell you the number he wants."

"Okay, sounds good," David Tyree replied and then continued with more information about equipment and uniforms. "All players will need to buy their own baseball pants, belt, cleats, and mitt. There are some team bats so no one will need to buy one unless they want their own. Also, there are some team batting helmets, but players often buy their own."

Vicki's thoughts turned to: *money and costs?* Her eyes narrowed as she asked, "How much did you say those will cost?"

"Cleats about $30, belt and pants about $15, and batting helmet about $12. The bat could cost from $45 to $200, depending on the brand. I recommend not buying the helmet and bat until the player gets a feel for what is needed in this age group. They also may not stay with it."

Satisfied with his answer, Vicki said, "Thanks. I will get Peter if you can hold on."

"Sure. Go ahead. I will hold."

Vicki laid the phone down and hurried excitedly up the stairs to Peter's room. *Peter will be on a team! He will be on a team!* She knocked joyfully, and peeked inside. *Good, he is awake.* He looked over at her when she entered.

"Peter," she said excitedly. "There's a man on the phone." She could hardly get the words out. "He's a coach in the league where you tried out this morning. He said you are on his team."

Peter immediately sat up and asked loudly, "What?" He couldn't believe what he just heard his mother say. "What, Mom?"

"There's a man on the phone who says he's your baseball team coach, and..."

Before she finished, Peter jumped to his feet and ran past her on his way down the stairs. He reached the phone before she recovered from her excitement and started back down.

"Hello, this is Peter," he said apprehensively.

"Hi, Peter. I'm David Tyree and I drafted you to play on my baseball team if you still want to play." He paused, but Peter couldn't get any words out so he asked, "Do you?"

Peter yelled excitedly, "YES! WHEN DO WE START?"

"Tomorrow," Coach Tyree replied. "At 2:30 p.m. Can you make it? Short notice."

"YES!"

"Great. We will finish the registration, order jerseys, and try to practice if we have time. What number do you want?"

Without hesitation Peter blurted out, "46."

Vicki was now nearby and heard much of the conversation.

"Okay, coach, see you tomorrow." Peter slowly hung up the

phone, and turned with a huge smile plastered across his face. His eyes met his mom's, and he yelled excitedly, "Mom, I'm on a team!" He said it again, "Mom, I'm on a team!" as he leaped into her outstretched arms. "I have a coach, and we start tomorrow!"

"I'm on a team!"

She hugged him and replied, "That is terrific, Hun. Didn't I tell you something good is going to happen to you?"

They hugged for a long time. Then Peter wiggled out of her arms with a look like he was late for something important. He picked up a ball and his mitt, and went outside without a word. Vicki looked out the window and wondered, *what is he doing?* She saw him toss the ball in the air and catch it. Then she heard him say again, "I'm on a team. I'm on a team."

Vicki said a big prayer of thanks. Soon, thoughts kept coming back to her. *How am I going to pay for this?* She remembered, *Peter's saved enough from mowing jobs in the neighborhood to cover the $35 registration, but I don't think he's saved for the other expenses.*

She decided to call Coach Tyree for some clarification. "Hello. This is Vicki Marshall, Peter's mother. You called a few minutes ago." She paused to hear his response and continued, "Yes." … "Thank you." … "No, nothing's wrong. I just wanted to know if Peter needs to bring the jersey money tomorrow?" She paused again, "Okay, thank you." … "I'll try to be at the parent meeting at 3:00." … "Okay, see you tomorrow. Goodbye."

What a relief, she thought with a deep sigh as she hung up the phone. *Peter only needs the $35 tomorrow. We will worry how to pay for the other things another day. Today, we are going to celebrate. My Hun's on a team, and he gets a chance to get his base hit.*

Vicki picked up a few oatmeal-raisin cookies and went outside to celebrate with Peter.

"Look," Charley hooted to Caroline. "Peter's eating cookies and laughing with his mom, and listen what they're saying." He paused and continued, "And Peter's on a team!"

"Let's go tell Cla'ence," Caroline hooted joyfully.

[CHAPTER 7]

Coach Tyree and his son, John William, arrived early Sunday afternoon at the ball field to greet players and parents when they arrived. "Here," he said as he pulled an equipment bag from the pickup and handed it to him. "Take this to the dugout."

"Ooo-kaay," John William replied as he took the bag and trudged slowly away. He added over his shoulder, "Dad, going to the courts 'til players come."

"Okay. Listen for my whistle to begin practice."

Coach Tyree glanced at his watch. *Have time to check out the place.* He stepped on the field and gazed slowly around. One team was just finishing practice An adrenalin rush hit him. "Wow!" he mumbled excitedly. "This old ball field, sitting among tall pines and majestic oaks, is an impressive picture. Something like Norman Rockwell would paint."

The comments of the coaches about its condition came to mind, and he nodded in agreement. *Fence is rusty and dangerously short. Outfield grass has patches of dirt.*

Dugouts, scoreboard and seating are in poor shape. But, he thought as he stopped at the fence in centerfield, *the history and character of the place trumps those negatives. ... Wonder how many dreams have occurred here? ... And now my team will be part of it.*

He realized what he just thought, and wondered,

With the players on this team, how will we be remembered?

Clarence, Caroline, and Charley watched Coach Tyree as he walked the field. "Whaud'se he do-un, Cha'lee, Doll'un?" Caroline hooted curiously as she turned her head to see.

"Just looking around," Clarence answered before Charley responded. "Watch."

Coach Tyree leaned against the fence, closed his eyes, and took in the setting through his other senses. A cool breeze from the creek down the hill kissed his face and fluffed his hair. It caressed the branches and leaves of trees. The buzz of wildlife and the musical chirps of birds seemed everywhere. A soft clanging of the rope rings against the flagpole kept a steady beat. The fragrances and sounds of Spring were beginning to break.

Coach Tyree opened his eyes and looked around again. *There is that majestic oak with limbs that hang over the right field fence.* He studied its branches for a moment and thought about the homerun rule. Then he turned slowly in a circle taking in all he saw. *This picture of trees gently swaying in the breeze and sunlight shining in patches of golden light on the field after being filtered through the branches gives the feeling this place seems a little like heaven.*

Suddenly, a voice called out, "Coach Tyree." It was Jason Sanders standing by the dugout. Their eyes met, and they started walking towards each other.

A big guy, Coach Tyree observed sizing him up. *Glad he will be on my side,* he thought with a subtle smile, *if we get in one of those adult disagreements about youth league play.*

"I'm Jason Sanders," the man said as he stuck out his big hand.

Coach Tyree did the same and, as they shook, he said, "Glad you are willing to give it a go as our assistant coach."

"Glad to help anyway I can. Anything particular?"

"Today, help on the field when the players arrive. We will add to the basics as we learn their abilities. You mentioned you pitched in high school."

"Yes, small town in Alabama; but I was just an average pitcher. My experience since has only been with my son, Jake, so I may not be as much help as you need. "

"Truthfully, except for a woman offering to help organize the team, you are the only one willing to help coach. We are on our own right now and maybe all season." He paused, looked at Jason with a serious expression and asked, "Can I introduce you as Coach Sanders?"

"Well, yes. I want to provide the best experience possible for my son and for the others."

"Great," Coach Tyree said with a relieved tone to his voice. "Now let's go over the roster and draft picks. Here's a copy for you."

After some discussion, Coach Sanders said with an "I have more to add" tone to his voice, "So the draft was held in the business office of Terry and Priscilla Smart?"

"Yes. Do you have a connection to them?"

"Only indirectly. I'm in construction and real estate. Do you know anything about them?"

"Not much. She seemed pretty involved with Jerry Cramer and the league officials, and loaned their business conference room for the draft. She was there most of the time. My guess is they're well connected in many circles."

"Your first impression is on target," Jason acknowledged. "Priscilla is the wife of Terry Smart, a long-time state political party official. They are well known in Tallahassee and across the North Florida area. They are often involved in the wheeling and dealings of business, civic affairs, and government decision-making. They own a large development company, and their clientele includes recognizable government officials—even governors and senators of the state."

"Explains the opulence," Coach Tyree expressed. "When I stepped into their conference room, I was wowed. It was something to see. Huge inlaid mahogany table that'd sit twenty, tuck'n-roll red leather chairs, hard wood floors, and a rug with the state seal, and glass display cases built into the walls." Coach Tyree paused for a moment, rolled his eyes and continued, "That room and furniture probably cost more than my house."

Jason nodded his head in agreement. "I'm sure they do, and that rug with the seal was probably a gift from a high-up politician."

Then he continued to tell about Priscilla, "She runs the day-to-day business, and people call her Prissy." He paused, raised his eyes, and looked about as if he was checking whether anyone was nearby. Then he continued, "From my limited interactions, I know she's tough as nails, and both are accustomed to having decisions work out to their advantage."

"Oh, really?" Coach Tyree's eyebrows raised as he asked, "Tell me how they, or guess I should say, Prissy became so involved in the league? From what I've seen so far, league officials jump when she pulls their chain. Correct?"

"Your observation is pretty accurate," Jason replied with a sly grin. "I'm sure they know them from other city-county functions. They became involved in the league when their son, Billy, was a nine-year-old. This is his third year, and he can play next year. Hear tell he's one of the best players in the league." He paused again and shifted his big frame on his feet and continued, "Billy's on the defending league champions, and I suspect it was through their connections. I'm sure she had a big hand in building the team. Talent-wise, it is the best team again this year. … Surprise. Surprise."

> *"Prissy's son, Billy, is one of the best in the league."*

"Yeah, I got a dose of that reality at the draft," Coach Tyree expressed, "when that team announced they were full and I still had half my team to draft." He paused, rolled his eyes in a hopeless look and continued, "Six of our players are from the bottom ten in the draft. Four were the last picks."

"Oh, nooooo," Coach Sanders replied disgustedly and dug angrily at the ground with his shoe. "If the key to winning is drafting few players," he paused and looked seriously at Coach Tyree, "let's find a way to draft only one or two players next year—because our sons return."

"Hope that's not the key to winning," Coach Tyree said trying to reassure himself as an "I've been suckered" frown crossed his face. "If true, our team won't win many games." He paused and responded to Coach Sanders' last point, "Let's look into how we can do it."

Meanwhile at the Marshall house, Peter was on a countdown to leave for the ball field. He wanted to arrive early. He wolfed down his last bit of lasagna and chased it with a gulp of milk as he stood to leave.

Mom met him at the door and said, "Don't forget this," as she handed him the registration form, copy of the birth certificate, and the $35 fee that he'd earned from odd jobs in the neighborhood.

Peter took the items and pecked her quickly on the cheek as he opened the door.

"Hold on, young man!" mom expressed with a stern look on her face, "Don't you think this deserves more than just a peck?"

Oops, Peter thought as he froze in his tracks. He goofed, and turned to give her a hug and a kiss and said warmly as they embraced, "Love you, Mom."

"Me, too." They were quiet for a few moments and then she pushed him out the door. "Time to go get 'em," she said loudly like a cheerleader at a ballgame. As Peter pedaled away, she shouted, "Don't forget. I'll be at the field to meet Coach Tyree and the other parents."

Coach Tyree greeted each parent and player as they arrived.

"Nice to meet you, coach. I'm Marilyn Davis, and this is my daughter Sakine."

"Good to meet you too," he replied, He faced Sakine, and said, "I'm glad you are on our team." He motioned towards Coach Sanders on the field, and said, "Put your ball bag in the dugout and we will start in a few minutes."

As Sakine walked away, he turned back to Marilyn and said, "Mrs. Davis, I'm so thankful that you offered to help with the player registration and organizing the parents today."

"Call me Marilyn, coach," she said softly and, with a facial look and tone of "This information's for you," added "I'm a single woman."

"Okay, sorry," he replied nervously.

"No thanks needed," she said with a warm smile and womanly flutter of her eye lashes as she looked up and into his eyes. "Folks need to chip in to help our young uns grow up."

"Great," Coach Tyree replied with a blush. *Is she flirting with me?* he wondered for a moment then he managed to say, "I've set up a table for you over here," he said as he walked her to it. "Please remember to get player jersey size and number, Okay?"

"Sure thing, sweetie," she said as she sat down. "Just send 'em my way."

Yikes! She is! he thought as he walked toward another player and parents arriving.

Meanwhile, Clarence, Caroline, and Charley anticipated Peter's arrival. "Here he comes!" Clarence exclaimed quietly.

"I seeum, I seeum," Caroline hooted as she bounced her body and head up and down.

"Shuuuuu," Clarence reminded them. "Don't forget our plan."

Peter coasted his bike to the large oak tree outside the right field fence. His heart beat rapidly from the excitement. He kept thinking, *I'm on a ball team, and we're practicing today.* He stood beside the big oak and looked slowly around the old ball field. An ear-to-ear grin appeared as he mouthed the words, "I'm on a ball team, I'm on a ball team."

Laughing and talking sounds of players and adults near a dugout jolted Peter back to the present. He grabbed his mitt and bat and the registration items and was about to trot off towards them when he heard that deep voice again.

"Good luck, Peter." Clarence encouraged Peter. It also was a test to see if Peter could hear and understand them.

Peter stopped in his tracks, and jerked his head to look left and then right. *No one's close enough to make the sound,* he thought. He asked anyway. "Who are you?" He listened for a few seconds, but there was no answer. He went on, "I can't see you. What do you want?" He paused a moment.

Maybe someone's hiding on the other side, he thought. He quickly moved around the tree, hopping over a couple of its huge roots that looked like large worms crawling along the top of the ground. *No one there, either.*

Maybe up in the tree, he guessed as he looked upward. He saw his two friends, Mr. Owl and Mrs. Owl, perched high on a branch. He smiled at them. *My two owl friends.*

As he continued to look, his voice quivered in frustration. He asked again, "Wha… what do you want?"

He stood silently listening, but there was no answer. He quickly looked all around the tree once again, and pleaded, "Where are you? I can't see you. Please come out." There was only silence.

He stood with a puzzled look for a few moments, and then he heard the dugout sounds again. *Better go,* he thought, and off he trotted.

As Peter approached the dugout, the sight of Sakine Davis among the players brought him to a screeching halt. His upper body sagged in disappointment like a flower wilts in the heat of day. "Oh, no!" he said in frustration. "Not her. Please not on my team."

As if that wasn't bad enough, Peter noticed she had been talking to another girl, who also was dressed as a player. "TWO!!" he said disgustedly as his eyes bulged. "Two girls on my team!" he mumbled under his breath. "That's all we need."

An idea came to him. *Maybe if I'm with the other guys and not close to THOSE GIRLS, coach won't pair me with them.* So he walked past them towards a couple of boys talking. Peter didn't know it, but the boys were two of the three players returning from the year before.

As he came near, the husky boy, with the name Tommy Lassiter, who also was like a giant compared to the other players on the team, turned his gaze to Peter. Tommy's face lit up like he didn't believe what he saw. When his eyes met Peter's,

he blurted out in a voice extra loud so the other players heard, "Baseball players don't wear jeans." He paused to let the statement hit home and continued in a humiliating posture, "Don't you have any baseball pants?"

Lacroy Carter was the other boy with Tommy. He pointed towards Peter's tennis shoes and followed with his own snide remark. "Yeah, and they don't wear tennis shoes either. Don't you have any cleats?"

The other players heard the extra-loud comments and turned their attention towards the three boys to see what was happening.

Sakine Davis looked amused and thought, *That guy again. He must be poor or stupid or both.*

Peter looked around for some friendly support. He even looked Sakine's direction. Their eyes met but, because her experience with him was negative and he had ignored her just moments before, she rolled her eyes and turned away.

At that moment Coach Tyree blew his whistle and motioned for everyone to come to the dugout. The players quickly picked up their bags, mitts, and stuff and hurried to him. Bags bumped against bodies on the way.

Coach Tyree pointed to a woman sitting at a table, and said, "This is Marilyn Davis. She's collecting registrations for the team, and she will start the parent's meeting for me. Make sure she has yours, put your bags in the dugout, and go out on the field to stretch and loosen up."

Then he turned and pointed toward Jason Sanders and said, "This is Coach Sanders. He'll be on the field with you. Listen to his instructions. I'll be there soon."

Coach Tyree stood at a distance and surveyed the team. *All thirteen here, and there's the number one draft pick, Rick Taylor. Need pitching, hitting—everything from you, Rick.*

There's the two girls: Sakine Davis and Angelica Turner. He looked at his notes. *Sakine seemed good, but Angelica was one of the last four drafted.* He mumbled, "Hope she's better than coaches believed."

His gaze fell on Lacroy Carter, and he wondered, *Only one I wasn't able to reach, so how did he learn about practice? Pitched last year. Hope he's good. If not, we're in deep trouble.* "Looks athletic," he mumbled, "so maybe he is good at other things too. We'll see."

There is the other two from last year: Larry "Scrubs" Johnson and Tommy Lassiter. Wow! Lots of groceries in Tommy; must be at least six foot and two hundred pounds. Played 1st base but nothing else about him. Hope he can hit. Can he pitch?

He wondered, *how did Larry get the nickname, "Scrubs?" Caught last year and has catcher equipment. Big plus if he is good. Who else can catch? Sakine's the other one I know.*

Coach Tyree observed the two coaches sons, Jake Sanders and John William. We want to be good coaches, he thought, *but—more important—good dads. Hope Coach Sanders doesn't push his son where he shouldn't go. Me, too, for that matter. Jake has potential and John William can develop gradually since he can play four years.*

His eyes settled on the twins, Terry and Larry. *Amazing. Identical. How're we going to tell them apart? Small, but they seemed eager to play.* He chuckled as he speculated, *Would they let me put a marker dot on one to know who is who?*

He sighed deeply as he read the last four names: *Phillip Edwards, Angelica Turner, David Petri, and Peter Marshall.* His face flushed in anger for a moment as he remembered. *These were the last four players left in the draft.* He moaned quietly, "One-fourth of our team graded out to be the four worst players in the league. We'll be lucky to win any games."

At that moment, Coach Tyree noticed the blue jeans and tennis shoes on Peter Marshall. *He wore them in the tryouts, too. Why instead of baseball stuff?*

He closed his notebook, blew his whistle, and motioned the players to gather around. They came bouncing his way. "Take a knee," he instructed. *Not many athletes,* he thought with a deep sigh. *I hope I don't regret bringing John William up to the league a year early.*

As the group settled down he said, "Look at the players around you. These are your teammates." *Hmmm,* he thought, *not much reaction.* "Our season'll depend on how well you work with each other and how well you learn the game and improve."

Still not much reaction so he paused to let the message sink in to their young mushy brains. He continued, "How good we become and how many games we win, will depend on how well each of you pull for each other. We will be only as good as our weakest player."

They are not getting the idea, he thought as the players all had a puzzled look. *Maybe I can demonstrate it another way.*

He motioned to a spot and said, "Stand in a line here and I will show you what I mean." As they formed a line he said, "Coach Sanders take one end. Tommy Lassiter take the other. Now everyone take hold of the hand of the player on your left and right." Slowly they grasp the player's hands on each side. He continued, "Hold tight and don't let go."

Pointing to Tommy and Coach Sanders, he said, "Now start pulling." Then he yelled, "Everyone hold on tight."

Instantly, there were ughs and grunts and laughs as the players strained to hold.

"Hold on! Don't let go!" Coach Tyree yelled.

The yells and giggles continued as the players struggled to hold on to each other. A couple fell to their knees, but still held. Finally, Angelica and another player couldn't hold any longer, and their hands were pulled apart. The line on both sides of them fell down from Coach Sanders pulling one direction and Tommy the other. All laughed.

Coach Tyree asked, "Understand now what it means about supporting the team? Only as good as our weakest player?" He looked around, but continued before anyone responded. "As long as we were connected, we were one team. When our hands broke, our team broke apart too. The team depends on each of us. We're only as good as our weakest player."

"…only good as our weakest player."

He asked "Understand?" as he looked around slowly into the eyes of each player. Each nodded "Yes" whether they did or not.

"Good. Now everyone jog a couple of laps around the field to loosen up and then we'll do some exercises. Need to strengthen those legs and get in shape. It will help our running, fielding, and batting. We want to be in better shape than the other teams."

He blew his whistle and the players took off, dropping their mitts behind on the ground. He immediately blew his whistle. The players stopped and looked back at him. He yelled, "Pick up your mitt and take it with you. It is your best friend. Take care of your friend. It goes with you when you run."

They hurried back, picked up their mitt "friends" and took off again. He yelled after them, "Stay near the fence." Soon three players were in the lead. Peter was near the front of the second group, and Sakine was running along side of him. Angelica brought up the distant rear.

As the players turned the right field corner, a deep voice said, "Come on Peter, you're faster than that. Show the coaches what you can do. Catch up to those players in front."

Clarence, Charley, Caroline, and Maggie's plan was to encourage Peter to perform at his potential. Peter was the only player who glanced around at the voice. They knew for sure now that he was the only human that could understand Clarence speak.

Peter picked up his pace, and caught the front players after one lap. He ran the rest of the way with them and, yes, Coach Tyree noticed.

After the run, Coach Tyree said, "Pair off and throw to each other. Start with short throws and then back up a few steps."

He noticed the parents gathered by the dugout, and he glanced at his watch. *Oops. Time for the meeting.* "Coach Sanders will work with you in throwing and catching. I'm with your parents, but I will be able to watch you from there."

Marilyn Davis saw Coach Tyree coming and moved towards him as he walked up to the parents. She spoke loud enough for the parents to hear, "Coach, the registrations and $35 have been turned in for all thirteen players."

He looked at her and replied, "Thanks. Would you keep them until after practice?"

She answered, in a softer voice, "Yes, I will meet you later." She was close enough he could smell her perfume.

Coach Tyree nodded he understood, and he turned to face the parents. Then momentarily he looked back at her, and a question popped into his mind, *Is she flirting with me? Here?* He answered himself, *No, can't be,* but before he thought more about her, his gaze took in the players on the field.

He was stunned. *Can't believe what I'm seeing.* Balls were thrown over the heads, wide to the side, and at the feet of the player trying to catch them. *My gosh,* he observed, *most of them can't throw, and even fewer can catch even when it's thrown right to them.* More players ran to retrieve balls than they were able to throw and catch them.

He was dumbfounded. *Most can't catch or throw a ball. It's a nightmare. If I wasn't the coach, I'd be laughing.*

As he turned to face the parents, he wondered, *what is their reaction?* He didn't see any.

He looked slowly over the group. *Most are women.* An inquisitive look appeared on his face. *Where are the men? Playing golf? Fishing?*

Are these single parents? His thoughts quickly returned to the field. *They see what's taking place on the field?*

He began to speak, and the ones sitting on the bleacher seats leaned forward. "My name's David Tyree. I'm the coach of the team. I'm glad to meet with you about your players and give you some idea of what to expect over the season."

"First," he said, "I have a son who is playing in the league this year and, since I would be at the ball field, I agreed to coach." He turned toward the field and pointed, "the man giving instruction is Jason Sanders. He agreed to be an assistant coach." He turned back to the group and continued, "Coach Sanders also has a son on the team, and that is why he's involved."

Still can't believe what I'm seeing on the field. He sighed deeply. "As you can see, we have lots to work on to become a team. Coach Sanders and I need help. If any of you have an interest in helping coach, please come talk to me."

He shuffled his papers and continued, "Second, the ball league requires that each team operate the concession stand when it is the home team for a game. This is a money-maker for the league, and it helps to pay the expenses. Every one of you must be involved, to do your part, and..." he paused and turned toward Marilyn Davis, "...a sign-up sheet is being passed around for the days that you can take your turn."

"Next, we'll wear white ball pants and a crimson belt to match our jerseys. Let's wear black cleats, but remember the rules don't allow metal spikes. We have a few team bats and batting helmets, but it's ok if you buy these for your player. Any questions so far?"

"What's the price for these things?" a parent asked.

"Jersey's $15. We order all of them at the same time, so give that to me. Do it today or by next practice. Pants cost about $13. Belt about $7. Cleats about $40 depending upon the brand. Batting helmets cost $20. Bats can be expensive. Recommend that you shop around."

He looked at the group and concluded the answer satisfied them. But *Hmmm,* he thought, *the woman in the back has an anguished look on her face. Wonder what her problem is?*

"Now let's talk about your player," Coach Tyree continued. "Each team will have thirteen players, but only nine can play at the same time. Means four players will be in the dugout. If one of those four is your child, both you and your child will be frustrated until they get to play. Now a player needs opportunities to play in order to learn and develop their skills. This league recognizes that, and has adopted special rules that require each player be provided the opportunity to play. For each game, each player must have at least one inning in the field and bat at least one time. If for some reason these two things do not occur, like shorter games because of high scores by one team, then the player left out must start the next game.

You can say that one inning is not enough since games at this age level usually are only six innings. As a parent, I tend to agree, but as a coach, I'm on the other side of the fence." Coach Tyree looked around and it looked like they were about to revolt. "Before you tar and feather me, let me explain." He paused as several in the group laughed.

"You should understand being on a team is about competing for a position and playing time. When a player works and produces better results than other players, the reward is more innings. Competition makes the player better and, in turn, the team gets better. I will coach the same way for our team. Each player will have to compete with the others for playing time. If a player outperforms others, the result will be more playing time.

Practice is important to improving. So, if your child doesn't come to team practices, you need to know now they may not play in the next game. Or, they may play only the minimum amount. Please understand, though, missing practices or games for legitimate reasons will be allowed. If any of you have a problem with playing time, come and talk. Okay?"

"The most important thing, your son or daughter needs your attention. They need to practice on their own, and they need your help. They can't do it by themselves. They'll need someone to throw and catch over and over with them. They won't improve very much without it. They need this every day that we don't practice."

> *"...your son or daughter needs your help.*
> *They won't improve much without it."*

He pointed towards the players on the field and said, "There is lots of room for every player to improve. For some, it will take more work than for others. As you can see, they're not even catching and throwing very well. The time we spend catching and throwing means less time for fielding and batting practices, not to mention live-game practice. We can't beat anyone if we don't throw well or catch the ball."

"Any questions?" he asked hoping there would be none.

A hand shot up and the question followed, "Do we have a sponsor for the team?"

"Thanks. Forgot to mention it. It's Rosie's Café. It is near the middle of the old part of town. Has a colorful history; kind of a throwback to Arlo's Alice's Restaurant."

No other questions he said, "Thanks again for letting your player be on our team." Then he headed to the field, and he was at the dugout when a woman's voice sounded behind him.

"Coach Tyree, do you have a minute?"

He thought it was Marilyn Davis, and an impatient look came to his face. *What now?* he wondered. He turned and was about to say, "I don't have time to talk with you at this moment," when to his surprise, it was the quiet woman from the back of the group. Before he caught himself, he answered in a sharp voice, "Yes, I have a minute." *Oops*, he thought.

"I'm Vicki Marshall," she replied with some hesitation. "Peter Marshall is my son." She had difficulty speaking and paused again. "Thank you for inviting Peter to be on your team. He has looked forward to playing for a long time."

"You're welcome, ma'am," he replied in a calmer voice and expression. "What's up?"

"Well, I ... uh ... I'm not sure how to say it." She paused, then blurted out, "About the money for those things you mentioned."

He recognized quickly where she was going with her comments, and he spoke with a softer tone, "Don't worry about this right now. We can order the jersey without the money being turned in, but Peter will need to pay for it when they arrive."

She seemed relieved with the information, but he could tell she had more concerns. He went further to ease her mind, "As for the ball pants and belt and shoes, Peter can practice in his blue jeans and tennis shoes until you can buy them. The league has a rule, though, that he'll need them in a game. The first one is in ten days. This help?"

A slight smile replaced the tenseness in her face, and for the first time she seemed relaxed a bit. She was grateful that Peter could practice. "That's great!" she said with a warm smile. "Thanks. Thank you so much."

"Good. Glad to work this out. Peter will have a good year," he tried to reassure her about the season and Peter playing.

She turned away and, as he walked towards the team on the field, he thought, *Needs to dress herself up a little.*

Coach Tyree blew his whistle and he motioned the players to take a knee as they arrived. He gave them the same message he gave to their parents about practice, competition, performance, and playing time. Then he dismissed them.

Later in comparing notes, Coach Sanders express frustration, "We have only four players who can throw and catch very well. Two-three others are fair, and the rest are flat pitiful. How can they be so bad?"

"Yes, I could see that even speaking to the parents. Not good." Coach Tyree replied in an anguished tone. "Looks like we'll spend most of our practice time just throwing and catching. I'm okay with learning the basics, but most of the other teams are far ahead of us and will be playing practice games and having team scrimmages."

As Vicki walked home, she thought about the parents' meeting and later with Coach Tyree. *Intended to ask him why the coaches made fun of Peter at the tryouts.* She walked about a block and sighed deeply. *Oh, well, there will be another time to ask him.*

Suddenly, Peter pedaled up on his bike. "Hi, mom," he said as he circled around her. "Glad you came," he said gleefully. "See my team? Meet Coach Tyree?" Before she could respond, he rattled off other questions that weren't easy to answer. "Coach Tyree said to practice on our own. Can you throw with me when we get home? When can we buy my uniform stuff?"

Her voice choked as she replied, "Let's talk about this at home, okay?"

"Sure," Peter answered and peddled off yelling over his shoulder, "See ya at the house."

Questions engulfed Vicki's mind. *How am I going to pay for these uniform and equipment costs? Hun can't play without them. Have until first game. Ten days doesn't help. How do I juggle two jobs and come up with more time to help him? Don't have time to do many things around the house now.* Her eyes teared and her lips quivered. *Already sacrificed personal time. What's left?* She stumbled teary-eyed into the drive.

[CHAPTER 8]

Opening Day, Team Pictures, and More
Taunts; "How did Mom pay for my uniform?";
Papers from the Mortgage Company

"Tomorrow is my first game," Peter mumbled joyfully half asleep. It was a dream finally coming true. He had awakened several times already from the exciting thoughts. *My first real baseball game. Will I start? What position will I play? Coach has played me mostly in right field in practice. What's the batting order? How many base hits will I get? Any home runs?*

Each time he awakened he recalled something that led to this moment. *After I put on my jersey, pants, and cleats for the first time, Mom said proudly, "You look like a real ballplayer."*

When he saw himself in the mirror, it struck him that, *Yes, I do look like a real ballplayer.* Then in a confident voice, "I may haf'ta wear blue jeans in practice, but no one will laugh at me with my uniform."

Before bed, he spread his jersey out beside his dad's on the curved lid of an old trunk. Mom had given it to him and explained, "Your dad got the trunk from his dad, your granddad. He brought it with him when his parents immigrated from Old Austria."

Several times during the night, Peter would go over to the jerseys, move his fingers along the numbers and say, "46." During one of those times, he touched his jersey to his cheek. *I wonder if dad knows. Hope so.*

Wish I could wear them in practice, too, Peter thought sadly as he remembered money being tight in the family. *How did Mom pay for my uniform and the other things like leggings, socks, and this protector-cup thing?*

Sure was uncomfortable when I first put it on, he recalled, *and embarrassing when the clerk said with a sheepish grin, "It might be on upside down if it feels uncomfortable."*

And there was a batting glove. *I wasn't going to ask for one, but Mom insisted. "The other players use one to bat, so you're going to have one too."*

Peter recalled how he struggled to convince her he didn't need a batting helmet or bat. "I have a bat, mom. Remember?" he asked as he showed her his Savoy bat. "I can use it or one of the team bats. And I can use a team helmet."

Still, he wondered, *How did mom pay for the other things?*

Years later, when he reflected on this time, he realized the answer. Mom sacrificed so he could follow his dream to play ball. *How did she do those things to make it happen?* Then quickly he knew the obvious—*Mom gave up things for herself to provide the same equipment all the other players had. Even seemingly unimportant things like a batting glove.*

Peter dozed off momentarily, but soon woke again. This time Coach Tyree's comments about the opening of the season were on his mind.

"All eight teams will play, and there'll be four games. Our team plays in the second game about noon. It will be a big day. All eight teams will be on the field at once for the opening ceremony. Each team and player will be introduced over the Public Address system. No other park or high school in Tallahassee has one. The flag will be raised and National Anthem played. Lots of spectators, and the concession will be open to satisfy every delight of junk foods."

Peter pictured in his mind what the day'd look like because he had watched the opening ceremony several times from Big Fella, the old oak tree in right field. *The aroma of fresh popcorn filled the air. Smoke from hamburgers and hotdogs cooked on the grill drifted over the field, and filtered slowly away through the trees. Food smells would entice both humans and animals to come. The humans'd spend lots of money at the concession stand, and animals'd sniff for morsels dropped to the ground after the humans had packed up and left.*

He rolled over and tried to sleep, but the anticipation of the exciting day kept him sky-high and wide awake. Must've looked at the clock a hundred times.

Meanwhile, Mom couldn't sleep either, but it was for another reason. She had received mail from the financial company that held the mortgage on their house. It was a registered notice for failing to make mortgage payments. The papers read:

Dear Mrs. Vicki Marshall,

This registered letter is to confirm that you are three months delinquent with mortgage payments and the next payment is due at the end of this month. By this registered letter, the Company gives notice that the overdue payments must be made current. The Company requests that, if there is a problem in making the payments, it be contacted. Failure to bring the mortgage payments current or work out an acceptable solution will result in foreclosure being initiated to recover the balance of the loan. Respectfully...

Vicki slipped a robe on and quietly made her way to the kitchen where she reread the letter. Her face and lips tightened with the stress. *Knew it would come soon,* she thought as she sighed deeply. She gazed through the window at the breaking dawn. *But reading its contents is far worse than I'd imagined.* The tears flowing down her cheeks glistened in the sun rays coming through the window.

The money I've earned the last three months was only enough to pay for our utilities, food, a few bills, Hun's uniform and cleats, and some personal things for Sally and Elizabeth. Peter's life insurance money is gone. Nothing left!

Up stairs, Peter rolled over and looked at the clock. "Finally, 7:30! First game'll start soon." *Gotta get up,* he reasoned. *Besides Pokey's barking loudly at something outside and I can't sleep anyway. Probably a squirrel. She chases them, but I think they're really friends.*

He slid out of bed, went through the motions of brushing his teeth and hair. He started *to dress. It is unbelievable—this feeling!*

He posed in front of the mirror, held up his arms, and pretended to bat. He swung. *It's a base hit and the winning run scores.* Then he grabbed his cap and cleats and tiptoed down the stairs past mom's bedroom. *Don't want to wake her if she's not working.*

The house was quiet, but Peter still heard Pokey's occasional bark. "Shuuuu, Pokey," he mumbled. "You are gonna wake everybody." As he walked into the kitchen to get a glass of juice and eat some cereal, he was surprised to find his mom. She didn't see him come in, though, as her back was to him and deep in thought.

Probably making some breakfast, Peter thought as he said, "Hi, Mom."

Vicki jumped, startled by his voice, and turned away from him quickly. *Mom's eyes are red. She has been crying. Why?*

He noticed she had papers in her hands and asked him a question to divert his attention, "How about an extra treat with your breakfast on this special day?" She put the papers into its envelope while she waited for his reply, casually placing it on the counter by the doorway.

Peter hurried to his mom and gave her his usual big hug and kisses on the cheek, and said, "Yes" to the offer. Then while she prepared it, he picked up the trash sack and hurried off to do outside chores. This included feeding and watering Pokey.

Pokey knew Peter'd be coming outside about that time of day, and she was waiting to greet him with the usual anticipation and wag of the tail. She wanted to play, and she jumped at him with a lick to the face and a sharp bark. The message was something like, "Tag—you're it!"

Peter giggled and wiped the lick off. He loved Pokey, his trusty playmate. She was his devoted friend, but he said, "Not this morning. I have a game to play. Later, okay?"

Pokey cocked her head to one side and looked at him as if she understood. Then she trotted alongside as Peter carried the sack to the trash can at the back edge of the yard.

"Slow down," Vicki admonished Peter as he downed his breakfast in two bites, chased by one gulp of juice. "I have your things ready and you'll get there in time," she added as she walked to the backdoor where she was going to give him a special send-off.

As Peter placed his glass on the counter beside the envelope his mom held earlier, he noticed the return address. *What's a mortgage company? Way Mom looked, must be something serious.* Two steps later, his mind was on the events of the day and, in a flash, he was pedaling fast to the ballpark.

The morning coolness was giving way to warmer temperatures as the sun climbed in the sky. "Where are those pesky owls?" Clarence wondered in his rumbling voice as he stretched his branches and shook the night due off his leaves. He knew the likely answer, but he said it anyway, "Catching a few extra winks in the golf course woods." He shook his branches again. "First game's underway. Peter will be here soon."

Those words still echoed through the woods when Peter pedaled into sight. Moments later, he parked his bike against Clarence's massive trunk. "Gently, gently," Clarence mumbled with a chuckle as if the bike could hurt him.

Peter untied his bat and mitt from the bike handle, pulled his cap down almost over his eyes, and hitched his pants up.

What is he doing? Clarence wondered. *He can barely see where he is going. Are all human ballplayers this strange, or is Peter different? And what is he smiling about?*

Clarence didn't know it, but when Peter first tried on his uniform, his mom said, "The way you hitch your pants up reminds me of how your dad hitched his when he played ball." Peter would think, *Dad is with me,* and a warm smile'd come to his face.

The sound of "Hey batter, hey batter," by the players on the field caught Peter's attention. They were crouched over and ready to spring into action if the batter hit the ball their way. "It's like what Coach Tyree said, 'Be like lions stalking a prey.' Hafta 'member that."

He glanced at the old rusty scoreboard: *Bears 2 and Lions 1, second inning.* After a few more pitches, he noticed, *My team is already getting together behind the 3rd base dugout,* so he jogged in that direction.

Along the way, Peter had to pass by the concession stand where a few players from the Tigers team, the defending champions, were snacking on popcorn.

One noticed Peter jogging their direction, and he made a loud taunting comment. "Hey guys, look. Mr. Blue Jeans now has baseball pants." Then he purposely stepped in Peter's path and asked with a laugh, "Where's the jeans? You will play better with 'em."

A second Tigers player followed with another taunt, "Mr. Blue Jeans, where are your tennis shoes? Those cleats won't help your play. Better go home and get your tennies."

By that time, other players and fans around the concession stand heard the taunts and, by the sounds, Peter thought, *Everyone's snickering at me.*

Taunts like these weren't new to Peter. Besides his blue jeans and tennis shoes, he had also received jabs about his dad's baggy shirt and his old baseball glove. Even some of his own teammates made comments when coaches weren't in hearing range. Today, dressed in full uniform, Peter thought it would be different, but it wasn't.

His face flushed red with anger, and his impulse was *Gonna punch you in the nose.* He took a few steps towards one of the Tigers players, but he trotted on his way when he remembered what Coach said, "Any player who gets in trouble off the field will sit next game."

Peter heard another taunt over his shoulder as he trotted on his way, but he couldn't make out the words. *I will show you on the field someday,* he promised. *Just wait.*

Some of Peter's teammates heard the taunting and had smirks on their faces as he arrived. Tommy Lassiter and Lacroy Carter were about to make comments, but Coach Tyree and his son, John William, walked up at that moment.

"Okay team," Coach Tyree said as he pointed toward his pickup.

"Get the equipment bags, and take them down by the pitcher's bullpen where we'll warm up for the game."

"I'll take this one," Big Tommy Lassiter said bragging tone as he threw the largest bag over his shoulder. "Takes a man to carry it."

Not to be outdone, the small Smith twins each grabbed a bag, but its size was a problem. "Help me!" one yelled desperately as he fell and the bag rolled on top of him. The others laughed, and the other twin dropped his bag to help his brother. They were the last ones to the bullpen, so Big Tommy came to their rescue. It seemed, though, he carried them too.

Coach Tyree pointed and said, "Photographer is taking team pictures. If you want to buy an individual picture, do it now. When through, stretch, and toss a ball with another player."

I would like to have a picture, Peter thought, *but don't think mom has the money.*

Photography was over, Coach Tyree observed. "Everyone in and grab a knee." He paused for a moment to let them get settled, and then he handed a sack of bubble gum to pass around. They giggled as they took a piece and started chewing.

Coach Tyree looked around at the joy on player faces. Thoughts of how each one performed in practice were going through his mind. After a while, he spoke, "We've talked about the player line-up before, and what I expect out of each one of you. This is our first game, and we have thirteen more before we play in a tournament for the league championship. Most of the other teams have played practice games while we've been mostly catching and throwing."

He looked around at the parents. "We have made good progress, but don't have much game experience so we know our team play'll be rough at times. The players who have performed best in practice will start. No favorites." He held up the line-up. "This will be in the dugout so you can see where you play and what order in the line-up you'll bat. Be ready to go on to the field or to bat. Everyone understand?"

Each player either nodded or said, "Yes, sir."

Coach Tyree softened his voice, "Only nine players can be on the field at one time." He paused and looked around, "That means four of you wil be on the bench, but you will replace four others after three innings. Everyone should get the opportunity to bat at least once. If not, you will start the next game."

With a stern look, he continued, "No matter if you're in the game or on the bench to start, hustle and give it your best effort. How well you play in the early games will help Coach Sanders and me set the line-ups in later games and determine the amount of playing time for each player. No one has a lock on a position. Understand?"

All players nodded, "Yes," but Coach Tyree observed some did so with little enthusiasm.

"The more games we play," he continued, "the better I expect each of you to become. All of you can improve. If you do, we'll be a better team as the season progresses. When we take the field, go to your position on the line-up. Four positions will have two players listed."

Coach Tyree looked at Lacroy Carter and said, "You will start as pitcher, and Jake Sanders will replace you. Give us your best, Okay? Let's hold the runs down on the other team. Stay here, and work with Coach Sanders."

At that moment, whooping noises came from the field. Peter glanced at the scoreboard, *Game's over. Bears won.*

As soon as the players shook hands with the opponent, they packed and left the dugout. Coach Tyree smiled and said, "Okay, this is it. Let's go get 'em."

Peter's mind raced as the players walked into the dugout. *What position will I play? Will I start? Do I havta share with someone?* As he scanned down the list of names, his breathing became heavier and his eyes opened wider with each name he passed. Down, down, down. *I don't see it!* He panicked and his heart pounded so hard it seemed it was trying to escape his chest. Frantically, he wondered, *Where is it? Sakine Davis's starting at 2nd!* His eyes reached number nine. *I'm on the bench!* Disappointment crushed his heart. *I'm on the bench! I'm sitting on the bench when the game starts. A girl is ahead of me!*

Peter continued to read down the list, and confirmed what he knew already. *I'm one of the four players on the bench and I share right field position with David Petri.* He tried to console himself, *At least I get to play the last three innings.* Then agony swept over him as he suddenly realized, *I'm the last on the team to bat! Even Angelica'll bat before me. She's terrible!*

While other players enjoyed the moment, Peter fought back tears as he walked to the far corner of the dugout, leaned his bat against the wall, and mumbled, "Won't need you for a while." After a time of sulking, his face lit up with a positive thought, *When I get my base hit, Coach'ill start me next game.*

Soon Coach Tyree yelled, "Okay, gang. Let's go."

The players left the dugout yelling and hollering as they ran to their positions for the warm-up. Peter and David Petri did the same as they trotted to right field.

[CHAPTER 9]

Rosie's Café, a Historical Place Where…;
Peter's First Real Baseball Game;
Coaches' Review the Game

"B out time you showed up," Clarence bellowed impatiently to Caroline and Charley as they sailed towards him. "Peter's game is 'bout to start. Where you been?"

"Aww," Charley squawked in a sharp tone. "We had a rough night," Charley added as they landed softly on their favorite branch of Clarence's. He stretched his wings, yawned, and continued. "There was a loud noise around the Cascades basin, and nothing was stirring. Had to hunt further away. Up most of the night.

"Not surprised," Clarence replied in a frustrated tone. "That noise was from what some humans call a 'concert.' They call it 'music.' Made everything in the woods uneasy."

Caroline fluffed her wings and feathers to get comfortable and hooted, "It's a problem fo' Cha'lee an me. Maht havta nest fu'tha off if food's scared away."

"Hope not," Clarence replied and then turned to the subject at hand. "Peter's game against Quincy's Bombers is about to start. His team's about to take the field."

"Is he starting?" Charley squawked.

"Not sure yet. Find out soon."

Caroline saw a name on Peter's team jerseys and asked, "Whad's a Rosie's Cafe?"

"It is ... uh ... er ... a," Charley stammered as he tried to think of an explanation.

Clarence noticed Charley's beak had tighten and his eyes had crossed so Clarence interceded for his feathery friend, "Well, Caroline," he said in a fatherly voice, "it's the name of the sponsor for Peter's team. A sponsor provides money to help buy equipment and things."

"But whad's the name mean, and wha's it on the ju'sey?"

"I have heard about Rosie's Café over the years. It began as a breakfast and coffee shop about the same time the first Model T rolled into Tallahassee. It's still in business today and located about six blocks from here in 'Old Town.' It is about a block down the street from the old State Capitol building."

Clarence paused to let Charley say something. He didn't, so he continued, "I overheard some humans back in the 1950s, right here at this ball field, talking excitedly about Rosie's. They said, 'Rosie's had been remodeled into a counter-and-stool soda fountain place. Small wood tables and wire-frame chairs were added along with a new jukebox for playing 45s. The pine floor was great for dancing!' Hear tell Rosie's still looks the same today, and the old jukebox still works: plays 45s for a dime each and three for two bits. Johnny

Horton's 'Honky Tonk Man' and Buddy Holly's 'Peggy Sue' are popular record choices, and the old pine boards creak with each jitterbug step. The old shoeshine stand still sits next to the jukebox, but it's only for looks now days since folks who can give a good buff are rare."

Charley finally made a contribution, "Must be a special place to have survived so long."

"Yeah, it was, and is," Clarence replied but with a sad tone as he reflected for a moment about some changes that've taken place nearby over his lifetime.

He perked up, though, as he continued describing Rosie's, "I have heard humans say, 'Going to Rosie's on a Saturday evening is like stepping back in time. Thick malts and soda drinks are made like in the 1950s. Chairs and tables are shoved against the wall, and the jukebox struts its stuff while sock-hopping dancers joyfully relive history.'"

"Be'cha those humans enjoy that," Caroline hooted as she fluffed her feathery wings.

"Ya be'cha," Clarence bellowed joyfully as he was getting more and more into the spirit, "and it wasn't just for the common folks either. Eat at Rosie's regularly and you're likely to look up and see the Governor of Florida plop down on the stool next to you and casually remark, 'How's it goin?' like the two of you met every day for grits 'n fixins or a short stack, a little chit-chat and Rosie's famous hot black coffee that has an aroma and kick out of this world."

"Wow!" Charley exclaimed. "With all that colorful history, the players on Peter's team must be honored to have Rosie's Café as their sponsor."

"You would think, but not so," Clarence replied, "The players wanted to be called 'The Mustangs,' and on the downside, the name has brought taunts from other teams."

"By the way," Clarence asked, "where's Maggie?"

"Said couldn't get here until later," Charley replied. "but definitely wouldn't miss the treats left by the humans."

"Okay; just wondering."

"Look," Charley hooted as he pointed a feathery wing towards the dugout, "They're about to start. The coach's circled the team, and Quincy's batters are warming up."

Coach Tyree extended his hands, and said with an excited voice, "Everyone put them in here, and let's give a yell." It was another way of building the idea of "team" among them.

The players squeezed their sweaty bodies forward, and piled hands one on top of another.

"All together now," he yelled as they joined with him, "One, two, three, team!"

"Louder," he yelled, "one more time."

"ONE, TWO, THREE, TEAM!" they screamed. The starters trotted gleefully to their field positions while Peter and the other three bench sitters walked sadly into the dugout where they turned towards the field and watched through chain link fencing.

"Look," Clarence grumbled, "Peter is not starting."

"The deaah boy looks sad," Caroline squawked mournfully.

Charley's head twitched and he added, "Hope he stays alert and ready to play later."

Meanwhile Coach Sanders encouraged Rosie's pitcher and catcher. "Okay, let's get 'em," he yelled to Lacroy Carter pitching and to Scrubs Larry Johnson catching.

The game was on as the umpire pointed to the first Bombers batter, and said, "Batter up."

After only three pitches, Coach Sanders called "Time" in a frustrated tone in his voice, and went to the mound to talk with Lacroy and Scrubs.

When he returned to the sideline, Coach Tyree asked. "What's the matter?"

Coach Sanders looked at him with a frustrated expression and replied, "We're in deep trouble." He paused, took a deep breath to settle down and continued, "Neither one can remember the signals I'm giving of what pitch I want thrown."

"You mean..."

"Yeah," Coach Sanders replied before Coach Tyree could finish. "And after all the time we have practiced the signals, neither one can remember right now."

"First game jitters?" Coach Tyree inquired in a hopeful tone. Then he followed with the all-important question, "what do we do now?"

Coach Sanders looked at him, shrugged his shoulders, and replied with a sheepish grin, "A wise coach recently told me when I asked a similar question, 'We will hafta wing it.'"

Coach Tyree understood. He was the "wise coach." He glanced at Coach Sanders with a "That's not a good answer" look, but couldn't hold it. Soon both chuckled at their coaching predicament. "It figures," Coach Tyree said with raised eyebrows. After a few moments, he added, "This is going to be interesting to watch you pull the rabbit out of the hat."

As it turned out, didn't matter what Coach Sanders tried. "He is only throwing fast balls to the batters," Coach Sanders muttered in frustration. "Lecroy has a decent curve ball and an off-speed ball so why doesn't he use them?"

"Don't know," Coach Tyree responded. Then, knowing Coach

Sanders didn't have an answer, he followed with a little sarcasm, "YOU ARE the pitching guru. You tell me."

No matter what Coach Sanders tried, Lacroy only threw fast balls. They went everywhere: in the dirt, over the batter's head, behind the batter, and sometimes across the plate for strikes. Coach Sanders mumbled, "At least the wild pitching's kept the batters hopping and they are not getting many hits."

"You are right," Coach Tyree agreed. "And Scrubs is earning his spurs today," he added referring to Scrubs literally getting down in the dirt to block and catch the balls. Some got by him to the backstop, and he had to run after them.

After a while, the extra stretching in Scrubs' ball pants caused the crotch to split. The spectators and players close by laughed. Players on the Tigers team heckled especially loud, but Scrubs kept his focus. "That a boy," Coach Tyree yelled encouragingly, "keep doing your job."

Peter kept looking through the crowd for his mom during the game. "Hope she can get off work to come," he mumbled sadly each time he didn't see her.

Soon the third inning ended. "You players are in for the rest of the game," Coach Tyree reminded the four on the bench. Peter was delighted but, unfortunately, the player he replaced had just batted.

Peter ran happily to right field, *Finally playing!* Then suddenly a negative thought struck him, *I won't get to bat until eight other batters do. May not until the last inning.* Panic set in, *Maybe not at all!*

"Look!" Charley hooted excitedly and hopped up and down on the branch. "Peter's in the game, in the game."

"Ah see'um, ah see'um!" Caroline squawked loudly while bobbing her head around.

"Shhhh," Clarence said quietly. "Don't distract the lad."

Nothing was hit Peter's direction until the last inning when a big left-handed player came to bat. Everyone gasped when he hit a bomb high in the branches of Clarence for an automatic home run. Two runners were on base, so three runs scored.

Clarence said, "Ouch" when the ball hit him, even though it obviously didn't hurt him.

Peter heard the voice, and looked backward towards the fence to see who said it. *Same one I've heard before, but no one's around.* His brow wrinkled and a curious look appeared on his face as he wondered, *Who said that?*

He didn't wonder long as the next voice he heard was Coach Tyree yelling across the field where everyone could hear. "Peter, get your head in the game. Next batter's ready to bat."

Finally Rosie's got three outs on the Bombers, and Clarence said to the three friends, "Peter'll get to bat."

"Yea-a-a-a-a-a!" howled Maggie as Caroline and Charley squawked enthusiastically.

Peter slipped on his new batting glove, grabbed his Savoy bat, and hitched up his pants. *Now I will show 'em.*

As he left the dugout with his Savoy bat, he brushed by Sakine holding her own bat. She whispered out the side of her mouth, "Maybe you can hit better then you can catch."

Peter's face instantly turned red with anger, and he momentarily glared at her with a piercing look. "Weren't so hot yourself," he mumbled. As he walked on, he angrily thought, *If you weren't a GIRL, I would...*

Sakine must have read his mind as she shot back, "Don't let that stop you!"

Her words didn't penetrate as his thoughts were on his moment of glory. He had watched batters many times from outside the fence by Clarence and put himself in their positions. He dreamed of getting a base hit in a real game and driving in the winning run.

Come on, he thought with bat ready as he stared at the pitcher. *Throw me a ball to hit.*

Suddenly, the Bomber's catcher snickered and whispered as he pointed to Peter's feet, "Hey batter, gum is stuck all over your cleats."

Peter was distracted momentarily and, as he looked down, the first pitch hit the catcher's mitt with a thump. The sound startled him, and he jerked backwards and almost stumbled to the ground in a reflex action.

"Strike," yelled the umpire as he held up his hand. Then he bent over and cautioned Peter, "You must watch the pitcher, son. You can get hurt if a ball hits you.

"Come on, Peter," Coach Tyree yelled sternly. "Keep your eyes on the pitcher."

"Oh, my," Clarence moaned to the friends. "Peter wasn't ready for the first pitch."

Peter was upset about not seeing the ball pitched, but he made the mistake again when he glanced over his shoulder back at Coach Tyree. By the time he refocused on the pitcher, he realized the next pitch was almost at the plate. He whipped the bat wildly at the ball, but it had already hit the catcher's mitt with another thump.

"Strike two," the umpire called with raised arm.

Peter was even more upset now, and was determined to be ready for the next pitch. He tightened his jaw and looked at the pitcher with steely eyes. *No distractions this time!*

Unfortunately, his body was wound so tight, like a trap, it would snap into action at the slightest thing. The Bomber's coaches noticed, and signaled, "*Throw outside the plate.*" Sure enough, Peter swung even though the ball was so far outside he had no chance of hitting it.

"Strike three. You're out," the umpire yelled.

"Yikes! The boy struck out in three pitches!" Charley squawked agonizingly as he almost fell off the branch from the moment. "Worst batter of the game! He's terrible! Has one time at bat, and he never came close to touching the ball with that special bat of his."

"Now, don't throw in the towel so fast," cautioned Clarence calmly. "Remember? It's not what he is, but what he can become. That is why we're allowed to help him."

"Well, the job may be impossible," Charley hooted as he tried to refocus his eyes from his near fall. "Looked like the ball created a vacuum and sucked his bat into the path it just traveled." He paused for a moment and pondered Clarence's reminder, "What can we do?"

"One step at a time," Clarence replied. "Patience and one step at a time."

I looked terrible, Peter thought as he slowly walked with his head down back to the dugout. Out of the corners of his eyes, he could see some players on the Tigers team laughing. "I really showed them," he sarcastically mumbled.

To make matters worst, Tommy Lassiter and Lacroy Carter tormented him with puckered lips and crying expressions. Peter ignored them, and walked on to the far end of the dugout.

The game ended soon, and Rosie's lost by a score of 9 to 1. Once the teams shook hands and Rosie's moved out of the dugout, Coach Tyree called them together for a pep talk.

Team parents also gathered nearby. Most were there, being opening day, but Peter didn't see his mom. *Guess Mom couldn't leave work early. Glad she didn't see how badly I played.*

Peter's gaze fell on Sakine talking to her mother, Marilyn Davis. *Wonder why she didn't pick on me too after my pitiful batting?* He didn't know that her mother was upset because messed up hair and dirt and grass stains down the front of Sakine's jersey was not the neat, clean, and feminine look she wanted for her daughter.

Coach Tyree gazed slowly around at the players and parents, and his first words were to pep the team up. "We did some good things today. That was a good team we played. They had seven players from last year, and the coaches considered them one of the best in the league. We hung in there for a while, but they have had lots more game practices than us. Result: We couldn't stay with them, so hold your heads up." He looked around and continued, "Coach Sanders and I think you did really well. We will get better. I promise you, and . . ." to break the tension he added with a chuckle, "we will clean their plow next time."

Coach Sanders looked up quickly, and wondered, *What is with the corny country talk?* Players and parents also laughed.

"Couple more things," Coach Tyree continued, "We have a game Monday evening. Be on time. Also, the opening ceremony begins in a few minutes so be ready to go on as a team."

As soon as the ceremony was over, Peter retreated to his bike under the security and shade of Clarence. "Wha'ze do'in?" Caroline asked quietly from their branch over Peter's head.

"Dunno," replied Charley. "Watching the Sharks and Tigers."

After three innings, the Tigers led by ten runs. Peter wondered

What it'd be like to play for them? I'd probably be really good with all those good players. Wish they'd drafted me.

Soon he hopped on his bike. "Look," Caroline hooted softly, "Boy's leavin'."

Meanwhile, Coaches Tyree and Sanders dissected their first game. "Had some good play today," Coach Tyree said while reviewing his notes.

"Sure did," Coach Sanders responded. "Playing experience makes a big difference. Our returners and our first pick, Rick Taylor, made some good plays, but we still can do better."

"Agree. Your son, Jake, pitched well for the first time, and that Sakine's a scrappy player. Liked how she dove at those hits between 1st and 2nd."

"Yeah, but did'ja notice her mom giving her a 'what for' about the dirt and grass stains on her jersey front and pants?"

"No. Really? When was that?"

"Yeah. After the game. I heard her say to Sakine, 'You look like one of those long haired hippies from the nineteen sixties who had been rollicking in the meadow at Woodstock.'"

Coach Tyree chuckled as he agreed, "She did kind'a look like one after the rubber band holding her hair broke, but I doubt Sakine knows anything about that history." He paused to make a note and continued, "We will need to head off Sakine's mom or we won't get much out of her rest of the season." Then he made another note. "Difficult for Tommy Lassiter to get that big body moving so we need to adjust player at 2nd to reach balls away from him at 1st."

"Good point." Coach Sanders chuckled. "Felt like pushing him a couple of times,"

"Maybe we can hide a cattle hotshot on you," Coach Tyree replied with a laugh.

"Not sure that would get him to moving fast enough."

Coach Tyree became serious again as he looked at his notes. "For the experience of the Bomber's, the score seemed close, but..." He paused again, "in all honesty, Rosie's performance was a comedy of errors." One-by-one the coaches discussed them.

"Sakine is a hustler, but she was on the ground more than standing. Dove many times before finally snagging a ground ball. Needs ground ball fielding practice, but I still see her on the ground lots in a game so need to talk to her mother."

Coach Tyree paused for a moment. *Since she's flirting with me, don't want to go there.* He looked at Coach Sanders and said, "You heard her getting after Sakine, so how 'bout you talking with her?"

"Well-l-l-l-l," Coach Sanders replied, and then joked, "I will take one for the team."

Coach Tyree didn't react and continued with his notes. "Another time was when Terry Smith was playing 3rd base, and charged toward a slow grounder coming his way. He stumbled forward as he bent to scoop the ball into his mitt, but instead stabbed it into the ground."

"Yeah, that was funny. When he fell face down and rolled over spitting red dirt, I laughed with everyone else. I shouldn't have done it, but it was just to funny."

"Don't fret too much. I struggled to hold it in too. Bottom line, though, we need lots of practice fielding ground balls."

"You are right, and maybe then we'll get the out instead of runner on by fielder's error."

"I'm not sure that practice is the answer for some players," Coach Tyree lamented as he described another comedy. "How many times has Phillip Edwards done the same thing in trying to catch a fly ball? No matter where we place these last draft picks, the ball finds them."

"I know whatcha mean. When that fly ball was hit towards him in left field and he ran forward to catch it, I thought maybe he will remember and do it this time."

"Yeah, thought the same. But Phillip's trying to catch a fly ball is *like that bad dream in the movie, Groundhog* Day. Each time it turns out the same. Phillip *always* runs in to far, the ball's over his head, he realizes it—I think. He gets his body moving backwards but not his feet so he jumps backward with his mitt in the air as the ball flies overhead."

Coach Sanders' laughed as he interrupted him and he choked, too, but he managed to continue, "Where was I? Oh, yes, ... Phillip falls to the ground, the ball rolls to the fence, he lies face down and pounds the ground and cries instead of jumping up and running after it, and some other player gets it and throws it in."

By now both choked with laughter, but Coach Tyree finally managed to ask, "How many more times is Phillip going to have that *Groundhog Day* moment?"

"No answer for you," Coach Sanders managed to reply through more laughs. Then he jested, "Maybe our head coach should do a better job in drafting players."

"Can say that again, podner! Hav'ta give'em a piece of our mind 'bout that." Then he looked at his notes and continued. "Our hitting wasn't very good either. Only a couple of hits in the top of the order. Have to work on that, too."

He paused for a moment reflecting on the game. "Ya know, that Peter Marshall runs pretty well and has great intensity, but he plays like he's never seen a baseball, let alone catch or throw or hit one. Needs lots of practice on his own. I've seen his mom, but where's his dad?"

"I've not seen him either," Coach Sanders replied. "Peter was so anxious to bat, and then strikes out in only three pitches. He'll improve if he can get some one-on-one help." He paused for a moment. Know any coaches we can recruit?"

"You know that answer already," Coach Tyree replied in a matter-of-fact tone. "Going to be a long season if we're not able somehow to get our last six picks to perform better. Don't have the hitting or fielding to carry 'em, and the two of us don't have enough time."

When Peter arrived home, the house was quiet and he found a note from mom on the kitchen counter.

"Hun, if you find this note, then I wasn't able to leave work early to come to your game. I know it was a special day, and I wanted so much to be there. I'm sorry I couldn't. I'll explain later. I hope you had a good game. Left a plate of food in the fridge and will fix more later. Sally and Elizabeth are overnighting with friends so just you and me tonight. Can't wait to hear about the game. L ya, mom."

A curious frown mixed with the sad look on Peter's face. *Mom's still at work? What's up? She is usually off by late-afternoon.*

What is a mortgage company?

As he reached for a juice glass in the cabinet, he saw the envelope his mom had placed there that morning. His attention fell on the return company name. *What is a mortgage company? And why was Mom crying?*

Peter didn't know it, but his mom had taken a second job to help pay their bills. When she finally came home late in the evening, the first thing she did was go straight to Peter and ask, "Hun, how was the game?"

"We lost," Peter mumbled. Then added, "gotta go feed Pokey," 'cause he didn't want further questions.

On her way home, Vicki stopped by the ball field. She learned his team lost and that he didn't do well. *I will bathe and talk to him later,* she reasoned, *when he can talk about it.*

When she did, she said, "Hun, I'm sorry I couldn't be at the game. I wanted so much to see you play your first game and bat, but right now I need to work extra hours when I can. You may not understand right now, but in time you will."

"I know, Mom," Peter said with a shaky voice. "You would have if you could. It's okay."

By the sound of his voice she knew he was hiding his great disappointment, and her emotions sent her on a guilt trip. She continued to explain, "I even tried to get off for a few minutes to maybe come to the field to see you hit, but I couldn't even do that."

She noticed he had tears, so she decided to talk about his next game. "Your next one's Monday evening. You will do much better. I promise, and I'll do everything I can to be there."

[CHAPTER 18]

Peter Dislikes History; Sakine Fires a 'Hot one' to Peter; Team Loses. Coach Instructs to Practice with Parents; Peter Reminisces over Dad's Photos

Peter hustled home after school on Monday. *Glad Mom left me a snack,* he thought as he pulled it from the fridge. *Hungry, and a note, too.* He grinned as he gobbled the food down and walked upstairs to his room to do homework. He read the note again.

"Hun, I hope you have a great game today. Think about good things and they'll happen. I will try to get off work early so I can come before the game ends. I will be thinking of you all the time so do well for me. Okay? And oh yes, remember your coach wants players to come early if they can for some batting practice. Love ya bunches, Mom. X X X X."

Seeing the Xs brought another big grin. "Love you too, Mom," he mumbled.

Peter finished math homework and looked at his other book. "History!" he exclaimed with a sourpuss face. "Hate history!" *Why does anyone need to know about what happened long ago? Gonna help me get a base hit?* He glanced at the clock. *Time to go. I will study it later.*

He changed quickly into his uniform, strapped his mitt and bat to his bike and soon was at the ball field. *I'm late. Team is already having batting practice and warming up.* He hopped off and let his bike roll to its side at the foot of Clarence's massive trunk.

"He didn't even look up to see if we were here," Charley squawked disappointedly as Peter trotted towards his dugout.

Peter looked for the player line-up as he walked into the dugout. *There it is. I will do better this game.* He repeated those words over and over since the first game. *Mom said, "I was just nervous, and I would do better with experience."*

His eyes scanned down the batting order list and, with each name he passed, his anxiety increased. Down, down he looked. He mumbled angrily after not seeing his name in the top nine, "On the bench again. Not fair. If I hav'ta share a position, I should at least get to start this time."

"Look," Clarence said to Caroline and Charley as Peter walked slowly out on the field. "Peter looks depressed. Must be on the bench again when the game starts."

Peter shagged balls with the other players for batting practice. Soon it was his turn. Of five pitches, he hit one foul and missed the other four.

"Kid couldn't touch a wadda mellun with that swing," Charley hooted in his sometimes southern drawl when he was exasperated.

"Yeah, you are right," Clarence replied, "but don't be too hard on him He has some bad habits. See how he stepped back from the plate with his left foot before swinging?"

"Head flies out too, looking to see where the hit goes like he was taking a photo."

"No wonder he swings wildly and doesn't come close to hitting the ball."

Caroline fluttered her eyes and asked, "Y'all still gonna do somethin' about it?"

"Will if we can, and if Peter doesn't improve over the next few games," replied Clarence. "But whatever happens, that young'un sure needs some special help."

Charley bobbed his head in agreement.

Peter looked around to find someone to throw with and warm-up his arm. He saw Sakine Davis without a partner. At this point he didn't care that he'd be throwing with a girl. He waved his arm and yelled her name, "Sakening. Sakening."

Sakine heard something that sounded like her name and saw Peter's wave. *Oh, no! I'll pretend I don't see him.* A few moments passed. *Yikes, there's no one else.* So she drew back and fired a hot one to him. *What? He didn't drop it!* Her surprise was short-lived as his return throws were still the same loopy ones she experienced before. *Oh, well. Only be a minute.* The time seemed like an eternity, though, as she had to run to catch Peter's wild throws.

Soon Coach Tyree called the team to come to the dugout. As the players ran, Sakine yelled to Peter running beside her, "My name is Sakine. You're not saying it right."

"Huh?" Peter asked in a confused tone.

"I said," she shouted this time, "my name is Sakine. You are not saying it right!"

"Whata you talking about?"

"Oh, forget it!" she replied disgustedly as they arrived at the team dugout.

"Listen up," Coach Tyree said. "We can beat the Pirates. They lost their first game. They have lots of new players, and learning to play with each other. Sounds like our team, huh?"

A few floppy haired heads nodded.

"We can win if we play like I think we can." He looked around at the young faces and continued, "We want Rosie's to be the best it can be when the season ends. To do that, everyone of you needs to improve. Your place in the line-up'll change if you get better, so hustle all the time. Everyone understand?"

"Yes, sir!" They yelled.

"Good. The line-up's the same because we still don't know how well some of you can play. So the only change is the pitcher." Then he leaned forward with arms extended and said, "Together now, let's give a yell."

"ONE, TWO, THREE, TEAM!"

"One more time!"

"ONE, TWO, THREE! TEAM!" they yelled, and broke from the circle. The first four players put on batting helmets because Rosie's batted first, and they started swinging the bat. They pretended to hit a ball being pitched toward them. The other players walked into the dugout. Five waited for their turn. The other four slouched to the far corner and out of the way.

"Sure 'nough, Peter's not starting," Clarence whispered.

"Yeah ... I see," squawked Charley. "Bet it is not fun to sit on the bench and watch others play the game."

"You are right, my feathery friend. It is an emotional roller coaster ... tough to ride. I have overheard young humans, including their parents, agonize about sitting and watching others getting playing opportunities to improve. Many have sleepless nights, and some quit."

After one inning, the announcer called out across the field, "Pirates 2 and Rosie's 2. Top of the second. Up to bat for Rosie's is Sakine Davis."

"Bet she strikes out, too," Peter grumbled under his breath and with a sourpuss look. She swung at the first pitch and his mouth gaped open when she hit the ball over the short stop's head.

It's a base hit! ... She is a girl! ... It's not fair!

Sakine was safe at 1st base, but the inning ended with no score. Both teams added three more runs by the end of the third inning, and the score was tied 5 to 5.

"Both teams are closely matched," Clarence observed.

"Yeah," Charley squawked over his shoulder as he caught sight of Maggie crouching in the bushes by the creek bottom. He pointed a wing and hooted, "It is our four-legged friend."

"Hello, Maggie," Clarence bellowed and shook his leaves. "Glad you could join us."

"Hi, Maggaee deaah," Caroline hooted softly. "Missun a great game."

"Hellooo friends," Maggie whispered. "Glad to join you. Had to wait until the coast was clear."

Meanwhile, the fourth inning was starting, and Coach Tyree reminded the players, "Don't forget who is in the game now."

An adrenalin rush hit Peter as he looked

at the batting list. *Eight other batters before me, but I will get to bat. I'm going to do well this time. Is Mom here?* He looked around the corner of the dugout where most parents were sitting, but he didn't see her. *Hope she gets to see me.*

There were two outs and Rick Taylor was on base when Big Tommy Lassiter hit a homerun high over the centerfield fence. Both Rick and Big Tommy scored.

"That was a bomb," Clarence bellowed.

"Boy, was it ever," Maggie howled. Then she added showing her mouthful of teeth, "Lucky it didn't hit you, Big Fella."

"Yeah, that woulda hurt," Charley hooted gleefully knowing it was a tease.

"Not me," Clarence boasted. "You forgot, I'm tough."

"Whatcha y'all tawkin' 'bout?" Caroline asked softly. "What'za bomb havta do with baseball?"

"Ask Charley," Clarence replied with a chuckle. "He will explain everything."

"Later, dear," Charley squawked with a gulp and quickly changed the subject. "Look. Peter's trotting this way to right field with his mitt."

As a Pirates player walked up to bat, Peter scanned the crowd again. *Hope Mom gets off in time to come.* Suddenly, he panicked. *I can't see the batter! Sun's behind home plate, and blinding me! What if a ball is hit my direction? Can't see a thing.* He held his mitt up to block the blinding rays. *I will look terrible, but it won't be my fault!* Fortunately, none were hit to him.

When the fourth inning ended, Rosie's led 7 to 5; and the coaches, parents, and players yelled and had joyous looks on their faces.

"Look, Peter will be the next batter!" Charley squawked excitedly.

Caroline could only manage to hop up and down like it was one of the best moments of her life.

"You are right, but..." Clarence replied sadly, "batter just grounded out and Peter will havta wait 'til next inning."

Peter was in the on-deck circle, and his spirit took a nose dive when the third out was made. *Ah, fooey.* But he quickly regained excitement. *I'm the first batter next inning. Sure hope mom gets here by then.*

The sun was still in Peter's eyes when Rosie's took the field, but again, no balls were hit his direction. The Pirates scored two runs, and the fifth inning ended tied 7 to 7.

Peter outran all the Rosie's players to the dugout. *My time to bat.* He tossed his mitt in the corner, grabbed a batting helmet and his Savoy bat, and trotted onto the field where he warmed up by pretending to swing at imaginary pitches.

Coach Tyree walked up to him, looked him in the eye and gave him some encouragement and instructions. "Peter, you have been improving, and I know you can hit this pitcher. Watch him, Keep your eye on the ball and tag it just as it gets to the plate. Swing like you did in our toss drills. Remember how well you hit the ball?"

Peter nodded and walked to the batter's box with chest out and a strut like he was the best in the league.

"You can do it," Coach Tyree yelled encouragingly. "Team needs you on base."

The Pirates coach looked at his scout note about Peter's hitting. *Gets impatient and will swing at almost any pitch.* The coach motioned to the catcher and pitcher, "Throw fast balls to Peter, but make them high and low around the hitting area."

To everyone's surprise, Peter hit the first pitch hard, but it was a foul ball and ricocheted with a bang off the 1st base line fence. He quickly dug his cleats and cocked the bat ready.

"Oh, no-o-o-o," Clarence moaned. "Peter is too anxious to hit the next pitches."

Sure enough, he swung wildly at the next one high and outside. "Boy has lost his focus of the strike zone," Clarence agonized. "Goose's cooked now."

That proved true as Peter chased the next one in the dirt. "Oh, my! Struck out in only three pitches again!" squawked Charley as his eyes crossed.

Coach Tyree spoke encouragingly to Peter as he trudged back to the dugout, but Peter's mind was far off. *Glad mom wasn't here to see me.* He walked to the far corner of the dugout. *That is all I will get to hit today. One sorry time.*

As he leaned his bat in the corner, he heard Big Tommy behind him say to the other players, "He can't hit anything. Even the girlies hit better." Other players snickered agreement.

Peter pretended not to hear. He felt miserable. He was alone at the end of the dugout. He stuffed the feeling and thoughts away inside his private box of 'bad memories.' *Glad mom didn't see me!*

The next two batters made outs, too, but they were both hard and exciting hits instead of a wimpy strikeout like Peter's. One was a grounder to the shortstop who scooped it up and threw the out at 1st base. The other was a high fly ball to center field a few feet short of the fence, where the center fielder caught it for out three.

Why can't I hit like that? Peter agonized as the players gathered around Coach Tyree.

"Listen up. We are tied with the Pirates so let's make good defensive plays and keep them from scoring. Ok?"

Everyone nodded and whooped it up as they ran to their positions on the field.

"Sun is still in the boy's face," Charley squawked. "Hope nothin's hit to-um."

Things were going good for Rosie's as the first Pirates batter struck out and the second one hit a grounder to 1st base for the second out.

The next batter hit a line-drive towards Big Tommy at 1st base. *Over his head*, Peter thought. *Gotta stop it from rolling to the back fence.* His speed helped him to block the ball.

"Great going, Peter!" Clarence bellowed excitedly even though no human could hear him. Charley, Caroline, and Maggie all joined in with joyous hoots and howls too. Charley even did a little country two-step hop that'd make Buck Owens proud.

Rosie's coaches, the parents and players were ecstatic too until ... well ... yes, you guessed right. Peter's throw to the 2nd baseman was wide to the side, and it gave the batter the opportunity to run to 2nd safely.

"That po' boy," Caroline hooted sympathetically.

The next Pirates batter hit a ball over the short stop's head, and the runner at 2nd ran all the way home for the winning run. Game over: Pirates 8 and Rosie's Café 7.

Rosie's players were discouraged with the loss. As they trotted slowly off the field, a couple purposely moved close to Peter. "You throw like a sissy. Sakine is better'n you. You cost us the game. Why doncha quit?"

Coach Tyree heard a little of what the players said to Peter, and he hollered in a harsh voice, "Hey, that's enough of that!" He looked angry and discouraged and, after a moment he said, "Let's go down by the scoreboard for a talk."

Soon players were on a knee. Parents stood a little ways behind them, but close enough to hear the coach's comments.

Coach Tyree began. "Guys, we came close to getting a win today, and I want to congratulate you for trying your best. We will win next time when we play them." He looked around as he talked. Sometimes his gaze fell on a particular player for a moment or two when he made a point.

"We made some good plays today so don't get down on yourselves. Yes, we made some bad ones too, but remember we win and lose as a team. No single player wins or loses a game. Y'all understand?"

A few heads nodded "Yes."

His gaze fell on Peter as he made the next comments, "I want each of you to think about how you played. Think about what you did well, and think of how you can improve. Maybe your batting needs to improve. Maybe it is your defense or throwing. Our team will not improve—until each of you improves your part."

Coach Tyree then turned his head several times side to side looking at each player as he talked, but Peter felt he still was talking to him. *After all, it was me who lost the game. If I hadn't made that bad throw, that runner wouldn't have scored.*

Coach continued, "If you want to help the team, you need to improve. You need to practice on your own. Understand?"

The players nodded.

"Our next game is Friday night, and we play the late game against the Tigers. If you all bring your best game, we'll make them struggle. Any questions?" Seeing none, "See you then."

Peter imagined the owls were talking to him.

Peter slowly trudged around the ball field fence to his bike at the foot of Clarence. He noticed the two owls sitting on a low branch in the tree. A smile crossed his face. "You guys are pretty neat." To his surprise, he saw them move and heard them squawk, and he imagined they were talking to him, thanking him. Actually, they were, but his imagination wasn't there yet.

On his way home, Peter rehearsed an answer to a question he knew his mom'd ask about the ball game. He was in for a surprise. *The kitchen is dark? No Mom. Why is she still at work?*

He grabbed some juice and cheese-n crackers and climbed the stairs to clean up and study his history lesson. *No need to put my ball pants in the laundry. Didn't get dirty.* So he dropped them on top of his cleats by the bed and picked up his history book. After reading the same page over at least three times, he put the book down. *Can't remember this. Dull stuff.*

Peter's thoughts shifted to his dad, and he reached under the bed for a long box where some of his dad's pictures were stored. He found a small picture of his dad dressed in a baseball uniform and stared at the face captured forever in time

Slowly the emotions of Peter's game surfaced through puckered lips and tears. "I've wanted to play baseball, get a base hit, and be the hero," he mumbled. "Now I'm playing, but I am terrible. Even the girls are better. I lost the game today, and no one likes me." He paused for a moment as if hoping for a response from the figure in the picture. ... "I wish you were here to help me."

Vicki wanted to be at Peter's game, but she had to choose between it and working a second job she had taken because of their financial problems. Within moments of walking into the house, her first concern was to check on her babies even though she was dog-tired.

The lights were on in both bedrooms. Sally and Elizabeth had finished studying and cleaning up for bed. Vicki gave them hugs and said, "I'll be back later."

She gently knocked on Peter's door, but she didn't hear any response so she pushed it open a crack. There eyes met, Peter looked away. She concluded he was hurting, and hurried over and gave him a warm hug. "I'm sorry I couldn't get off work to come to your game."

"That is okay," Peter mumbled, trying to make out like it didn't matter. It did, though, and he buried his face into her neck and released his frustrations. "Coach's not giving me a chance. Other kids may be better now, but with a little help, I can improve. Not fair! Coach plays me only at the end, and I think about not making a mistake. So, that's what I do!"

He raised his head, nodded to the picture of his dad in the baseball uniform propped up on the night stand, and blurted out angrily, "I wish dad was here to help me." Then he buried his face in his pillow on the bed and sobbed.

A blur of thoughts and memories ran through Vicki's mind. She was angry, flustered, and sorrowful. *What can I say that I haven't said a hundred times already?* When his sobs subsided, she patted Peter on the head, bent down and whispered, "Me, too, Hun. Me, too."

Outside the bedroom door, Vicki leaned her exhausted body and head against the doorframe, and said a little prayer for some special help for Peter and the family.

After a while, Peter pushed his dad's picture box back under the bed. Unknowingly, Peter's baseball pants and cleats were behind the box, out of sight.

CHAPTER 11

*"Where's my ball pants and cleats?"; Tiger
Players Taunt Peter and Team Clobbers
Rosie's; Peter is Beginning to
Understand His Imaginary Friends*

Peter's excitement had been sky high for his first two games, but he moved slowly in putting on his uniform for the game with the Tigers. Negative thoughts rolled through his mind. *They're the best in the league. What is the fun of being stomped? Mom had to work and sisters have other school activities. I won't start anyway.*

His pace was like a snail as if the game was hours away, and he fiddled with school supplies on his desk. He casually glanced at the clock, then panicked. *I'll be late for my game!*

Frantically he rummaged through his closet like a starving pig looking for food in a pile of leaves and nosing things out of the way. "Where's my ball pants and cleats?" he mumbled. "Here's my jersey. My cap. Mitt."

He stood erect with a puzzled look and tried to recall. *Took them off in my room, . . .* he looked about, *but where? They havta be here some place.*

He forgot he had kicked them off by the bed after his last game, and he didn't realize he'd pushed them under the bed and out of sight behind the box of his dad's pictures.

Peter's nervous level increased with each passing moment. He glanced at the clock. *Gonna be late, and Coach won't play me.*

There is my blue jeans and tennis shoes. He was used to playing in them since he didn't have a practice uniform like the other players. *I will wear them! But hope Coach doesn't get mad at me.* Then another concern hit him. *But what if I have lost them. Can't tell mom 'cause we don't have money to buy more.*

Meanwhile, Clarence, Caroline, and Charley were concerned about Peter's absence. "Where is that boy?" Clarence asked nervously. "He is late for his game."

After a while, Caroline squawked loudly. "Ah seeum. Jus pedaled inta sight."

"Whee, I'm glad. Thought something was wrong 'cause he wasn't here to warm up, and the game is about to start."

Peter saw Rosie's players meeting with Coach Tyree. *No time to put my bike by Big Fella. Havta leave it by the dugout.*

Billy Smart, son of Terry and Prissy Smart, saw Peter coming and motioned to some of his Tigers' teammates.

"Uh-oh," Charley hooted. "Peter's headed towards those Tigers players, and they're acting like they are going to do something."

"Hey guys. Look," Billy said in a loud, heckling voice. "It is Mr. Blue Jeans and he's on his old rusty bike."

Following the player tryout, Billy and other Tigers teased Peter about how he dressed. How he batted. How he threw the ball. How his bike was old and rusty. How sorry a mitt he had. How his bat was cheap looking. On and on. *No time to mess with 'em.* Peter thought as he pedaled around them to his team dugout.

Didn't stop the taunting, though, as over his shoulder he heard Billy yell, "Chicken-n-n, cluck, cluck," and the other players laughing in delight.

"I will get you guys back someday," Peter mumbled as he slid to a stop.

Coach Tyree interrupted his comments as Peter joined the team. "Glad you could finally make it," he said sternly and with a facial expression that matched. *Why is he wearing blue jeans and tennis shoes?* he wondered. Then in the same breath he resumed explaining who was starting and pitching. He closed with some positive comments.

"Guys, this is a good team, but Coach Sanders and I believe you can compete with them if you play your best. That is all we ask; each of you try to play your best. Okay?"

The silence surprised him, and he glanced at Coach Sanders to see if he noticed too. He did, and responded with a not-sure-what's-up look on his face.

Coach Tyree wondered, *What is going on?* Then just as quickly, he knew. *They're intimidated. Scared of this team. This isn't good.*

Before the players arrived, Coaches Tyree and Sanders talked about Rosie's pitchers. "The Tigers are good. Let's not put our best pitchers in against them. Don't want them to get discouraged and pitch poorly the rest of the season."

"Tommy Lassiter'll start at pitcher, and Scrubs Johnson'll pitch after a few innings. We want Scrubs fresh so we're moving a few of you around to other positions. Scrubs'll play 1st base, Sakine will catch, and Jake Sanders'll play 2nd base."

"Yes!" Sakine yelled with a wide grin and a fist pumping the air. "Finally!" She'd been bugging Coach Tyree about letting her catch in a game to show what she could do.

Peter looked at her and mumbled through clinched teeth, "That's great. She gets to play other positions, and I'm probably still sharing one."

Coach Tyree tacked the line up to the wall and the players squeezed against each other to see where they are playing and when they batted. Each hollered gleefully when they found out.

Peter was sure he knew what was on the line up card, but looked anyway. *I knew it! Share right field with David Petri. Won't play 'til the fourth inning, and last on the team to bat.*

He trudged sadly to the corner of the dugout. *How can I get better if Coach doesn't give me a chance? If I'm always last?*

Didn't help that Sakine purposely plopped down beside him to strap on her catcher shin guards. She looked up at Peter momentarily as she snapped one into place and sent him a "I'm better'n you" grin. Then she quickly left him stewing on the bench before he could respond.

Rosie's batted first. The good news: they scored 2 runs; and the players, coaches, and parents were laughing and having fun. After all, they were ahead of the best team in the league. The bad news: The Tigers hadn't yet batted.

The hope that Tommy would pitch well lasted only through his warm-up. After two innings, the score was Tigers 10 and Rosie's 2. Scrubs Johnson pitched about the same as Tommy, and the score after three innings was Tigers 15 and Rosie's 2.

The fourth inning started, and Rosie's was batting.

"Look," Clarence said excitedly to Caroline and Charley. "Peter's got his bat and swinging it. Must be coming into the game."

"Yeah, but this game's all but over." Charley squawked. "They will never catch the Tigers." Then he hooted over his shoulder as he hopped off the branch and flew towards the ball field lights outside center field. He'd caught sight of some moths and insects attracted by the lights. "Caroline, let's get some of these tasty snacks."

"Come-un, Cha'lee deaah."

Both swooped and made sharp turns as they chased the moths, and the humans, young and old, were mesmerized as they watched the owls' aerial acrobatics high over the field.

When play resumed, Rosie's first three players made outs, and Peter mumbled a sigh of frustration, "Drat!" He looked at the line-up list as he headed to right field. *Fourth batter in the next inning.* He ran to right field with a step of excitement. *Hope I'll get to bat.*

Billy Smart, one of the top hitters in the league, was batting for the Tigers. He smacked the ball high into center field, and it was headed into the trees for a homerun.

Clarence saw the ball moving fast towards his feathery friends. *They don't see it coming. May hit them!* He bellowed loudly, "CHARLEY! CAROLINE! LOOK OUT! BALL'S COMING AT YA!"

Charley immediately banked to the right as the ball brushed by him. "Yikes! That was close!" he exclaimed and fluttered in the air as he struggled to get his balance.

Caroline could barely squawk a reply, "Oh, ma' honey! Are ya'll rite Cha'lee?"

Charley bobbed his feathery head and stuttered, "Ye... ye... yes dear." Then he plopped his shaking body down on a branch of the tall pine tree outside center field. Caroline joined him, and they sat there without moving, as if they were statues, the rest of the game.

Meanwhile, Peter, unnoticed by Clarence or Charley or Caroline, stood frozen in right field also like a statue, with eyes wide open and a shocked look on his face. *Who yelled those words?* he wondered. Clarence's voice was one he'd heard before, but now he heard others.

The next two Tigers batters made outs, and Butch Anderson, the best batter in the league, was batting. He smacked a fly ball high in the air and deep in right field.

Peter made up his mind early in the week to make good plays when he had the chance, and this was the only ball hit his direction. He tracked the flight of the ball and mumbled, "Ball's going to hit the oak tree branches." He moved under the ball as it started on its downward path. "Don't care if it hits the tree. Still going to catch it."

Sure enough the ball hit the branches, and ricocheted back and forth before dropping down. "OUCH!" Clarence bellowed, pretending as usual it hurt him.

Clarence's voice startled Peter again, and he momentarily glanced in the direction where the voice seemed to be. Just as he looked back up, the ball clonked him on top of the head.

"Oops," Clarence said trying to hold his laughter back.

The ball didn't hurt Peter, but the scene was hilarious. He looked around. Everyone he saw was laughing: the spectators and all the players and coaches—even those on his team.

Clarence choked off any laughs, but Charley and Caroline's laughing squawks could be heard deep into the woods. It was what they needed to get their minds off the fright they had experienced a few minutes earlier.

During the week and leading up to the game, Peter had practiced tossing the ball in the air and catching it. He did not practice for what just happened to him. The laughter and teasing shouts embarrassed him. *I played terrible again.* The clonk on his head would be what players and fans remembered along with Rosie's blowout loss to the Tigers.

The umpires waved in a circle to signal a homerun for a ball hit into the branches over the playing field. The next batter made the third out, and the score after four innings: Tigers 17 and Rosie's 2. The game would be over by the ten-run rule unless Rosie's scored at least six runs.

I'm fourth to bat, Peter thought. *One of those ahead of me has to get on base.* He put on a batter's helmet, picked up his Savoy bat and hollered, "Come on guys. Get on base." *Please get on base,* he pleaded.

All of a sudden, he thought of his mom. *Was Mom able to come see me play?* He quickly looked around at the crowd of parents and rationalized when he didn't see her. *Glad she didn't see me get clonked on the head.*

He yelled encouragement again to the batters ahead of him, "Come on guys—get a hit!" His hopes rose as the first batter hit a grounder but took a nose dive as the batter was thrown out at 1st base. "Two outs left, and two batters in front of me," he mumbled through tight lips. Adrenaline pumped through his body, and he was wound tight with excitement. If someone popped a bag, he'd explode. Thoughts of batting rushed through his mind. *Soon it'll be my time.*

"Oh, noooo. Two outs," Peter moaned as the second batter struck out. He walked to the on-deck circle, and began to swing his bat pretending to hit the ball as the pitcher threw it. Exciting thoughts raced through his mind as he looked at Billy Smart crouching down at 2nd base. *I am going to hit this ball past that bully and out of the park. And when I run by him, I'm going to give him a big grin and say, "See ya."*

About that moment, the batter hit a pop-up just over the head of the pitcher and Billy ran forward to make the catch for out number three. Game over! Score: Tigers 17 and Rosie's 2.

Peter stood stunned in the on-deck circle. *I don't get to bat? Everyone batted except me!*

He didn't move as players on both teams formed the usual lines after a game and passed in opposite directions to shake hands. Slowly Peter walked to the end of Rosie's line. When he came to Billy, all Peter could see was a wide smirk.

Billy couldn't resist one more verbal punch, "Nice catch on the noggin, Mr. Blue Jeans." Other Tigers players snickered.

Charley heard everything from his perch high in the tree, and he knew Peter felt humiliated. He squawked loudly, "I'd like to do something, like punch Billy in the nose."

"Nah, Cha'lee, deaah," Caroline hooted calmly, "Stay calm."

Peter kept walking, and managed to put on a good face before he reached the dugout.

"Hey, guys. Those owls were something, huh?" Coach Tyree expressed to the team to get their mind off the game for a moment and perk them up.

A few laughed briefly. Tommy Lassiter tossed a dirt clod at his buddy, Lacroy Carter, and teased, "Yeah. Looked like they were copying Lacroy's smo-o-o-o-oth moves."

"You wish ya had 'em!" Lacroy fired back with a laugh and as he flipped his own dirt clod at Tommy.

Coach Tyree let the bantering go back and forth for a few moments and then brought up the game. "We took a lickin' today," immediately the group was silent, "but you know what? We're improving with each game. By the end of the season, we're going to be good, too; but we must work on basics and have faith in ourselves. You have to practice extra on your own because we don't have time to do enough as a team. Get your dad to throw to you and help with your hitting." He paused to let the point sink into the young players. "Everyone understand this?"

A few mumbled unenthusiastically, "Yes, sir." The others had looks of being far away.

"WHAT?" Coach Tyree snapped as he didn't like their reply.

It startled them. "Yes sir!" they responded, but this still wasn't good enough for Coach.

"WHAT WAS THAT?" he yelled even louder.

"YES, SIR!" they yelled so loud that people across the field looked to see what happened.

"Okay, that is better. Remember, we have a game next Tuesday. We play the Sharks. Ours is the first game so be here earlier for batting practice. See you then."

The players nodded, and walked off each one going their own way. Some with parents and grandparends, some with a single parent, and a couple alone.

Coach Tyree remembered another point he wanted to make and he shouted as they walked away, "Do your homework and study."

Meanwhile, Charley and Caroline had returned to sit on one of Clarence's branches. "Thanks, Big Fella, for the shout-out," Charley hooted. "May have saved my feathers."

"Awe, don't mention it. You would have done the same. Besides, what would I do without you two crazy love birds and Maggie to keep life interesting and fun?"

"Well, Cla'ence, honee," Caroline hooted softly as she moved to get comfy on the branch, "I dun'o what I'd do without ma Cha'lee."

"It is what friends are for," Clarence replied and then he shifted the subject. "Peter is having a tough time playing ball. Remember how he'd sit on one of my roots and talk about playing baseball and getting base hits. Nothing close to that is happening for him so far."

"I remember," Charley hooted, "but hav'ta admit, that clonk on his head was funny."

"Look," Clarence replied, "Coach Tyree's with Peter by his bike. Let's listen."

"Peter, where's your ball pants and cleats? We are supposed to be dressed in a uniform, not blue jeans. I was reminded during the game it's a league rule. Players must be in uniform." Prissy Smart delivered the message.

Peter looked up at him and stammered, "Coach, I couldn't find them, and Mom was at work. It's why I was late, and hoped I could play in them."

Coach Tyree paused for a moment, reflecting that he hadn't seen Vicki Marshall since the parent's meeting, then he said, "It is okay this time." Then he gave Peter a pat on the head, chuckled and asked, "How is the noggin?"

"It is all right," he replied slowly, but didn't want to talk more about it. He wanted to leave, but Coach Tyree started to say something else.

"Next game, you will..."

"Coach Tyree," a woman's soft voice interrupted from behind.

He didn't need to turn around to see who it was. *Oh, no-o-o-o.*

Marilyn Davis. Sure hope Coach Sanders talked to her since Sakine was in the dirt a lot today as catcher.

Her appearance surprised him. She had a Rosie's jersey on with her daughter's name on the back, and she wore a ball cap with her hair pulled through the back just like her daughter. *Coach Sanders talked to her,* he concluded, *and ... she still has those extra tight jeans.*

"Coach Tyree" she said with a flirtatious flutter of her eyes and a warm smile. "I have the new parents schedule and ... You can come by my house for them at any time."

Coach Tyree's hearing shut off momentarily, and he forgot about Peter until he noticed him near the big oak in right field. Before refocusing on Marilyn, he made a mental note: *I need to talk with his parents.*

As Peter tied his mitt and bat to his bike, he noticed the two owls up in Big Fella. He smiled for a moment as he recalled their aerial acrobatics. "You guys are pretty neat." They made cackling sounds at that moment, and Peter pretended, *Awesome! You're thanking me!*

"Too bad he doesn't understand us," Charley squawked.

"I think hez beginnun to, Cha'lee deaah."

[CHAPTER 12]

*Peter's Enthusiasm Wanes; Players Who Don't
Bat Start Next Game; Peter Definitely Heard
Clarence; A Dragon at the Ballgame*

Vicki slid the lasagna into the oven, and leaned her weary body against the counter. Peter moping around the house had been in her mind constantly. *He is not excited about playing baseball as he was at the start of the season. Not even wearing his dad's old jersey. Something is amiss. What happened?* She asked about his game against the Tigers, but he didn't say much.

She washed a few dishes. *Tomorrow is their next game.* Vicki abruptly stopped. *I'll call Coach Tyree to find out if anything happened that would explain Peter's mood.*

"Hello, this is David Tyree."

"Hi, Coach Tyree, this is Vicki Marshall. Peter's mom."

After a few cordial exchanges, Vicki got to the point. "I'm calling because I'm concerned about how Peter's acting since his last couple of games."

Coach Tyree's defensive instincts quickly surfaced. *Oh, no. An unhappy parent wanting to know why their youngster is not starting.* He took a deep breath. "What's wrong?"

"...no talk about getting a base hit. Why?"

"Not sure. Peter has not said much, and that isn't like him. He has been excited about playing ball. All he talked about the last couple of years is getting a base hit. Not now. Why?"

She paused, and he thought, *Now she's about to ask why isn't Peter playing more?* To his surprise, she mentioned something else.

"Maybe it is because I haven't been to his games. Had to work, but hope to attend soon. Or maybe it is something else." She paused for a moment and added, "Also, I needed to check about my turn helping in the concession stand."

Coach Tyree's impulse was to take her to the proverbial wood shed. *What do you think the coaches are, baby sitters? Peter and all the players need their parents helping them and attending their events. Not just dropping them off or sending them alone.*

Fortunately a calmer response won out. "I hope you and Peter's dad can come to some games soon. Peter and all players need encouragement from parents, but I do understand about the need to work. We have families to feed and bills to pay, and that takes priority."

The comment about Peter's dad caught Vicki off guard. *Coach Tyree doesn't know I'm a single parent; that Peter's father died in a car accident.*

He continued, "About team drinks and the concession schedule, please check with Marilyn Davis. She's coordinating this for the team."

He didn't hear anything for a few moments, and he asked, "You there?"

"Uh, yes." Vicki managed a response while clinching her lips to keep the hurt subdued. *Will I ever stop grieving? Stop missing Peter?* … "Okay, I'll check with her."

"Good. Now about Peter, we were beaten badly in our last game. It is probably the reason for his mood. Losing by such a big score hit us all pretty hard." He paused again. *Should I tell her about the funny event where Peter was clonked on the head by the ball falling through the tree branches? Guess Peter didn't tell her since she didn't mention it, so I'm not either. Besides, her voice changed; sounded like she wanted to end the call.*

"Not fun to lose," she replied. "Anything I can do to help him out?"

"Yes. Peter runs as good as anyone on the team. I think he can be a decent player if he gets lots of practice in catching, throwing, and hitting. Practice in any of those will help. The coaches don't have the time to work with players individually."

"I will see what we can do to help," she responded quickly. "Thanks for your time."

"Good luck, and call me any time. Bye."

As Vicki hit the off button, she made a promise, "I have to reserve some time to practice with Peter." Realistically, though, she already knew she didn't have enough time to work two jobs, run the house, and see that the basic needs of her kids were being met. The girls and Peter already were doing lots around the house to help. Before she could think more about it, she noticed the clock. *Got to hurry. Almost time for work.*

The Tuesday evening game with the Sharks was near, and Peter knew he needed to leave soon for the ballpark. He panicked. *I have searched the house for my ball pants and cleats. Where did I lose them? Coach Tyree said I couldn't play if I wasn't in uniform.*

He shrugged his shoulders in a hopeless motion, and sat down on the bed. *I won't go. I'll tell coach I was sick, or had lots of homework, or something like mom gave me extra jobs around the house that had to be done today.*

A few minutes passed as he thought about the reasons. Finally, he concluded, *No, I can't use those excuses. Mom would find out and give me a "what for."* He slipped on his blue jeans and tennis shoes. *Maybe coach'll let me play one more game in them.*

Clarence, Caroline, and Charley were discussing how they could help Peter improve his baseball skills when Charley spotted Peter pedaling rapidly towards them. "Here he comes."

"Ah see'um, dah'lin," Caroline hooted softly as she fluttered her eyelashes and did a fancy back and forth step on the branch like she'd been practicing a square dance do-ce-doe.

"Shu-u-u, he's close," Clarence cautioned. "We know he's heard me speak. Now let's see if he can understand what you say, too."

Charley and Caroline nodded their heads in agreement.

Peter noticed the two owls on a lower branch of Big Fella as he coasted up to its trunk where he'd leave his bike. I can almost jump and touch them. Why aren't they afraid and fly away or perched higher in the tree?

Instead, the owls sat there, moving their heads back and forth, up and down, and quietly hooting. They seemed like they were used to Peter being around. Like a couple of southern folks sitting on a porch and extending their unique hospitality to a neighbor walking in front of their house. "Cu'mon up 'n rest a spell."

Peter started on his way to the team dugout, but Charley's loud squawk stopped him briefly in his tracks. "No time to talk now," he said over his shoulder as he jogged away.

Charley hooted disappointedly this time, "He didn't understand us."

"Maybe he did," Clarence replied. "He might have been thinking so much about his game he didn't realize it. Let's see what happens during the game."

"Who is the game with?" Caroline asked.

"Rosie's plays the Sharks," Charley replied. "They are the visiting team, and bat first."

Several of Peter's teammates were in the dugout when he walked through the gate. Sakine Davis was among them. All glanced at him. Peter was puzzled. *They looked at me differently than before previous games. What's up?*

Then he noticed the game line-up card already was tacked on the wall, and he walked over to it. A note from Coach Tyree was written at the bottom. "I will be late for the start of the game, and Coach Sanders'll be in charge."

Peter's eyes looked directly at the bottom of the list where the non-starters'd been written for the previous games. He was stunned. *My name is not there!* The worst came to mind. *Did Coach Tyree not list me because I wore blue jeans and tennis shoes last game?*

His eyes scanned upwards, and he spotted his name. He couldn't believe what he saw.

I'm starting! Playing right field, and batting ninth! A moment of disappointment hit him. *Drats, David Petri subs me in the fourth inning.* But Peter's jubilation soon returned with an ear-to-ear grin. *I'm starting! Who cares if I play only three innings. At last, I'm starting!*

As he placed his mitt and bat on the bench, he passed Sakine. He couldn't resist the comment, "Hey, Sakining, I'm starting. Batting a couple after you. Don't make an out."

"I told you before," she retorted angrily, "my name is Sakine. Since you can't remember it, call me Channing. Maybe you can remember that name!"

"Well, snooty," he replied with a purposeful upturn of his nose and upper lip. "I'll just call you…

"Oh, do what you want," she shot back loudly. She turned to

leave, but stopped and burst his happy bubble. "You are only starting because the league rule requires any player who didn't bat in the last game, must start the next one."

Peter was stunned. A shocked look flashed on his face, and his mouth gaped wide open. He slowly slumped down on the bench as she walked away. *Starting because of a rule, not because I'm good?* The game was soon underway, but the thought of why Peter was starting was in his mind the whole time. *At least it's okay to play in my blue jeans and tennis shoes.* Turned out Coach Sanders didn't say anything to Peter about the blue jeans and tennis shoes was because he didn't know Coach Tyree'd spoken to Peter about being in uniform for games.

All nine of Rosie's players, including Peter, batted in the first two innings, but the team had only one hit and one run. Peter was the only player to strike out.

The Sharks scored five runs in two innings. Only three balls were hit Peter's direction. One was a home run that hit into the branches of Clarence, and the other two were fouls.

Score after two innings: Rosie's Café 1 and Sharks 5.

In the third inning, Rosie's scored two runs. Coach Tyree arrived while the team was on defense, but didn't notice Peter in his blue jeans until the players ran in from the field.

Peter thought as he ran towards the dugout, *Didn't hit the ball, but at least I didn't screw up today playing defense.*

Peter is subbed out in fourth inning.

Coach Tyree stared at Peter as he ran passed. *I won't say anything in front of the others since David Petri's subbing him out in the fourth inning.*

Score after three innings: Rosie's 3 and Sharks 7.

Rosie's gained on the Sharks in the fourth inning. Nine players batted, and three runs scored. David Petri made one of the runs when he walked and was on base as a runner.

Peter watched David as he scored his run. *How lucky! Why can't that happen to me? I'd like to get on base. All I do is strike out.*

The Sharkes didn't score and after four innings, it was Rosic's 6 and Sharks 9.

Coach Tyree called Rosie's players together before batting in the fifth inning, but he didn't notice David Petri was by the fence, throwing up. "Everyone huddle up." He looked around at the eager eyes on the young faces, "Guys, we're fighting back. We're only three runs behind, and we're closing the gap. Let's give them the best game each of you has. Okay?"

As the players prepared to bat, Coach Sanders said to Coach Tyree, "David Petri's sick, and his parents have taken him home. Also, David was to bat fourth in the fifth inning."

Coach Tyree expressed his concern, "Sick? Hope he'll be all right. Also, not contagious." He asked, "Who will replace him?"

"Peter Marshall is the only player eligible to re-enter for David."

Coach Tyree studied the line-up for a moment and wondered. *What do I do? Either I don't let Peter play because he's out of uniform and that means an automatic out when David's up to bat and we have only eight players on defense, or I allow Peter to play and the league officials give us another reprimand.*

Coach Sanders broke the silence. "Want me to tell Peter?"

Coach Tyree decided, *I'm letting Peter play. It is only a game.* "No, I will talk to him."

Coach Tyree called Peter over to him and said, "David is sick, and you will be re-entering the game in his position."

Peter wasn't sure he heard correctly. "I play again?"

"Yes, now get ready to bat. David bats fourth."

There was one out and two runners on base when Peter batted. Sakine was one of them.

"Look!" Charley squawked excitedly, "Peter is back in the game and batting."

"Sure 'nough," Clarence added,

Coach Tyree gave Peter encouragement right before he stepped into the batter's box. "You can hit this pitcher, Peter. You can score those two runners. Keep your eye on the ball, and smack it between 1st and 2nd base. You can do it."

Peter nodded and strutted to the plate with a flair like he was the best hitter in the league. He scratched the ground with his shoes like he had seen other good hitters do, bounced the bat on the plate a couple of times, raised his bat ready to hit and stared at the pitcher. *Come on, I can hit anything you can throw. I will come through for the team. I'm going to drive in Chan Chan and the team will be proud of me.* Then he promptly struck out in four pitches.

"The po' boy," Caroline said with a tear in the corners of her big eyes, "Looks like a deflated balloon."

As Peter neared the dugout, he caught sight of Chan Chan standing on 3rd base with both hands and arms in the air, and he imagined it to mean, "*What did anyone expect?*"

Fortunately, they had one out to go. Three more batted, and two base runners scored. The Sharks didn't score in the inning and, after the 5th, Rosie's was 8 and the Sharks was 10.

In the 6th and final inning, Peter was the fifth batter. Three runners were on base with one out when he came to bat.

Clarence, Caroline, Charley, and Maggie, who just arrived, bellowed, hooted, and howled for Peter to get a hit. No one noticed their sounds because all the humans pulling for and against Peter to hit the ball were yelling too—even Sakine and his teammates.

So what'd Peter do? He fouled off the first pitch, and raised everyone's expectation. *Maybe he will be lucky and hit one,* Coach Tyree thought jubilantly. "Come on, Peter," he yelled.

The encouragement didn't help, though, as he whiffed at the next two pitches.

"Not again," Clarence moaned. "Struck out a third time."

With each strike out, the walk back to the dugout seemed like a journey that became longer and longer. This time, Peter noticed the displeased look on Coach Tyree's face. *I've let everyone down. ... Again.*

Big Tommy whispered as Peter passed, "You are terrible. Help the team and quit."

Peter was soon forgotten, though, as four other teammates batted and three runs scored in the inning. Rosie's was ahead 11 to 10, but the Sharks still had their time at bat to win.

Things looked good for Rosie's as Rick Taylor struck out the Sharks first two batters. Then Maggie howled an alarm, "Clarence, the next two batters are left-handed, and Peter looks like he's too far to center field to make a play."

Peter heard the howl, and looked back for a moment as he knew the sound. *My friend, the fox. She's brave to come this close so early.* Then he resumed his defensive crouch like a tiger and joined the chant of the other Rosie's players, "Hey batter, hey batter."

Suddenly, a deep voice whispered from behind near the fence.

"Peter, the next batters are left-handed, and they hit near the right field line. You are too far away to the center, and you need to move towards the right field line."

Peter glanced back for a moment, but didn't see anyone. *Coach must've sent a parent to tell me to move over.*

Coach Tyree also noticed Peter was out of position, and he had been looking back at the fence. He was about to holler for him to move when Peter took several steps the right direction. *Good. Now keep your head in the game.*

The first lefty didn't hit the ball very often but, when he did, the ball was hit hard. He swung so hard at the first pitch he almost fell down. Rosie's players continued their chant, "Hey batter. Hey batter."

Wham—the batter hit the next pitch in a line drive down the right field baseline.

Ball is coming right at me, Peter concluded. *Slightly above my head,* He raised his glove up to catch it. "Whop," he heard and felt it hit the mitt but, when he reached for it to throw it to the 2nd baseman, he was stunned. *It wasn't there!* He looked around on the ground and saw it had rolled to the fence. By the time Peter ran and retrieved it, the batter had made it to 3rd base.

"Oh, my," Clarence mumbled sadly. "Should've been an out, and a win for Rosie's."

"Yeah, ah know," Charley squawked and rolled his eyes. "Not sure we can hep that boy."

Coach Tyree threw up his arms, and yelled in an angry tone like never before, "PETER, WHAT'RE YOU DOING? STOP

LOOKING AROUND. GET YOUR HEAD IN THE GAME!" It was obvious to everyone within hearing distance Coach Tyree had lost his cool.

The next lefty was the best hitter on the Sharks team. He took a couple of practice swings, and on the second pitch hit a deep fly ball to center-right field. Peter watched the ball sail over the fence for a homerun. One swing of the bat, two runs scored, and the game was over. The Sharks won 12 to Rosie's 11.

Rosie's players slowly trotted to the dugout. Every one of them acted dejected, and some blamed Peter. "You lost the game," a player whispered when Peter passed by in the dugout.

"Can say that again."

Another whispered, "No one likes you" as Peter packed his stuff.

"Lissen to 'em," Caroline squawked with a tone of motherly anger. "Peta's teem's saying mean thangs to him."

"Yeah, I know," Charley squawked, "Players are upset. Had a chance to win, but they could have lost on other plays, like a pitch that allowed a homerun. Not fair Peter is blamed."

Slowly the players dragged themselves to the team meeting. The objective of Coach Tyree was to be positive, but today his anger carried over from the game and how it ended. Also, it didn't help that he had words again after the game with a league official about Peter playing out of uniform in blue jeans and tennis shoes. "The Sharks coaches brought up the dress code infraction, and were playing under protest in case they lost. Since they won, though, they decided against filing it."

The remarks disturbed Coach Tyree, and he wondered as he walked to his team. *What's the character of adults who'd file a protest about the uniform of a youngster just to have a win recorded in the books?*

For that matter, same question for league officials who would allow it. Coach Tyree's talk to the team was confusing, and he rambled from point to point.

"Wonder what the coach is saying," Clarence rumbled in his deep voice. "He looks hot under the collar. Face's red, and he has looked mostly at Peter. Never seen him act this way."

"Wonder, too," Charley hooted as he wobbled around on Clarence's branch to get a better view. "Want me to fly over there and listen?"

"Nah. Not sure we want to know. Besides, Peter'll be here soon to get his bike, and maybe he'll give us a clue to what the coach said."

As Coach Tyree dismissed the team, he added in an unfriendly voice, "Peter, hold up. Want to talk to you."

Coach Tyree's harsh tone caught the attention of the other players and parents, and most tried to listen as they walked slowly away.

Coach Tyree towered over Peter, and looked down into his face as he spoke. "Peter, if you can't find your ball pants and cleats, your dad needs to buy you new ones. You can't play if you come again in blue jeans and tennis shoes." He paused to let Peter think about the message, pointed his finger and pounded home the question, "DO YOU UNDERSTAND ME?"

Peter tried to reply, "My da ... da ... dad ..." but he couldn't say, "died." The word wouldn't come out of his mouth. His lips quivered and cheeks puckered, but he managed to fight back the tears. After a noticeably long struggle, he forced a mumble, "Yes, sir."

"Good! Remember what I said." Coach Tyree turned quickly and walked away. After a few steps, he turned slightly, and hollered angrily over his shoulder, "And tell your dad to come to the games, if he gives a rip about his son, and help him."

All of Rosie's players and parents who were still nearby heard every harsh word Coach Tyree spoke to Peter. Sakine Davis said to her mother, "Glad I'm not in his shoes."

"Well," Marilyn replied with a huff, "I would give him a what for if he was speaking to you that way." She paused a moment and added under her breath, "Even though he's a hunk."

In a short time, everyone had left the park except Peter. He stood, unmoving, in the same spot. "Peter is dazed. He's not moving," Clarence bellowed angrily.

"Ya mean hez daid?" Charley asked sadly.

"No! I mean it's like he's frozen to the spot. Don't know what Coach Tyree said to him, but it wasn't good." Clarence took a couple of deep breaths and shook his branches and added a little parental philosophy. "If I was human, I'd turn that coach over my knee. He has forgotten youngsters, like Peter, don't think and reason and act like adults. When the adult stands over the youngster and speaks down like Coach Tyree did, it might as well have been a large dragon with blood-shot eyes and smoke steaming out the nostrils, towering overhead, and looking to devour anyone foolish enough to wander nearby."

Clarence paused to catch his breath. After a moment, he continued, "Young humans, like Peter, shouldn't have to battle dragons along with everything else."

The yell of players in the next game startled Peter out of his trance. *How long have I been standing here? My team's gone. I remember Coach Tyree saying something to me. What was it?* He shrugged his shoulders, shuffled his bat and mitt from one shoulder to the other, and slowly walked toward his bike parked under Big Fella.

[CHAPTER 13]

*"...not my fault!"; The Imaginary Friends are
Able to Talk to Peter, and They Have a
Plan to Improve His Skills*

Tears dripped from Peter's nose. He wiped them with the back of his forearm as he stumbled in a daze towards his bike under Big Fella. He replayed the game in his mind the whole way. "Glad mom couldn't come," he mumbled through puckered lips. When he plopped down on one of the large roots that was above ground, the mitt and bat slipped from his hands.

Clarence and the animal friends watched Peter's movements. Caroline and Charley leaned over the branch almost to falling off. Maggie peaked from near by bushes.

What is he thinking? Clarence wondered.

Caroline's motherly instincts filled her thoughts, *The po' dollin need za hug.*

Impatient Charley wanted to yell, *Big Fella, get on with it! Say something to 'im!*

Maggie was cool as usual, and sat back on her haunches and watched patiently.

Clarence was about to break the silence when Peter mumbled and kicked at the dirt in a spurt of anger at himself, "I know I played poorly. Struck out three times, and... And not catching that line drive lost the game."

Peter didn't say anything after that for a long time. Finally, he broke the silence. "Not fair Coach and the players blamed me for losing the game. ... Other players mess up, too."

He was silent for a spell as he kept replaying in his mind the game and Coach Tyree's comments. His face took on a look of deep anguish. "Why can't I do something good?"

Suddenly, a sound overhead startled Peter. Caroline squawked, "Coooks-fo'u," and flapped her wings to regain her balance. She had leaned over too far to watch Peter.

"Oh, it is you guys!" Peter explained. "You still here?"

Charley and Caroline bobbed their heads and hooted like they were responding to him. He grinned as he momentarily forgot about the horrible game.

Soon, though, his mind was back on the game. "Why did Coach stare at me like that and chew me out?" He paused and added, "Didn't do it to anyone else."

Peter leaned back against Clarence's trunk and was silent again. *Hmmmm, what's he thinking?* Clarence wondered. *Gazing across the park woods like he's studying something.*

After a while, Peter picked at the bark on Clarence's root, and sailed pieces on the air like small frizbees. Clarence decided, *didn't hurt, so best give him time to recover.*

Peter blurted out in an angry tone, "Doesn't coach know my dad isn't alive?"

He replayed his batting performance. *Three strike outs? ... Worst yet!*

His outfield play came to mind and, in the wink of an eye, a puzzled look replaced the frown on his face. "I was in position to catch that line-drive. It hit my mitt. Why didn't I?"

He replayed the moment in slow-motion, frame-by-frame. He remembered, jumped to his feet, and exclaimed. "Yes! The ball hit my mitt. What happened? Why didn't I catch it? I've practiced. Tossed balls in the air and caught them."

Charley wanted to hoot, *Ya got a point,* but kept it as a thought to talk about later.

"I want to play good," Peter moaned. "Seems the harder I try, the worse I do. What's wrong?"

Maybe you are trying too hard, kid, Clarence thought.

Peter kicked hard at the dirt as if it would help him feel better. His sight fell on his mitt as he turned around. *Something's not right!* He picked it up, and noticed the webbing between the thumb and big finger was ripped. The leather strap that held the webbing in place had broken. Suddenly, it dawned on him, *No line-drive could have been caught with this mitt.*

"THAT IS IT!" He yelled and jumped excitedly. "IT WASN'T MY FAULT! I DIDN'T MISS THE BALL! IT RIPPED MY MITT, AND ROLLED ON TO THE FENCE!"

He looked around to tell Coach Tyree and players about his discovery, but he realized they had left the park. "They are gone," he expressed in a sad tone, "They won't believe me anyway. But, it is the truth! I didn't catch that line-drive because the ball ripped my mitt. It's not my fault." He repeated as his voice tailed off in a whisper, "…not my fault!"

Peter's eyes watered with tears again, but this time there was bitterness in how he felt. "I was blamed for a mistake I didn't cause. It was no different than when other players make a blunder. Errors occur all the time on the ball field."

Peter slumped on the root again and mumbled, "Playing baseball isn't fun like I thought it would be. Maybe I should give up, and quit like they said."

Clarence wanted to ask Maggie, Caroline, and Charley, *Did you hear him?* as if they couldn't understand Peter themselves. *He's really down on himself.*

Peter remembered what his mom promised about playing ball. *Be patient, Hun. Things'll work out, and eventually you will play good.* "Glad mom wasn't at the game. She would have been embarrassed if people knew I'm her son."

He sat quietly against the tree trunk for a long time. Every once in a while he would stand and kick the dirt. Eyes were red from being rubbed, and dry streaks down his cheeks testified to the river of tears he had a few minutes earlier.

"What now? Coach said 'Get practice help.' Where? Where do I get help?"

Peter didn't do anything for a long time after that. The second game ended, and teams and parents were leaving. Soon the concession stand'd close and the field lights'd be turned out.

After a while, there was a faint whisper from Peter, "Dear Lord, Mom says you're real, Says she talks to you all the time about problems and things. Says you've helped her in so many ways." Peter paused, then added, "If you're real, would you help me?"

He paused as if time was needed for the words to register. Indeed, they grabbed the attention of Clarence, Maggie, Caroline, and Charley. Not a leaf, hair, or feather moved.

"Coach Tyree said I couldn't play out of uniform again. I don't know where mine are, and Mom works a lot. No money to buy them again. I have only blue jeans and tennis shoes."

He remembered his play, and he appealed for help there, too. "If you can't help with those, would you help me to play better?"

Peter decided he needed to explain, "You see, Mom can't help me with that either. If Dad was alive, he could help me, and I wouldn't need to ask you. If..." Peter paused again thinking of all the things the Lord does, "If you are not too busy, would you help me?"

Peter didn't say anything else or move. The field lights had been turned off, and only the dim light from those cleaning and closing down the concession stand remained. Clarence knew it was time to speak. 

"Come now, Peter. Things can't be all that bad." Clarence's voice was a loud, rumbling sound like a train approaching not far down the track. Wild life took flight or scampered to safety.

It seemed to Peter like the sound was on top of him, which it was. "WHO IS THERE?" Peter yelled as he jumped to his feet like he had been shot out of a cannon. He looked quickly back and forth, but didn't see anyone. *Maybe someone is hiding on the other side of the tree.* He hopped over the tree roots and peeked around the large trunk. *No one is there, either. Only people near are the ones at the concession stand.*

"Who is there?" Peter shouted again. "I can't see you. Come out." He listened for an answer. *Nothing.* "Where are you?" he asked nervously.

"I'm right here," Clarence answered. "Can't you see me?"

The voice seemed everywhere. Peter looked around again. *Don't see anyone.* His eyes bugged out in fright. He stepped backward, and fell over a root. He didn't realize it was the tree talking. Fear was in control. *Gotta get outa here,* then realized, *My bike and ball stuff.* Peter's lips quivered as he stuttered to get the words out, "Are you God?"

"God?" Clarence laughed and shook his branches. "No," he replied still chuckling, "I'm the tree you're standing under. I'm part of God's creation. You've played around me many times and you park your bike here before going to the ball games." Clarence paused momentarily to let Peter catch up then added, "My name is Clarence."

Peter was stunned and couldn't respond, so Clarence continued. "The owls in my branches also can talk, and their names are Charley and Caroline."

Peter's mouth gaped wide open, but he forced himself to look up at the two owls

"Hoo-loo-ooo," Charley hooted staring down at Peter with his big eyes. Caroline could only flutter her wings, ruffle her feathers, and mumble a squawking sound.

Clarence continued, "There is a grey fox hiding over there in the bushes. She can talk, too. Her name is Maggie. We are all friends and you have seen and greeted us many times."

Maggie stepped from behind a bush, gently tossed her sleek head in the air and sent a muffled howl his way, "How-da-doo, Peter." Soon, she was at the base of Clarence.

Peter couldn't believe what he saw. *They are not real!* He rubbed both eyes and looked again. *There is the fox!* He looked up into the tree. *The owls!* He stepped back from the tree trunk. *Did this tree talk to me?* He looked at them again. *There is the fox! The owls! The tree!* He opened his mouth to speak. His lips moved, but nothing came. Finally, in a shaky voice, he stuttered, "Y-y-you ca-ca-can ta-ta-talk?"

"Sure 'nough, son," they all said together.

"We have always talked to each other," Clarence added, "but humans can't understand us unless there is a special reason. You're able to understand because of your imagination, and you have a special need. We..."

"You forgot something, Big fella," Charley interrupted as he hopped up and down on the branch. "Humans, ALSO, must ask for help like Peter did."

"You are right," Clarence replied.

Peter was now in deep shock and couldn't move.

Charley fluttered down to the root by Peter and hopped closer to look into his face. "Eyes are open," Charley hooted softly. "Anything wrong with 'im?"

"Doubt it," Clarence replied. "It is too much to absorb so quickly for the young lad."

After a few minutes, Peter moved his head slowly and gazed again at each of them. He gently slapped his face with his hand, and looked at them again. Then he pinched himself to make sure he wasn't dreaming. "Am I making you up? Are you my imagination?"

"NO!" Clarence bellowed to make sure Peter understood. "WE'RE REAL. YOU'RE NOT MAKING US UP, BUT YOUR IMAGINATION DOES PLAY A PART."

"Y-ye-es-s," Peter answered in a quivering voice. He was noticeably shaken by the things taking place. "I'm n-no-ot used to talking to a tree or to owls or a fox."

"You are right," Clarence responded in a soft voice. "We will slow down so you can get used to us. Sit down, and let's talk."

Clarence began, "Peter, we became special to you because you often saw us in your wild bike rides through the park woods." He paused to give Peter time to reflect. "Remember how you gave us names and talked to us? We could understand you."

Peter nodded his head and began to grin.

"You would say, 'Hello, Big Fella' and 'See ya, Big Fella.' You did it so many times, my three friends here have teased me with that name."

Peter's grin was ear-to-ear now, and a chuckle came from deep within his chest.

"Well, you didn't know it, but I'd reply, 'Hello, Peter.' What humans heard was my branches creaking and leaves rustling in the breeze."

Peter nodded yes. "I loved to play around you because your trunk's massive, and your branches are fun to climb."

Charley waited impatiently to say something to Peter, but couldn't hold off any longer. "Remember how you would speak to us? You would say, 'Hi Mr. Owl,' and 'Hi Mrs. Owl.'" He raised a wing and pointed, "Well, this is Caroline and I'm Charley."

"Hello, Caroline," Peter replied and waved. "Hi, Charley."

"Hi, Peta, honey," Caroline hooted softly as she twisted her head around and fluttered her big eyes at Peter.

"Az-ya know," Charley continued, "Caroline and I sit in Clarence's branches, tawk to 'im and snooze until hunt'n time."

Peter grinned as he replied, "Seen you lots of times, and I

have heard your hooting squawks many times: 'Who-o-o, who-o-o hu-u-nts for u-u-u-u-u-u?'"

Maggie wanted in on the talk and maneuvered her head. "Hi, Peter. Remember how you'd call me, 'Madam Fox? You'd race your bike across the golf course in the evening, see me and yell, 'Can't catch me, Madam Fox! Can't catch me!' like I was nipping at your feet."

"Yeah, that was fun," Peter replied excitedly. "I would look back and see you standing calmly in the distance and staring at me. Then one day, I was close enough to see your eyes. One is grey. Looked like you stared right through me. Spooky."

Peter paused for a moment, looked at each slowly again, and said, "Okay, you guys are real. I'm not dreaming." After a short pause, he asked, "Can I tell my mom about you?"

"Maggie, Caroline, Charley," Clarence inquired of them, "Any problem with Peter's request? Doesn't bother me."

"Fawne with me," Charley hooted. Turning to Caroline he asked, "Okay with you, hun?"

"Yes, Cha'lee deaah," Caroline hooted softly as she turned her head aside to hide her blush from Charley's romantic comment.

"Okay with me, too," Maggie howled quietly.

With that, Charley hopped closer to Peter. He wanted to help Peter feel at ease and believe he was able to talk to them.

Also, Maggie moved to the same root Peter sat on and crouched down so no one else could see her.

"Seems fine, Peter. Now tell us about your baseball problems," Clarence said.

Peter sat quietly for a few moments looking first at Charley and then at Maggie, both within touching distance. He also glanced up at Caroline and Clarence. Then he spoke. "Mom brought my sisters and me to the park to play lots of times, ever since I can remember. It is a fun place. The playground offers lots of things to do, and you can play games and sports like tennis and basketball and baseball and softball." He reflected for a moment and added, "I have even seen folks in some type of sword fighting."

He paused to catch his breath and continued, "As I got older, I watched the boys and girls playing ball on the field. They were having so much fun. When a player caught a ball, there was a big yell from the players and the people watching outside the fence. When they ran to the dugout, they would pat the player on the back for making the catch."

Peter's chest heaved deeply with another breath. "When a player batted, everyone watched. Players had big smiles when they hit the ball. The players and coaches patted them on the back and said good things as they ran around the bases."

At this moment, a gleam appeared on Peter's face as he explained, "Those players seemed to be special, and the whole world stopped to watch them. I want to play ball so I can be special too. I want to do something good. But..." Peter paused and a frustrated look appeared on his face, "I can't hit the ball or catch it or throw it very well."

He paused again as if thinking about what he said, then continued. "I stink! I keep failing and letting the team and coaches down. I'm not any good." He paused again and added more negative stuff. "I can't even find my ball pants or cleats, and I don't look like a ball player in blue jeans and tennis shoes."

Peter stood with his arms raised and hands on the trunk of Clarence. He was quiet, but his mouth moved like he wasn't through. Before long, he whispered.

"I want to play good, to be special. I want to stand at the plate, look out at the pitcher, swing the bat a few times, and have all the eyes at the field looking at me like I was the hero come to save the day. I want to hit the pitch high and watch it sail over the fence for a homerun. That would feel so good. I want to be someone special."

He finished talking and seemed calm and relaxed like he was glad to share his feelings with someone. Someone who would listen.

"Hmmmm, interesting," Clarence replied in a voice like he was deep in thought about what Peter told them. "Now tell us about your mom and dad."

Peter didn't answer for a few moments. A sad expression was on his face as he spoke. "My dad isn't living. Mom told me I was about a year old when he died in a car accident, but..." He paused and a small gleam appeared and his voice became excited, "I have

pictures of him, and mom tells me what he was like. I think of him often."

Tears welled up in both Maggie's and Caroline's eyes, and they turned their heads to hide their motherly emotions.

A bigger gleam appeared, "Did you know he played sports when he was young? I have an old ball jersey of his; number 46. I wear it all the time, even to bed."

"And what about your mom?" Charley asked. "We haven't seen her at your games."

A respectful look came to Peter's face and he replied in a serious tone, "Mom would like to come, but two jobs and taking some classes and..." he paused momentarily. "And I have two older sisters. Mom doesn't have time to practice with me or come to games. We don't have extra money to buy things, but Mom did buy my ball pants and cleats."

He reflected for a moment, "Mom is pretty, but seems tired all the time. Think our family money problem is worse."

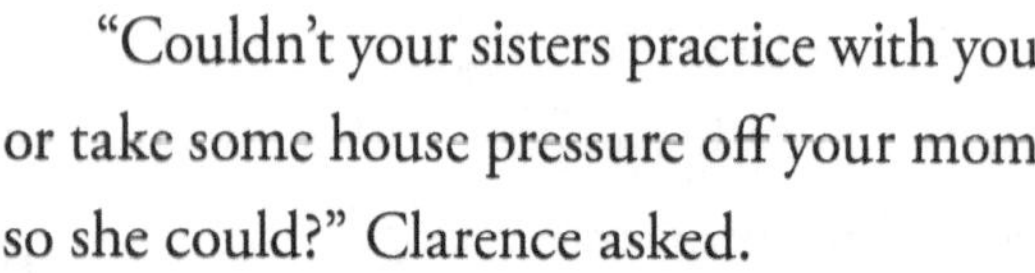

"Couldn't your sisters practice with you or take some house pressure off your mom so she could?" Clarence asked.

"Sally and Elizabeth help around the house, but their ball throws are worse than mine."

"Oh, my." Maggie whispered. "No help there."

"I see other boys and girls practicing and having fun with their dads. If mine was here, he could help me play better, and maybe I wouldn't stink it up like I do now."

"No money? That is why you wear blue jeans and tennis shoes?" Clarence asked.

"Yes. The pants and cleats are someplace in the house, but I can't find them. Don't want to tell Mom 'cause she doesn't have the money. Hope I find them before she comes to a game."

"So when your coach mentions wearing blue jeans and tennis shoes," Clarence inquired, "he says you're out of uniform?"

"Yes," Peter said sadly as his thoughts returned to the game and comments of Coach Tyree. "If I wear them again, said he won't let me play. He also was angry about how I played."

As if on cue, Maggie snuggled against Peter's leg to comfort him, and Caroline fluttered down and perched next to him. Their moves shocked Peter and he choked with gratitude of the warmness and friendship. "You guys are awesome!"

Suddenly, the concession stand outside light went out, leaving only the lights inside.

Clarence stayed on track, "'Bout out of time. We will talk more about your uniform problem another day. Let's talk about your ball playing. We've watched your practices and games. What do you think you need to improve?"

Peter had a ready answer. "Well, I run good, but I need help with everything else. I can't catch a fly ball or field a grounder very good.

My arm's strong, but I throw wildly when I try to throw hard. When I try to throw with control, I throw what players call a 'banana-ball.' Think I'm getting better, but I need practice. Batting, I can't hit the ball at all. I struck out three times today, and let the team down. So far, I've struck out every time. Only times I've hit the ball, they were foul, and then I'd strike out."

Charley wobbled to Peter's knee, looked him eye-to-eye and hooted, "We caun help ya."

"That is right," Clarence added. "We believe with a little help, you can make lots of improvement. We also can help in a few other ways, too."

"How doz-zat sound?" Charley asked.

The conversation with these new friends was difficult for Peter to believe. The owls next to him and the fox at his legs. *Am I really talking to a tree, owls, and a fox?*

"The voice I heard when I was on the field playing, was that you?" Peter asked.

"Yes," Clarence replied, "We wanted to know if you could understand me. You did. Now, Peter, for our efforts to be successful, there's one thing you must do."

"What's that?"

"You must have faith in yourself and believe, like your mom

said, 'Good things will happen.' Do you believe you can improve your baseball playing?"

Peter raised his eyebrows, shrugged his shoulders and replied sheepishly, "I will try."

"You MUST believe you can do it!"

"NO!" Clarence bellowed. "Trying isn't good enough! You MUST believe you can. Say it. I can do it. I can do it!"

The stern sound and loudness of Clarence's voice shook Peter's attention. "Okay. I can do it. I can do it."

At that moment, the lights in the concession stand went dark, and Peter realized, *It's late and I need to go home.* He was excited and mumbled, "Can't wait to tell Mom about my new friends, and they're going to help me." He jumped to his feet and said, "I have to get home, guys. Mom will wonder where I am."

As Peter pedaled away, he yelled over his shoulder, "See you, friends!"

Clarence yelled after him, "Come Thursday evening after school and after you finish your homework and we will begin."

Peter hollered back, "Okay. See you then."

Clarence spoke in a soft voice to Maggie, Caroline, and Charley, "Friends, this young human needs lots of help, but I believe we can help him if he works with us."

Charley fluttered his wings and squawked, "Agree, Big Fella."

Caroline wiped tears from her big round eyes, and nodded her feathered head in agreement, too. She was moved so much by Peter's life and problems she couldn't speak.

Maggie yelped over her shoulder as she trotted off to hunt for food morsels the humans dropped around the field, "I will help. He's a sweetie. Let me know what I can do."

[CHAPTER 14]

*Peter Tells Mom About His Terrible Game, the
Dragon, and His New Friends; Vicki Chews
Out Coach Tyree for His Treatment of Peter*

It had been a long work day for Vicki. *Can't wait to collapse my tired body for awhile into an easy chair at home.*

"What a day," she mumbled as she placed her purse on the kitchen counter. She was too tired to wipe her hair from her eyes, so she blew a puff upwards instead. Didn't help.

"Glad finally home." She flipped on the light, and realized, *No lights on downstairs? Hun is not home yet, or all would be on.* She decided to check up stairs and coaxed her body to further action with a bribe. *I will let you relax longer than planned.*

Lights on in the girl's room, but not in his. "Hi, dears."

Sally and Elizabeth greeted her warmly, "Hi, Mom." They talked about their day and studies and other important teenage girl things.

Suddenly, it dawned on Vicki that her little girls were no longer little. Momentarily, memories of her teen years popped into her mind. *Oh my gosh! What am I going to do? Dear Lord, please not so soon, and...* She lamented, *They are growing up without their father's influence. Help me.*

"Peter home yet?"

"No," they replied in unison.

Hmmmmm, not like him to be so late. His game was the first one. After night hugs and kisses, Vicki somehow managed the journey back to the kitchen. She glanced at the clock. *Second game has been over for a while. Peter's was the first. Where is he?*

She opened the fridge door. *Hun's after-game snack is still there. Where is he?* Her motherly concern rose several notches and masked her tiredness. *I will call Marilyn Davis. She might know of Peter's whereabouts and she will give me blow-by-blow details of the game.*

"Hi, sweetie," Marilyn greeted Vicki. She eagerly shared how the game turned out—and how Rosie's lost. Then she dropped a bombshell. "Coach Tyree and all the players, except my Sakine, seemed to blame Peter for the loss. My dawling'd never do a mean thing like that." She paused momentarily and asked, "Is Peter okay?"

Vicki's head spun from the rapid delivery of information, and she was caught off guard by the question. When she didn't speak, Marilyn continued. "Coach Tyree was really, really mad, and he talked that way, too. When he spoke to the players after the game, he stared at Peter most of the time. Later, I noticed he talked with Peter alone."

Marilyn had to catch her breath, and paused for a second. "I declare, Vicki dear, the way that man stood over Peter and shook his finger at him while he spoke. Peter looked upset." She paused again, and asked in a softer tone, "Is he okay?"

Vicki was exhausted from the long strenuous day and in shock from the revelation her daughters were growing into the challenges of teenage years. Those realities were nothing, though. Her dander quickly rose to the boiling point as she listened to

Marilyn describe the game and events afterwards. The adrenaline was flowing from her motherly, protective instincts. *How dare he speak that way to my baby!*

She mumbled a response, thanked her, and politely said, "Goodbye."

Vicki had the phone in hand to call Coach Tyree and give him a piece of her mind when Peter burst through the back door yelling excitedly, "Mom! Mom! Where are you?"

She didn't want him to see her upset so she straightened her clothes and hair, took a deep breath, and calmly walked out of the kitchen to greet him with a warm smile.

Peter rushed towards her, slamming the outside door shut behind him. "Mom! Mom!" he said excitedly as he looked into her face. "I have some new friends, and..." He choked to catch his breath, "And they are helping with my ball playing!"

She was shocked! *What is this? Peter is in good spirits?*

Mom planned not to mention the game right away, but the topic popped out of her mouth. "Hi, Hun. How was your game?" The goof caused her eyes and mouth to open wide, and she wanted to kick herself. *What am I doing? How could I put my child on the spot like this?*

Before she recovered, Peter answered in a carefree manner. "Oh, the same." ... "We lost again. I struck out three times. A ball hit my mitt, and broke it when I was playing defense. The winning runs then scored." ... "I did start the game, though."

Hun's response puzzled her. *This is all bad news. Why is he so perky, like something great has happened?*

A sad look came on his face as he added, "Mom, I stink, and Coach yelled at me in front of everyone. I felt so bad I wanted to quit, but..."

Now he's letting it out, she thought and she threw her arms open as she said, "Peter."

He rushed into them, warmth like a security blanket, and they hugged deeply. She stroked his sweaty cheeks with her fingers, and touched her face against his. "I know how badly you want to play baseball, Hun. Sometimes things don't work out like we want, and it takes more time to accomplish our goals."

She had a pep talk prepared but, before she could deliver it, Peter leaned back and looked up into her eyes. They stood quietly looking deeply at each other. Mom had tears in her eyes, and Peter knew they were for him.

"Mom, I was trying to tell you I'm okay, now. Yes, I was angry with Coach for awhile, but not now."

He paused for a few moments, with an unusual look on his face, as if deciding to say the next thing, "I was angry with God, too, for Dad not being here." He paused again for a short time. "It isn't fair not having a dad to help me. I thought about quitting baseball."

He paused to collect his thoughts, and Vicki started to say something when he continued in an excited voice. "I said a prayer, and know it wasn't God's fault. ... And then, mom, you won't believe what happened!"

Vicki's emotions had been like a roller coaster—up and down. She asked with a puzzled look, "What, Hun?"

Peter's body moved excitedly about as he rapidly fired off his next comments. "It is like God sent me some help."

"Huh?" Vicki asked in a shocked tone of voice and with a puzzled look.

"I have four new friends! I met them right after my prayer. They're going to help me with my ball playing. They believe I can improve. You have to meet them. They are really neat!"

"Whoa—slow down." His comments confused her, but she was happy he wasn't sulking and down on himself. "New friends? What do you mean?"

"Their names are Clarence, Caroline, Charley, and Maggie. Clarence is a huge tree, Charley and Caroline are a couple of owls, and Maggie is a grey fox."

Peter never noticed how his mom's head snapped up and her face and eyes bugged out in shock. Never phased him of the questions flying around in her head. *New friends? A tree? Two owls and a fox? … Oh, my gosh. Something drastic's happened to my baby!*

She cautioned herself. *Stay calm, Vicki. Stay calm. Don't trigger a meltdown.* "That's great, Hun. How did you meet them? When can I meet them?"

Peter said so many things, but her thoughts kept coming back to him saying his new friends were owls, a tree, and a fox. *Imaginary friends? Did he say what I thought he said?*

At that moment, she remembered the counselor's words about her husband's accident. "You and the children may have some psychological issues. They could come soon, or later in life. Could be expressed as abnormal behavior, like make-believe or even depression. If that happens, it doesn't mean you, or they, have some deep mental disorder. Rather, it will be a way of coping with the stress and loss of your husband and their dad."

> *"Is Peter escaping reality and turning to imaginary friends?"*

Vicki wondered, *Is Peter so hurt with the way he's playing, and now Coach Tyree speaking angrily to him, and not having a father like the other players, he is escaping reality and turning to imaginary friends?*

Peter continued to talk about his new friends helping him, but his voice seemed to be muffled as she kept thinking, *That settles it. I'm calling Coach Tyree right now!*

"When do you want to meet them?" Peter asked. When she didn't answer, he looked into her eyes, shook her gently and said, "Mom! Mom! Earth to mom!"

She regained her focus, and Peter asked again, "When do you want to meet my new friends?"

"Uh. Uh, whenever is best for them." She paused for a moment to think about what he asked. "Maybe the next game?" She thought for moment, and added, "Tell you what. Check and let me know when is best for them."

"Okay."

"Great, now go feed Pokey and I'll freshen up your after-game snack."

With that, Peter grabbed a cookie and off he went outside with a joyful look on his face. *I can hardly wait to see my new friends again and start practice.*

The moment Peter went outside, Vicki picked up the phone to call Coach Tyree, but before she placed the call, it rang. "Hello," she answered.

"Hello. This is Coach Tyree, and..."

Vicki's mouth gaped open. *The jerk I was going to call.* She responded coldly, "Hello, this is Vicki Marshall."

Before he could say anything, she began to unload her motherly anger on him. "I was about to call you. I want you to know I don't appreciate how you treated my son today. I heard he didn't bat well and..."

He interrupted her, "That is why ... uh..."

The intensity of Vicki's voice interrupted him back, "...and Peter didn't catch a ball and you chewed him out at the team meeting and again when you were alone with him but everyone at the field heard you."

"That is why I'm..."

"How dare you?" She was on fire now, and had his ears pinned back. "How dare you speak to my son like that! Or anyone's son? Peter is trying to play ball the best he can, and he could be better if I was able to help him. But I have to work two jobs for us to make ends meet, and he doesn't have a father to practice with him like all the other players do."

Coach Tyree could hear her sobbing now, and he was upset. *I deserve this.*

"You coaches have beaten him down," Vicki expressed loudly, "and now he comes home talking about some make-believe, imaginary friends to escape reality! That's a fine way to tear down a player. You are doing a great job!"

Finally she paused either out of words or breath or maybe both. Before she could say anything else, Coach Tyree spoke.

"That is why I'm calling you and Peter. I want to apologize. I have called a team meeting tomorrow evening at the field. I lost control of my emotions at the game today, and spoke harshly to the team and especially to Peter afterwards. I'm not proud of how I acted." He repeated, "I want to apologize, but to everyone together. I hope you and Peter will come."

Vicki didn't remember any more of the phone call. When she realized the call was over, she put the phone down, changed clothes and went back to the kitchen to finish Hun's after-game snack. For a moment, she forgot her husband wasn't there, *Peter will take care of this.*

CHAPTER 15

Coach Tyree Apologizes to the Team; Peter
Tells Mom More About His Imaginary Friends

Coach Tyree finished the calls to set up the special team meeting, and he collapsed into a well-worn leather recliner. *Wow! Emotionally drained,* he thought as he rubbed his eyes and sipped, now cold coffee. *I want to apologize, but how do I say it? Sound sincere?*

He replayed the call with Vicki Marshall. "Boy howdy, she lit into me."

Her comment about "Peter not having a father" jarred his memory. A coach had mentioned it at the player draft. "…in a car accident, and Peter was only a toddler."

Coach Tyree frowned in disappointment of his forgetfulness. *How did I not remember? I didn't make the connection she is a widower even though I learned she worked several jobs because of financial difficulties.*

He sat upright and momentarily reflected on her traumatic experience. *Had to be a heartache to lose a loved one in a tragic accident and leave her to raise three young'uns.*

> *A single parent. Fatherless!*
> *Explains lots of things!*

His thoughts turned to losing his wife, Mary Beth, to cancer and raising John William alone. He gazed at a picture of her on a nearby table. *Traumatic enough to lose a partner. Then being a single parent. Explains why Peter's baseball skills are so undeveloped. Also, why he wears blue jeans and tennis shoes.*

Wednesday evening came, and players and parents were beginning to arrive at the ball field for the team meeting. Players came dressed for practice.

When Peter and his mom arrived, he grinned, made a comment about Clarence, and waived. Clarence returned the greeting, but all Vicki saw was branches moving in a breeze. Peter still wore the blue jeans and tennis shoes as neither could find his ball pants and cleats.

Coach Sanders blew his whistle and motioned for the players to join him on the field. He said, "Coach Tyree will be out here in a few minutes, so I will start the practice."

Coach Tyree soon pulled up in his pickup, and John William hustled to join the team. Coach Tyree was dressed in his coaches' team jersey, but this time he had on blue jeans and tennis shoes. After a short practice, he called the players to join the parents. "Grab a knee." He also motioned for the parents to move closer.

"There is something important I want to say to the team and to each player and parent." Coach Tyree's voice quivered and had a serious tone unlike any he had used before. The players and parents looked at each other curiously as they moved closer.

At that moment, a couple of owls sailed high overhead to a nearby tall pine tree and settled on a branch. Clarence wanted them to listen in on the meeting. Peter grinned. *It's Caroline and Charley. Wonder if Mom sees them?*

"I appreciate you coming to this special meeting. I didn't say much over the phone because I wanted to speak to you face-to-face and to the whole group at once." He looked nervous, and shifted his weight more than usual back and forth on his legs.

"You see," he paused for a moment, and then stunned the group. "I was a jerk last Monday at our ball game. I'm not proud of how I acted and what I said both during the game and afterwards. I did the opposite of what I try to coach your sons and daughters to do." He paused again. "I lost my temper! To make matters worse, I spoke harshly to the team." He paused and turned toward Peter, "ALSO, I humiliated Peter Marshall in a separate meeting afterwards."

Coach Tyree stopped speaking and slowly looked at each player and parent. After making eye connection, he continued with a choke in his voice, "I made a lot of mistakes last game, and I apologize to each one of you for my actions and words."

His gaze stopped on Peter Marshall. "Peter, I especially want to apologize to you and your mother in front of everyone." He glanced back and forth to Peter and Vicki. "I put too much pressure on you before you went to bat by stressing how much we needed you to hit the ball. Same with playing good defense before you even took the field. All it did was make you fearful of making a mistake, and that set you up to make them."

"But," he paused again, "since the last game, Peter, the rest of you, I've learned in that play where I thought Peter missed the ball and it rolled to the fence, it actually hit his mitt and tore the webbing. Few if anyone would have caught it."

He inhaled deeply and continued, "Yes, a coach should encourage players to push themselves to higher levels of performance—especially if the coach believes the player can be better. And, yes, I said the same to other players, but not as often or forceful as I did to Peter. I also said team players need to do lots more work on the basic skills of catching, throwing, and hitting, but everyone thought I meant especially you, Peter, since I stared at you the whole time."

His voice choked again as he continued, "Peter and Mrs. Marshall, I mentioned Peter's father needed to help him. I forgot about your family situation. My words hurt. I'm terribly sorry and hope you will give me a chance to make it up. Maybe in time, you will forgive me."

Vicki responded with a slight nod, and mumbled, "Thank you."

Coach Tyree looked around at the other players and parents, and said, "I hope you will also forgive my stupidity. If you think I've pushed your player too hard, please come talk to me. And..." his voice quivered as he added in a solemn tone, "I will resign if you feel best."

No one made a sound.

After a few moments of silence, Coach Tyree continued, "And Peter, your coming to ball games and practices in blue jeans and tennis shoes irritated me in a personal way I didn't realize. I am fond of wearing blue jeans and western boots, but yours reminded me of an unpleasant memory from my youth.

"When I was your age, the kids would play baseball or softball on the school playgrounds. After lunch, we played ball—work-up or choose sides. I would be one of the first chosen as I was as good as any of the others, including most who played organized summer ball.

"I never could play in the summer, though, because I lived on a wheat and dairy farm in Western Oklahoma and there was no time to practice or play in games because I had to work. One day a dad, who coached his son's ball team, called about my playing with his son and team. He didn't have enough players for a game that evening, and he wanted to know if I could go this one time. They could travel by our farm on the way to the other town. I got the okay if I finished my chores for the day."

A gleam came to Coach Tyree's face as he talked. "I tell you,

I was so excited! I was playing in my first organized game of baseball. I didn't have a uniform, though, but they brought me a team jersey." For a few seconds, his eyes and mind returned to that time, "I remember how special I felt when I pulled that jersey over my head and looked down at the number. Wow! I'm a real ballplayer. However, I only had blue jeans and some old tennis shoes to wear. I also had an old ball mitt, but none of those things mattered. I was playing in an official ball game!"

Coach Tyree's excitement dropped several notches as he continued, "Well, it rained on the ball field about an hour before we arrived. We played anyway, but there was a good-size rain puddle along the 3rd baseline and just outside 3rd base. You guessed it. I played 3rd base."

His excitement now was replaced by a tone of disappointment. "I remember only a few things about the game. I was really nervous, and I struck out three times. Never touched the ball except for one foul ball. I knew I was a better hitter than that. On defense, the only ball hit my way was a high foul ball. I could see that it would come down somewhere outside 3rd base, and I knew I could make this catch as I had caught balls like that before on the school playground. It was my chance to show everyone I was a good player by catching this one. It was an easy catch, but I had to walk into the rain puddle to move under the ball. I looked up tracking the ball the whole time, but I made a mistake and overplayed it. I had to reach backwards quickly over my head if I was going to catch it. I took a couple of steps backwards, but my tennis shoes slipped in the mud. I fell down on my bottom smack in the middle of the puddle. I was wet and muddy, and so was my mitt. I heard everyone laughing at me, even the players and coaches on my team. I don't remember much after that except being wet, muddy, embarrassed, and not making the catch. Also, we lost the game."

He paused briefly and continued in a sad tone. "I was never asked again to play with the team." His voice became a whisper, "That was the only game of organized baseball in my life."

A serious look came to Coach Tyree's face. "Maybe as a coach I have tried to have a baseball life through my son and other players I coach. When one of you has success in a game, in a way it's like I'm doing that. I'd want to do well, to be the best. In looking back at my coaching, I have put too much emphasis on each player being perfect every time. Instead, I should be helping each one of you get better and better than what you were before."

Coach Tyree paused and took a deep breath. "Now you know the story, and reasons why I wanted this meeting. Again, I apologize and ask you to give me a chance to make it up to you."

No one said anything for a moment. Then Vicki Marshall spoke. "I would like you to stay as coach." A few others expressed the same, and then everyone. Including the players.

Coach Tyree beamed and choked out the words, "Thank you. And, thanks again for coming." He nodded to his son, and they walked to their pickup to leave. From that day on, Coach Tyree and Coach Sanders wore blue jeans and tennis shoes to practices and games.

No one said much to each other, and within a few minutes all left the park, too.

Neither Peter nor his mom said much as they walked home. Coach's apology and Peter's imaginary friends kept going through Vicki's mind. *Maybe I misunderstood him. Glad I spoke up. ... Think my Peter would be proud.* About half way home, she felt her forehead. *Hmmm, tenseness I had before the meeting is now gone.*

She glanced at Peter. *He's mentioned imaginary friends several times now, even waved to them. Was this to hide his true feelings about Coach Tyree and playing baseball?* "Hun," she asked softly, "what do you think about Coach Tyree's comments?"

Peter glanced at her momentarily, shrugged his shoulders and mumbled, "Duh-know."

She pressed for more response as they walked to the rear door of the house. "Sounds like he didn't remember about our family and your dad."

Pokey started their way, and Vicki hurried the next comment. "That explains coach expecting your ball skills to improve with extra practice away from the team." She was eager for him to talk, and pushed gently for a response. "What do you think?"

"Uh, guess he didn't know," Peter replied as he avoided Pokey's charge. "Not now, Pokey," he giggled as he dodged her and took off for the back door. "Maybe later," he yelled over the shoulder as she nipped playfully at his heels.

By the time Vicki walked into the back door, Peter had bounded up the stairs to his room. She called to him, "Hun, I'll have a little time in an hour. Want to throw the ball with me?"

Peter appeared at the top of the stairs. "Thanks Mom, but no need. Remember? I have a practice with Clarence tomorrow after school and when my homework is done."

Peter's words caused a worried look to appear on Vicki's face. *What am I going to do about these imaginary friends? Maybe I should talk to coach again.* She made a mental note to ask Coach Tyree for a meeting soon after the next game.

This caused her to think again of Coach Tyree's comments. A warm feeling came over her. *I appreciate his apology and what he said. Seems to be a better guy than what I believed.*

CHAPTER 16

Peter Practices With His Imaginary Friends

Peter was nervous all day at school about his practice with Clarence and friends. Doubts had crept in. *Are they real?* First thing at home, he put his dad's old jersey on because it comforted him. He goofed off for a while, then remembered. *Oops, forgot. Clarence said, "Finish homework before practice."*

His growling stomach reminded him of his hunger. He hurried to the kitchen, slapped together a peanut butter 'n' jelly sandwich, grabbed a half-filled bottle of juice from the fridge, and bounded up the stairs to his room to study.

His body squirmed and twisted as he tried to recall what he just read. "Ugh, hate history! Can't remember this." He settled on a compromise. *I'll study more tonight.* Once he let himself off the hook, he was out the door and pedaling fast to practice with Clarence and friends.

"Glad to see you, Peter," Clarence bellowed as he rode into sight. "Ready to begin?"

Charley and Caroline hooted their welcome, "Hoo-lo, Peter."

"Y-ye-yes," Peter replied nervously and said hello to the owls.

"Great!" Clarence exclaimed. "First, a refresher. Remember our talk about believing good things will happen when you have faith in yourself?"

"Yes."

"Good. You must always remember those two things. Now let's begin. We'll teach you some small steps and, when you learn those, you will figure out bigger steps yourself."

Peter asked with a puzzled look, "What do you mean, small steps?"

Clarence hesitated for a few seconds and wondered, *How do I explain so he'll understand?* An idea came to him. "Peter, see where Charley and Caroline are sitting?"

"Yes," he answered as he looked up at them.

"Well, I want you to climb up there and sit with them."

"Huh?" Peter's brow wrinkled and he asked in a doubtful voice as he looked up and pointed. "Sit way up there?"

"Yes, up there."

"But. They flew up there. … I can't fly."

"I know that," Clarence said with an impatient tone to his voice, "but you can climb."

"But … I have never climbed that high before."

Clarence responded in a stern tone, "No buts! Get to it. Say it. I can do it. I can do it."

Peter slowly joined in, but softly. "I … can … do it. … I … can … do it."

"Good. Now decide what steps to take and how to begin."

Peter stood without saying a word, so Clarence continued, "Come on. Get moving. You have climbed to my lower branches while playing."

With that, Peter used his bike as the first step. He leaned it against Clarence's trunk, climbed to the seat, stood on it, and pulled himself up to Clarence's lowest branch. Then he climbed to the next two lowest branches where he had been before.

"See, you took several small steps, and already you are off the ground by several branches."

"Yeah," Peter replied, "but that part was easy."

"Come on, where is that self-belief? Now steady yourself against my trunk, and pull yourself to the next branch."

Peter had to stretch to reach the next branch, struggled to get his feet over it, but soon was sitting on top of it.

"Way ta go!" Caroline hooted softly as she rotated her head to watch Peter's moves.

"Now do you see how a goal can be reached by taking small steps?" Clarence asked.

"Sure," Peter replied as he stared up at the branch where Charley and Caroline were perched. *I can reach them after a few more branches,* he concluded, and began to climb without any more of Clarence's prodding. Before long, he was only two branches below them. He put his hands up and started to pull himself up when suddenly he jerked a hand back and looked at it. "Yuk!" he exclaimed loudly.

"What's wrong?" Clarence asked.

Caroline peeked over their branch and squawked when she understood what happened, "Oh, my, Cha'lee, you di'dant."

"Ooops," Charley hooted in a guilty tone.

"Bird poop!" Peter yelled as he stared at his hand smeared with it.

Clarence's branches and leaves suddenly shook violently as he laughed. Peter, Caroline, and Charley had to hold on to keep from being shaken off.

"Cha'lee, deaah..."

"I know, I know," Charley interrupted with an embarrassed look. "I should'a stuck my tail feathers further out from the branch so it'd fall to the ground. ... Sorry, Peter."

"Just wipe it off on my trunk," Clarence chuckled, "and get on with your climb."

Peter soon made it to the branch with Caroline and Charley, and they snuggled up to him. "Still friends?" Charley asked.

"No problem," Peter replied patting Charley on the head. Then a big grin of accomplishment came to his face. "I see what you mean, Clarence."

"*...learn how to play, one step at a time!*"

"This is what we want you to do in baseball. Learn and practice each skill, one step at a time, just like climbing to my high branches. You have to remember what you learn, though."

"Let's do it!" Peter replied excitedly.

"Good. Now hustle down to the ground."

Peter looked down, and gulped. "Remember your steps," Clarence expressed.

Before long Peter was back on the ground. "What now?"

"We'll start with what you've mentioned: fielding grounders, catching fly balls, throwing with accuracy and power, and hitting," Clarence said. "We don't have time to practice all of them today, but we'll teach you how to practice on your own. You ready?"

"Yes!" Peter exclaimed in a giddy tone. A thought was heavy on his mind, *It's the first time anyone has ever spent some one-on-one practice with me.*

Clarence chuckled at Peter's enthusiasm, then continued, "The practice steps we'll teach you are ones we've seen work for other players. They'll work for you too, Peter, but you have to practice and believe in yourself." Clarence wondered, *Am I going too fast for him? . . . We'll see.*

"You'll be able to hear me from anywhere in the park, but

remember ... other humans won't understand. Same in hearing Charley and Caroline. Understand what I am saying?"

"Uh-huh," Peter mumbled and nodded his head.

"Good. Fielding ground balls will be the first steps we'll practice." Clarence raised a branch slightly and pointed towards the tennis court. "See the practice wall over there?"

Peter turned his head that direction and nodded, "Yes."

"First drill is a throw and catch. Stand about fifteen feet in front of the wall with your mitt. Bend your knees, squat down with your rear end low, and put your mitt in front of you to catch a ground ball coming towards you. Throw the ball against the wall, and catch it. Do this drill about five times. Then take a step to one side and throw and catch another five times. Then take a step to the other side, and repeat the throw and catch drill."

"The ball you will use is a tennis ball. Throw it at the bottom of the wall so it will bounce back low along the ground toward you. Move in front of the path you think the ball'll follow when it bounces back. Bend your legs and squat down. Put your mitt down and let the ball come into its pocket. Do these steps over and over. After you're able to catch all the balls that bounce back to you, throw harder and harder. These steps will improve your throwing and sharpen your eye for placing your mitt in the right position to catch it. After a while, move towards the wall and try to scoop the ball while you're moving. Do this over and over until it becomes a habit—a muscle memory. Then in a game, all you need to do is remember the first step and believe in yourself. Understand?"

"Yes, I believe so, but that is a lot to remember."

"Yes, but we'll be watching you. I can see you from here and talk to you if you need it. The more you do these drills, you will remember, and can practice them against a brick or concrete wall at home or someplace else."

"Now let's talk about throwing with accuracy and power. Peter, my squirrel friends tell me you sometimes throw rocks at them but, fortunately, your accuracy isn't good. Same with your throws on the ball field.

"Practice these steps. Go to the basketball court over there when no one is playing. Take some tennis balls with you, and stand at the free throw line. Throw a ball easy at the backboard. Do this until you hit the backboard ten times without missing. Then back up to the top of the free throw circle, and throw at the backboard again until you hit it ten times without missing. After these steps, repeat throwing at the free throw line and at the top of the circle, but try to catch the balls. After you're able to hit the backboard and catch most of the balls, repeat with harder throws. Keep throwing and catching the ball until you can throw as hard as you can, and hit the backboard target each time. If you need help to remember these steps, holler out to me or Caroline or Charley or Maggie."

"Yes, Peter—just ask us," Charley squawked.

Clarence added a warning, "If I see you loaf or form a bad habit, we'll scold you."

Peter took a deep breath and nodded he understood.

"Now, let's cover catching fly balls. Start by tossing a ball in the air and catching it. Make small tosses at first. When you're able to catch it most of the time, throw it higher and higher. After you are able to catch most of them, close your eyes, throw a ball up, then open your eyes, find the ball, and catch it. These steps will improve your eye focus and body movement to get under the ball to catch it. Work on these steps in your backyard or in an open space. After you work on these throws for a while, walk and toss the ball up and catch it. Remember this?"

"Yes, I believe so," Peter responded, "but can I ask if I forget some of it?".

"Absolutely! Now let's talk about hitting. Find an old broom and remove the broom straw from the handle. Use it as a bat, and practice hitting small pebbles. The idea is if you learn to hit the small pebbles with the small broom handle, you will improve to hit a baseball with a bat."

Charley added, "Peter, there are lots of pebbles down by the Cascades waterfalls."

"Oh, yes, Peter," Clarence cautioned, "make sure not to practice these steps in an area where you might hit a house or cars or people. You don't want to get in trouble for breaking a window or hurting someone. … Stand like you are at the batter's plate. Hold the broom handle up and ready to hit. Hold it with one hand and a pebble with the other. Toss the pebble up, put both hands on the handle and swing it at the pebble when it comes down. Swing like you're going to hit a baseball pitched to you. You'll miss most of the time at first, but soon you will have better eye contact on the pebble as it comes down, and you will improve your anticipation of the right time to swing to hit it. Do this over and over until you can hit the pebble most of the time. These practice steps will help you to keep your eye on the pebble as it comes down into your strike zone. After this, you will use a baseball and a bat. Okay?"

"Yes, I believe so."

"Good. If you have a few minutes before you need to head home, go to the tennis practice volley board and practice throwing and fielding a ball. There is a tennis ball by the bushes some players left. We will watch how you are doing. After today, practice the other steps until you're ready for more lessons. Come tomorrow and we'll continue. Okay?"

Peter's head was spinning with all the information, but he was excited. "Okay!" he answered as he hurriedly put his ball stuff on his bike and pedaled off to the tennis courts. He yelled back over his shoulder, "Thanks, guys. See you!"

Clarence's instructions were on Peter's mind as he walked on to the volley court. *Start with fielding grounders. Throw the tennis ball low at the board and catch it.* His face and posture took on a confident expression. *This oughtta be easy.*

"Look," Charley squawked, "Balls are bouncing back too fast for him, and all over the place. His body's movun one way and legs another. Kid has no coordination."

"You may be correct," replied Clarence in a doubtful tone, "but he is probably that way because he is trying to throw hard for ball speed and has no control where it bounces back."

Clarence bellowed across the park, "Peter, slow down your throws. It is messing up your control."

Peter heard him, but was determined to do it his way. *I will show them I can throw hard.*

He lunged and threw with more force than before and, of course, he misjudged the returning speed. The ball bounced into his groin, hitting smack in his private parts. His first reaction was a deep sucking gasp, followed by a loud, "Ugh."

"Oops," Clarence said as he observed Peter's body double over and slump to the court.

"Oooh," Peter moaned through clinched teeth as his lips turned blue.

"He wasn't wearing that protector cup thing," Clarence added as he chuckled.

"Betcha that hurt," Charley squawked and lost his balance. He raised his wing quickly, but accidently caused Caroline to loose hers too. Luckily, Clarence noticed and moved his branch enough to keep them steady.

"What happ'n, deaah?" Caroline asked through a twisted beak and with eyes crossed. "Whaz'a protecto' thingy?"

"He'll explain later," Clarence answered with a chuckle. Clarence wanted to stay on track. "Maybe this'll teach Peter to follow instructions."

"Yeah," Charley added. "Sure hope he gets the hang of this before he hurts himself."

"You all right, Peter?" Clarence hollered.

From his sprawled position on the ground, Peter raised his mitt and mumbled in a high-pitched squeaky voice, "Oo-kay. Just taking a little break."

After a while, he struggled to his feet and began throwing the ball at the wall again. This time, with less force. He now had more control, and he fielded a few of the grounders.

"Look at him!" Clarence whispered excitedly. "Improved already. Learning to focus."

"Yup," Charley hooted with a cackle. "Nothing like being hit like that will get him to focus every time. Still needs lots of work."

Before long, Peter decided to practice throwing tennis balls against the basketball backboard and catching them in the air on the ricochet.

"Kid doesn't do this very good, either," Charley hooted. "He's not hitting the backboard. Needs to throw with less force to learn ball speed and control."

"That is not helping either," Clarence replied. "The ball doesn't bounce back far enough to catch. Our young ballplayer needs more improvement than I thought."

Charley nodded his head in agreement and added, "Can say that again, Big Fella."

"Gotta head home," Peter mumbled. "Can't wait to tell mom about practice with my friends. I will work on catching fly balls and hitting another day."

As he tied his ball equipment on his bike, he recalled being hit in the private parts fielding grounders. His face softened and his eyes faded to that moment.

Surely it'll be less painful to catch fly balls and hit pebbles with a broom handle.

Telling his mom about practice was on his mind, and he forgot to say "Goodbye" to his friends. Also, he never heard Clarence yell, "See you tomorrow after school for practice."

[CHAPTER 17]

Peter Learns More About Dad, and the Family
Possibly Losing Their House

Peter coasted his bike to the back of the house. *Hmmm, mom's car. What's up? . . . Said she would work late today.* He hopped off and hit the ground in a trot towards the back porch while the bike rolled to its side in the yard.

"Bow-wow," Pokey barked eagerly as she wagged her tail and beckoned him to play.

"Maybe later," Peter giggled over his shoulder as Pokey chased him to the door, nipping playfully at his heels.

"Mom, Mom, where are you?" Peter hollered excitedly while the screen door banged behind him. "My practice was awesome!"

She was not in the kitchen. Car is home. ... Maybe up stairs. Halfway up, he yelled again, "Mom, you up there?"

A faint voice responded from Vicki's bedroom.

Peter turned and was down the stairs in a flash. He tapped lightly on her bedroom door. "Mom, you in there?" He listened, but didn't hear anything. "Can I come in?" ... Still no reply, he opened the door a bit and peaked inside.

She was face down across the bed with a letter in her hand. "Mom, you all right?"

Vicki raised her head, and he saw the reddish, puffy face. *Mom has been crying.* He hurried to her side, and hugged her tightly. Friends and practice were no longer a thought.

Mom made a futile attempt to hide her anguish but, after mumbling, "It is nothing," the story gushed out.

"Hun, I wanted to keep you and the girls from being forced into adulthood so soon," she expressed in a teary tone, "but I can't any longer."

She slowly told him about their money problems. "They began when your father died in that car accident." She paused, and her eyes took on a far a way look as fresh tears appeared.

"It was devastating! ... They returned your dad's cell phone. It had a message from us of your first words. He and I had a little bet on whether you'd say 'Daddy' or 'Mommy' first. He won, but he was on a trip. I called, but he didn't answer. You said, 'Da, Da' on the recording." She paused as another far away look appeared. "I hope he heard it before..."

After a deep breath, she continued. "Anyway, it was a tough time. We lost our loving father and husband that day, and I lost a partner to solve problems with. Before long, I discovered we also lost his income to help pay family expenses."

She sat up and looked into Peter's eyes. "Remember my telling you about a mortgage?" Before he could respond, she continued, "Well, the life insurance monies have been depleted, and I have been unable to pay on the house mortgage. I'm four payments behind, and another is due soon."

She raised the letter in her hand. "It is from the mortgage company. If I can't catch up the payments and miss another, they will foreclose on the house. That means we will lose it. A rental with three bedrooms will cost more than a house payment."

This was a heavy dose of adult reality for Peter. Minutes earlier his concern was about base hits and wearing blue jeans and tennis shoes. Now: *We will lose our house?*

Vicki sobbed deeply, but the tenseness of her body and voice subsided as she shared the burden. "I've tried to work extra and Grandpa and Grandma have helped, but there have been too many costs this last year. I can't keep up with repairs and expenses."

Peter was stunned. He never thought much about money for groceries, the house, or other things. He was a kid, and parents took care of those things. His world took on a whole different meaning of what is most important at that moment.

Peter's ideas in how to help his family!

He put his arms around her and hugged her tightly. "Mom, I can help. I will quit the ball team and go around the neighborhoods near the park and look for jobs. Lots of people have leaves on their roofs and in their gutters. I can sweep and clean them. I can rake leaves in the yard, prune bushes, and mow lawns. I can ask about other odd jobs too. Done some of these already. I'm a good worker. I can help, Mom. You will see."

Vicki was exhausted from worry, little sleep, and hunger, but she wasn't about to let Peter toss his dream away. "Those ideas sound great, Hun. But, no," she said in a voice barely loud enough for him to hear. "I don't want you to quit the team. Playing has been your dream, and it is important to me, too. It's okay if you find some jobs, but you can't quit."

She put her hand on his chin, turned it firmly towards her and said in a stern voice, "Understand me?"

Peter's lips tightened as he nodded. *Still, I must do something to help.*

They sat quietly and hugged each other. Vicki gently brushed the hair from his face and broke the silence. "God will help us somehow," she mumbled as she slumped down into the pillow and faded away. "He always has," she said in a whisper.

"God will help us somehow. ... He always has."

She gazed up at him and mumbled, "You look so much like your dad. Be the man of the house soon. He would have been..."

Peter, now an eleven-year-old man, gently tucked the cover under her chin, kissed her on the cheek, and tiptoed out the room. A plan already was forming in his mind as he closed the door. *After school tomorrow, I will...*

CHAPTER 18

The Mortgage is More Important Than Base Hits

During school, Peter's thoughts kept drifting back to his family money problems. His English teacher noticed the absent-minded look on his face. She interrupted the lesson and asked him a silly question to see if he was listening or daydreaming. "Peter, would you take off your shoes and socks?"

Students who were listening looked up, stunned by the question. Everyone quickly turned in their seat to see his reaction. Peter was looking at her, but his mind was someplace else.

She asked the question again, "Peter, would you take off your shoes and socks?"

Peter's facial expression still didn't change, but the loud giggle of the students startled him. He glanced around quickly with a quizzical look of, "What is happening?"

"I thought so," the teacher stated sharply. "Peter, please pay attention to the lesson."

He replied sheepishly, "Yes ma'am," as he slumped in his seat trying to hide. *Why is everyone laughing and staring?*

In a short time, though, his mind was back on his plan to help with the family money problems. *Find work and give the money to mom. I will look right after school for odd jobs.* Suddenly he moaned under his breath, "Oh, nooo," as he remembered. *I have a practice with Clarence right after school.*

What do I do? ... I have it. Be honest. I will go by the ball field later and tell Clarence why I was late—and I can't practice much over the next week or two.

When the end-of-day bell rang, Peter was out the door in a flash. At home, he quickly changed clothes, did his daily chores, grabbed some cookies, and headed down the street.

Soon Peter knocked on his first door, Mr. Higgin's. *This place has been run down for a long time. Betcha they will be glad to have help.*

When the door opened, Peter was surprised Mr. Higgins was standing with a walker. *Didn't know he needed one!*

"Hi, son."

"Uh, uh ... Hi Mr. uh ... Hig-gins," Peter stammered as he nervously shifted his body weight from one leg to the other. It hit Peter that asking an adult for work wasn't easy.

Mr. Higgins smiled, and he came to Peter's rescue. "What can I do for you?"

"Uh ... I'm looking for odd jobs to earn money. Looks like you could use some help. I can rake, mow, clip hedges, clean gutters, or anything you might want me to do."

Mr. Higgins' smile abruptly disappeared. "Sorry," he replied curtly as he closed the door. "I don't have anything."

Peter was shocked at the response. *I was sure he would want help.* He didn't realize Mr. Higgins knew his place was run down, but disturbed he didn't have money to hire anyone.

Over the next few hours, Peter knocked on more doors, and was excited he had some success. *Have a flower bed to dig and clean for planting, haul trash from a shed to the curb, sweep leaves off a carport, and clip a long hedgerow. Maybe I will earn enough to make our mortgage payments!* Reality would teach him differently, though.

Meanwhile, Clarence spoke with Caroline and Charley, "Peter is late for practice. Not good of him. Any idea why?"

"Dunno," Charley replied. "Want us to check?"

"Good idea."

Soon they returned. "We found him knocking on doors, and perched nearby in a tree so we could watch. He asked for jobs to do. Some humans'd talk a moment and then shut the door. A few walked with him around their place and pointed to different projects."

Clarence mumbled. "Why did Peter do that instead of coming to practice as we agreed? Must be important."

Peter planned the work for the jobs he had as he started up the path to another house. *My team plays Saturday morning. I will start as soon as our ball game is over. Finish Monday or Tuesday after school.*

This knock also had a flower bed job for him, but a monkey wrench was thrown into the work plan. "No, your schedule won't work for me. I'm leaving town at 10:00 a.m. Saturday. If you want the job, Peter, you have to do it before I go."

Helping family is more important than base hits!

Peter was in a pickle. *Getting base hits is my dream! I want to play in my ballgame Saturday, but I must earn money! Won't be many jobs.* His heart ached, but he knew what he must do. "Okay, I'll come early in the morning and finish before you leave." They agreed to Peter's work plan.

Peter agonized over this commitment. *Coach Tyree said not to miss a game without an excuse. I've got to tell him I can't play tomorrow. What am I going to say?*

After the last knock-on-the-door, Peter noticed the time. *Late, but maybe Clarence will still practice with me.* So he hurried home to get his mitt, a broom handle and tennis ball.

Mom is at work. He left a note. "Mom, at the park to practice baseball with Clarence. Back about 8:00 p.m. L, P." He downed a couple more cookies with a glass of juice and headed off to the park.

A ball game was underway as Peter pedaled into sight. "Here he comes now," Clarence whispered to Caroline and Charley. "Wonder what his excuse'll be?"

As Peter rounded the outfield fence, Clarence bellowed in a stern tone, "PETER, . . . WHERE HAVE YOU BEEN? ... NOT GOOD OF YOU! WE AGREED TO PRACTICE RIGHT AFTER SCHOOL TODAY! DID YOU FORGET?"

Peter opened his mouth to speak, but Clarence had more to say. "To be a good ball player, Peter, you must have discipline, be responsible, and live up to your agreements with others. Your teammates have to know they can trust you."

Clarence was about to say more, but Peter managed to get in a few words. "Uh, hi, Clarence. I'm sorry." Peter noticed Caroline and Charley and mouthed a "Hello" to them. "I had something very important to do after school before coming here."

Clarence snapped back sharply with a shake of his branches, "Well, was it more important than living up to your agreement with us? We can't help someone who doesn't keep his word!"

The unexpected criticism caused Peter to freeze and Clarence asked again, "Well? . . . Was it?"

"Yes, we agreed," Peter finally replied, "but I didn't have a choice.

My family needs help to pay our bills. Mom says we may lose the house. I need to do my part to help even if it means missing a game." He gazed at the ground a few seconds and then up at Clarence and the two owls. "I looked for jobs to earn money, and I didn't have a way to let you know. I'm sorry."

"You mean? Uh..." Clarence had to think. "Hold on..."

Peter could hear Clarence jabbering with Caroline and Charley, but he couldn't make out the words.

"Okay, Peter," Clarence replied. "We understand your problem, and we will continue to work with you. But on one condition."

"What is that?"

"We work as a team from now on, and you tell us first if you have to break an agreement. Understand?"

Peter replied softly, "I understand. Thanks for staying my friends. ... I let you guys down." Tears came to his eyes as he struggled to get out the next words, "I love baseball. I always wanted to get base hits and be special. In the morning, I have to miss my game so I can earn money for my family."

He gulped for breath as he made the next comment, "My dad would want me to help mom pay our bills. He wouldn't want us to lose our house."

At this point, Peter was exhausted. He'd said it all. He sat down on one of Clarence's roots, and fought to hold the flood of tears back.

After a few minutes, Clarence spoke. His voice was calm and warm now. "Peter, we're proud you are putting your family over your own desires. I'm sure your dad'd be proud too."

Charley fluttered down close to Peter, looked him in the face, and squawked, "Ditto, Peter. Ya da man!"

Caroline was too emotionally moved to say much. She wobbled around a bit, fluffed her feathers, and hooted a tender note.

Maggie arrived during the back and forth with Peter, and she added a warm howl, "Peter, glad we're a team. Your family is lucky to have ya. You are going to be great!"

The warm gestures and words from the four new friends brought a boyish grin to Peter's face. It was ear to ear. *I'm one of the gang! Part of a team!*

Clarence interrupted the emotional moment with a shake of his branches, and said, "Peter, your coach is scouting the ball game. Best go tell him you can't be at your game tomorrow. If there is time after you talk, we will go over the lesson about hitting the pebble and protecting the batter's box. Okay?"

Peter looked in the direction of his coach and nodded he understood without turning around to face Clarence. Then off he trotted, lickety-split.

Clarence chuckled, "Young humans. They are interesting creatures."

"Yes siree," Charley hooted and Caroline nodded agreement.

"Sure are," Maggie added, "but some, like Peter, are neat."

Peter trotted along the ball field fence towards Coach Tyree and thought about how he would approach him. *Can't walk up to him and start talking. If I stand near him, maybe he'll say something.* When he looked up again, he grumbled in frustration, "Drat, too late! Now he's talking to a person in the concession line." *Have to wait until he returns to the game.*

Suddenly, players in one dugout yelled loudly. Peter turned to see the action. One had hit a home run and two teammates were on base. Three runs would score.

Coach Tyree looked back at the field when he heard the yells. He also made a mental note. *Need to remember that hitter and watch the pitches we throw to him.*

Players hustled from the dugout to home plate where they gave pats-on-the-back to the home run hitter along with high fives as the celebration run ended.

Peter visualized himself hitting the home run. *That would be so awesome! I would glide around the bases like I was on air, and teammates would smother me when I touched home plate.*

As he drifted back to earth, reality took hold. *What am I dreaming about? I don't even have a base hit yet!*

No longer the hero, he remembered what he was doing, and turned to look for Coach Tyree. "Where did he go?" he muttered as he looked in all directions. *There he is by his pickup.*

Peter took off, yelling as he ran, "Coach Tyree, Coach Tyree, wait."

Coach Tyree heard his name being called, and he turned towards the yell. *It's Peter Marshall. Wonder what he wants?*

Peter ran to him, and stood without talking for a moment to catch his breath.

"What is up, Peter?"

"Coach Tyree, I need to talk," Peter blurted nervously through gulps for breath. "I can't be at the game tomorrow."

"Why not?"

"Well, uh, I have to do some jobs and can't be here." He answered in a calmer voice.

Coach Tyree looked at Peter for a moment in a serious expression and inquired further, "Is this because of the way I yelled at you in our last game?"

Peter didn't respond for a moment, and Coach Tyree continued. "If that is the case, I want you to know I'm terribly sorry for those words. I was out of line, and they'll have no bearing on your being on the team."

The response gave Peter courage to answer. "No, that's not it. I really want to play, but I have to miss for something very important, and..." he paused for a few moments, "I can't talk about the reason right now."

Coach Tyree concluded, *Best not press for a reason.* "Do you remember our team rule is a player sits a game if he misses one without a good reason and isn't excused?"

"Yes sir," Peter responded with a subdued voice. "But I have no choice, and it's important. I really want to play. Honest. I just can't."

"Okay, I will excuse you for this game, but will you be at our next game Tuesday? It is the first one."

"Yes, I will. I won't forget," Peter responded gleefully and started off. "Thanks, Coach. See you Tuesday!"

Peter turned away and in a few steps was at full speed running around the fence towards Clarence like something was chasing him. *Wow! Glad that's over. Now we can practice.*

Peter's rapid departure caught Coach Tyree's attention, and he watched Peter run all the way to the big oak tree outside right field. A curious look came over his face. *Peter seems to be talking to someone, but who's he talking to? No one's near the tree.* After a bit, Peter tossed something into the air, and swung at it with a long stick. *Strange kid.*

Coach Tyree eased the pickup out of the parking lot, but

continued to watch Peter until he turned onto the road. *I better speak to Vicki Marshall and ask about Peter's strange actions. Want to make sure what I said to him isn't causing problems.*

Then his thoughts shifted to their similar situations as he drove down the road. *Wonder how she is making it with the house and family? It is tough raising John William, but she has three to raise as a single parent--two of them teenagers.*

The thought of her being attractive, even though he had never seen her dressed up, suddenly popped into his mind, and it startled him.

CHAPTER 19

Peter's Baseball Lessons Continue

Clarence didn't waste any time and asked about Peter's practicing the things he had mentioned. "How well can you hit the pebble with the broom handle?"

"I want to see his face," Charley whispered to Caroline as he leaned over the branch. Caroline leaned too. They had observed Peter practicing by the creek. "Wasn't very good, and down-right clumsy." They muffled their laughter when Peter almost fell into the water, so he didn't know they were watching.

Peter answered in a discouraged tone, "I'm not hitting them very well," He tossed one and swung to demonstrate. He muttered, "Too small," as he missed it.

"Kid missed by a country mile," Charley whispered into Caroline's fuzzy ear.

Clarence thought about what to say, *needs some positive strokes.* "Hmmm, your form needs a wee bit of adjustment."

Charley whispered to Caroline, "A wee bit is a stretch. He needs a lot!"

Clarence continued, "Bend over a little more in your upper body." Peter made the adjustment. "Good!" Clarence added approvingly.

"Now visualize you are at bat and facing a pitcher on the mound. Turn your head to face the pitcher, but not your body. That looks good. Now, keep your eyes on the ball as it leaves the pitcher's hand and crosses home plate."

Peter swung a few times, and Clarence said, "Looks smooth. How does that feel?"

"Better," Peter answered with a slight grin. His swing form began to improve, and his jerking habit was almost gone.

"Now toss a pebble in the air and try to hit it."

His body twisted with the swings, lost his balance and fell over one of Clarence's roots.

Charley and Caroline put their wings over their beaks to keep from cracking up with laughter at how funny Peter looked.

"I can't hit anything," Peter said disgustedly. "I'm terrible. I'll never get a hit."

"Stop!" Clarence shouted in a commanding tone. "You will hit no better than you believe. Go to the plate thinking you can't hit and it is exactly what you're going to do."

"But..."

"No buts! Think of yourself as a good hitter. Have faith in yourself and our help."

"O-kaaaay," Peter mumbled slowly.

"Yeah, Peter. Have faith," Charley added a supportive hoot.

Peter looked up at Charley and Caroline and nodded slowly.

"It will help if you have a better idea of the strike zone area." Clarence paused to focus. *Teaching humans isn't easy.*

"Peter, visualize yourself standing in the batter's box. … Next, picture a cardboard box about 18 inches on all sides, and it's hung by a string directly over the plate. The box is suspended where its bottom is about knee high, and its top comes to a few inches higher than your elbow. ... Can you visualize this box hanging over home plate?"

"Guess so," Peter answered with a quizzical tone, "but I have never heard of this before."

"That is okay. You will understand in time. The box is open on the front and back. If you were the catcher, you would see the pitcher through the box. A pitcher would see the catcher."

"Think of yourself at bat. In order to get a strike called on you, the pitcher must throw the ball through the box to the catcher. If it is not through the box, it is not a strike."

Clarence paused to emphasize his next comment, "The box belongs to you, the batter! You own it! Your objective is to protect your box—and not let any balls be thrown through the space to the catcher. You must keep all balls out of the box by hitting them with your bat. You don't care if the pitcher throws the ball over or under or to either side of it. Those pitches'll be called balls by the umpire. Don't swing at them. Only the balls through the box space are called strikes. The box space is the strike zone, and you hit any ball through it. ... Understand?"

"Yes, but ... how can I hit the ball if a box is there?"

Maggie howled with a chuckle, Charley's eyes crossed, Caroline didn't know what Peter said as she was staring at an unsuspecting young squirrel scampering not far away, and Clarence let out a big gasp of exasperation, "Uhhhh."

Clarence finally replied, "The box is imaginary! ... You will understand in time." *At least, I hope so.* "For now, remember to protect the space where your imaginary box is. Do it by hitting the ball if the pitcher throws it through the box. Don't swing if it isn't going to be through the box. It is a contest between you and the pitcher. Stare him down. Don't look away. The pitcher will try to fool you to swinging at pitches that aren't strikes. You have to be smart, and swing only at balls coming through the box space. Swing only when you want and not when the pitcher wants."

"Now practice swinging through your imaginary box space, and hitting a pitch. Swing over and over, and protect the box!"

Peter practiced and then swung at a few pebbles. To his surprise, he hit with better contact. *Wow! It works!*

Clarence noticed. "Peter, we have covered enough today. Come after your Saturday jobs if you can, and we will continue. Okay?"

Peter was excited with his improvement, but was tired and ready to go home. "Okay," he replied gleefully. For now, he had forgotten the family money problems. *Maybe mom will be home so I can tell her about the help my friends are giving me.*

CHAPTER 28

Plan to Help Peter's Family;
Practice and Historic Treasure

Clarence sighed deeply as Peter pedaled out of sight. "Wow! I'm mentally bushed. Peter's a good kid, but coaching him isn't as easy as I thought it would be." He paused to let Maggie, Caroline or Charley add their two-cents worth, but no one said anything. "Any ideas how we can best help him?"

Charley's eyes crossed and his beak opened like he had something to say, but only a muted squawk came from his throat.

Caroline stared at Charley and was irritated with his silence. "This isn't like you, Cha'lee," she hooted quietly where only he could hear, and prodded him with her wing. "Ya always have an answer to any question—even when you're wrong."

Clarence noticed and asked, "Any thoughts, Caroline?"

When Charley didn't speak, Caroline replied in a displeased tone, "Cha'lee mentioned Peta's mind was probably on his family's money problems." She blinked her big eyes several times, fluffed the feathers on her neck, and fluttered her eyelashes and continued, "Maybe he's not hitting the ball because his thoughts are on those problems."

Clarence rubbed his upper trunk with one of his branches like an older human rubs the chin with a hand when thinking. "Maybe so." He mulled the idea for a while, "Maybe so." Then in an emotional voice, he added, "Caroline, good point. You might have something there."

Charley was still thinking about Caroline's comments. *When did I say that to her?* The more he thought the idea came from him, the more his feathery chest puffed up, and soon it was almost twice its normal size. He forgot he and Caroline weren't alone, and he leaned over and gently touched her with his head in a show of affection like two lovebirds getting ready to nest.

Caroline blushed, blinked her eyelashes, and lowered her head to her feathery chest. She hooted a soft response, "Awe, Cha'lee, dah'lin," as they snuggled up to each other.

Clarence paid them no mind as he had witnessed many such moments in his lifetime. After all, he was a tree, and there were several nests scattered around in his branches. He was busy thinking about Caroline's comments on helping Peter.

A light went on and he said, "Gang, remember that old Indian and Spanish stuff you found a while back in the deep part of the swamp near the coast?"

There was no response, so Maggie howled, "Hey, you two lovebirds. Clarence asked you a question."

"Uh, huh?" Light headed Charley responded, "Oh, yeah, Sorry, didn't hear you."

"I will repeat," Clarence replied impatiently.

"Oh, you mean that old round stuff and those hard, rocky things?"

"Yes, remember we overheard a human once say things like those are valuable, historical treasures. Some collect them and display them in museums and private collections?"

"Sure do," Charley gleefully hooted while hopping up and down as he began to understand Clarence's plan to help Peter.

Clarence asked, "Think you and Caroline can find more of them?"

"Pretty sure we can," Charley squawked with delight. "No. Absolutely sure we can!"

"Well, if you can find them again, let's give some to Peter so he can help his family with their money problems. They can sell them and pay off the back debt on their house and have extra for other needs."

Caroline broke in, "Like buy'n cleats an ball pants fo Peta and some new dresses fo' his mom and sistahs. Maybe 'nuf so his mom can quit second job 'n devote more tahm on the nursing degree."

"Yes," Clarence replied gleefully. "Then, if you are right, Caroline, Peter's mind will be free to think about improving his skills. What do you think?"

No one made a sound for a few moments, thinking of the possibilities. Then they hooted, howled and bellowed loudly at the same time, "Sounds good! Let's do it!"

Caroline wasn't through though and said, "Here's anotha' idea. Cha-lee, Maggie and I can go on the golf course with Peta where no'un will see us. Cha'lee can hold da ball in iz feet, fly overhead towards Peta 'n drop it so he can practice catchin' fly balls. Howz this sound?"

"Great idea," Clarence responded. "Let's add it to the practice, along with hitting pebbles with a broom handle and fielding grounders from the tennis practice back board.

"How soon can you love birds look for that treasure stuff?"

Caroline quickly replied, "Today if okay with Cha'lee."

"Great. If you're successful, bring them here and hide them high in one of the bends of my branches. We'll give them to Peter soon as we can. Y'all agree?"

"Yes," the four imaginary friends said at the same time. Then Charley and Caroline flapped their wings and off they flew towards the coastal swamplands where they had seen the treasures, which had laid hidden in the swamp and muck for the last four centuries.

"We'll hunt for food along the way," hooted Charley over his shoulder.

"Good hunting," Maggie howled as she moved cautiously over towards Clarence to discuss the possibilities with him. "But what if they don't find the treasure, Big Fella?"

[CHAPTER 21]

Peter Keeps Work Commitments

Sweat beads slid slowly down Peter's cheeks and glistened in the morning sunrays that filtered through tall oaks and pine trees. He wiped his shirtsleeve across his face, clearing his eyes as he dug out and cleaned Mr. Fitzgerald's flower beds.

Mom's disturbed facial expression during their late night talk kept popping into Peter's mind. *Why did Mom act so flustered when I told her about my awesome practice with Clarence, Caroline, Charley, and Maggie?* His emotional juices began to flow, and a couple of tears joined the sweat beads. "Thought she would be happy I had someone helping me," he muttered with a tinge of anger as he tossed the shovel to the side.

A voice from behind startled him. "Looks like you've about wrapped it up," Mr. Fitzgerald said as he bent down to examine the beds. He looked at Peter. "You still hold to my paying you what I think the job was worth?"

Peter looked up at him. "Yes sir. Deal's a deal."

"Well, son, to be honest, I didn't think a young lad like you'd even show up so early on Saturday morning, let alone buckle down and do this work. Fooled me. Here's twenty."

Peter held out his hand and replied, "Thank you!"

Mr. Fitzgerald nodded, and Peter hopped on his bike and started towards home. *Twenty dollars. Hope it helps. I will leave it in the kitchen with a note to mom.* He noticed the dirt on his hands. *Gotta wash before I practice with my friends.*

Peter passed old Mr. Higgins' house. *No one is working.* An idea came to him. *Maybe I can trade work for his mower and mow his lawn.*

Thoughts of his other jobs came to mind. *I will do some after practice if I can, and the rest next week after school.*

"I'll trade work for his mower."

As he entered the house, he noticed the time. *If I hurry, I can get there before my team's game ends.* He quickly pulled on his jersey, grabbed his practice stuff, and hurried on his way to the ballpark.

CHAPTER 22

"Oh, just call me Channing!";
First Christmas in the United States?;
Indian and Spanish Treasures

Peter's team's fifth game ended as he arrived at the ball field. Unfortunately, Rosie's lost again, 4 to 6 to the Apalachee Indians team. He yelled "Hello" as he hurriedly parked his bike against Clarence and hurried to join the team meeting.

"Hi Peter. See ya when you are through," Clarence replied.

"We played better today," Coach Tyree said in a peppy tone. "We made some good plays, and Coach Sanders and I are proud of you for improving." He noticed Peter and smiled.

Peter walked up beside Sakine Davis. She did a double take, leaned towards him and whispered in a demanding tone, "Where you been? Coach didn't have you in the line-up."

Peter ignored her, so she hit him with a verbal jab. "Didja see my hit? Drove in a run."

Still no response—not even a blink. "We thought you had quit or something good for the team like that," she added sarcastically.

Nothing, not a peep! After Coach finished, Peter looked at Sakine and sternly expressed, "I was gone for a reason, and Coach excused me ... Sakining." Then he jogged away before she could reply.

Her dander exploded and she muttered

angrily through clenched teeth, "Told you to call me Channing if you can't remember my name! I'll get you, Dufus," she promised as she continued to stare at him.

Peter greeted his imaginary friends, as he approached them, "Ready for practice." He expressed as he sat down on one of Clarence's roots, "Need to catch my breath first, though."

Strange, Sakine thought with a curious look on her face. *He's talking, but I don't see anyone. Guy must have a loose screw.* Then her mother's voice diverted her attention.

"Coach Tyree, heard your favorite was apple cobbler so I baked one just for you," Marilyn Davis said softly and handed it to him. Their eyes met as he reached to take it.

He blushed as her hand came to rest on his arm and her perfume fragrance engulfed him. "Uh, uh, thank you, Mrs. Davis."

"Awe, Coach, call me Marilyn," she expressed with a flutter of her eye lashes. "Remember? Single mom—over a year now."

"Yes, I forgot, but..."

Sakine interrupted as she walked up to them, "I'm ready to roll, mom. We still shopping?"

Marilyn turned to her with a disappointed look of the timing of the interruption, and replied, "Yes, we're still going." Then she turned back with a subtle smile, "Havta run, sweetie. See ya next game." She took a few steps towards the parking lot and turned back again, "Don't forget. Call any time if you have any questions about the parents, or..." she paused, "anything."

"Oh, I will," Coach Tyree assured her nervously glancing at the pie and back at her, "And thanks for this." Quickly, he and John William tossed the gear in the pickup and drove away.

Meanwhile, Peter inquired anxiously to his friends, "We still practicing on the golf course next Monday?" Before they could respond, he continued, "Where and what time? What do I need to bring? My regular ball stuff or tennis balls, pebbles, and broom handle? What?"

"Whoa!" Clarence exclaimed. "Slow down! We have something important first."

"Huh?" Peter asked, "What is more important than practice?"

"Oh, trust us'n do what Big Fella, er, Clarence says," Charley hooted as he stretched his wings and yawned.

"Climb up to my branch where Charley and Caroline are perched," Clarence instructed.

"Up there? Again? But I thought..."

"No buts," Clarence cut him off. "It is something else. Climb up there, and you'll see."

Peter shrugged his shoulders, sadly grumbled, "Okay," and began the climb. *Thought we were going to practice today.*

Caroline and Charley hooted a "Hello" when he settled beside them. *They don't have much life. What is wrong?*

Before Peter replied, he noticed some unusual objects in the space where Clarence's trunk connects to one of his branches. "What are those?" he asked curiously.

"Peter," Clarence explained. "Those are old Spanish and Indian relics. Charley and Caroline found in a swamp near the coast." He paused and added, "Pick one up and feel it."

After Peter examined them a few minutes, Clarence continued. "You probably learned in your history studies of the Spanish explorers, Ponce de Leon and Hernando de Soto. They..."

"I hate history," Peter interrupted. "It is dull stuff."

"We'll talk about your dislikes later. Don't interrupt me again!" Clarence replied. "Uh, where was I? Oh, yes. Juan Ponce de Leon in 1513 was the first known European to set foot in what he called, *La Florida.* Two decades later, De Soto and six hundred Spanish Conquistadors came ashore in the area of what is now Tampa, and explored northward. Over the winter of 1539, they camped in the woods around what became known as Myers Park of Tallahassee."

"Really?" Peter asked with interest as he looked around. "Around here—this park?"

"Thought you didn't like history," Clarence reminded him. He continued before Peter responded. "Yes. De Soto's main camp was located about six blocks to the Northeast of here, and some of those Conquistadors would have moved about these woods like you do."

"Wow! That is awesome!"

"We know, Peter. Isn't it fascinating to know that history? But there is even something more exciting. You see, those humans probably celebrated something very special."

"What was that?"

"It was Christmas."

"Really? Christmas?" Peter asked astonished, as he looked around again.

"Right here in these woods?"

"Yes, but that isn't all. It would have been one of, if not the first Christmas in what would become the United States. That Christmas service would have been fifteen years before the French Huguenots temporary settlement at St. Augustine, sixty-eight years before Captain John Smith established the Jamestown Colony in Virginia in 1607, and eighty-one years before William Bradford and the Pilgrims founded Plymouth Colony in 1620."

Peter replied, "The first Christmas? In these woods? Wow! Unbelievable!"

"Now, Peter, do you have a better feeling for history?"

"Yes," Peter replied but with a hint of skepticism.

"Well, keep an open mind, and you will discover there is a lot of history within a few blocks of us. Take a little time, and you will be fascinated about what took place long before you were born and roamed around in these woods."

"Okay, I will try."

"Now where was I? Oh, yes. De Soto's group or someone else must have lost the treasure or buried it for safe keeping. Humans say these are historical treasures and are valuable. They spend lots of money for them and often display them in collections and museums.

"Peter, we decided to give these treasures to you. We want to help you with your family money problems. You can sell them and pay on the house mortgage and buy cleats and ball pants and new clothes for your mom and sisters."

"And," Caroline added, "your mom can quit the second job an finish the nursin' dagree."

Peter slowly picked up each treasure piece and looked it over. Neither he nor his friends made a sound. Maggie couldn't see what was taking place. She howled, "What are you guys doing? It is awfully quiet up there."

"These are valuable?" Peter asked in an unbelieving tone as he rubbed some of the swamp muck from one of the round pieces. "I see some yellow color in this one."

"That is what we understand from human talk," replied Clarence.

Charley hopped where he could look into Peter's eyes and squawked, "I've seen humans with something like that and they call it a gold coin."

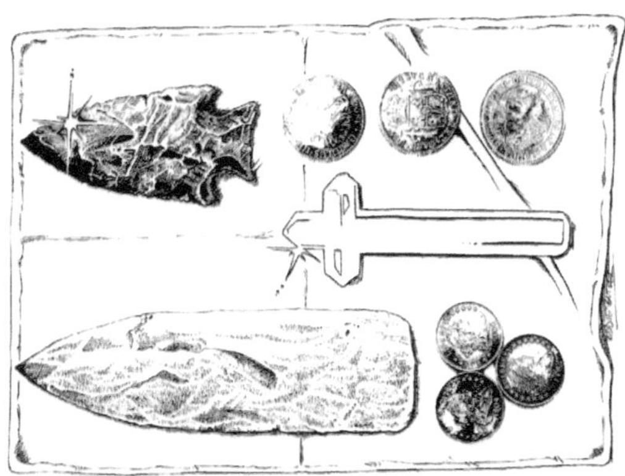

Peter pulled off his T-shirt and laid the items out on it as he talked. "This one is sorta like a cross," Peter said as he picked up another piece. He gently rubbed some of the muck away and said, "It is like some of my clear marbles. What are these?"

Clarence responded, "My ancestors said the Apalachee Indians established this area as their 'Capital' village before de Soto and his men arrived. Thirty thousand Apalachee lived around here, and things made of clear crystal-quartz held special properties for them. Humans hunted for treasures in these woods after State of Florida archaeologist Calvin Jones discovered the de Soto 1539 winter encampment. Apparently, things made of crystal-quartz are rare."

Charley yawned and hooted a question, "If these are made of crystal-quartz and from the Apalachee or some other Indian group, they are valuable?"

"Yes," Clarence replied. "Seem to be valuable to humans."

"Hey you guys," Maggie whispered. "What about plans for Peter's practice? Sun's getting up in the sky, and it's tough to make it past the barking dogs to the woods on the golf course."

"Okay, okay. Little patience, please," Charley replied.

"Easy for you to say up there where dogs can't get to you."

Clarence quickly spoke to stop the bantering between his friends, "Let's do what Caroline suggested. You three go up on the golf course early Monday right after Peter gets out of school. The course is closed that day. Sound okay?"

"Sure," all replied, and Charley added, "Big fella."

"Good."

With that agreement, Maggie, Caroline and Charley left. Peter gathered the treasures in his shirt. As he peddled away, he yelled back over his shoulder, "See ya Monday, Clarence."

Clarence responded to them with his loud voice, "See you all Monday after Peter's practice."

Peter's thoughts soon were on his mom. *Can't wait to tell mom how my friends are helping us with our family money problems.*

[CHAPTER 23]

Peter Tells Mom About the Treasures
From His Friends

"Mom, mom, you here?" Peter called out excitedly as the screen door bang shut behind him. "Look! Look what I have!"

He glanced into the kitchen, then down the hall. *Dark. Where's Mom?* His enthusiasm took a nosedive as it dawned on him. *Mom's still at work.*

Elizabeth stuck her head out of her bedroom and asked loudly in an aggravated tone, "What is going on down there? What is the yelling all about?"

"Oh, nothing. Wanted to tell Mom something."

"Well, if you remembered," she replied sarcastically, "Mom is at work." She added as she retreated back into her room, "Keep the noise down, or I will call the police riot squad."

"Yah, Lizzy. Yah, yah," Peter retorted as he climbed the stairs. He reached into his dresser and pulled out a clean old t-shirt. He quickly spread it on his bed and laid out the treasure pieces. *Nine round and three rock-like.* They were coated with swamp muck so he gently rubbed them in his fingers. *Hmmm. Seven round ones have yellow color. Are these gold coins like Charley said?* The other two round ones had a dull-blackish appearance. *Wonder what they are?*

The other three pieces were hard and showed different shapes. One was sorta like a cross, another like a large arrowhead, and the other even larger, like a spear point.

Peter studied each piece for a while. *What do they look like cleaned? Maybe Mom'll have an idea how to do it.*

The growl of his stomach reminded him of his hunger. He folded the pieces in his shirt and put them away. "Can't wait to tell Mom," he mumbled enthusiastically as he started down stairs. "If they're valuable, it will help with our money problems."

It wasn't long before he heard the car in the drive. "Mom, Mom," he yelled as he hustled to meet her before she even reached the back door. "I have something exciting to tell you!"

Vicki slowed her walk enough to peck him on the cheek, and said as she walked on into the house, "Let's talk later, Hun. I'm dead tired, and need to get these shoes and clothes off and grab a warm bath."

"But, Mom-m-m..."

The words fell on deaf ears as she walked to her bedroom and closed the door.

"It is really important." He pleaded through the door. "Need to talk now," he persisted with a gentle, pesky tap of the fingers.

"O-k-k-k-kay," she replied in a beat-down voice, "but give me a few minutes."

"Okay," Peter said as he heard her crash to the bed. A few seconds passed, but he pressed ahead outside her door, "How do you clean something that has been in the dirt a long time?"

She blurted out, without any curiosity of what he was doing, "Oh, soak it in some mild soapy water or something to loosen the dirt, and then gently wash with a little rub."

Peter knew that would be all from mom until later. Soon he delightfully expressed, "Ah-ha, Mom is right! It removed most of the swamp muck on this arrow head." *I will wear it around my neck to show her, and it'll be my lucky piece.*

Before long, Vicki called out, "I'm ready, Hun. ... What's up?"

Peter grabbed the other treasures and flew down the stairs. "Look what my friends gave to me!" he said excitedly as he thrust them towards her face. "They said these are valuable, and we can sell them and pay some of our bills. And..."

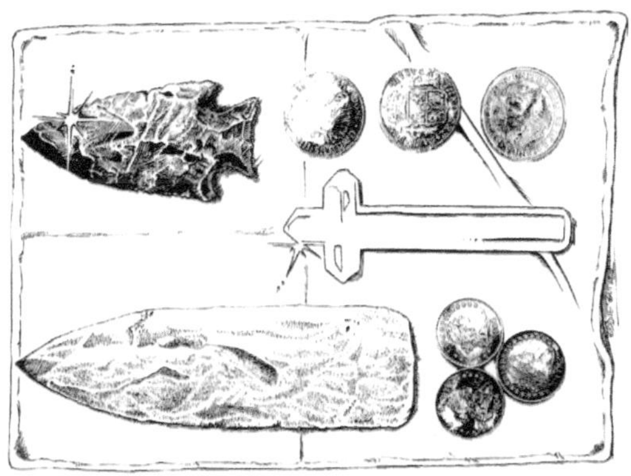

"Wait, Peter," Vicki interrupted him in a confused tone as she pushed his hands away and tried to follow what he said. "My head is spinning. What did you say these are and who gave them to you?"

Peter replied rapidly. "Clarence and my friends gave these to me. Said, "These are old Spanish and Indian treasures and they are valuable and we can sell them and pay some of our bills and..."

Vicki interrupted again, "Slow down. ... I thought that is what you said. Isn't Clarence your make-believe friend?" Before Peter could answer, she continued in a scolding tone, "I don't know where you got these, Peter, but you can't go around talking about imaginary friends like you have been for the last few days. It is not good."

"But, Mom, they're real," he expressed in a frustrated tone and an anguished look on his face. He raised his arms and hands. "My friends are real, Mom. They are all real!"

Vicki saw how much her comments upset him, so she backed off and softened her voice. "Okay, okay, Hun, they are real."

Her demeanor changed as she picked up a treasure, and wondered, *But where did Hun get these? … And they are valuable?* … "What did you say about these?"

"They are treasures, Mom." Peter handed a round one to her and added, "See the gold color? Clarence and Charley said this maybe a gold coin. I don't know about the blackish ones."

Vicki clinched her eyes slightly in frustration when Peter said "Clarence" again, but quickly focused on the coin. She examined it closely as she turned it over and over in her hand. *This seems real, and old. Somehow Hun has them. How?*

After a few moments, Peter picked up the arrowhead, and handed it to her. "Clarence said Indians made this and they lived here long ago." Peter then handed her the cross and spearhead and continued, "They also made these."

Vicki's lips tightened. *What am I going to do? He keeps mentioning Clarence, but where else did he get these?*

She managed to refocus, then he said it again, "Clarence said 'These have a special meaning to the Indians.'"

Vicki glanced at the clock as she examined the treasures. *It is late, but I need to get more information about them and where Peter obtained them. Hope his desire to help with expenses didn't cause him to steal from someone. Need time to talk to someone else about these, but I don't want Peter to think I don't trust him.*

"All of this is fabulous news, but it is late, Hun. Let's talk about this tomorrow. Okay?"

"Okay, but can I wear the arrowhead around my neck?"

"Yes, don't see any reason why not. Now clean up while I fix you a bite to eat."

Peter scampered upstairs, and Vicki thought more about the

treasures and friends. *Wonder if Coach Tyree knows anything about them?* She set about preparing Peter's meal. *I'll ask at his next game.*

As she set Peter's food on the table, she momentarily thought about her girls and a warm feeling came over her. *I'm glad they're old enough to fix something for themselves and help with the house.*

Her thoughts returned to contacting Coach Tyree. *No, I need to know before then. Calling now and ask if he'd meet next Monday at the ballpark.*

CHAPTER 24

Practice with Charley, Caroline, and Maggie

Monday afternoon rolled around quickly. "Let's wait for Peter at the edge of the golf course," Charley squawked to Caroline. No sooner did they settle in a tall pine tree then Charley hooted, "Here he comes."

"Hi, Peta," Caroline called softly. "Been wait'n fo ya."

Peter waived and replied, "Hi, Charley. Hi, Caroline."

"Maggie is meeting us on hole number two for your practice."

"Okay," Peter yelled as he pedaled furiously that direction. "Race ya."

Charley and Caroline looked curiously at each other with a thought like, *Does he really think he can beat us?*

"Let's buzz him," Charley hooted and Caroline nodded agreement. They quickly overtook him, and brushed each side of his head with their wing tips as they passed.

Maggie sprawled lazily on the bank of a sandtrap, warming herself in the sun. "'Bout time. Peter on the way?"

"Hello Maggie, deaah," Caroline replied. "He's pedal'n ovah the hill now."

"Hi, Peter," Maggie howeled a greeting as he arrived.

"Hi, Maggie."

"Let's get right to it. First, we will practice catching fly balls.

Peter, you set up like you're playing in the outfield. Charley will fly towards you with a ball, and drop it. You catch it. Understand how this will work?"

"Yup."

"Okay, let's go."

Charley snatched a ball in his claws, and flew high overhead. "Bomb's away," he hooted as he dropped it.

Now catching a fly ball hit by a batter was different than one dropped by a bird. It bounced off Peter's mitt, and ker-plunked off his forehead knocking him to the ground.

"Uh-o-o-o-oh," Maggie howled sympathetically.

"O-o-ops," Charley squawked as Peter shook his head.

"Oooooh, m'ahh" Caroline groaned. "Betcha that hurt."

"You know it," snickered Maggie with a mouthful of teeth showing. "but was funny."

"Good try." Charley called out to Peter as he flew down and grabbed another ball. "You will catch the next one."

The words proved untrue as Peter was clunked the same way four balls in a row, and he was getting discouraged.

Maggie's and Caroline's snickers grew louder each time Peter was knocked to the ground

"You will do it soon," Charley said. "Promise."

Finally, Peter caught the fifth ball. All of them froze from the shock. Peter stared disbelievingly at the ball in his mitt. Maggie and Caroline looked expressionless at each other, and Charley nearly flew into a tree.

When Peter realized he had the ball in his mitt, he jumped up an down, and yelled, "I caught it! I caught it! I caught it!"

The others chimed in, "He caught it! He caught it! He caught it!"

Peter caught four of the next six balls, and Charley was tired. "Why don't you practice hitting pebbles with the broomstick, Peter?" Before long, he hit every fourth pebble.

"Now use a ball and bat," Charley instructed. Maggie and Caroline took turns retrieving the balls.

"I'm pooped," Peter said after a while and plopped down beside his three friends.

Maggie decided to take advantage of a human presence and wiggled closer to Peter. "How 'bout a scratch on the back?"

Peter looked at her for a moment and said grudgingly, "Oh, all right. That's what Pokey, my dog, always wants."

"Down a little, okay?" A few scratches later, "Aw-w-w-w. Perfect. Feels good."

"Hey, you two," Charley interrupted. "Caroline and I are heading out to hunt. See you at the ball game tomorrow."

Peter and Maggie replied, "See you," as Charley and Caroline flew away. In moments, they were out of sight, and Maggie turned her attention back to a human being in her life.

"Peter, first time I laid eyes on you, you were riding your bike across this golf course. When you saw me, you yelled, 'Can't catch me, can't catch me,' like I was chasing you. What was that all about?"

"Yeah," Peter replied excitedly. "I was spooked by how you looked. I thought you were chasing me. I felt you nipping at my foot as I pedaled to get away but, when I peeked over my shoulder, you were standing calmly at a distance. Up close, I see it's your eyes. They're different colors. One's grey. They give you a spooky look. Seems like you can see through me."

"That explains it," Maggie replied.

"Explains what?"

"I thought you were screwy but, now ... well you are a pretty cool dude."

"Thanks. I think you're special, too." Then she rolled her body into Peter, and pushed her furry head and wet nose into his neck.

Mistaking Maggie for his dog, he hollered, "Pokey, stop! Stop!" he giggled with delight as she snuck in a few licks.

A cackling sound from their two feathery friends in the distance broke the moment, "Whooo, whoo-kooo-fo-uooouuuuuuu. Whooo, whoo-koooks-fo-uooouuuuuuu."

Peter jumped to his feet. "Gotta go," As he topped the hill on his bike, he yelled a tease over his shoulder, "Can't catch me-e-e-e. Can't catch me-e-e-e."

Maggie watched until he disappeared, and thought as she trotted towards her den, *He maybe a cool dude, but he is still screwy.* A few steps later her thoughts turned to the good practice. *Hope it carries over into his game.*

Little did she and the friends know that all of them would be confronted soon by big, life-threatening obstacles—monsters in the Myers Park woods!

[CHAPTER 25]

*Vicki Speaks to Coach Tyree About Peter's
Imaginary Friends and Meets Prissy Smart*

Vicki Marshall's Monday workday was filled with thoughts of her meeting with Coach Tyree to discuss Peter's imagination. *Should I also ask about the old treasures?*

Coach Tyree saw Vicki walking towards him, and hastily stuffed the last bite of two hotdogs into his mouth. He washed it down with a gulp just in time to say, "Hi, Mrs. Marshall."

"Uh ... oh ... uh," she stammered as the greeting caught her off guard. She was seldom addressed anymore as "Mrs." After regaining her composure, she replied, "Hello, Coach Tyree. I hope you haven't waited long."

"No. Been scouting the teams. We play each one twice during the season." He wiped relish stickiness from his hands, and confessed a weakness. "There is something about a ballpark that makes hotdogs and hamburgers and junk food taste better."

Vicki laughed slightly and joked, "You are human, after all!" Then noticing the cooking smoke floating over the area, she gave him an excuse. "It is probably the smell from the cooking pit. Stand here long enough, and it would trap anyone. My Peter loves the stuff, and he would eat it every day if he could."

Coach Tyree chuckled and said, "Then Peter and I have the same weakness. John William and I probably eat too many meals like this. Maybe ruined his eating habits."

"Could be," she agreed jokingly. Then her internal alarm clicked.

Need to move on to why I wanted this meeting. She pointed to a picnic table outside the first base line. "Do you mind if we talk over there?"

"That's fine," he replied, and they walked that direction.

Player yells were coming from the field, "Hey batter, hey batter." And the dugout, "Pitcher has a rubber arm. Pitcher has a rubber arm."

Coach Tyree suddenly thrust his arm in front of her, holding her back, and nodded to the ground. "Watch out for the bubble gum." She was about to step on a big wad. "It's one of the hazards of ballparks. Bubble gum is a big  seller, and some don't make it to the trash can when thrown away."

She mumbled, "Thanks."

Coach Tyree continued making small talk, but the majestic oak tree outside right field had her attention. *What did Peter call him? Oh, yes, Clarence.* She didn't know it, but Clarence heard every word they said.

"I imagine you are busy with coaching and your family and working and whatever else. I didn't want to take more of your time, but I need to talk about Peter."

"Peter? Something wrong, Mrs. Marshall?" he asked with raised eyebrows while studying her face. *Looks frustrated, not angry.* He was prepared for questions from an unhappy mother about the son's playing time. It is often the subject when a parent asks for a meeting. *I apologized for my anger and comments. Thought she forgave me.*

"Call me, Vicki. Been a widow a long time!"
"Only if you call me, David."

The words stopped her response. *Oh, he called me "Mrs." again,* she thought in frustration. *I have to end this now.* She turned, looked him squarely in the face, and exclaimed with a firmness to her voice like before on the phone. "Coach Tyree, would you please drop the 'Mrs.' and call me Vicki? As I said, I've been a widow for a long time."

Vicki's response caught him off guard, and he paused for a moment before replying, "Okay, on one condition. You call me 'David,' and not Coach Tyree."

"Oh, no you don't," she shot back. "I can't do that. You are the Coach for my son's team. I can't call you David. Has to be Coach or Coach Tyree. Peter wouldn't understand just 'David' and the other players or parents wouldn't understand either. Only a wife or a lady friend can call the coach by his first name."

"Okay, okay," he said in a frustrated look. "I see your point. I will try to live with that."

He wanted to avoid more on that hot topic. "Anything particular you want to discuss?"

Clarence rumbled with a slight shake of his limbs and leaves, "This will be interesting."

Vicki began. "Peter has make-believe friends. I think he has created them in his imagination to make up for his dad not being alive. He talks about them as friends, and he says 'they are helping him practice to be a better ball player.'"

"Imagination?" Clarence rumbled again, but louder this time. "So you think we are just Peter's imagination?"

Coach Tyree didn't respond to Vicki's comments right away. He turned her concern over in his thoughts. After awhile, he stood, faced her and said in a consoling way, "Vicki, everyone has an imagination. Especially, kids. Why should Peter be any different?"

She smiled slightly, acknowledging he had dropped the 'Mrs.' and mouthed, "Thank you."

His facial expression acknowledged acceptance. He continued, "It is not unusual for a boy or girl to have imaginary friends or to play a game against an imaginary foe."

After a moment, he continued. "When I was growing up on the farm, I loved basketball, but I didn't have anyone to play with. I practiced dribbling and shooting the ball by myself. I would pretend I was in a game, with an imaginary person guarding me. I would count the seconds out loud down to zero and, as the last second ticked off, I shot the ball to the hoop. The buzzer ending the game would go off while the ball was in flight. Down it came and, if it went threw the hoop, I won the game for my team." He raised his arms in the air. "I'd trot around the barnyard court like this to glorify my terrific feat and how awesome I was. If it didn't, I started the countdown again until it did. The game would end with me as the hero."

Vicki laughed. "I can see you trotting around the barn-yard." She joked, "Were chickens and pigs cheering you along?"

"Chickens, yes," he replied with a big grin. "But you had to watch where you bounced the ball or you stepped as their droppings were everywhere. Once you get some of that gunk on the hand or foot, you learn best to clear the court first."

She chuckled momentarily thinking about that picture. Then her facial expression turned serious. "I understand some of a person's imagination might be okay, but ... but it is more serious with Peter. His imaginary friends have names."

Hmmm, Peter told her about us after all, Clarence concluded.

Coach Tyree gestured with his hand, "What is wrong with that?"

Before she could reply, he asked with a chuckle, "Better to have names and keep them apart, don't you think?"

"But!" she blurted out. "Peter's friends aren't people and he says they are alive!" *Ooops,* she thought as she quickly covered her mouth with her hand. *Didn't mean to share that with him. No putting it back in the box now.* "One is that tree." She pointed to the large oak outside right field. "Peter calls him, 'Clarence.'"

Coach Tyree looked at the tree and thought, *Clarence is the name? … That's a fitting name for an old, majestic oak.*

Vicki continued, "Peter has three other friends. Two are the owls that are often around the field during games, and usually sit in Clarence. He calls them, 'Charley and Caroline.'"

"I have seen them," Coach Tyree replied. "Great sight. The players love them."

"The other is a gray fox that often comes to games looking for goodies dropped or thrown away. He calls her, 'Maggie,' and sometimes hides around the trunk of Clarence."

"I have seen her, too."

"Well, Peter talks a lot about Clarence, Charley, Caroline, and Maggie; and how they are helping him to be a better ball player."

"Glad to know that's how Peter feels," Clarence said as a warm feeling and calmness came over him.

Coach Tyree asked, "Is that right? How they doing that?"

What am I doing? Vicki wondered. *I can't believe I'm telling him all these things.*

Clarence moved his branches like he was stretching. *Humans are interesting creatures,* he thought to himself. *Wonder what they will finally make out of this?*

After what seemed like a long time, Coach Tyree spoke in a calming voice. "Vicki, let him have his imaginary friends. I don't see a problem with it. Peter seems fine to me. He is eager to play and it disappoints him if he doesn't play well." He paused and added an assuring comment, "He will outgrow them soon."

"I appreciate your advice, Coach." Then she remembered the treasures. *Should I ask about these too?* She answered herself by plowing ahead. "There is something else."

"More?" he asked with a puzzled tone that turned to a tease. "We have already solved a life problem."

"Yes, I know, but this is related."

"You've pricked my curiosity. What is it?"

"Don't know how to tell you so I will jump right in. Peter came home with some old treasures. Said he was told they are Spanish and Indian and are valuable. I trust Peter so I know he didn't steal them. Coach, have you heard anyone around the ball field say anything about them? Any missing treasures?"

"Treasures? Did you say, treasures? ... No—haven't heard

anything. Games? Yes. Winning or losing? Yes. Who's playing, pitching or hitting? Yes. But nothing about treasures. ... Did you see them?"

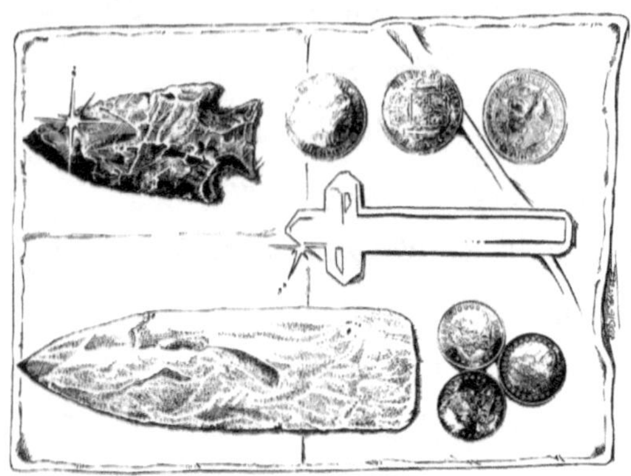

"Yes. They are real," Vicki answered in frustration. "I have held a couple. They look old. Some seem to be coins and the others look like some type of chipped rock-like crystal."

She hesitated for a moment debating whether or not to show him the ones she brought. *Can I trust him? I need to confide with someone. He seems trustworthy.*

"I have a couple with me," she said as she unwrapped what appeared to be coins and the spearhead. "Peter says the coin is gold and the spearhead is from quartz rock."

Coach Tyree didn't say a word. He sat down beside her and examined the coins and spearhead for a few minutes. "Wow! These look real and old, and ... there is a gold tinge color to the coins and they are heavy so I suppose they are gold."

He examined the spearhead. "I don't know anything about Indian treasures, but I would guess this is Indian."

An idea came to him. "I have seen some Indian artifacts that look like this spearhead in the business office of a couple who have a son who plays in this league. The coaches drafted players there. The woman's name is Priscilla Smart, and she is involved somehow in the league management. They call her, 'Prissy.' Maybe she would know something about these treasures."

"Do you want to talk to her about your treasures? I saw her earlier. May still be around."

"That sounds okay, but I don't want to go into a lot of detail yet or show her these."

"If that is what you want," he said as he looked around the ballpark. "I will introduce you, and then you take the lead."

"Good."

Coach Tyree suddenly hollered, "Watch it," as he stepped in front of her. "Foul ball," he yelled and caught it in his hands.

"Thank you. I never saw it coming."

Several youngsters ran in the direction of where the ball was hit. The one who returned it to the umpire would get a piece of bubble gum for a reward. Coach Tyree tossed it to the smallest youngster of the group, who probably wasn't fast enough to ever get one. An ear-to-ear grin appeared as he said, "Thanks mister."

Coach Tyree nodded to the youngster. Then he turned and said, "There she is," as he pointed to a woman in the scorekeeper's box. "I'll see if Prissy'll come and talk."

After a few minutes, he returned with a woman. "Vicki, this is Prissy Smart. Prissy and her husband are major supporters of the ball league, and they have a son on the best team."

"Prissy, this is Vicki Marshall, the person whom I mentioned. Her son is on my team."

Vicki and Prissy exchanged greetings of, "Nice to meet you."

Turning to Vicki, Coach Tyree continued, "I told Prissy you had questions about local history and specifically about Spanish and Indian treasures. Also said I didn't know much about them, but he thought Prissy Smart might."

Vicki looked at Prissy and, with a hesitant voice, continued the introductions, "Thank you for coming."

"Sure. No problem," Prissy responded. "Spanish and Indian histories are favorite subjects of mine. What is this all about?"

Vicki's intuition moved her to go slowly. "Well, my son, Peter, has a terrific imagination." She turned momentarily towards Coach Tyree, "Like most boys, as Coach assured me. Recently, Peter's included the topic of Spanish and Indian treasures when he mentions his imaginary friends."

As Vicki talked, she studied Prissy's facial expression and body movement to get an idea if her comments raised Prissy's interest level. She didn't see any reaction. Truth is, Prissy was interested, but had trained herself to appear calm and courteous.

Vicki continued, "Coach Tyree says you're an expert on Spanish and Indian relics, and you have quite a collection."

"Yes, Terry, my husband, and I have a collection of those items." She raised her head in a proud manner and continued, "probably best in Florida. We are always looking to add to it."

"Yes, it is impressive," Coach Tyree added.

"Well, maybe I can see it sometime," Vicki added.

"Any time," Prissy replied.

"Anyway," Vicki continued, "I'm not sure why Peter, my son, started talking about Spanish and Indian relics. I wondered if someone had been showing or talking about them around the ballpark and that is where he picked up the information."

"No, I haven't heard anyone talking about those." Prissy turned to Coach Tyree. "The player draft was in our conference room, and we have part of our collection there. Do you think some coaches talked about them in front of the players?"

"I suppose, Prissy. I remember coaches making lots of comments about them that day."

Prissy turned to Vicki, "I will ask around and if I learn anything, I'll get back to you."

"I would appreciate that," Vicki replied with a slight smile. "If I'm not at the game, would you share with Coach Tyree."

"Yes," Prissy turned slightly as she walked away and said, "Nice meeting you."

"You, too."

Prissy nodded as she walked back to the scorekeeper's box.

Clarence heard the conversation among Coach Tyree, Vicki, and Prissy. "Hmmmm," he mumbled. "Prissy has a lot of interest there. I better keep up with their talk about Spanish and Indian treasures."

Prissy, back in the scorekeeper's box, no longer watched the game. Now her sights were locked onto Vicki Marshall as Coach Tyree walked her to a car and she drove away.

Prissy wondered, *Did someone find some Spanish and Indian treasures? The mention of them wasn't merely a topic of conversation. There's something more to it. Why did Vicki Marshall and her son have this sudden interest? … His team has a ball game tomorrow evening. I will be there and accidentally bump into him. What did she say his name was? Oh, yes, Peter. I will talk to him and catch him off guard.* Prissy smiled with the sly look of a cat as she thought her plan through. *I'll find out if there are any treasures.*

CHAPTER 26

Prissy Tricks Peter to Tell About the
Treasures; Rosie's Wins a Game; Peter
is Confronted by Another Dragon

"Hi Peter," Clarence called out as Peter approach fast on his bike, "Charley and Caroline said you had a good practice."

"Hi, Big Fella. Think so, but can't talk," Peter replied as he hopped off and started jogging to his team gathered near the backside of a dugout. "Need to get to batting practice."

"Ouch," Clarence hollered in jest as the bike bounced off his trunk and fell to the ground, "You drive terribly!"

"Sorry," Peter yelled over his shoulder.

"No problem. Make sure we talk after your game. Something important is afoot."

Meanwhile in the scorekeeper's box, Prissy Smart had asked Jerry Cramer, a league official, to point Peter Marshall out when he arrived for his game.

"There he is," Jerry exclaimed as he pointed towards the big oak outside right field.

"Oh, THAT boy. The one with blue jeans and tennis shoes. I already know him."

"He is heading to his team," Jerry said, but noticed Prissy already had left the box. *What does she want with him?*

Charley and Caroline flew in for their afternoon snooze, and Clarence told them of the talk between Peter's mom, Coach Tyree, and Prissy Smart; and about the treasures mentioned.

Clarence suddenly shouted, "Look out, Peter! You are about to hit that..."

Too late. Peter stumbled over Prissy Smart as he tried to avoid running over her.

Caroline hooted softly, "Looked ta me, she stepped into Peta's path on purpose."

Prissy blurted, "Are you Peter Marshall?" as he retrieved his bat and mitt on the ground.

Peter recognized who it was. *The woman who scolded Coach Tyree for playing me when I was out of uniform. Coach sure was angry for my wearing blue jeans and tennis shoes.* Suddenly it dawned on him, *Oops, I'm in trouble again.*

His eyes locked with hers, and a knot choked his throat. He glanced around to see if Coach Tyree was nearby, too. He mumbled, "Uhm ... uhh ... yes m'am, I'm Peter Marshall." He expected the worst. ... What she did next surprised him, though.

This kid will be a pushover, Prissy concluded. A warm smile spread across her face, and she spoke softly, "Peter, I'm so glad to finally meet you. I'm Prissy Smart. I met your mother yesterday, and she seems to be such a wonderful woman. I bet she's a terrific mother too."

Peter's chest puffed a little but, other than that, he didn't move, and he didn't blink. His eyes were frozen wide open—another dragon moment.

Meanwhile, Rosie's players were almost finished hitting pepper tosses into a net. *Where's Peter?* Coach Tyree wondered as he looked around. *Saw him on his bike a few minutes ago.* Then he saw him on the other side of the ballpark. *Oh, no! Prissy Smart has him cornered, and he is dressed in blue jeans and tennis shoes. Probably chewing him out.*

He hollered to Coach Sanders, "Take over." Then he hustled to Peter's rescue. *Glad I brought these extra ball pants.*

"I see you have a game today," Prissy said to Peter. "I'm looking forward to watching you play." She asked in a soothing voice, "Will your mother be here?"

"Uhm ... uh ..." Peter stammered. He shifted on his feet, trying to think of a way to end the talk and go on to his team. *Don't want to get in trouble with Coach Tyree for being late.* "Mom is working, and I don't think she will get off before the game is over."

"Oh, I'm so disappointed. I was looking forward to seeing her again." Prissy could see Peter was anxious to leave, so she pressed the issue. "You see, your mom asked me about Spanish and Indian relics. She said you have an interest in them, too."

Stretching the truth, Prissy added, "But we didn't get to finish our talk. Your mom still had some questions, and I was willing to meet with you and your mom and answer any other questions you two might have about them."

Peter's reluctance softened. "Mom told you about those things?" Hesitating for a moment, he thought, *If mom spoke to her about them guess it is ok for me to talk to her, too.* Did mom show them to you?"

When Prissy heard that question, her body quivered, and she

sucked in a deep breath. … *I knew there was something to this*! She was so excited, she had to calm herself. *Settle down, Prissy. Ssettle down. Don't show your eagerness.*

She took another deep breath and said nonchalantly, "No, Peter. We didn't have time, so your mom never showed them to me. Do you have them with you?"

Clarence heard their talk, and was alarmed Peter was being tricked. "Peter," he yelled, "hold on! Don't tell her anything about the treasures!"

Unfortunately, Peter couldn't hear Clarence because of the loud yells at the end of the ball game, and Peter fell right into Prissy's trap.

"I only have this one with me," Peter said as he reached into his shirt and pulled out the arrowhead tied around his neck. He held it up for her to see, and said, "My friends tell me this was made by the Indians long ago. They said these brought special fortune to them. I'm wearing this for good luck in my games."

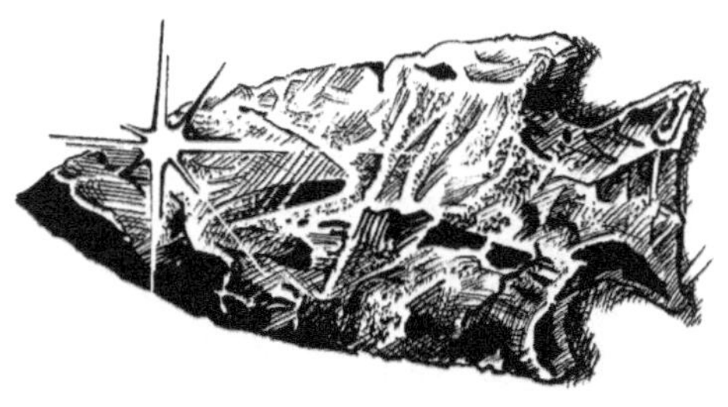

When Prissy laid eyes on the arrowhead, she gasped another deep breath and her body quivered. Her hands shook as they inched forward, and it took all her will power to keep from grabbing it and clutching it tightly.

Exquisite! Her excitement rose to its highest level when she recognized, *it is made of clear quartz crystal! Don't see any fractures!* Her face took on a whimpering look. *Priceless! Got to have it*! She was about to ask Peter if she could look at it closely and what other pieces he had and where he got them when she noticed Coach Tyree hurriedly walking towards them.

Acting fast, she said, "That is a great idea to wear it for luck. Put it back in your shirt. Maybe we can talk after the game even if your mom doesn't come. Okay?"

Coach Tyree began speaking as he walked up to them, "About the uniform, Prissy..."

She cut him off and said with a friendly smile, "Oh, there is no problem with the uniform, Coach. Boys sometimes lose their clothes and things. I have one of my own, you know, and he loses his bat, ball, or jersey all the time."

Her warm response stunned Coach Tyree, and he stood for a moment. "Well ... uhh ... our game is about to start." He turned to Peter and said, "Hurry and get some hitting practice."

Peter took off in a run, and Coach Tyree turned to face Prissy. He wondered, *What caused her to have a change of heart to allow Peter to wear blue jeans and tennis shoes?*

Prissy smiled like she knew what he was thinking, turned quickly and walked off without saying another word, leaving Coach Tyree to wonder, *What's going on here? Something's strange. Very strange.*

His thoughts repeated over and over as he walked back to his team. Prissy Smart was soon out of mind, though, when the game with the De Soto Conquistadors began.

Peter's team, Rosie's Cafe, finally won its first game, winning 5 runs to 4. Its record: 1 win and 5 losses. Not good, but the team seemed to be improving.

"Peter's play seemed better today," Clarence expressed to his three friends as they discussed the game. "Didn't start, but played his usual three innings in right field."

"Yeah," Charley added. "Fielded the only ball hit his direction, and that throw to 2nd base was on target."

"But it still was loopy and ... he didn't bat so hot," Maggie howled sadly. "Struck out both times, and ... leaders on his team still unfriendly."

"Yes, the po'boy," Caroline hooted agreement. "Izzie ev'a goin' ta get a hit, and will they eva be kind?"

Clarence added a positive note, "Peter did hit a couple of hard foul balls, and he will get better as we work with him. ... At least, think so."

Rosie's players, coaches, and parents were excited about the win. They high-fived each other and laughed, and players rollicked back and forth like young colts kicking their hooves up as they ran around in a pasture.

Coach Tyree walked into the team circle with a big grin on his face and spoke emotionally, "This is fun, isn't it?" Heads nodded with ear-to-ear grins. "This win's a big step for us. Coach Sanders and I saw so many good things today. And ... you know what? We saw something good from EVERY player." He slowly looked around and purposely into each player's eyes. "It took every one of you to do something good out there today for us to win. Shows how important teamwork is, and that each of you have practiced on your own." He paused to let the words and moment sink in. "Remember those good things you did today. If you do them again at our other games, we will have more wins like today."

These verbal pats on the players' backs made Peter feel good about himself. Soon the team pep talk was over. Peter slung his Savoy bat over his shoulder, tucked his mitt under his arm, and started towards Clarence.

As he rounded the corner of the dugout, all of a sudden, that woman, Prissy Smart, was standing in front of him again. This time, Coach Tyree was walking the other direction to the parking lot. Only one player, Sakine Davis, was near to them, but she was inside the dugout packing her gear.

"Hey, gang," Clarence said in an alarming tone to the other friends. "That Prissy woman has Peter trapped again."

"Nice game, Peter. Your team played a great game," Prissy said warmly trying to make him at ease.

"Yes, we won and it was fun."

She continued with the praise, "I saw that great throw you made to 2nd base. You kept the runner from going further around the bases." Her next words touched Peter's pride button. "Since your team won by only one run, your good throw probably was the play that won the game."

Sakine Davis's head jerked up when she heard Prissy say those words to Peter. "What?" she mumbled quietly. "You think Peter, the Peter I know, made the play that won the game? What game were you watching, lady?"

Peter's face and eyes lit up. "Do you think?" he asked for reassurance.

"Sure," she said recognizing he was warming up to her. Then she hit a home run that disarmed him, "It must have been that good luck arrowhead."

Peter's eyes sparkled, and he exclaimed, "Wow!" Then without realizing it, he said outloud, "Maybe they were telling the truth about this being a lucky piece."

"What is this?" Sakine mumbled. "A good luck arrowhead?" She stopped packing and looked through a peephole. Peter was touching an object under his shirt just below his neck.

Prissy tossed caution to the wind now as she thought no one was nearby, and bombarded Peter with questions. "Who told you it was a lucky piece? You mentioned you had more like it. What do you have? Where are you keeping them?"

Peter's guard was down now, and he never heard Clarence or the other friends yell to him, "Peter, don't tell her!"

He blurted out, "My friends told me. They also gave me a spearhead and one shaped like a cross and said they were made by the Indians."

"Really?" Prissy asked with a shocked look. "You have two more made of the same crystal material?" Her voice croaked with excitement. "And these friends just gave them to you? Why would they do that? Who are these friends? Do they know where the relics came from?"

Her excitement bubbled over to Peter and he couldn't hold back from telling her more, "They also gave me some round things they said are old coins. Some are yellow, probably gold."

Gold coins? Questions raced through Prissy's mind. *Who are these friends of Peter's? Where did they get these treasures? Why would they give them to him? Are there more?* She took a couple of deep breaths to gain her composure and slow the conversation down. She asked softly but pressed aggressively for answers, "But who are these friends?"

Sakine's curiosity was sky high, and she moved to a closer peephole in the dugout to get a better view and hear them speak.

Peter didn't hold anything back. "My friends are Clarence, Charley, Caroline, and Maggie. They gave them to me." He turned and pointed towards the majestic oak tree just outside the corner of right field. "They are over there."

Prissy stood erect quickly, turned, and scanned the area. After a few moments, she asked impatiently, "Where? I don't see anyone."

Sakine looked too. *I don't see anyone, either.*

"Over there," Peter said with a laugh. "Clarence is the oak tree

by my bike. Charley and Caroline are owls, and are perched out of sight up on one of Clarence's branches. Maggie is a fox. She is hiding in those bushes down the hill."

Prissy looked at the large oak tree and scanned the area again. After a moment, she bent close to Peter's face,

thrust her finger at him and snapped, "Don't get cute with me. Do you understand? Tell me where you really got them."

The harsh tone of Prissy's comment startled Sakine, and she pressed her eye into the peephole to see them better.

"But ... it ... it is true," he stammered.

"You want me to believe you got them from a tree, two owls, and a fox? Don't you know it is not nice to tell lies, Peter. Your mom wouldn't like you to tell a lie."

"But ... but ... I'm telling the truth," he stammered again. This time almost in tears. "Those are my friends. They gave them to me."

Prissy decided to press him more, and maybe he would break down and tell the truth. "Well, we will see what your mom thinks about this." She added another threat, "I have been too kind to you. If you don't tell me the truth, I'm going to tell Coach Tyree you must play in your uniform from now on or you can't play."

Prissy presented an imposing picture as she stood silent, towering over him with arms on her hips. She thought, *Who do you think your dealing with?* She assured herself, *He will soon realize it is in his best interest to cooperate.*

She asked him again, but Peter didn't change his story. Fact is, he was a boy intimidated by another towering dragon. He stood frozen in place, barely breathing. His eyes looked at her, but he had checked out mentally.

She finally concluded, *He is not going to say anything different,* and she blurted out, "Okay, if that's the way you want it, you will be sorry." She turned abruptly and stomped off snorting like a dragon blowing flames from the nostrils.

After a few steps, she whipped out her phone and began to make a call. She stopped abruptly, looked down and slowly lifted her shoe. "Bubble gum!" She screamed angrily. "Just great!" she yelled as she stomped off talking over the phone. "No," she shouted harshly, "I didn't say that to you."

"Wow!" Sakine exclaimed. "She was a hot tamale! Hope Peter is okay."

Peter's name being yelled by Clarence and his friends snapped him back to his senses, "Great going Peter. That will show her!"

When Peter finally made it to Clarence and his friends, Clarence cautioned him, "Peter, you must be careful and watch out for that Prissy lady. She was really angry with you about not telling her where you got the Spanish and Indian treasures."

Charley hooted in delight though, "Sure was funny to see she didn't get her way."

Caroline hooted too, "And you should've seen the angry look on her face when she stepped on that bubble gum! It was so funny I almost fell off Cla'ence's branch." Pausing for a moment and snuggl'n up to Charley she added, "Lucky Cha'lee saved me."

"Oh, you lovebirds, cool it," Clarence said chuckling so much his branches shook. He added, "She sure was frustrated when you told her who your friends were and pointed to us. I thought I was going to lose a branch or two laughing so hard."

Peter laughed too but soon he became serious and asked them, "Well, what am I going to do about her? She kept asking about the treasures and also threatened me about playing in my blue jeans and tennis shoes."

Clarence responded, "Well Peter, we gave the treasures to you so you could help with your family money problems. You can sell them and also buy some new ball pants and cleats."

The friends shared ideas about how to sell the treasures, then a joyful Peter pedaled home. "I can't wait to tell mom we won our first game," he kept saying over and over. "And I did something good. I might have saved the win for the team."

No matter the other things that Prissy Smart said to him, Peter could still hear her words, "Since your team won by a run, your good throw probably was the play that won the game."

Peter's eyes sparkled as he was excited about being a hero for the team. He reached up and touched the arrowhead tied around his neck. "Wow! Mom will be excited."

Sakine had watched Peter as he hurried to the large oak tree. She mumbled, "He seemed to be talking to someone as he tied his bat and mitt to the handlebars of his bike, but I ddidn't see anyone. There was no one around the tree or close enough to talk to him. ... He must be nuts!" When her mom called her name, she mumbled again. "Here, Mom. I'm in the dugout packing."

Sakine continued to wonder on the drive home and into the night, *Why was Prissy Smart so angry with Peter, and who was he talking to by the tree?*

[CHAPTER 27]

Sinister Plot to Learn More About
Peter's Treasures

Prissy was on the phone with Jerry Cramer as she walked away angrily from Peter. "I'm at the ballpark. Meet me in twenty minutes in the scorekeeper's box." She was silent for a moment. "No, I don't care if you are on the golf course with your buddies! Now! Not after you finish your round." She added a reminder, "You know who butters your bread." She paused to let him absorb that bit of reality. "And bring Tom and Larry."

She scraped her shoe on the bleacher frame to remove the bubble gum. This was futile, and she mumbled a few words that would have brought on a mouth soap-washing for some youngsters. "No, I don't know where Tom or Larry are. Find them. Be here in twenty minutes."

Prissy put the phone in her pocket and grumbled, "Great! Smeared it all over my shoe." She made a promise, *Don't care if kids like it and the league wants it as a money maker, bubble gum will no longer be sold in the concession stand.*

As twenty minutes ticked off the clock, Jerry Cramer walked into the scorekeeper's box. He still had his golf shoes on and a golf glove was hanging out his hip pocket. He was not a happy person but seeing Prissy he forced a friendly face and said, "Tom and Larry will be here in a few minutes."

"Good," Prissy replied without looking up. She was bent over and trying to scrape the bubble gum from her shoe.

Jerry saw what she was doing, grinned in glee since she wasn't looking, *Serves you right for ruining my golf outing.* In a serious tone, though, he said, "Lighter fluid will remove it." She looked at him with a quizzical expression and he blurted, "The bubble gum. Lighter fluid will remove it. If you want, I will take your shoe home and remove the gum for you."

"That will work?" she asked in a disbelieving tone.

He nodded and said, "It will take it all off."

She stood, looked over her clothes, and said, "That is a relief, but I even have it all over my clothes."

"Don't think lighter fluid will be good for your clothes."

Tom and Larry walked through the door at that moment, and Prissy nodded her gratitude at their coming on such short notice. She motioned everyone to sit. "Let's get to it."

Tom noticed Jerry's golf shoes and glove and, since he knew it would rile him, he asked, "Kinda late for golf, isn't it?"

Jerry fired him a threatening look and replied, "We were on the sixteenth hole."

Once everyone settled into their seats, Prissy added, "This project is to be kept only among the four of us." She paused and added, "Understand?"

The three fellows glanced at each other with a "What is up?" expression, but nodded they understood what she expected. Besides, they knew there would be consequences if anything was mentioned to anyone else.

"Good. As you know, Terry and I are collectors of old Florida artifacts and treasures. Some of our collection is in our office. Well, a ball player in our league by the name of Peter Marshall found some old Spanish and Indian artifacts, and he showed one to me. I asked where he obtained them, and he said some friends gave them to him."

She paused for a moment then said, "Fellas, I want your help to find out who these friends are of Peter's. This part gets a little sticky. You see, he says these are from his ..." Prissy lowered her voice to a whisper like she was embarrassed to say the next words "... his IMAGINARY FRIENDS."

She paused to let the words sink in then continued, "Doesn't matter to me if these are imaginary friends. I want to learn where Peter found the artifacts."

Jerry Cramer chuckled and asked in disbelief, "Imaginary?"

"Yes, imaginary," Prissy affirmed. "That is what he said."

The three guys sat quietly for a moment and didn't ask more about the imaginary friends.

"What is the name of Peter's team?" Tom asked.

"Rosie's Café, and David Tyree is the coach."

Larry asked, "Any suggestions in finding this information?"

Prissy rolled her eyes and thought, *Don't you men have any creative ideas at all?* Then she laid out her plan.

"I want you to shadow Peter and his mother, Vicki Marshall, every minute they are at the ballpark. Maybe in a relay so they won't get wise to you. Get close enough to hear what they say when talking. Keep track of everyone they talk to, and…" she emphasized, "I mean everyone. Peter's mother probably will not be at many games because she works a lot, so you'll need to be on your toes to observe her when she does come. You have the schedule showing when Peter's team plays, so make sure you are around. I'll be here, too; watching most of the time from here in the scorekeeper's box. Report to me after each of his games, but don't say anything if anyone is around. Questions?"

"How long?" Tom asked.

"Until I tell you to stop," Prissy answered. "It won't be a long time. The season is half over and then there will be the tournament games. Maximum, about six weeks, so plan on all that time if it is necessary."

From that day onward, Prissy's three spies shadowed Peter and Vicki before, during, and after each of the ballgames of Peter's team. They even shadowed Peter when he came to watch other games. They listened for any clue that might reveal where Peter got the treasures.

Prissy soon had some reports from their reports.

Larry: "Peter rides a bicycle to the games and always leaves it by the huge oak tree that stands outside the corner of the right field fence."

All three: "Peter spends a lot of time before and after each ball game around the huge oak tree by right field."

Tom: "Peter seems to talk to someone when he is by the oak tree, but I never see anyone close enough to talk with."

Jerry: "I have seen Peter look back when he's playing in right field during a game. He speaks like he's talking to someone by the oak tree, but I don't see anyone. Strange kid."

All three: "Peter's mom, Vicki, only came to a couple of games as we expected. Interesting part is she sometimes sat or walked out near the outfield where Peter played. Also, she spoke to Coach Tyree a couple of times after the team's end-of-game meetings."

Jerry: "I overheard Vicki talking to Peter through the ball field fence. Something about a lucky arrowhead. Then he touched something around his neck and under his shirt."

Larry: "Peter and his mother walked to the oak tree after one of his ballgames, and they seemed to be talking with someone else. At least Peter was, as she didn't do much talking. She was sorta standing, awe struck. Strange family."

Tom: "I heard Peter talk to one of the girls on his team. Think her name is Sakine. He showed her an arrowhead tied around his neck, and said it was his lucky piece."

Jerry: "The girl's name is Sakine. I heard Peter say to her his friends gave the arrowhead to him, and he pointed in the direction of right field."

Jerry: "Peter told Sakine his friends were the oak tree, the two owls, and a fox. The girl just twirled her finger beside her ear and mouthed, "Crazy.""

Tom: "I saw Peter on the golf course with his mitt and a stick. I followed at a distance and, I swear, two owls and a fox joined him when he was out of sight. They disappeared to a secluded area that I couldn't get to without them seeing me. Never seen anything like it."

Prissy read the reports over and over. After a while an idea popped into her head. *The oak tree is mentioned in most of the notes. Maybe ... just maybe, Peter found the artifact treasures somewhere around that tree. And if he didn't find them there, he must be fond of the tree since it is where he leaves his bike all the time. He even sits on it to watch other games.*

She put together a plan that would force Peter to tell her where he obtained the treasures. She laughed in a sinister way as she mumbled, "What a great plan, and everyone will think Terry and I are wonderful citizens."

CHAPTER 28

*"Be the best you can, and good
things will happen."*

Clarence stretched his branches and yawned loudly as his feathery friend landed on a branch. "Hello, Charley. Where's that boss of yours?" He asked with a chuckle.

"She is remodeling the nest. I'm hunting alone. Thought I would come by and check on Peter's team as it practiced."

"They have finished and about to have their team meeting," explained Clarence. "Peter is coming here afterwards."

"I will be gone, so tell 'em Caroline and I think he's do'un good."

"Will do, but..." Clarence added in a negative tone, "but time is running out."

"Is there a problem?" Charley asked.

"Yes. Rosie's has one regular season game left, and Peter doesn't have a base hit. Thought he would by now. Next up is the tournament. Lose one game and they are out."

"Big Fella, you are usually the one positive and calm. Why so much fret over Peter's performance? He has improved with our help. If you don't stop, you are likely to get some stress fractures in your limbs or trunk. They will break off or your bark will wrinkle too much and crack and allow those pesky infections to get to your innards." He added, "Then some human will say you are sick and need to be cut down to keep from falling on someone."

"Okay, okay!" Clarence exclaimed. "I won't fret! I won't stress out!"

"Good. Just don't screw up." Charley paused and then added with a chuckle. "After all, Caroline and I don't have the time or patience to break in another tree where we can snooze."

"Yeah, yeah." Clarence laughed. "Anyway, you can tell the pressure is building in Peter. He has hit the ball good lately, but to someone or foul. Then he becomes frustrated and strikes out. He will be ok once he gets over this hump. When he gets his first hit."

"Yeah, agree. It will happen, but when? Surely he can't go the whole season and not get one." Charley paused momentarily before he asked in a doubtful tone, "Is that possible?"

"Hope not," Clarence replied as a gentle breeze swayed his branches. "Let us ramp his practice up during the spring break and prepare him to end his season with a base hit."

"Good plan," Charley hooted as he spread his wings to fly away. "Back to hunting. See ya later."

Coach Tyree began the serious part of his talk. "We are in 7th place, with 5 wins and 8 losses." He paused for a moment and added, "That record doesn't sound so hot, but we are better than it indicates."

"How is that coach?" a player's dad asked with a frown on his face. "We're under 0.400 for the season."

"Glad you asked. Like you said, 'for the season.' It doesn't reveal our improvement. Our record in our last 8 games is 5 wins and 3 losses. That is great improvement; especially, when you consider we lost our first 5 games!" He looked around into each player's eyes and said, "Most important, it means you have improved, and that is the goal we've worked toward."

He paused again to let the positive news sink in and added, "Coach Sanders is passing out a game-by-game statistic sheet so you can see how each of you has improved."

A buzz started to rise among the players and parents as they looked at the stats. Players compared with one another.

"I have the most hits."

"I have the most triples."

"I have the most doubles, home runs, and runs batted in."

"I have the most strike outs as a pitcher."

"I have the most wins as a pitcher."

"I have the most double plays."

As the buzz continued, players moved from one group to another giggling and ribbing each other. That is, all except Peter. He was the only one without a base hit. He did, however, lead the team in one category—strike outs.

Peter stood alone and thought, *They could at least show how many good defensive throws I have made. That Prissy lady even said "I saved the game."*

When Sakine saw Peter standing by himself with a sad look, she walked up to him with a snide look that said, "I'm better than you and here's the proof." She whispered in a mean tone, "Hey Dufus, if you want, I will tell coach to give you one of my hits since you can't get one."

Peter nudged her away with an arm and threw a verbal punch back. "They are just easy on you, Sakining, since you are a girlee."

He hit a home run with the words. Sakine's dander shot through the roof, and she upped her attack. "I told you to call me 'Channing' since you can't remember my name."

He struck back, "Oh, girlee can't take it, huh?" Then he said, "Chan Chan," with a grin because he knew he got the best of her and wanted to rile her even more.

Chan Chan stood fuming as Peter walked away.

Coach Tyree yelled above the buzz, "Anything else?"

Coach Sanders responded, "Don't forget the field repairs."

"Oh, yes," Coach Tyree yelled to the team. "The field will be closed over the break for improvements. Getting a new irrigation system. Don't know about other improvements. We'll be in touch about practice. Any questions?" He didn't see any, and added, "Everyone enjoy your break but keep practicing on your own."

As the team scattered, Coach Tyree walked up to Coach Sanders and asked, "Know any place where we can practice?"

"There are cub league fields on the southwest corner of the nearby golf course. I will check to see if we can use them."

"Good. Let me know, and we will call..."

"There you are, ya Big Hunk," a woman's voice interrupted from behind.

Oh, noooo, Coach Tyree thought as he recognized the voice. *Marilyn Davis. Thought Coach Sanders had a talk with her.* As he turned, he noticed she was striding towards them in the usual, extra-tight jeans.

"I baked your favorite," she expressed, "a Key Lime pie, just for you."

Coach Tyree was beside himself as he raised his hands to take it. "I can't thank you..."

"Sorry," she said softly as she brushed passed him and handed it to Coach Sanders. "This one is for this big hunk."

Coach Tyree's jaw dropped and his eyes locked with those of Coach Sanders, who shrugged and raised his eyes in delight, like a kid who'd been caught with his hands in the cookie jar.

Coach Sanders blushed. "Uh, uh, thank you, Marilyn."

"Just wa-unta please ya, Sweetie," she replied with a flutter of her eye lashes. "So ya won't forget."

Sakine walked up and expressed in a huff, "I'm ready to go, Mom. I'll be in the car."

"I will be there in a moment." Then Marilyn turned back to face Coaches Sanders and Tyree with a subtle smile, "Havta run. See ya tomorrow night."

As she walked away, Coach Sanders' face and eyes connected again with Coach Tyree's, and he explained with a sheepish grin, "You did ask me to talk to her. Remember?"

Coach Tyree laughed loudly, "No need to say more."

Coach Sanders laughed along and he confessed, "She's one heck of a cook. Something Jake's needed for a long time."

"Sure. Now you're taking one for Jake, huh?"

They both giggled like little kids as they loaded the team's gear into their separate pickups. Each nodded, and a warm smile was on the face of both as they drove away.

Meanwhile, Peter talked to Clarence, "My stats are terrible. I lead the team in strike-outs. Wished I had at least one base hit."

"It will come in time," Clarence replied warmly. "Just be patient. Sometimes the more you think about something, the more difficult it is to do it. It will be that way for you. Be the best team player no matter how you bat and bingo, it will happen."

"Think so?" Peter asked for reassurance.

"You bet. Do the best you can and something good will come. Promise."

A relaxed grin appeared on Peter's face. "Big Fella, you're the best. I don't know what I'd do without you and Caroline and Charley and Maggie. . . . You're my best friends."

"Same here, Peter," Clarence responded with an emotional choke in his voice, "Same here."

CHAPTER 29

Monsters, Giant Ones, are about
to eat Clarence!

Maggie licked her lips as she trotted in the dawn light along the creek that meandered through the golf course. *Maybe night scavengers haven't gotten all the food at the ballpark.* Suddenly she froze in her tracks and thrust her ears into the air. … *What is that loud bellowing sound?* After a moment, she howled, "It is Clarence! He sounds terrified!"

She ran frantically through open woods without regard for her safety. "Oh, my gosh!" she yelped the instant she laid eyes on Clarence. She turned on her heels and howled as she ran to find Charley and Caroline, "We have to save our friend! We have to save our friend!"

Charley and Caroline were doing some nest repair, and they heard Maggie's alarming howl before she came into sight. "Charley! Caroline! Come quickly!" she exclaimed out of breath. "Monsters are tearing up the forest! The ground shakes when they move. Their feet smash everything in their path and leave deep tracks in the ground. One monster has lots of sharp teeth. … They are headed towards Clarence!"

Charley and Caroline flew immediately towards Clarence. "I can't believe what we're seeing," Charley squawked. "Clarence is in danger!" They sailed above Clarence and hooted franticly, "What can we do, Big Fella?"

"No idea!" Clarence bellowed in a terrified voice.

Caroline squawked, "Cha'lee, maybe Peta can do som-thun."

Charley agreed and after a rapid flight, he banged at Peter's bedroom window. "Peter! Peter! Wake up! Wake up!"

"What ... uh ..." Peter mumbled coming out of a deep sleep. "What is the...?" Slowly the bed covers were pulled downward, and Peter's half-opened eyes peered out.

"Wake up, Peter! Wake up!" Charley squawked frantically as he banged on the window. "Monsters are going to eat Clarence!" He exclaimed.

"What? Monsters?" Peter mumbled as he dragged himself out of bed to the window. *It is Charley.* "Why are you making so much noise? Practice is later."

"Come quick! Monsters are about to eat Clarence. We have to save him!"

"Okay. Okay. I'm coming," Peter grumbled lazily like he would rather get back into bed. Suddenly it dawned on him, *Clarence eaten by monsters? He must be in serious trouble.* In seconds, he was dressed and pedaled to the park as Charley flew ahead.

Peter heard the roar before reaching sight of the ballpark, but he wasn't prepared for what he saw. Huge machines crawled on heavy steel tracks, "Clack, clack, clack," along the fence. They tore down trees and stirred up clouds of dust as they slowly worked their way toward their friend, Clarence.

One of the two large pine trees outside center field was pushed over with a large bulldozer, and it hit the ground with a loud thud. Peter's heart sank as he thought, *Charley and Caroline would sit on it during ballgames.* It next knocked down the small trees along the fence.

Another large machine, with a front end that looked like the giant pinching jaws of a monster, grabbed the trunk of the other tall pine tree, nipped it off at ground level, and let it fall to the ground with a heavy crash.

Several men with chain saws moved in and cut the tree trunks and thick branches into small logs and branches. Another large machine had a huge mouth and men fed branches and small limbs into it. The machine ground and spit them into piles of wood chips.

Clarence cried out in helpless agony, "Stop! Stop! Ooooooooooh, stop this!" He pleaded loudly, "Stop this carnage! You are destroying my tree friends!" He shook his branches and leaves violently to scare these humans, but all was lost in the machinery's roar.

Another machine loaded the larger tree logs and branches onto a big truck. "It will be hauled away," a worker said, "to be chipped into pieces, cut into lumber, burned, or left to rot."

Charley buzzed Peter and yelled, "The monsters have almost reached Clarence! We havta' do sumpthin' quick to save our friend!"

An idea popped into Peter's head, but he didn't have time to tell Charley. "Follow me!" he yelled.

Clarence saw him coming and bellowed, "Peter, I'm glad to see you, my boy. Things are a little uncomfortable here!"

Peter slid his bike to a stop between Clarence and the front of the mechanical jawed monster, but it was still moving—about fifteen feet away. Peter closed his eyes. *Sure hope the man sees me—and doesn't want to run over a boy.*

The deep roar of the huge engine crept closer and closer until it seemed it was on top of Peter. "I'm a goner," he mumbled. Suddenly it turned into a purr. The monster stopped!

Peter slowly peeked. He expected to see the monster's jaws inches away but, to his shock, it was the face of Prissy Smart.

Ever since she last spoke to Peter about where he got the Spanish and Indian treasures, she had worked on a plan to get the information from him. *If Peter found the treasures around the huge oak tree,* she reasoned, *my workers'd find them for me by digging up the area. If he found them somewhere else, he would tell me to keep the huge oak from being bulldozed down.*

Anyone could see the ballpark needed a total makeover, and it was easy for Prissy to persuade league officials and others already in her hip pocket. "Everything must be removed and rebuilt." She even presented a petition signed by hundreds of uninformed citizens, and she raised money to fund the renovations. She counted on the weakness of public servants not wanting to turn off her money faucet. Prissy and husband, Terry, also called in favors, and her project quickly was rubberstamped for approval.

Prissy knew, *The trees outside the outfield fence weren't a problem in renovating the ball field, but public sentiment wouldn't approve only taking down the largest patriarch oak in the area. Especially, the one outside right field that had been seen by thousands of people and ball players over the years.*

So I will insert wording into the plans that will give me cover: "Disease in tree has created dangerous situation from branches falling on walkers and spectators."

Yes, it was Prissy who stood directly in front of Peter. She shook her finger at him, almost poking his nose and said in a deep voice, nothing like he had ever heard by a woman.

"So this pile of wood is one of your friends is he? … And he gave those Spanish and Indian treasures to you, did he?"

"Uh … uh … yes," Peter stammered.

"Well, see these big machines?" she asked harshly as she pointed to the one purring a few feet away. Then she pointed at Clarence.

"Unless you tell me where your friends found those treasures, I'm going to make a wood pile out of this one. … Do you understand?"

Clarence gulped and his branches shook nervously, "Peter, she won't believe you, but go ahead and tell her your friends found them near the coast in swamp muck."

Peter nodded he understood. "But I already told you. They found them in the coastal swamp land."

This response irritated Prissy even more, and she shouted, "Don't play me for a fool! How could this tree go to the coast?"

She bent down again with her face just above his. She was so close he could feel the hot air snorting from her nostrils just like his make believe dragons.

In a gruff voice, she threatened. "See those workers over there? I'm sending them to eat. If you haven't told me where you really got those treasures by the time they return, I'm going to have them bulldoze your tree friend down and cut it up into a pile of wood pieces."

A wicked smile came upon her face as she added, "And then…" with a laugh, "we're going to burn them! … Understand?"

Peter was in a shock now, as the tone of her threats were equal to any imaginary dragon or monster he'd ever faced. All he could manage was a nod that he understood.

Prissy and the workers left for lunch, and Peter collapsed on one of Clarence's roots. Charley and Caroline flew in and perched beside him, and Maggie joined them.

"What are we going to do?" Peter asked in a frantic voice.

"Can't think of a thing," Charley hooted.

"Me either," Caroline screeched in a 'woe is us' tone.

"Brain is a blank," Maggie howled sadly.

Clarence was silent. Maybe he recognized his hours as the majestic tree in this forest were numbered and soon he would be no more—only a memory in the minds of his friends, and a pile of charred wood pieces scattered on the ground.

"Time's running out."

Suddenly, Caroline started hopping around and hooting, "Cha'lee, deaah. I've an ah-de'ah! I've an ah-de'-ah!"

"Well, Hon, tell us. Tell us. Time's running out."

"It is somethin' we saw awhile back on the unive'sity campus. It's..." she explained. "Peta, you will need to..."

"That might work!" Clarence bellowed with a little hope to his voice. "At least it might give us time to think of some other idea, but we have to hurry."

"Okay," Peter said as he hopped on his bike and pedaled furiously towards his house. "See you guys in a bit."

"Charley and Caroline, how about watching Peter and making sure he gets back before Prissy and her worker bees return?"

"Sure thing," they hooted as they flew after Peter.

In one hour sharp, Prissy and her worker bees returned. "Kid is nowhere in sight," Prissy mumbled. *Guess he didn't want to see his friend torn down and chopped up.* Prissy yelled instructions as she pointed at Clarence, "Okay, fellas, push down that tree, and chop it to small pieces in that grinder."

Clarence gulped and shook nervously as he said to his friends, "I'm in a heap of trouble if they don't get here fast and if this plan doesn't work."

The driver of a bulldozer looked at the majestic oak tree and questioned her commands. *She wants to push down this tree? Chop it up? Does she see its size? It will take forever to push it down, let alone cut it up and haul it away?* Then he asked to make sure, "All of it, Ma'am?"

"Yes," Prissy barked. "All of it. Every piece. Nothing left. Understand?" … She paused for a moment then added, "…but if you find something unusual, stop and let me know."

The worker bees nodded and went to work. The engines of the two largest monsters were revved to maximum power and started crawling towards Clarence. Two owls suddenly flew out of nowhere and buzzed the lead driver's head. Caroline swooped close in a dive and Charley dropped poop on his face. "Yuk! Bird poop!" he yelled and stopped immediately.

Caroline hooted gleefully when she saw the target had been hit, "Atta boy, Cha'lee!" Maggie also howled in delight.

Prissy stomped towards the driver and asked sharply, "Why are you stopping?"

"Those crazy owls almost hit me. One pooped all over me. Didn't you see?" he asked in an angry tone as he wiped his face.

"I don't care. Get to it and this time don't stop." She threatened, "Or I'll have your job!"

"Okay, whatever you say," the worker said as he revved the machine and started it forward again. Under his breath, though, he mumbled, "You are a witch."

At that moment, another worker ran to Prissy, and pointed upwards into the tree. Peter was sitting high on one of the branches and next to the tree trunk.

Prissy shouted angrily at him, "What are you doing up there? Get down! Do you have an answer about the treasures?"

"Be calm, Peter," Clarence spoke softly. "There is nothing she can do ... at least nothing quickly with those chains around you and my branch. Don't let her have the padlock key."

"I hope dose newspaper and TV folks show up soon," Charley squawked. "Need 'em here now. ... You did call, didn't you, Peter?"

"Yes, I did. I also called Sakine Davis on my team. Made me apologize before she'd help. Said she would call the team players and coaches and then come right away." Peter turned to look at the parking lot. "No one is there. Hope help arrives soon."

Peter yelled at Prissy, "I already told you my friends found the treasures at the coast in the inland swamp land."

"Is that so? Well, come down out of that tree," Prissy commanded harshly. "Now! We're going to push your friend over."

"No! I won't come!"

The workers gathered around now, and Prissy commanded, "Bring that front loader machine, and get him out of that tree!"

"But he is chained to the tree," one worker exclaimed. "And it's padlocked. We'll have to cut the chain or padlock."

"Well, get to it," Prissy yelled.

"Have to go to the shop and get a bolt cutter big enough to cut them."

"Hurry and get it," Prissy replied loudly.

"Boy, she is steaming," Charley squawked gleefully.

"You can say that ag'in, deah," Caroline hooted softly as she snuggled closer to him. "Cha'lee, you made that driva stop, and you bravely saved Clarence."

Charley's chest puffed to almost twice its size in pride as he hooted, "Think so?" Before she responded, though, he took credit, "Uh, guess I did."

"Been thirty minutes, but seems like seconds," Clarence moaned. "Need time for others to arrive."

"Oh, nooooo," Maggie howled from the woods as she sounded the alarm. "Worker bees returned with the bolt cutter."

"Cut it and drag him out of there," Prissy demanded.

Three workers stepped onto the bucket of the front loader, and it moved forward to a place under Clarence's branches where they could be hoisted up to Peter's level.

"Oooh-mah, oooh-mah!" Caroline shrieked.

At that moment, Sakine Davis and several of Peter's teammates ran up and stood, right in the path of the mechanical loader before it could reach Clarence and Peter. It had to stop or it would run over them.

Prissy hustled towards them and yelled, "What are you kids doing? You are going to get hurt! Get out of the way!"

Newspaper and TV reporters arrived at that moment and hustled over to the group. "We received a call a child had been run over by one of these large machines. Where is the child?"

Clarence asked, "A child run over? Peter, is that what you told them?"

"I had to say something drastic that would get them to come. ... It worked didn't it?"

The worker bees moved out of the way as this was Prissy's gig. "Not reporters, too!" she exclaimed under her breath when a microphone and camera were pushed her way.

Prissy knew how to think and act quickly on her feet in the public arena. She collected herself and calmly explained, "No one has been run over. We are renovating the ball field and the seating/dugout areas. The plan was approved by the elected commissioners as well as the ball league officials." *They can take the heat if any fallout occurs.*

The TV reporter followed with the question, "Why are these kids on the ground and in the path of these machines?"

Neither reporter yet knew Peter was in the tree and chained to it. Sakine yelled at them, "Ask Peter."

Both reporters walked to the players before Prissy answered. "Which one is Peter?"

"He is up there," Sakine said and pointed into the tree. "He chained and padlocked himself to a branch."

The cameraman started shooting footage of Peter in the tree, and the reporter asked, "Young man, why are you chained to this tree?"

A crowd of curious humans had formed by now. Vicki Marshall had a message from Peter and rushed to the park. Coach Tyree arrived at the same moment, and caught up to her, "What is this about?"

"I don't know for sure," she replied as she glanced at him. "Peter left a message to 'Come quick to the ball field. His friend, Clarence, is being cut down.' He sounded extremely upset."

Coach Tyree replied, "I had a call from Sakine Davis about an emergency at the ball field." He nodded towards the players under the tree, "Looks like she contacted the other teammates, too." He paused and wondered, *Should I ask? Yes.* "Peter still insisting he can talk to the tree and also to those owls?"

Vicki nodded, "Yes," and then they hurried to the group near the huge oak tree. A reporter asked Peter questions. He waved when he saw his mom and Coach Tyree.

The reporter asked again, "Young man, why are you chained to this tree?"

"To save it!" Peter shouted.

"I can't hear you," the reporter responded because of the machinery motors.

Peter leaned down as far as the chain around him would allow, and repeated, "To save this tree!" When he did that, the crystal arrowhead tied around his neck dangled out from his shirt and reflected the TV camera light.

"Why do you want to save this tree?" the reporter asked. "They say it's diseased and have a permit to remove everything, including the trees along the outfield fence."

Clarence interrupted at that point, "Say nothing is wrong with me, Peter. Tell them that Prissy lady just made it up."

"There is nothing wrong with this tree. It has no disease. That is made up."

Clarence gave Peter another instruction, "Tell them to bring a tree doctor, or whatever they call them, to examine me to see if I'm really diseased like Prissy says."

"Bring a tree doctor to check to see if Clar... er ... uh ... this tree is diseased," Peter yelled into the camera. "It's a majestic, old oak, and shouldn't be destroyed on a mistake!"

Prissy heard everything. *Ah-ha! I will promise to bring a tree specialist and, after everyone is gone, I will have the workers push the tree down if he doesn't tell me where he got the treasures.*

While the camera was still rolling, Prissy looked up at Peter and said in a nice voice, "Okay, we will bring a tree specialist. Come down and we will go contact one."

She made an effort to keep a smile on her face as she thought, *It will give me one more chance to change his mind about telling me where he got the treasures. And if he doesn't, his tree friend becomes a pile of matchsticks.*

"Peter, don't trust what she says," Clarence cautioned. "Stay where you are until the tree doctor comes."

"Okay," Peter said to Clarence. Then he realized that everyone thought he agreed to leave with Prissy. "I mean, no! I'm not going anywhere until someone I know, like my mom or Coach Tyree, tells me nothing is going to happen to this tree."

The reporters now had their news story: "Boy chains himself to tree to save it." They put a wrap to their comments, packed their equipment and left. The story made the TV evening and late news and also was front page in the next newspaper issue. Anyone watching also could see the arrowhead treasure dangling from Peter's neck.

Before anyone else was close enough to hear, Prissy whispered to Peter, "You can't protect your friend forever. I will be back when everyone is gone and we are going to cut down your tree friend unless you tell me where you got those treasures."

Peter was stunned by her threat, and he would have fallen if not chained to the branch. Clarence's shaky voice stunned him in another way. "Pe-Pe-Peter," he stammered, "you and my friends saved my life. ... At least for now, but please don't leave me!"

Charley and Caroline hooted excitedly, too, over the temporary victory. Charley said, "Atta boy, Peter. Ya da man, but we gotta stay and protect Clarence!"

Peter replied in a worn-out voice, "A team effort, Big Fella, and... we won't leave ya."

After the reporters left, Vicki turned slightly towards Coach Tyree and asked, "Any idea what Peter has gotten himself into?"

"Not sure, but looks like he is determined to stay chained to that tree until he knows it won't be cut down."

He stopped by his players sitting on the ground, and Vicki continued to where she could see Peter up in the tree. When they made eye contact, she said, "Hun, I'm proud of you for protecting your friend. I know he is special to you."

"Thanks, Mom, and thanks so much for coming. Didn't know if you would hear my message in time or if you could leave your work."

"Have you eaten anything today?"

Peter shook his head, "No."

"I will make some sandwiches and bring a drink."

"That would be great, Mom."

They talked more about why he was in the tree, and she began to understand.

Coach Tyree finished talking to his players and walked over to speak with Vicki and Peter. "Sounds like the health of this tree is an issue. Tell you what. I will arrange for a tree specialist to come and examine this tree. Is that okay?"

Vicki looked up at Peter and both said enthusiastically, "Yes!"

"When? How soon can you do this?" she asked anxiously.

"I will make calls right now. If lucky, maybe someone will come today. I will call you."

"Do you have my number?" Vicki asked.

"Yes." As he responded, he noticed a look on her face of: *Why would you have my number?* He added, "from the list of team parents. Remember?"

She nodded in understanding, and they left to carry out their missions.

Sakine shouted to Peter, "Hey, Dufus. How long ya gonna stay up there?"

"Don't know. Long as I hav'ta, and," with a big grin he added, "thanks for calling the team ... Chan Chan."

Even Big Tommy Lassiter, who had been one of Peter's biggest tormentors, came. He asked, "All night?"

"If I hav'ta."

"Here, Dufus. Catch," Sakine said as she tossed a phone to him. "Call me and I will pass the news to the team. Just push that green button and punch my REAL name. It will dial me."

A smile crossed Peter's face as he thought, *She is okay—for a girl.* "Okay. Thanks for coming to save Clar... uh ... this tree."

Several hours passed before Coach Tyree phoned Vicki, "I have good news and bad news. I finally reached a tree expert, but she can't be at the ballpark until tomorrow."

"Oh, that is not good!" Vicki moaned.

"Doubt anything will happen now until the expert comes."

"Maybe so, but Peter will stay in that tree until the tree expert comes; even all night."

"Tell you what. If you will take care of John William tonight, I will stay with Peter so he won't be alone."

"Well, uh," she hesitated, "I'm not sure..."

Coach Tyree cut her off, "I have some sleeping cots or, if Peter wants to stay chained up in the tree, he can have a sleeping bag and pillow."

"Well, that sounds okay, but you sure you want to do this?"

"Yes. You would do it for me. Right?"

"Not so sure," she replied in a confessional tone. "Okay, I will get Peter's bag and pillow and send some sack lunches. They will be ready when you drop John William off at the house."

A few hours later, Coach Tyree hollered to Peter as he returned for the night, "Peter, I'm back. You still up there?"

"Yes, Coach. I moved to a larger branch."

Coach Tyree maneuvered to where he could see Peter. "Your mom sent some sandwiches and a sleeping bag. She was worried about you being alone overnight in the tree, so I said I'd stay with you. I brought a cot and I will sleep down here."

"Coach, you don't need to stay. I will be okay My friends will keep me company, and Chan Chan gave me her phone if I need help."

Coach Tyree wondered, *Who is Chan Chan?* "Peter, I know you will be okay, but I promised your mom. So unless you object, I will spend the night."

"Okay, Coach, but you don't hav'ta."

"We will rough it together," Coach Tyree replied. *At least he won't fall since he is chained to the branch. Bet it's uncomfortable, though.* "Yell out, Peter, if you need me." He paused for a moment and thought, *David Tyree, what have you gotten yourself into?*

Coach Tyree unfolded the cot directly under Peter, but stopped abruptly. *My, gosh! Look at all the bird poop under these branches.* He moved the cot a few feet to the side, rolled the sleeping bag out, and slid his body into it.

He squirmed to find some comfort as thoughts ran rapidly through his mind. *At least there is few mosquitoes. This cot is not very comfy, but it beats sleeping on the ground. How do the military guys and gals do it? And they don't even have a cot! Is that Peter's voice? Who's he talking with?* "Peter, something wrong?" No answer. *Maybe my imagination.*

Over the next couple of hours, Coach Tyree faded in and out of sleep. Suddenly, loud squawks broke the silence of the night and jerked him upright. He fumbled for his flashlight and looked up into the tree. He rubbed his eyes in disbelief. *It is the two owls that come around the ballpark, and they are on a branch close to Peter. Coach*  *Tyree's jaw dropped when he notice, they seem to be eating what looked like a large mouse.*

Wow! Peter did mention two of his friends were owls. What did he call them? Oh, yes—Charley and Caroline…. Maybe his imaginary friends are real after all!

After a while, Coach Tyree laid back on his cot. *Hope that tree expert comes tomorrow. Not sure my body can survive another night out here.*

Later, the owls flew away without making a sound, and continued their nightly hunt for food. Their silence moved stealthily across the forest. Their shadows along with those cast by gentle breezes on trees and shrubs as well as other critters scampering about, moved along the forest floor. Day break would come soon. Would Peter and his friends be able to save Clarence?

CHAPTER 38

Can they save Clarence?

The monster machines suddenly roared back to life after their night's sleep, and Clarence yelled in fright. "Peter, wake up! Wake up! The worker bees are back!"

Prissy kept her word. "You can't protect your friend forever," she yelled up to Peter still rubbing his eyes. "We are going to cut down your tree friend unless you tell me right this second where you got those Spanish and Indian treasures."

Peter wondered, *How come Coach Tyree is not saying anything?* He peered over the branch he had been on all night long and discovered Coach Tyree and his sleeping cot were gone. *Where is Coach? How can I stop these machines by myself?*

"Well! You going to tell me where you got those treasures?"

Clarence grumbled, "Wasting your breath, Peter. She's beyond believing us." Suddenly, he managed a small chuckle as he added, "Serves her right she walked around in Charley's and Caroline's bird poop."

"Yeah," Peter responded in a brief moment of satisfaction, "She is going to be angry when she discovers it all over her shoes."

Clarence's voice perked up, "The tree expert may be here! Coach Tyree and another human are headed this way from the parking lot."

"I see them." Peter yelled, "Hurry Coach, they are back."

Prissy saw them too. *Must be the tree expert.* She started towards them, but stopped immediately when she noticed her shoes and screamed in anger, "Bird poop!"

Clarence laughed loudly at Prissy's reaction at the poop smeared over her shoes. "First good laugh I have had in a while." He saw Charley and Caroline land at that moment to help and added, "You two love birds did good."

"Jessica," Coach Tyree said as he pointed to Clarence, "that is the oak tree and that woman," pointing to Prissy Smart, "said it is diseased. She has a permit to take it down. I don't see any disease, but I don't have the expertise you have. I do know it'd be terrible to destroy such a magnificent oak that has been here longer than us or anything else in this area."

Coach Tyree and Jessica walked quickly to Prissy Smart and spoke briefly with her. Then they continued on to the tree.

Clarence instructed Peter, "Tell them nothing is wrong with me. That Prissy woman made it up so she could blackmail you into telling where you got the treasures."

Coach Tyree spoke before Peter could say anything, "Hi, Peter. I left early to bring Ms. Jessica Foster. She's a tree expert. She will determine if this tree has any diseases."

Peter nodded his head when his eyes met those of Ms. Foster, and then blurted, "There's nothing wrong with this tree. That is just made up."

"Hi, Peter," she replied. "Maybe so, maybe so; but let us look to make sure. Okay?"

She started about her work and, after a while looked back up at Peter, "How about you coming down now?"

"Not until those machines leave," Peter responded.

"Suit yourself, but be careful not to drop anything." She turned her attention to the tree and started to checked for any diseases.

"I will be close by if you need me," Coach Tyree said.

A small crowd gathered near Clarence and the machinery. Some humans were there for the first time after they heard the news on TV or read about it in the morning paper. Others, like Sakine Davis and Peter's teammates, returned from the day before. Peter waved when he saw them.

Sakine shouted, "How was the night?"

"Get any sleep?" Tommy Lassiter asked with a giggle.

Sakine asked, "You staying up there?"

"If I havta."

As the crowd grew, the humans in front were forced closer to Clarence and the machinery.

A policeman stepped from his cruiser and hurried towards the crowd. Prissy Smart intercepted him and said, "Hi, officer. I'm the person who called." She handed him the work permit. "These people are obstructing our work. Please move them."

He scanned the permit and handed it back to her. Prissy pointed towards the tree and said, "One person is up there."

The policeman walked to the crowd and said, "You folks have to move back behind the ball field fence corner." He then walked under the tree, and said in a stern voice to Peter, "Young man, come down. You are preventing these workers from doing their jobs."

Before Peter replied, the tree expert introduced herself and handed him her business card, "Hi, officer, I'm Jessica Foster. I'm here to determine if this tree's diseased."

He looked at the business card, then turned and looked at Prissy Smart to obtain some explanation. Prissy raised the work permit. He turned back to Ms. Foster and said, "They have a work permit to put in a field irrigation system and to take down this tree. I'm only here to provide security for her work crew so they can do their approved jobs."

"But sir, even if they have a work permit, it is illegal to take down a tree this size unless there's an exception such as the tree is diseased. So far, I haven't found any diseases."

"It is my job, ma'am, and it is only to provide security. Their work has been approved by the commissioners."

The size of the crowd had doubled by this time, and a man called out from it. "Officer, officer—over here, please."

The policeman recognized the individual, walked over, and said, "Good morning, Commissioner."

The officer's name was on the badge pinned to his uniform, and the commissioner replied after sneaking a peek. "Officer Randle, good morning. I'm Commissioner Jules Johnson. I saw this protest on the news, and I came to help resolve it."

"I understand, sir."

"Is the boy still chained up in the tree?"

"Yes, he is. His name's Peter Marshall and central dispatch has been called to locate his parents or guardians."

"You don't need to do that. I'm his mother," a woman near the front of the crowd stated. She stepped towards them. "I'm Vicki Marshall. The boy's mother."

Commissioner Johnson introduced himself, and Vicki nodded that she recognized him.

Officer Randle spoke, "Ma'am, you must remove your son from the tree. He has stopped these workers from doing their jobs, and they have a legal permit for the work."

Commissioner Johnson noticed that more people had arrived. *This must be a hot issue. Best head this thing off. My vote to take down the tree won't look good if that tree turns out not to be diseased.* "Officer Randle, let me see if I can resolve this problem."

"Okay. I will work crowd control."

"Good idea." Commissioner Johnson motioned to Vicki, "Let's talk to your son." After a step, he asked, "What is his name?"

"Peter. Peter Marshall."

Vicki smiled approvingly at Coach Tyree.

Coach Tyree walked out of the crowd and caught them in stride. Vicki glanced his way, smiled approvingly for his support and asked, "Everything okay last night?"

"Had an owl concert for a while, but yes. How about you?"

"John William did well. He is at the house playing an old video game of Peter's. The girls will look after him if this takes long."

"Commissioner, I'm Coach Tyree. Peter is on my team."

"Hello, Coach. Glad to meet you. Hope you can help with this problem."

They stopped where they could see Peter. "Hi, son. I'm Commissioner Johnson. I'm here to talk about why you are up there."

Peter nodded to the commissioner but looked at his mom. He smiled, "Hi, Mom. Hi, Coach."

Before he could say more, the tree expert introduced herself and handed them her business card. "Hello, I'm Jessica Foster. I'm checking this tree to see if it is diseased like the permit states." She paused for a moment and then continued, "Yes, I know what you're thinking, Commissioner. You approved taking it down because it is diseased, but maybe it is not. Sometimes mistakes are made."

Prissy joined them just as the tree expert finished introducing herself, and Commissioner Johnson suddenly became tense. Jessica Foster assumed it was due to her comment about commissioners making mistakes. *I better think of something to let him off the hook.*

She continued, "After all, Commissioner, you have to rely on staff and their recommendations. But, as you know, it is illegal to take down an oak tree this size except for something like disease. So far, I haven't found any."

"Did you guys hear that?" Peter whispered excitedly.

"Yes I did!" Clarence replied in a giddy tone.

Charley and Caroline also hooted delight.

"You have not found any disease?" the Commissioner asked as he directed a curious glance at Prissy.

Oops, Prissy thought. *He suspects something's not right with the permit.*

"No, not yet."

"How much more needs to be done before you're sure?"

"Well, Commissioner, I can tell you here and now there is no disease in this tree—unless something unusual pops up later when I re-examine the samples in my lab."

"How long will it take to complete your lab work?"

"I will confirm if there's any disease by mid-day tomorrow, and my written report will be completed by mid-afternoon."

"Please call me when you have the final results. My number is on this card. Also, please send me a copy of your written report so I can submit it to the commissioners."

"I will do that."

"Great, I appreciate your work and your service."

Jessica Foster turned back to her inspection and Commissioner Johnson turned his attention to Prissy. "Based on Ms. Foster's initial findings, it is fair to say the commissioners made a mistake in approving the work permit to take down this tree."

Prissy was politically wise. *I best get on board with this information.* Before Commissioner Johnson could continue, she spoke, "Yes, it is fortunate she found the mistake in the analysis that was used to draft our plans. I would regret taking down this magnificent oak and later learn it wasn't diseased. Commissioner, will you work with me to correct this error?"

Peter couldn't believe what he was hearing. Neither could Clarence, "I told you. We can't trust this Prissy woman."

"Yes," Commissioner Johnson replied. "Let me know when."

"I will call and come by your office."

"Sounds good."

Peter caught the attention of his mom and Coach Tyree and their eyes rolled as they heard Prissy Smart go on and on about being grateful in catching the mistake.

"I will tell the work crew to finish the irrigation system," Prissy said as Commissioner Johnson turned his attention to Vicki, Peter, and Coach Tyree.

"The tree is saved for now--at least through tomorrow. Here is my card if you need to get in touch with me."

Clarence, Charley, and Caroline let out a big "Hurrah!" and Maggie howled with delight from her hiding place down the hill.

"Thanks so much for your help," Vicki said gushingly.

Coach Tyree nodded in agreement, "Yes. Very helpful."

"My pleasure." Commissioner Johnson then looked up at Peter, "You can come down now, son. Nice work in saving this tree. Really good work."

Peter was too excited about saving Clarence to say much. He nodded his head, mouthed a big "Thank you," and unraveled the chain from around his waist and legs.

Commissioner Johnson thought about his vote. *Where did Prissy get the information the tree was diseased? And what's the big reason for plowing down all these other trees? Oh, well; what is done is done. Need to stop by the crowd.*

Peter dropped the chain and lock to his mom and Coach Tyree, and then spoke excitedly to his friends, "Clarence, you're safe for now, but we need to be on guard if those machines come back. Charley, you and Caroline and Maggie watch and come get me if they return. Okay?"

"Sure thing," the four said almost at the same time.

Clarence choked as his near-destruction emotions caught up with him. "Pe... cough, cough ... Pee ... ter. You... and..."

"What's the matter, Big Fella?"

"I'll never forget you guys. You saved my life."

Peter couldn't say a word. He sat on Clarence's thick branch for a few moments and leaned into the rough bark of his massive trunk. Charley and Caroline hopped onto Peter's lap, being careful not to hook their claws into him. Maggie howled sympathetically from her hiding place.

Peter struggled with his emotions. "Have to go. You guys are the best friends I ever had."

Vicki and Coach Tyree heard Peter talking, and then looked at each other. Neither said anything as they already had enough excitement. Little did they know, more excitement waited just a few steps ahead by the crowd.

[CHAPTER 31]

The Arrowhead is Real

Peter dropped from the tree, and walked over to his mom. They hugged like they hadn't seen each other for a long time. After a while, Vicki asked, "Ready to go home?"

"Yes."

"I will take these," Coach Tyree said as he picked up the chain and lock.

Commissioner Johnson, Prissy, and Officer Randle had already left the ballpark, but the crowd remained sizeable. Most of Peter's teammates were still there.

"Way to go, Peter," yelled Sakine Davis.

"You showed them," added Big Tommy Lassiter.

"Yeah," other teammates mumbled, and slapped Peter with high fives as he drew near.

Coach Tyree motioned for the team to gather around. Then he looked at Peter. "You already know about the things I'm going to say, so you don't need to stay."

Peter nodded and Vicki said, "Let's go home." As they walked away, she glanced back at Coach Tyree and said, "See you when you pick up John William."

Coach Tyree nodded and turned his attention to the team.

A woman, who had watched from the back of the crowd, stepped toward Peter and Vicki as they approached. "Excuse me, please. I would like to have a moment of your time."

Peter and his mom stopped and looked curiously at the woman.

Clarence noticed and said to Charley, Caroline, and Maggie, "Oh, no. Something is afoot. Another woman has Peter and his mom cornered. Look over there."

"I'm Samantha Peters," she said as she handed her business card to Vicki.

Vicki examined the card for a moment, handed it to Peter, and replied, "I'm Vicki Marshall and this is my son, Peter."

"Please call me 'Sam.'"

Vicki raised her eyebrows in a puzzled expression.

"Long story on the name," Sam responded and then turned to Peter. "Young man, your effort to save the tree was on the news last evening, but I'm here to talk about something else."

Vicki replied cautiously, "Well, I don't know," she said as she glanced at Peter and back to Sam. "It has been an exhausting few days, and..."

Sam cut her off, "This is very important. I promise—won't take a lot of your time."

"Well, if you hurry," Vicki reluctantly approved.

Clarence asked his three friends, "You guys hearing this?"

"Yup, but whaddas that Sam woman want?" Charley asked.

Peter heard Clarence and Charley, looked their direction, and shrugged slightly.

"Thank you," Sam continued. "I'm an archaeologist with the State. I specialize in historical artifacts of this region, and always have my eye out for them. These include items made by the Apalachee Indians." ... Then Sam looked intently at Peter, "Young man, I saw something dangle from your neck when you were on TV that looked like a real arrowhead."

As she spoke, Peter raised his hand to his chest and touched the arrowhead under his shirt.

Sam saw his reaction and asked with an excited tone in her voice, "Could I see it?"

Peter shook his head and mouthed, "No."

"I won't take it away from you," Sam replied to reassure both Peter and Vicki. "I promise. I want to confirm whether it is what I think it might be."

Clarence bellowed, "Peter, be careful. Remember your experience with that Prissy lady."

Now a total stranger was inquiring about the same thing. *What do I do?* Peter wondered as he looked at mom for help.

Vicki sensed his question, and she nodded, "It is okay."

Sam's hand quivered slightly as Peter put the arrowhead into her palm. "Oh, my! Oh, my!" she exclaimed as she examined it with an eyepiece like something a jeweler would use. She held it up to the sunlight, and the expression on her face looked like that of a child surrounded by numerous Christmas gifts. "Oh, my! It is real! … And in perfect condition!"

Vicki coughed to get Sam's attention.

"I'm sorry," Sam responded with an embarrassed look at Vicki. "I got carried away." She handed the arrowhead back to Peter and said, "This is a magnificent piece. The Indians made it from clear quartz crystal. That is why it reflects the sunlight like a prism. They believed these crystals had special, even mystical, properties."

Peter tied it back around his neck and let it drop behind his shirt and said, "That's what my friends told me when they gave it to me."

"Your friends gave it to you? Who?" Sam asked in a puzzled tone.

Clarence bellowed, "Careful, Peter!"

"Oh, just some friends," Peter responded.

Sam continued, "The Apalachee Indians lived in this area. Did they find the arrowhead around here?"

Peter squirmed and hesitated in answering, and Vicki spoke, "Peter is not comfortable in talking about that information right now. Perhaps when we learn more about you he will share."

"Yes. I understand. You have my card. Please call me soon. I can tell you the State would like to obtain this arrowhead and any other crystal items you have that is made by the Indians. This piece is valuable because it is rare and in perfect condition. I know the State would make a fair purchase offer, and the piece would be placed in the museum for public viewing. Please call me soon. At least, you would get an idea what the State would offer for it."

"We will look into what you say," Vicki replied.

"Great. Please call me soon." Sam repeated as she walked away. Then she turned, "Peter, please don't lose it or damage it!"

Clarence and the gang were ecstatic. "Did you hear her?"

"Just like we planned," Charley hooted with a puffed chest.

Peter heard his friends, turned toward them, raised his arms and mouthed a big "Thank you."

Vicki noticed Peter's actions. She wondered, *Are they real? If not, where did he get these treasures? What about...?*

A firm squeeze of her hand interrupted her thoughts. Peter looked at her with a Cheshire cat smile, and spoke so fast it made her head spin. "See, I told you the treasures are real, and we can sell them and save our house, and you can quit those extra jobs, and buy some new clothes, and go back to school, and buy sisses some new stuff, and you can come to my games and... if there's some left ... maybe I can get some ball pants and cleats."

His words stunned Vicki, and the ones at the end caused tears to flood her eyes. "If there is some left, maybe I can get some ball pants and cleats." *My Hun put himself last!*

Peter wondered why his mom was crying, but she didn't say and he didn't ask. Soon his mind was on Rosie's last game of the regular season. *Will I start? ... Is this the game I get my base hit? Can't wait! I'll be a hero!*

[CHAPTER 32]

Coach Strategy to Get More Pitching;

Bad News is Coming to Peter

"Coach," Sakine Davis asked, "with Peter out of the tree, is our last game of the season still on for Monday?"

"Yes, definitely. Please spread the word."

"Who do we play," Phillip Edwards asked.

"Phillip!" Coach exclaimed. "Which team is next on your schedule?"

"I da no," he replied with a shrug of the shoulders.

Sakine giggled, rolled her eyes and piped up with a sarcastic tone, "It is the Eagles, dummy. Don't you ever look at the schedule?"

"That is enough," Coach Tyree half-heartedly admonished them. "Let us talk about our last game. We are in 7th place, but we'll still be in 7th place even if we win."

"7th place! That sucks," Tommy Lassiter exclaimed.

"Let's not talk that way." Coach Tyree admonished the team.

"O-o-o-kay, Coach," Tommy mumbled with a sour face.

"Here is our choices as a team: Do whatever is necessary to win our last game, or do things to improve for the tournament?"

Jake Sanders shot his hand up to ask a question, but blurted out, "I want to win tourney games, Coach."

"Me too, Jake, but what is your question?"

"Umm-uh ... we have lots to improve, so whadda we do?"

"Good question," Coach Tyree responded. Then he looked around at the team and said, "One place is pitching. Yes, I know, Lecroy Carter and Rick Taylor have pitched well at times. When they threw strikes, we have won or stayed close in games. But during the season, they had several days to rest between games so they could back each other up. The tournament is three days in a row. All eight teams play the first day, the four winners the second day, and the final two winners play the third day in the championship game. If Lecroy and Rick pitch good like I know they can, we have a great chance of winning our first game and playing the second day. Our pitching'll be weak the second game if both Lecroy and Rick pitch the first game. So you see, we need more pitching when we play games every day."

Larry Johnson waved his arm in the air.

"What is your question, Larry?"

"How we going to get more pitching? No one else pitched much 'cept in the bull pen."

"Good point. I believe we can get an inning or two out of a couple of players who I've seen throw strikes."

"Who is that?" Tommy Lassiter asked in a doubtful tone.

"Jake Sanders and Larry Smith are two possibilities."

"Larry?" Terry Smith laughed in disbelief. "My brother can't throw hard enough to strike anyone out! His pitches look like lobbed banana balls, and so slo-o-o-ow."

"I can do better than that!" Larry shouted as he charged toward his brother.

"Hold on now," Coach Tyree cautioned.

"Those two are the smallest players in the league," Sakine added. "I can throw twice as hard as Larry."

"You are dead meat!" Larry Smith yelled at Sakine, as he glared at her.

"Come on, guys," Coach Tyree responded quickly. "Let us not get personal." Then he addressed the concern, "Larry does throw slow, but he can throw strikes—and none of the teams have batted against him so they don't know how he pitches." *Hmmm. Maybe we better keep him in the bull pen so it will be a surprise to batters when he does pitch in a game.* "Look, gang. We might not be able to get a little more pitching, but we need to try. That is the best plan right now. We will use our last game to improve so we can win some tournament games. Do you agree?"

"Guess so," a few of the gang mumbled softly.

"What?" Coach shouted back loudly. "I can't hear you."

"Yeeesss sirrrrrr," they yelled.

"Glad to help a teammate. Peter did great."

"Good. Now everyone go home, get some rest, and be ready for a busy week. See you Monday evening." Immediately, he held up his arms, "...and thanks for supporting your teammate, Peter, when he really needed our help.

Players sound off as they headed away, "Glad to help a teammate. Peter did great."

Rosie's lost its last regular season game 4 runs to 6, but using additional pitchers seemed successful since game pitching experience was the objective. Peter was so upset with his performance he spent little time with his friends after the game.

"I know. I know," Clarence said to his three friends as Peter peddled away. "I was supposed to break our bad news to him, but he was so down on himself in not getting a hit."

"Yeah," Charley squawked, "he didn't even say something funny like after most games."

Maggie added her two-cents worth, "Thought he would be bubbly since his family money problems would be helped by selling those historical treasures."

"We hav'ta do som'thin, deaah," Caroline hooted sadly. "Peta needs to know whads ahead before it happens."

"You are right," Clarence replied. "You and Charley let him know we want to talk to him before his next game. Okay?"

Peter went straight to his room. He picked up his Savoy bat, laid down on the bed, and slid his palm across its smooth surface. Tears rolled off his dirty face. After a long while, he whispered, "Dear Lord, there is only the tournament left. If it is not asking too much, could ya help me get a hit? I'm the only player on the team and in the league who doesn't have one."

[CHAPTER 33]

The Awesome Splendor of the Field;
Game Schedule for End of Year Tournament;
Peter Receives the Bad News

The head coaches met at the ball field to discuss the tournament rules. *Will this meeting never end?* Coach Tyree wondered. *Lots to do. Need to pick up John William, prepare a meal, do homework, wash clothes needed tomorrow, and whatever else.*

The sound of shuffling chairs startled him. *Finally over!* He was outside the second floor of the team building in a flash, but what he saw from the top of the stairs stopped him. "Wow!" he exclaimed as he looked slowly around the field. "Never seen it look anything like this!"

The late afternoon sunlight filtered through the large oak and pine trees. The beams penetrated at angles, and looked extra bright, like they were from powerful spotlights. Each one highlighted the aerial dances of tiny particles and insects. A brilliant patchwork of light and shadows covered everything. This picture would've been special by itself, but there was something else Coach Tyree or few others had ever seen before. It was absolutely breathtaking!

A white brilliance, which looked like snow, covered the field and nearby area. While the coaches had their early evening meeting, a dense fog had risen from the cool creek below the outfield fence. It covered the field in a layer about two feet deep. The patchwork of sunlight and shadows added to the brilliance. Altogether, the scene was breathtaking! … Simply breathtaking! … Maybe once in a life time experience!

"Is this Heaven?"

What an awesome sight! A chill moved along Coach Tyree's back and neck, and his mouth gaped open. *Does heaven look anything like this?*

Suddenly, he noticed movement by the large oak tree outside right field. *It is Peter Marshall. ... What's he doing?* Coach Tyree watched for a few minutes. *He is gesturing and acting like he is talking to someone. ... Hmmmmm—could they actually be real?* he wondered as he recalled his talk with Vicki Marshall about Peter's imaginary friends and later Peter camping in the tree to save it from Prissy's bulldozers.

A few minutes earlier, Peter had gleefully yelled, "What is up guys?" as he hit the brakes and slid his bike sideways up to Clarence's huge trunk. They didn't have time to answer, but he wouldn't have heard them anyway as his attention was on the fog covering the ground. He acted like a little boy seeing his first snow, and a barrage of questions poured out of his curious mind: "Isn't this awesome? Where did it come from?! It is all over the ground! Did you see me ride through it? Did you...?"

Clarence broke in, "Hold on a second. Hold on, Peter. You are going too fast. Catch your breath. Slow down, son. Yes, the white ground cover is a fabulous sight, but... We have something important to tell you."

"Yeeessss," Charley hooted in agreement while lifting his wings over his feathery ears and rolling his big brown eyes. "Oh my. Ya make me dizzy!"

Caroline's motherly instinct moved her to Peter's defense. "Ah, ma deaahs," she softly hooted, "Let 'em enjoy the beau-ti-ful look. It is so bril-li-ant in the sunlight."

Peter looked into her big round eyes, sent her a cheek-to-cheek grin of appreciation for her support, and continued, "Ever seen anything like this? It is so beautiful."

"Yes, but not this early in the evening," Charley hooted, and Caroline nodded her feathery head in agreement.

"I have many times," Clarence bellowed in his deep voice. "But only once early in the evening like this. It usually happens about midnight or later when few humans are around to see it. A cool moist air forms a fog in the creek bottom and it slowly moves up the slopes of the hill as temperatures drop with the night. The curve in the creek matches the curve in the outfield fence. When the fog gets to the fence, it filters through the wire its entire length about the same time. Looks like some unusual creature as it slowly moves across the ballfield to home plate. Not sure what keeps the fog from mixing with air above it to keep it within a couple feet to the ground as it moves along. Over time, as tempertures rise, the white fog just disappears.

As Coach Tyree recalled Prissy's bulldozing attempts to destroy the old tree in right field, anger flushed his face. He glanced at the time. *Late. I'll watch Peter from the pickup.*

Clarence continued, "I have only seen fog like this early in the evening one other time. About ninety years ago."

"Wow! That is a long time," Peter exclaimed. He walked around Clarence's trunk a couple of times, and then laid down on one of Clarence's roots that protruded above ground. "Look," he shouted excitedly to his friends, "I'm below the fog." He laughed and cut up for a while, but soon noticed that he was the only one laughing. He was puzzled. *Why are they acting strange?* They usually laughed and cut up and teased each other.

Then he remembered why he came to see them, "Charley said

you wanted to see me right away." Even this serious moment, though, couldn't keep Peter from staring at the fog cover on the ball field. He was mesmerized, much the same way a young child would be who plays in a rain soaked yard and makes mud pies for the first time. It's near impossible to dampen their glee and remove them before they are exhausted and soaked head to toe.

Peter's expressions were like that. "Isn't this fog awesome? It was like riding on a cloud. My head was above it, but my bike wheels were in it and stirring it up."

Then Peter saw Maggie nearby in the bushes. "Hi, Maggie," he waved and called out as he raised himself above and below the fog. "Haven't seen you for a while."

"Hi, Peter. Been busy preparing for the pups."

"That is awesome!" Peter replied, but he never made the connection that Maggie wouldn't come this close to the field or leave her den very long during broad daylight unless it was for something very important.

He did notice Caroline's unusual movement of her head. It bobbed gently up and down. It hit him that, *She is crying!* and his jovial expression changed instantly to eyebrows raised and an inquisitive stare. "What is wrong, guys?"

What they said next caused him to forget the fog and everything else until he slipped into his room at home.

Clarence began to explain, but he choked as he spoke. His usual deep and bellowing voice was somber and somewhat muted. He spoke like a friend who was trying to say goodbye to a dear friend. One who knew they would not see each other again.

The task was not easy or fun for any of Peter's friends. In moments, it wouldn't be fun for Peter, either.

"Peter, you are very dear to us, and we think you're terrific.

Uh..." He paused for a moment and gave a forced laugh as he said, "...that is, for a human."

"Ya can say that again," Charley teased.

Clarence continued, "Remember the time you first were able to hear us talk? How we became friends and we became part of your world?"

"Ye-e-e-s," Peter replied hesitantly, "but what you getting to?"

"Well, we heard your talk with others around the ball field. You needed some special friends, and we wanted to help you improve your baseball play. We heard your plea to God for help. We told you we are not God, but we knew we could help you and wanted to do that. We had no doubt we would do this when we learned that your father died when you were just a toddler."

Clarence began to choke again and stopped to gather himself. Maggie and Charley had sad faces and sniffed, and Caroline sobbed uncontrollably. Tears flooded her big brown eyes and fell on Peter below. Clarence dipped a branch to Charley, and he plucked a soft leaf for Caroline to blow her beak.

Clarence cleared his throat and continued, "Where was I? Oh, yes. Peter, you've really improved your baseball playing. Soon the final game of the year will be over, and that's when our friendship ends." Clarence paused, then said quickly, "There, I've told you."

"Not true!" Peter exclaimed loudly and jumped to his feet.

The response puzzled Clarence and the other friends. It wasn't what they expected. "What do you mean, not true?" Clarence asked.

"I'm not a good player!" Peter replied. "I still don't have a base hit. The season's almost over and I'm the only player who doesn't have one. Even that girl, Sakine Davis, has several."

"But your catching and throwing have improved so much. Why,

even your hitting has improved," Clarence countered. "We have seen you hit the ball well in the last games. It just happened to be at someone, who made the play to put you out. That happens to all ballplayers. You will get a base hit sooner or later."

Both Maggie and Charley were teary-eyed now and made sad sounds because they knew their friendship with Peter would soon end. Caroline's tears kept flowing.

Peter saw how they acted, and won-dered, *Why are they so sad about my not getting a hit?* His mind was blank for a moment. Suddenly he remembered the rest of Clarence's comments, "...that is when our friendship ends."

This statement stunned Peter, and his body sagged slowly to one of Clarence's roots. The words were rolling through Peter's mind, "*...that is when our friend-ship ends.*" His head tilted down, his eyesight clouded with tears, and his lips began to quiver. After a moment, he looked up and asked through tears running down his cheeks, "What do you mean, our friendship ends? ... I will still be your friend after the ball season ends."

Peter's teary reaction devastated his friends. Clarence could hardly speak. He choked so much he blurted out through tears of his own, "You don't understand. When your last game ends you will only remember us as friends whom you made up in your imagination."

"Why would I do that?" Peter begged for an answer, "You are my best friends. How could I ever forget you guys?" He repeated over and over, "You are my best friends. You are my best friends. You are...!"

"Yes, we know that. You've become our dear friend, too." Clarence assured him.

"Yes! That is right, sweetie! Ya betcha!" Maggie, Caroline and Charley howled and hooted.

"Then why do you want to end our friendship?"

Peter pleaded as he thrust his arms in the air. "Why can't we be friends for life?"

Clarence groaned in anguish and his deep voice reverberated across the forest. It was loud enough to flush some turtle doves from their perch half a mile away. "Oh, my," he moaned and shook his massive branches as if to stimulate his thinking.

"Hang on, dear," Charley said to Caroline and moved to brace her from being knocked off. "Clarence is having one of those body adjustments."

"This is more difficult than I remembered," Clarence said out loud. He gathered himself and continued to explain what would take place. "Peter, you are not getting the picture. Listen carefully. It is not up to us or you. When your last game ends, you will not just forget us, but you won't even remember we were once your friends. You won't remember talking to us or anything. We became friends because you needed us. Soon you will no longer have that need."

None of them said a word after Clarence finished. The silence spread through the forest nearby as if all the other birds and animals and trees were their friends, too.

Peter didn't move or say anything. He just stared across the ballfield. Minutes passed, but the silence made them seem like hours.

Caroline hooted softly, "Iz-ze alive?"

"Don't no," Charley hooted. Then he fluttered down beside Peter. "You okay?" he asked poking his feathery face into Peter's.

Maggie wiggled her head up through his arms, put her wet nose on his face and as an extra 'love' measure, she licked his chin.

Peter snapped out of his trance, "But I love you, guys. Don't you like me any more?" he pleaded through tears streaming down his cheeks.

"Yes! Yes! We love ya, too," the friends all said together.

"You even saved my life!" Clarence exclaimed warmly. "I wouldn't be here if you hadn't climbed into my branches and saved me from those monsters and that dragon lady."

"Then why don't you still want to be friends with me?" Peter begged for an answer.

Clarence, with wisdom from many years of living, finally understood. *Peter doesn't see the big picture.* Clarence began to explain what was taking place.

"Peter, we don't have any control of what is going to take place among the five of us and our friendship. It is the natural order of things, and we don't have any control in how this works out. If we could, we would remain friends and talk with you for life. But please understand, it is not our choice. This is your field of dreams—to get base hits and win games. Our friendship is only a part of that dream. When your last game ends, so does your memory of our friendship."

A puzzled look came over Peter's face and he opened his mouth to ask another question. But Clarence broke in, "Like I said, it's the natural order of things. All humans have imaginary companions from time to time in their lives. This happens most often in their young years. Sometimes these companions become friends because the human talks and plays make believe games with them. On rare occasions, these imaginary friends become so special to the human they even seem real and have names. They talk back and forth. That is what happened between you and us. We became real to you and you were able to see, talk, and interact with us. Remember all the things we talked about and did?"

"Yes," Peter responded sadly. "But you are real, and the things we said and did together were real. They weren't make believe—not just my imagination!"

"That is true. That is true," Clarence affirmed. "It is also true that the natural order for young humans is their world expands to include many different humans as they mature and grow older and bigger. The need to have imaginary friends gradually dwindles. And those..."

"But," Peter broke in but was stopped by Clarence.

"Let me finish," Clarence rumbled in a firm tone. "And young girls, like Sakine Davis, who are pesky and nuisances now, will soon become a big part of your world. You won't have time for imaginary friends, because you will be busy with life, growing into adulthood."

Peter jumped to his feet and shouted, "I will never like girls!"

"Yes ya will, deaah," Caroline hooted melodiously. "Girls become attractive oldah girls and then young women."

"Yup," Charley added with a giddy one-two hop, "Some day soon you will walk by one, ya'll turn 'round to look without thinking why, and your world will never be the same again."

"Yuk! Never! Never!"

Clarence continued, "So you see, Peter. It is not up to us or you. It is the way God created you. It will happen and you will not realize it at the time."

Peter and his friends were in tears now—hooting, howling, and bellowing in agony. Even the other birds and animals and trees of the nearby forest joined them.

After a while, Peter was silent again. His friends became silent, too. A long time passed and Peter asked, "When will this happen? When will I no longer remember you guys as my best friends? If you know, tell me."

"The end will come when..."

Clarence answered, "The end will be when you play your last game of the year. When the final out is made and you step across the base line at the end of the game, your memories of the friendship with Caroline, Charley, Maggie, and me will be just part of your imagination."

"You mean I won't have any real memories at all of you guys?" Peter asked through deep sobs. "Nothing?"

"That is correct. You won't remember us as real friends who talked to you, teased each other, and shared your dreams of playing baseball and learning how to be the best you can be. But, yes, you will remember us as pretend, imaginary friends you once had," Clarence managed to get out through big rumbly sobs.

After a moment, he continued. "It will be like a pleasant time when you walk through the park and see a big oak outside right field, two owls, or a grey fox. Maybe someday you will have a picnic under my shade, and I will get to hear how your dreams are turning out."

"If I do, drop some acorns to see if it triggers some memory," Peter mumbled while forcing a smile on his tear-drenched face.

The friends laughed at the idea even though it was a sad moment.

Peter suddenly stiffened. He jumped up, knocking Maggie and Charley away without realizing it, and shouted, "I don't believe you! You just don't want to be my friends."

His statement shocked them, and before any regained their senses to reply, Peter grabbed his bike, hopped on, and screamed over his shoulder as he pedaled furiously away, "I hate you. I don't want to ever see you again! I hate you! … I hate you! … I hate you!"

The four friends were stunned, and silence gripped the forest. Maggie maneuvered quickly to her den where pups'd soon occupy her time and mind. Caroline and Charley snuggled close together in comfort, and Clarence sadly drooped his branches like he was preparing for an approaching hurricane-force storm. Each was in deep morning.

As Coach Tyree recalled Prissy's bulldozing attempts, anger flushed his face. He glanced at the time. *Late. I'll watch Peter from the pickup.*

His eyes, though, soon fell on the tournament game schedule handed out at the coaches' meeting. *What is our strategy?* He snickered. *Can a 7th place team even have one?*

Unconsciously, he reached for his thermos in the pickup holder, popped the lid, and took a swig of coffee. "Yuk. Should have known. Cold. Been there since morning." Without looking up, he poured it out on the ground, and continued to study the bracket.

Tournament First Game Opponent and Team Rank: Apalachee (4) vs Pirates (5), Tigers (1) vs Conquistadors (8), Sharks (2) vs Rosie's Cafe (7), and Quincy Bombers (3) vs Eagles (6).

Tigers seeded 1st, Coach Tyree observed. *No surprise there! Won the season like the coaches thought they would.* … A touch of anger flushed his face as he thought, *easier to coach a team loaded with good players. Rosie's had to spend most of our practices and early season just learning to throw and catch the ball. Hopefully those coaches'll get their due some day. Surely justice'll level out.* A doubtful look appeared on his face. *Won't it?...* "Enough of that thinking," *he chastised himself out loud. "I like my Rosies Team, and we have a tournament to play."*

Coach Tyree's attention returned to the schedule. *At least Rosie's won't play the Tigers unless we get into the championship game.* He paused for a moment and snickered again when he realized what just came to mind, *Rosie's in the championship game!* ... "With our players?" he asked skeptically out loud as if someone was there to answer. "Why, our players haven't even pulled together as a team. Rosie's in the championship game would be a miracle!"

A grin spread across his face as he studied the bracket. *Rosie's plays the Sharks in the first game. They are seeded 2nd, but we can win since we lost by only 1 run each time we played. Who starts at pitcher? They have seen Lecroy Carter so go with Rick Taylor and, if he falls behind, bring in Lecroy. Who starts the game and who sits on the bench? Not much choice now since Angelica Turner and David Petri decided baseball wasn't for them. Wonder why David's father insisted he play baseball when David is so talented in music and wanted to do that?*

Hmmmm—All eight teams play first game Thursday evening, and the last game isn't over until after 11 PM. Bet the parents aren't happy with that decision with school the next day. Glad we are not in the last game. Why didn't the league officials start on Saturday and play the two second-day games on Sunday afternoon? Lots of parents sleep in on Sunday anyway. Oh well, not my call.

Suddenly, a dose of reality hit him. *Gads! If we win, we'll play the winner of the last game Thursday, and I will need to stay to scout it. Can't keep John William at the field that late. Maybe Vicki will figure she still owes me a favor, and take him to her house until I'm through.*

A side thought popped into his mind. *It will give me a reason to call her.* He looked up quickly from the bracket, stunned, and wide-eyed. *Where did that thought come from?*

Peter came to mind again, and he glanced at the oak tree. *Not there. Guess he has gone home. I will call Vicki later to see if he made it home okay.*

CHAPTER 34

Vicki's Last Dance with Peter's Dad

The back door banged shut, and Vicki barely caught a glimpse of Peter's back as he disappeared up the stairs. "He just walked in the door. See you at the game, Coach Tyree. Bye." A puzzled look appeared on her face. *Something is definitely wrong. Hun always gives me a hug before heading upstairs to his room.*

Vicki knocked softly, "You okay, Hun?" She didn't hear anything so she put her ear to the door and, after a while, knocked again. Still no sound and she asked, "Can I come in?" Silence! Nothing! She opened the door slightly and peeked inside. Her "baby" was sprawled across the bed, and he sobbed into a pillow.

She was shocked. Then tiptoed to the bed, sat down beside him, and gently caressed his face and hair. Peter threw his arms around her and clung desperately. No words were exchanged. Just a "Love ya" feeling learned through their mom-son moments over the years.

Peter finally managed to tell her what took place between his friends and himself. "Mom, they don't like me anymore." As the story unfolded, new streams of tears dripped off his chin and mingled with hers.

He repeated in an agonizing tone, "They don't like me anymore," and rambled on and on until he had said it all and slumped to the bed.

"Hun, I can't explain what happened between you and your friends. I do know you really enjoyed them. You described fun times with them, and you insisted they were real. You often said they were your best friends."

She paused to let him think about her words. "Remember how you told me they worked with you to improve your baseball playing? Would they do that if they didn't like you?"

She touched the arrowhead under his shirt. "And don't forget about these treasures. Why they gave them to you? Would they do that if they didn't care deeply for you?"

His breathing relaxed some. "Don't forget how you saved that tree you called Clarence. Only a friend would do something that brave."

Vicki paused and took a deep breath, but this time she said in a firm voice. "Hun, please don't let a bad moment ruin these wonderful times and friendships you have with them."

She paused again, and the look on her face changed. "Remember my telling you that your father looked forward so much to teaching you about baseball—about life?"

Peter sat up slightly, as the mention of his father always grabbed his attention. Hearing what he was like, his interests and actions and dreams helped to fill the void in the father-son relationship that never had a chance to develop.

The emotions Vicki experienced with the mention of Peter's father caught her off guard. Over the ten years since the accident, she had buried the painful memories in a box deep inside, but she was never able to lock it. To her agony, it popped open at that moment, and those memories gushed to the surface.

Now this very room seemed to her as it was when Peter senior stood over Little P's crib. *Oh my gosh! I had forgotten we called him Little P!*

"He had two daughters, but..." she smiled warmly. "You were a boy! It was like he had a new precious toy the way he picked you up and talked to you."

She paused to take a deep breath, "Well, he didn't live out

his dreams, but..." she choked with the next words ... "but... God provided you some friends to replace your dad in helping you learn how to play baseball." She stood and continued, "I think they have done a pretty good job."

She started towards the door, "Tell you what. I will bring my picture of your dad and put it by your bed for tonight. Okay?"

Peter nodded, "Yes," as he was all out of words.

"Good. Now rest. Be back in a jiffy."

Vicki picked up Peter senior's picture from her nightstand, and her eyes studied the dashing figure. Memories of that terrible night and the struggles she had experienced over the years flooded her mind.

At that moment, it seemed to her imagination as if he were dancing with her and talking. "Peter, we have missed you so much."

"I know, Honey Pie."

"Somehow we made it through that first year, but it was like reliving the same nightmare each day. Elizabeth, Sally, and Little P have grown so much. You would be proud of each one."

"Yes, they have. You've done so much to take care of all four of you. I'm sorry everything fell on your shoulders. Not easy. I'm proud of you."

"Little P wasn't old enough to know much about you, but I have told him so many stories about how great you were." She paused and forced a laugh. "Made up some, too."

"I'm sure you did," he chuckled in return. Then he shifted the mood to a more serious tone. "How are you doing, Honey Pie?"

"Insurance moneys ran out, but managed so far. Things better now, though. And, I'm going back to nursing school to get a better-paying job."

"That is what I figured if something happened to me, but..." he paused for a moment, "that is not what I'm asking. You are young and beautiful. A young woman needs to dress up and receive attention and have outings with men. You doing that?"

"No. I have been too busy getting our family through each day, and..." she paused for a moment as tears filled her eyes, "and I have missed you, too—so much."

"Have to let me go, Honey Pie. I can't be there."

Vicki pretended not to hear, "I have missed your touch, arms sliding gently around my waist, and your face snuggling against the back of my hair. Drove me nuts you know!"

"You have to let me go. Why don't you go out again? It has been ten years now. You have been faithful, but it is time to move on with your life."

"Just felt so guilty. Loved you so much. Still do. It has been so difficult without you. I would finally get the kids to bed, clean up for the night, fix my hair the way you liked, dash some of your cologne on one of your shirts, snuggle down inside it, and cry myself to sleep. The next day, I would start over again. It is the only way I could keep going.

"By day, I was the confident and determined mother and provider to our children. But at night and when alone, I struggled to survive emotionally and still be a woman with feelings and dreams and wanting you."

"Time to move on, Vicki. Time to let me go."

Peter senior's picture suddenly slipped from her hands and gently dropped to the floor. It jolted her out of the dream. She felt warm like they had just finished a dance and his arms had been around her. *It seemed so real—like he was here.*

She made sure the picture wasn't broken, and then she went back to Hun's room. He was asleep. Vicki kissed him softly on the cheek and sat the picture of his father on the nightstand. It would be the first time she wouldn't have it through the night. As she closed the door, she peeked back at the two Peters and whispered softly, "Good night, Hun. ... Good night, love."

[CHAPTER 35]

*A Dragon Raises Its Head Over Blue Jeans
and Tennis Shoes; End of Year Tournament
Starts; Peter Chases His Dream*

Clarence gazed around the ballpark at the hoopla surrounding the end-of-season tournament. "Ummm," he muttered as he sniffed the tantalizing smoke drifting from the hamburgers and hotdogs sizzling on the concession grill. *If they taste anything like they smell, eating one must be heavenly.* He took another sniff and mumbled, "I love these games."

"Me too, Big Fella," Charley hooted as he and Caroline landed softly at that moment.

"Oh, it is you love birds," Clarence expressed in a startled tone, "You have to squawk or something so I will know you are near." Then he asked, "Maggie coming?"

"Don't know. Soon to have pups, but said she wanted to be here since it probably will be Peter's last game."

"Hope she's wrong. These games lift my spirit. The excitement fills the air; and the buzz of players, parents, and fans slowly builds like the sound of a train approaching from far away."

"Yeah, know what ya' mean," Caroline hooted softly. "Ev'ry-one's a winner, at least 'til the first game ends."

"Yeah. Four games today and four teams will walk away, sad their season is over," Clarence added. Then his spirit fell somewhat. "Hope Peter's team isn't one of them." Clarence paused for a moment, then continued, "Anyone heard from him since we last watched him peddle away after telling him our friendship would end with his last game?"

"No!" exclaimed Charley and Caroline sadly, "Nothing."

At that moment, Peter pedaled into sight. He breathed heavily and mumbled, "Hope my friends forgive me."

Clarence heard and his voice bellowed across the ballpark, "We already have, Peter. Your mom came and explained everything to us."

"Really?" Peter asked in an unbelieving tone as he slid to a stop by Clarence's trunk. "Mom came to talk to you?"

"Sure did," laughed Clarence with a roll of his branches. "Nice lady. You should have seen her standing there, looking up at me, and talking like she knew we are real and could understand what she said. She looked around nervously, though, to see if anyone noticed what she was doing. It was funny!

Your mom also shared the great news that you two worked out an agreement to sell the treasures to the State, and how grateful she was for the financial help."

"Yes, we did, and..."

Clarence broke in, "We will talk later. Your team is about to take the field."

Peter noticed Charley and Caroline, and said, "Hi, guys."

"Hello," Charley hooted in a happy tone. "Glad we are still buddies."

"Helooo, Peta," Caroline added with a flutter of her big brown eyes. "Me, too. Play well, sweet deaah."

Peter replied over his shoulder as he hustled towards his team, "Thanks. See ya later."

"Wait!" Clarence suddenly bellowed. "There is that..."

"Can't, Clarence. No time."

"But it is that..." Clarence responded as his voice tailed off. "Too late," he added in a hopeless tone.

Caroline sighed, "O-o-oh, my-y-y-y," when she saw what was about to happen.

As Peter rounded the dugout corner, he had to stop in his tracks. "Hello-o-o, Peter," Prissy Smart said coldly as she blocked his path. "Remember me-e-e-e-e?"

Her voice and presence sent a chill down his backside. "You have one last chance to tell me where you found those Indian and Spanish treasures."

Coach Tyree counted heads to see if all the players had arrived for Rosie's game. *Peter is missing. Not like him after all we have been through lately.* Then he noticed him by the dugout. "Oh, no!" he exclaimed in an aggravated tone. "Prissy has him cornered again."

"I already told you," Peter replied bravely. "My friends found them. I have no idea where, except in a marsh near the coast. You can ask them, but they won't talk to you."

Prissy saw Coach Tyree hurrying toward them. She subtly

stepped aside from blocking Peter's path, and she changed the cold look on her face to one of warmth. "Hi, Coach. Good luck with your game," she said in a friendly tone. "I talked to Peter about those treasures again, and offered to buy them."

Peter was shocked. *What! She never said anything about an offer to buy them.* He blurted out, "They are not for sale!"

Prissy calmly replied, "Well, you guys are busy. We will talk after the game about this. Will your mother be here?"

Peter persisted, "They are not for sale 'cause we already sold them."

"What!" Prissy frantically expressed. The calm look was gone, and her voice tone turned downright hostile. "Well, what is that around your neck?" she snapped sarcastically. "Isn't that the Indian arrowhead?"

"Yes it is, but it's sold."

Prissy looked at Coach Tyree for an explanation, and he moved his head and eyebrows in an expression, "That is the way it is." He turned to Peter and said as he started to walk towards the team, "Come. We need to warm up for the game."

They took only a couple of steps when a dragon's harsh voice from behind commanded their attention. "Just wait a moment! Peter cannot play with you!"

Coach Tyree turned to face Prissy and asked in a stern voice, "Why not?"

"Because," she replied with a smug smile, "he is not in the same uniform as your team on the field. League rules require he has to be in uniform to play." She paused to let that reality register. "Your team will forfeit its game if he plays," she added with a fiery voice, "and I will have the league officials stop the game the moment he sets foot on the field."

Coach Tyree's anger was beginning to boil. He challenged her bluff, "Well, Prissy Smart, you will have to do that because Peter plays tonight." Then he turned to Peter and said, "Come on. We have a game to play."

Prissy stared as they disappeared into the dugout. She was unaccustomed to being challenged like this. *I will show them!*

Clarence, Charley, and Caroline observed the exchanges between Peter, Coach Tyree, and Prissy. Clarence said, "Gang, I can hear everything, but you two fly over there. This might get nasty, and Peter may need our help."

"Okay, Big Fella," Charley replied. "Ready, Dear?"

"Yes, Da'lun," Caroline answered and they flew to a tall pine tree and settled on a branch directly over the dugout area.

Coach Tyree waved the players over and explained what happened. As he finished, a man's voice called out, "Coach Tyree, we need to speak with you. Please step out."

Coach Tyree stepped part way around the dugout corner to see who had spoken. It was Jerry Cramer, and he was with Prissy and several other league officials. Coach Tyree looked at Prissy with a message in his eyes, *"Looks like you carried out your threat."*

Coach Tyree put on his cool and asked, "What is up, Jerry?"

"You have a player dressed in blue jeans and tennis shoes. As you know by the rules, all players must be in the same uniform."

Peter knew the comments were about him, and he eased to the side of Coach Tyree. Most of Rosie's parents heard the confrontation and gathered nearby too.

Vicki Marshall had arrived and was with them, and she wondered, *What is up with this? Coach assured us blue jeans and tennis shoes were okay this late in the season.*

Coach Tyree continued to speak, "Yes, but he has been dressed that way for several games. We understood it was okay since the family had some unusual difficulties."

"That is telling them, Coach," Charley squawked as he hopped up and down on the pine branch and flapped the air with his wings. He accidently pooped in his excitement, and it fell like a bomb. "Oops, look out below," he squawked. "Hope no one's under it."

Peter heard Charley, and glanced up in time to see where the bomb landed. An ear-to-ear grin flashed on his face as he snickered uncontrollably.

Prissy was irritated by Peter's reaction. *Disrespectful kid.* It added to her determination. She interrupted Coach Tyree, "Yes, that is correct, but the league agreed everyone would be in uniform for the tournament."

What? Jerry Cramer wondered with a frown, *league officials never discussed this issue.* Neither he nor the others would challenge Prissy, though, or override her statement.

As the talk between the adults took place, the rest of Rosie's team gathered unnoticed, except by Coach Tyree, in front of their dugout, and faced the field like they were being introduced.

"I'll be," he mumbled as a big smile spread across his face. *They have finally become a team!* Joyfully, he rebuffed Prissy's comment. "But, he's not out of uniform!"

Her eyelids narrowed and she replied in an angry tone, "What do you mean, he is not out of uniform?" She pointed a finger at Peter, "Just look at him! Blue jeans and tennis shoes! That is not the Rosie's team uniform!"

Coach Tyree looked calmly at Prissy and then at each of the other league officials. All of them had their eyes fixed on Peter and his blue jeans and tennis shoes. *Boy howdy, are they in for a surprise!*

He smiled and pointed over the dugout to the players lined up in front of it, and said, "Take a look. He is in the same uniform as our entire team and coaches."

Every one of Rosie's players had an ear-to-ear grin and was dressed in blue jeans and tennis shoes. Rosie's team was ready to take the field and warm up for its game.

"Look," Clarence bellowed across the field, "Prissy's foolish look is priceless. Might say it's a little payback for the misery she's given to every team and player not in her good graces over the years."

Coach Tyree gazed slowly at each league official, enjoying their stunned looks. He turned to Peter and said disgustedly over his shoulder as they walked into the dugout, "Come on, Peter. We have a game to play." He added, "Enough of these adult games!"

Jerry Cramer and the league officials departed quickly without a word. Prissy was left standing by herself, and fumed about what took place. Suddenly, she felt something warm oozing down her forehead. *What is that?* she wondered as she felt with her hand. She screamed as she jerked her hand back, "Bird poop!"

"You were great, Charley!" Clarence exclaimed and shook his leaves as he laughed. The park forest came alive, laughing, too, as word spread.

Prissy stomped off toward the restrooms, and made agonizing

sounds all the way, "Ooooooooo." Everyone, except those on the Tigers team, giggled after she passed.

As Charley and Caroline flew back to Clarence, he asked, "Did you see the foolish look on their faces when they saw the team dressed in blue jeans and tennis shoes? Never seen humans look so stupid."

"Yeah," Charley replied. "Priceless, and did you see the stare Jerry Cramer gave to that Prissy woman? If it could inflict injury, it would have been deadly."

"Yes, I saw it, too," Clarence responded. "Now, let us see what we can do to help Peter with his game."

"Yes, let us help him," Caroline hooted gleefully as she bounced around the branch with a lively country two-step action.

As Rosie's players trotted on the field, Peter asked Sakine Davis, "What is with the blue jeans and tennis shoes?"

"We overheard Prissy Smart talking about doing that to you. The team didn't want it to happen, so we made plans to stop it." She added with a grin, "Worked out pretty good, huh?"

"Yeah," Peter said warmly. "Did. Thanks." A curious look appeared, "How did you change with the guys in the dugout?"

Sakine sent him a "Don't ask" look.

Peter then turned to find another boy to throw with. He took a couple of steps towards one, stopped abruptly, looked back at Sakine and asked, "Want to throw with me?"

Clarence smiled like a proud parent.

Sakine did a double-take and looked at him. *What? He's asking me—a girl—to throw with him?* Then she replied enthusiastically,

"Sure," and fired a ball extra fast to let him know she wasn't letting up.

Didn't bother Peter as he thought, *Mom is here. Coach has me starting, and I'm playing all the first game. Tonight, I'm getting my base hit.*

Marilyn Davis walked up beside Vicki Marshall, who hurridly was walking to the ballfield to watch the Rosie's Team warmup. She'd missed most of Peter's baseball games, and wanted to be present his last few games.

"Hi Sweetie." Vicki turned her head to reply, but Marilyn continued, "Glad Coach Tyree was able to head off that problem."

"Hi. Me too. Thought I was in for a fast trip to the sports store, but..." she laughed softly, "with my little knowledge of baseball, I'd probably get football pants and cleats."

"So you are a newbie?"

"If that means someone who knows little about the game, that is me," Vicki confessed. "Peter says things I don't have the foggiest idea about, and I nod like I understand. I hear terms like: fielder's choice, on by error, sacrifice out, double play, interference with runner or batter, on deck, strike zone, player's cup, balk, rubber arm, and so on. It is frustrating!"

"Well, you will pick up what they mean quickly."

"Hope so," Vicki said in an exasperated tone. "I found an old disc of my husband's and I played it to help me learn about the game. Lot of laughing, but language was confusing."

"What was it?"

"Baseball. Something by Abbot and Costello. They talked most of the time about who is on 1st and who is on 2nd."

Marilyn laughed, rolled her eyes and replied, "Honey, forget that old baseball disc. Just stick with me. I will teach you."

"You have a deal."

Rosie's played exceptionally well and, after three-and-a-half innings, led the Sharks by a score of 3 to 1. Coach Tyree gathered the players around. "Rick, you have pitched well, but we are not pitching you anymore tonight. We are going to win, and want you available in another game. Jake Sanders is pitching next inning, and you take his place at short stop." Coach Tyree reasoned to himself, *Besides, we have Lacroy as a backup and I can always return Rick if he hasn't left the game.*

Rick and Jake replied, "Yes, sir."

"Good. Jake, warm up. Rick, relax that arm and let's give it more care after the game. Larry and Terry Smith, you are out of the game. Warm up in case we need Larry to pitch."

"Aww, Coach, both of us?" Terry asked as he kicked the ground in frustration.

"Yes, we need both out at the same time so other coaches won't remember which one of you pitches and which one hits."

"O-o-oh ... ah, right."

"Good. Phillip Edwards and John William, you are in the game. Everyone pull for each other. Understand?"

All players nodded their heads and prepared to bat.

"Look," Charley squawked gleefully to Clarence and Caroline. "Peter is on deck and warming up with his Savoy bat. Hope he finally gets a hit."

"Me, too," Clarence replied. "That boy's game has improved a lot, but he's been unlucky batting. He hit a hot grounder to 3rd base his first at bat, but was thrown out at 1st. Maybe this time it will be different. Cross your branches, er ... uh ... your wings."

"Hope so," Caroline hooted softly. "Hope so 'cause he has had a great addatude."

"Strike three. You're out," the umpire yelled. Phillip was out in three pitches. Now it was Peter's turn. He stepped into the batter's box. The spotlight was his.

"Nervous, huh?" Marilyn whispered to Vicki who was fidgeting on her bleacher seat.

"Yes. Didn't realize how anxious a parent becomes when their child bats or when a ball's hit to them. It's kind of like being in their shoes. ... Being them."

"It will be there every time, Sweetie. No matter their age.

Vicki looked disbelievingly at Marilyn and asked, "You mean I will never get used to this? The feeling will be there each time?"

Marilyn raised her eyebrows, tilted her head, and nodded.

Vicki sighed and replied, "Oh, my... and this is fun?"

Peter swung at the second pitch and smacked it hard in a line-drive between 1st and 2nd base. Vicki stood quickly and screamed in delight.

That felt good, Peter thought as he dropped the bat and started running towards 1st base. Two steps later his body sagged to a stop. The 2nd baseman dove and caught the ball in the air.

Vicki's delight was gone in an instant. She agonized with her baby still not having a hit.

"Out number two. Top of the batting order," sounded loudly and formally over the address system.

"Cha'lee, announce'a was cold," Caroline hooted softly. "No empathy fo' the batters."

Charley didn't have a ready response, so Clarence came to his rescue. "After the announcer watches sixteen thousand pitches in a season, there is not much emotion. Just another brush stroke on the final canvas of a win or loss."

Three Rosie's batters managed another run before the third out. End of four innings: Rosie's 4 and Sharks 1.

"Top of the 5th inning," the announcer blared. "Bottom of the order up for the Sharks." The announcer soon sounded, "Three up and three outs."

Rosie's was batting again, and Peter was sixth in the order. Clarence bellowed encouragement, "Hang in there tough, Peter. This is your time."

Peter waved from the bench and mouthed, "Hope so."

Sakine noticed, and elbowed his ribs. "You wave to your imaginary friends?"

"Yes," he replied and elbowed her in return, "and they are not imaginary!"

Sakine elbowed him again, but more forceful than before. "Come on. I know you saved the tree, but don't kid me you can really talk to them."

"Yes, I can," Peter replied in an angry tone. "Clarence and the two owls and fox have helped me to play better."

"O-o-o-o kay," she teased as she rolled her eyes. "If you say so."

Crowd noise grabbed their attention as Big Tommy Lassiter belted a pitch high towards the center field fence.

"Wow!" John William exclaimed. "Ever see a ball hit so high. May never come down!"

"Give us a break, Dumbo," Sakine replied sarcastically as she looked at him. "It will come down. Ever hear of gravity?"

Peter's eyes and mind were fixed on the flight of the ball, and he didn't hear their exchange. *Wish I could hit like that.*

"Homerun," Tommy gleefully blurted as he slowly rambled towards 1st base. He raised his arms in triumph.

Coach Sanders, who was coaching at 1st base, yelled, "Run, Tommy, run!"

Tommy finally built up some steam and rounded the base with his big torso. Then the worst thing happened.

"Oh, noooo!" Clarence moaned loudly. "The ball bounced off the fence top rail and back on the field. No homerun! Big Tommy will be thrown out at 2nd base unless somehow he can stop that big body and get back to 1st."

Coach Sanders yelled, "Back! Tommy—come back!"

The next worst thing happened. Big Tommy's feet tangled as he turned around, and he fell to the ground about eight feet away from 1st base.

Coach Sanders was only a few feet away, but the rules didn't allow him to touch Tommy. He could only point to the base and yell, "Back! Get back!" When he saw Tommy on the ground and the ball was on its way to the 1st baseman, Coach Sanders fell to his hands and knees and yelled, "Crawl! Tommy, Crawl!"

"Too late!" Charley squawked. "Big Tommy's outstretched arms were six inches from the base when he was tagged out."

Coach Sanders helped Tommy struggle to his feet. His clothes and face were covered with dirt. "Snot is oozing from your nose, son."

Without a thought, Tommy wiped his dusty jersey sleeve across his nose and smeared the snot and dirt across his face. *Coach is gonna chew on me for not running,* he thought.

Coach Sanders tried to look serious, but he couldn't keep from laughing. He patted him on the back and sent him to the dugout.

It was contagious, and Big Tommy laughed, too, as he walked brushing dirt and snot away. Soon the whole team teased and laughed with him.

Coach Sanders chuckled as he watched Tommy jabbering with the team. *Wonder if he knows he has torn the crotch in his jeans? They will let him know soon.* To his surprise, no one said a word.

Four other players batted before the third out, but no one scored. Phillip made the final out. Score: 4 to 1.

Caroline gleefully hooted to Clarence and Charley, "Look, Peta will be the first ta bat next time."

"Yes, dear," Charley responded. "We know. But he bats only if the other team scores three runs and ties the game. Don't want that to happen."

"Oh, not good," she hooted softly.

The Sharks lead-off batter in the top of the sixth smacked a line-drive over Tommy Lassiter's head at 1st base. "Hot potato coming your way, Peter," Coach Tyree yelled.

"Look!" Clarence said excitedly, "Peter scooped the ball on the run and threw to Sakine playing 2nd base. Runner had to stop at 1st."

"Way to go, Peter," Charley squawked. "Nice play."

Peter turned and mouthed a "Thanks" to his friends.

The next batter bunted and made it safe to 1st base. "Drat!" Coach Tyree exclaimed as he kicked the dirt in frustration. He followed that with, "Dag-nabit," when he realized the runners were at 1st and 2nd and no outs.

The next batter hit a hot grounder at Sakine, who was in the gap between 1st and 2nd base. "Make the play, make the play," Coach Tyree mumbled.

"Oh, Sakine!" Marilyn muttered in a disappointed tone as she watched the ball roll through Sakine's legs.

Coach Tyree saw Sakine make the error, and kicked the dirt in exasperation. "Guess that will teach me about changing pitchers. Counted my chicks before the eggs hatched." He grimaced as his mind raced ahead, *One runner will score and the other'll make it to 3rd.*

Then he saw Peter had charged forward to backup Sakine. He scooped the ball on the run, and threw it accurately to the catcher in time to keep the lead runner from scoring.

"Way to go, Peter!" Coach Tyree exclaimed as others yelled the same.

"He saved a run!" exclaimed Marilyn Davis as she tugged on Vicki's arm and pointed towards Peter. "Maybe the game."

"Really?" Vicki yelled excitedly. "Just for throwing the ball to that other player? Way to go, Hun!"

Peter nodded, and ran back to his outfield position. "Thanks, Clarence, for reminding me to back her up." He grinned and added, "They think I did that all by myself."

"We are a team," Clarence replied warmly.

Three on base and no outs. We need a miracle, Coach Tyree agonized as he studied his notes of the Shark's batters. *Next two are their best hitters.* "Time," he yelled to the umpire as he hurried towards the pitcher's mound.

"Jake, you pitched good, but we need to change now." As Jake trotted off the field, Coach Tyree's thoughts gave way to doubt. *Have to dump the game plan now.* He turned to motion for Lacroy playing center field when he noticed Larry Smith running towards him. "Coach Sanders has faith, so game plan back on."

The umpire said, "You have eight pitches to warm up."

A frenzy of laughter and jokes was building among the Sharks' team and parents as they watched the warm up pitches.

"Looks to me like there's good and bad news there," Charley hooted woefully as he observed Larry's pitches. "The good: he threw eight strikes. The not so good: all were slo-o-ow lobs."

The first two hitters licked their mouths like they were about to eat a delicious dessert. One yelled, "Homerun derby, here we come! We're gonna cream this guy."

"Yee-haaa, can't wait," the other batter replied and pointed his bat to the outfield fence. "Homerun to left."

An anxious father hollered from the bleachers, "Knock it out of the park, and bring in those runs!"

Larry wound up and threw the first pitch. The batter swung so fast his bat was past the plate before the ball arrived.

"Strike one," the umpire yelled.

The batter looked foolish, and stared at Larry with a "You are not going to do that to me again." He scratched his cleats into the dirt, and cocked his bat ready to hit. The slo-o-o-ow, lobbed pitch was enticing, and he swung before he realized it would drop in front of the plate. He fell forward to the ground on his knees as he tried to hold back.

"Strike two," the umpire yelled.

"Stop chasing those bad pitches," the Sharks' coach yelled. "None have been strikes."

The batter dusted himself off, and everyone could see he was steaming as a teammate yelled from the dugout, "Come on! The runt is making you look foolish."

Come on runt, he thought, *throw me a strike.* He didn't swing, though, as his coach's admonishment, "Don't chase those pitches!" made him watch it go by.

The pitch plopped into the catcher's mitt, and the umpire yelled out, "Strike three—you are out!"

The batter stared at him in disbelief, and Rosie's team and fans hooped and hollered.

"Well, I'll be," Coach Tyree mumbled to Coach Sanders who had joined him from the bull pen. "Do you think?"

The next Sharks player batted the same way and struck out also. This time, though, he swung at a couple of pitches that weren't strikes. Two outs, but three players still on base.

"Good coaching, huh?" Coach Sanders said half joking.

"You can say that again," Coach Tyree replied in an unbelieving tone. "Can't believe this is working. They don't know whether to swing or hold up. One more out and game over."

Clarence expressed to his friends, "Look at the anger of the Sharks coach."

"Hot under the collar," Maggie howled gleefully.

"Hi, Maggie," Clarence replied.

"Glad you could make it. Peter would be disappointed if he didn't see you," Charley added.

"Guess everything is okay, Maggie deaah?" Caroline hooted.

"Sure is. Soon though," Maggie replied softly.

"Hi, Maggie," Peter yelled out as he heard their comments. He was about to say more, but the next Sharks' batter was up.

Clarence shook his branches and bellowed with a laugh, "Maybe that'll distract him."

The batter barely connected, and the ball rolled back towards the pitcher's mound. "Make the play!" Coach Tyree yelled loudly as Larry scooped the ball and threw it in a slo-o-o-ow lob towards Big Tommy at 1st base.

"Get there," Coach Tyree anxiously mumbled. "Get there."

The ball hit Tommy's mitt almost at the same time the runner's foot. An eternity seemed to pass before the umpire made the call, "Out!"

The announcer called out loudly over the address system, "No runs scored, three runners stranded, and Rosie's wins to advance to the next game."

"And," Clarence added what the announcer left off, "the 7th placed team upset the 2nd placed team!"

"We are a team," Peter replied . . .

Rosie's players and parents and coaches were delirious with glee. "Guess the good Lord thought we paid enough dues during the season," Coach Tyree said with a chuckle to Coach Sanders as they walked to meet with the team.

As Rosie's players trotted in from the field, Sakine said to Peter, "Thanks for saving my bacon."

"We are a team," Peter replied and added a grin.

Big Tommy brought up the rear and said to Peter as he passed, "Nice play."

Coach Tyree said to the happy guys, "Larry gets a game ball for his pitching, but truthfully, all of you did something good in this game for us to win. We won because you pulled together as a team. Coach Sanders and I are proud to be your coaches." He looked around, "and that includes you parents, too. The players can't do this without your support."

He paused for a moment to catch his breath and let them enjoy the excitement of the win. Then he continued, "Tomorrow evening we play in the second game. Hustle home and get some rest." He quickly added with a big grin, "Let's wear the same uniform. It is lucky for us."

After the meeting, Peter and Vicki hugged deeply. "Glad you could make it, Mom."

"You were great, Hun. Marilyn Davis said your play to keep the runners from scoring probably saved the game."

Peter didn't reply. He just hugged. After a while, Vicki asked, "Ready to walk home?"

"Yes, but..." he replied as he started to jog towards Clarence, "I'll catch you. Hafta get my bike."

"Great game, Peter," Clarence said. "That pitching strategy of your coaches worked out perfectly."

"Thanks." Then a big grin spread across his face. "Sure did, didn't it?" He laughed, "Did you see those guys try to hit Larry's lob pitches? That was funny."

"You had some super plays in the field," Charley added.

"Sho enough, sweetee," Caroline hooted.

"Amen, Peter," Maggie added. "You have improved so much."

"I owe it all to you guys. Thanks, bunches. You are great." Then the tone of his voice became solemn as he continued in a whisper, "I don't... but I wish... uh, um..."

"You won the game and played well, Peter. Why so sad?" Clarence asked. "Is it because of that Prissy lady?"

"No. That is over now. I hope. It's, uh, it is..."

Clarence coaxed softly, "Come on, Peter, tell us. We are your friends, and we want to help if we can." He paused for a moment, "We are still friends, aren't we?"

"Absolutely!"

"Well, is it because you still don't have a base hit?" Clarence asked.

"Yes," Peter blurted out. "I practice hitting the ball, but it hasn't helped. I have hit the ball hard in the field a few times, but it's always caught or an error or I'm thrown out."

"Well, son, a hit will come some day," Clarence said encouragingly. "Just go out and play the game and support your teammates and try to do your best like today."

"You think maybe?" Peter responded. Then all of a sudden he hopped on his bike and started off, "Hafta catch Mom and John William Tyree. He is staying with us so Coach can watch the next game. We play the winner. See ya tomorrow."

The second evening of the tournament came quickly. In the first game, the Tigers team easily beat the Pirates 13 runs to 3. Afterwards, the Tigers coaches and players stayed to watch the second game between Rosie's Cafe and the Quincy Bombers.

"Listen to those Tigers," Charley squawked angrily. "They are making fun of Rosie's blue jean and tennis shoes uniforms."

"What is the matter? Can't you goofs afford real uniforms?"

"Our practice uniforms are better than your game ones."

"Better hope you don't win today, 'cause we will whip your tails badly."

"I have a mind," Charley added with a fluff of his feathers, "to fly down there and peck them on the noggin."

"Awe, hold on, Charley," Clarence cautioned. "They will get their due someday."

"Yeah, maybe in about ten years."

Coach Tyree heard the taunts and told his players, "Don't think about them. They want to get into your mind." Then he threw in a jab for confidence, "Must be afraid to play us."

Lacroy Carter pitched the complete game against Quincy's Bombers, and Rosie's kept the Bombers score to two runs. Rosie's scored five runs, won the game, and now faced the Tigers in the championship game.

Vicki had an anguished look on her face. "So tell me, Marilyn," she pleaded. "Peter was on base twice. One was a walk. Was that other one a base hit?"

Marilyn's eyes revealed the bad news before she spoke. "Sweetie, I, uh, wish I could say 'Yes,' but it was one of those fielder's choices I told you about. Sorry."

He still didn't get a hit, Vicki thought sadly. *And his other at bat was a caught fly ball.*

Clarence heard their comments, and said to Charley, Caroline, and Maggie. "Peter has only one game left, and he is the only player in the league not to get a hit in the season."

"Oh, m-y-y-y. Po' boy," Caroline hooted as she wiped her eyes with a feather tip.

"We have to do something to encourage him," Maggie yelped.

"Yes, you are right, but gang," Clarence expressed with sadness in his voice, "don't forget what happens at the end of Peter's last game. The next one is his last. And, remember? He loses memory of our friendship."

"Awe, I had forgotten," Charley squawked. "The next game?"

"Me, too," Caroline added sadly as she snuggled close to Charley for comfort.

"Yes," replied Clarence sadly.

CHAPTER 36

*Championship Game: Rosie's Café (7) vs
Tigers (1); Peter and His Imaginary Friends*

"Aw-w-w-w-h-h, at last," Clarence sighed as a breeze gently pushed his leaves. "Gets a little old, though," he grumbled as he stretched his branches, "camouflaging my movements so humans won't see them."

He gazed at the hoopla around the ballpark. *Already busy with coaches and players warming up, and early arriving spectators. Parents and grandparents never change. A few come early to obtain the choice bleacher seats or places to set up their lawn chairs. They sit up cameras to hopefully record actions of their young heroes. … How many actually view them?*

The concession stand already was open for business. Hotdogs and hamburgers sizzled on the grill, and the smoke floated away with the breeze to entice everyone, even passing joggers and walkers, to come and enjoy a delicious bite on this special occasion.

A nostalgic mood settled over Clarence. *This field—this place has lots of history. Will Peter's game be anything special to remember, or something horrible one wants to forget?* He stretched again and mumbled, "Not long 'til game time." His thoughts turned to his friends. *They should have been here by now. Hope they arrive before Peter does.*

Meanwhile Peter was about to leave the house. "Bye, Mom!" he called out as he landed at the bottom of the stairs with a loud "Thud." The squeaks revealed he was headed toward the backdoor. "Cleaned my room like you said." He added a muffled comment as the back door squeaked open, "Glad you're coming to the game."

"Hold on!" Vicki yelled anxiously from the kitchen. She hurried through the door with arms stretched forward. "Haven't you forgotten something?"

"Oh, yeah," Peter replied as he turned in his tracks. "My snacks," he teased.

After a warm hug, Peter expressed, "You smell good, and..." he leaned back and looked into her eyes, "And you look extra pretty."

"Even with blue jeans and a jersey on?" Vicki asked with a slight laugh. Then before he could reply, she said, "Better scat before we get emotional. I will see you at the game. Play well and..." she paused, "and tell Clarence and your friends hello."

"Okay," he hollered over his shoulder as he...

"And don't slam the..."

...closed the door with a bang.

"...door!" *That boy! Never can say it quick enough.*

As Peter pedaled to the ball-park he looked up to see Caroline and Charley flying overhead. "Hi, Mrs. Owl," he teased. "Hi, Mr. Owl."

"Hello, Peter," Charley squawked as they buzzed him like they did on the golf course."

"Yeah, Peta," Caroline teased, "Just hav'n a little fun."

Peter yelled with a laugh, "I'll pull your feathers when I get to the field."

"Not today!" Charley squawked as they flew by. "See you there."

Charley and Caroline soon landed on one of Clarence's branches. "Hi, Big Fella," Charley hooted as he folded his wings and tucked them to his body.

Caroline settled in beside him. "Hellooo, Cla'ence," she hooted softly. "Maggie said she would be late. Hoped to howl som-thin to Peta befo' the game is ovah."

"'Bout time you love birds arrived. Peter on the way?"

"Sure is," Charley replied, "be here soon." Before Clarence could respond, Charley continued, "Field looks great! New lines and ready to see who's the champs."

"It is pic'tu'esque," Caroline hooted with a warm glow.

Charley raved some more, "Balloons and team flags make it seem like big time."

"And if the breeze kicks up," Clarence chuckled, "they will float away." Then he brought up the sad topic that was on their minds, "Don't forget why we wanted Peter to come early."

Charley choked as he replied, "Been regret'n the moment."

Big drops of tears revealed Caroline's feelings. She nuzzled her head into Charley's neck and never made a peep.

"I see him now. Hi, Peter," Clarence bellowed in a friendly voice like just another day.

Peter didn't hear him, though, because of taunts hurled his way by Tiger's players at the concession stand.

"Hey, guys. Look! It's Mr. Blue Jeans," Billy Smart shouted as he purposely dropped his ball bag in Peter's path.

The mean act didn't cause Peter to crash as he was second-to-none in riding bikes. He jerked the front of his bike in another direction, regained control before crashing, and slid to a stop. His adrenalin pushed his anger to the boiling point as he thought, *There'll be no more taunts and facial expressions of, "What you gonna do 'bout it, Mr. Blue Jeans?"*

Clarence saw what unfolded. "Oh, no-o-o-o!" he moaned.

"What is up, Big Guy?" Charley asked.

"Look over by the concession stand. Tiger players are giving Peter a hard time."

Peter rushed at Billy and was about to punch him when a person stepped between them. He looked up, and was stunned. It was Prissy Smart.

"Now boys," she smiled, but looked mostly at Peter, "we can't have any problems. You have a game to play. Why don't you let your play on the field speak for you?"

Prissy noticed the commotion had attracted onlookers, and she smiled at their approval of her actions to stop the ruckus. *The dummies don't realize my Billy wouldn't be allowed to play if a fight broke out with Peter, but who gives a hoot for Peter if he can't play?*

"Now shake hands and go on your way," Prissy instructed.

They reluctantly slapped hands, and Peter headed on to Clarence and his friends.

Billy kicked the ground and responded with a smug expression, "Oh, Mom. I could-da handled him."

Prissy didn't respond until they were out of hearing from the other Tiger players. "I know you could, son, but do that on the field. Your team is far better and you can humiliate them like you did in the regular season games."

"Okay," Billy said with an ear-to-ear grin. "Can't wait. We're gonna score big time. Me an Tony Spanoza are pitching."

"I can't wait, either," Prissy said gleefully, and added with a sinister smile as she looked toward Rosie's dugout, "there may be a few surprises, too."

As Peter parked his bike, Clarence sighed, "Whe-e-e, that was close. Thought you were going to punch him. Glad that Prissy lady stepped in, but something about her. I don't trust her."

"Me, either," Peter replied.

Coach Tyree arrived early. *Bad case of the butterflies, and this is only a youth championship. Bet those big games in high school, college, or the pros create ulcers.*

He noticed Peter's movement by the majestic oak tree, and he reflected on the time when he and Peter spent the night to save the tree. *Is it possible Peter can really talk with them? Naw ... no way,* he concluded. He stepped into the visitor dugout, as Rosie's was the visiting team, and soon, he forgot about Peter as his mind was preparing for the game.

Clarence, Caroline, and Charley each recalled their friendship with Peter and all the things they had done since the moment he could understand them.

"Remember how we first spoke to you, and...?"

"How you, Peter, thought I was God?" Clarence asked.

"Yes."

"That was sumpin! Wazzin it, Cha'lee," exclaimed Caroline.

"How we started your practices, and teased each other?"

"And," Charley cackled, "how you doubled over when you was hit in the private parts because you weren't wearing one of those protector cup thingies?"

"An when you wuz bonged on the haid when we practiced catch'n fly balls on the golf cou'se?" Caroline added with a joyous squawk.

"Absolutely!" Peter exclaimed, "And, when Coach Tyree and I spent the night with Clarence?"

That comment caused the joyous mood to suddenly become solemn. After a moment, Clarence spoke, "Peter..." his usual bellowing voice choked to get the words out, "you saved my life. If you hadn't chained yourself to my branches, I would be only pieces of wood spread over the ground or hauled off to some forgotten pile and left to rot or burn."

Clarence shook his branches in an attempt to clear his throat and then continued, "Peter and the rest of you, I want you all to know I never dreamed I'd become so fond of a human."

"Ya can say the same for us, too," squawked Charley as he hopped up and down and flapped his wings.

"Yes, sweet Peta," Caroline hooted in a gleeful tone as she gazed lovingly into his eyes.

Meanwhile, Coach Tyree's deep thought was interrupted suddenly by the arrival of Coach Sanders and his son, Jake, hastily entering the dugout.

"Thought the teams weren't allowed to practice today on the field," Coach Sanders expressed in a frustrated tone. "Heard the Tigers had batting practice on it, and we came early in case we missed a call from you to get the team here."

The news stunned Coach Tyree, but held any response until after Jake took the balls to the pitcher warmup area. Then he turned to Coach Sanders and asked, "The Tigers were allowed to practice on this field?"

"Yes," Coach Sanders replied sternly and with a nod.

"Teams were told they couldn't use the field today. Who allowed that? Why didn't they tell us we could use it? Don't we ever get to play by equal rules? Bet I know who ... what person was behind this."

"Going to do anything about it?"

"Not much we can do now. I will say something later. Right now, we need to put the final thoughts to our game strategy."

They sat on the bench in the visitor dugout, and reviewed again, for what seemed like the hundredth time, their game strategy for how to beat the Tigers.

Coach Tyree leaned back momentarily and looked at Coach Sanders. "It is unbelievable," he pointed out. "The Tigers still have their two best pitchers available for this game. Tony Spinoza can pitch three innings and Billy Smart five."

"I know," Coach Sanders replied. "What a luxury! How did they come to have so many good players?" he asked sarcastically and roll of his eyes. "Oh, we know."

After a few moments, he asked the all-important question, "Who are you pitching after Rick Taylor?"

Both knew the league rules allowed a player to pitch only six innings in a week, and Rick had only three left. Lacroy Carter, Rosie's other good pitcher, could not pitch today.

"Not sure," Coach Tyree replied with a deep sigh. "Maybe we can get a few outs with Larry Smith, then put in a thrower."

Coach Sanders abruptly set up straight and asked in jest, "We have a thrower left?"

Coach Tyree answered half-heartedly, "You know the answer. None whose pitches come close to the plate."

"If Rick's pitching is on and we play decent defense, the score will be close through three innings. After that," he paused reflecting on a potentially devastating outcome, "the Tigers have the hitters to score many runs. We have to some how keep them off their stride."

Coach Tyree asked with a sarcastic snicker, "Think we could put your son's jersey on you and sneak you in to pitch?"

Both chuckled and Coach Sanders added, "That is probably the only way we could possibly win, but not sure even I could shut their batters down. Besides," he added with a note of humor to his voice, "...think the jersey would be a little tight."

"Well," Coach Tyree piped in, "the good news is..."

"There is good news?" Coach Sanders interrupted.

"Yes, everyone, except our Rosie's players, knows it will take a miracle even to stay close in this game, so we need to keep telling them to believe and they can win. And..." Coach Tyree paused briefly and a twinkle came into his eyes, "maybe the Tigers will be so overconfident of this game being a cake walk they won't play very good."

"Think so?" Coach Sanders asked in a tone like he half-believed Coach Tyree's pep talk.

"What else do we have? They won all but one game by ten runs. If we somehow stay close, the pressure will build on them." He glanced at the time, "Need to round the players up."

Peter's eyes flooded with tears as he asked about the subject Clarence and his friends avoided to that moment. "Is it really true that at the end of the game, when I step across the baseline for the last time, I will only remember you guys as my imaginary friends? ... Please," he sobbed, "please tell me it's not true!"

None spoke for a moment. Then Clarence stuttered sadly, "Ye-yes, it is true."

"But, you are my best friends."

"You are our best friend too," Charley hooted softly.

"My heart feels like it's going to break," Peter moaned. "Like how I miss my dad. I love you guys."

"We love you too," Clarence whispered warmly. He repeated, "We love you, too!"

[CHAPTER 37]

*Championship Game: Rosie's Café (7) vs
Tigers (1); Memory of the Friends
Comes to an End*

Coach Tyree spoke softly to his Rosie's players, "Grab a knee." They did quickly and quietly without the usual shoving and teasing. *They are serious,* he thought while he glanced around into their eyes. ... *A coach's dream. They have come to play.*

"The two best teams in the league play today and," he paused as smiles spread across the young faces, "and Rosie's is one of them!" He let that reality sink in for a moment.

"We are playing because we came together as a team. So remember, no matter what happens during the game, even mistakes, if we play as a team, we will be winners in the end."

An umpire walked up at that moment. "Coach, your team has the field to warm up as soon as the Tigers come off. Then we have introductions and the National Anthem."

"Yes, sir," Coach Tyree replied and turned back to his team. "Rick Taylor is better than any pitcher on their team. Remember: Good pitching will beat their good hitting."

A player's hand shot up. "What is it, Jake?"

"Who is gonna pitch afta Rick?"

"Oops," Coach Tyree said under his breath. *They know Rick can only pitch three innings. When I tell them, hope they don't panic.* "Good question. We have others who can pitch, and we will put in the best player for the moment. It might be for only one batter or one inning so all pitchers be ready to come in and out of the game. Might have to play other positions too."

Coach Tyree noticed, *No shrugs or negative looks. Answer satisfied them.*

"Just keep scrapping," he added. "We'll beat the Tigers if we play as a team and help each other out. Okay?"

There was no response. *Hmmmm. No hands up. No one staring off into the trees. Intimidated? We'll find out soon.*

An umpire broke the silence, "Ready, coach?"

"Okay, let's go get 'em."

"Glad you could make it, Maggie," Clarence said as he had failed to greet her when Peter was with them.

"Hi yah, Maggie," hooted Charley and Caroline.

"Couldn't miss Peter's last game. Did you remind him to stay focused?"

"Sure did," Charley squawked.

"Good. Tell me when you think there is a good time to encourage him."

"Shoa, honee," Caroline replied.

"It has bothered me that Peter hasn't had a hit for the year," Clarence confessed. "And there is only this game left. Any ideas how we might help today?"

"Well," Charley responded, "only things come to mind is your knowledge, Big Fella, of the strike zone and where to play on the field. Think it will help if you remind him about them."

"Yes, reminders would help," Maggie howled softly. "So," she added showing a mouth full of teeth as she teased, "Big Fella, you are the man."

"Well, I'll do what I can, but..." Clarence added in a solemn tone, "don't forget, Peter loses memory of our friendship at the end of the game."

Charley and Caroline didn't say a thing as they had shared their thoughts already. Maggie mourned, "I will miss him."

"We will watch from that tall pine tree outside center field," Charley hooted. "It is the only one that Prissy lady didn't tear down with her giant monsters."

"Leaving me-e-e-e?" Clarence asked in a teasing tone.

"This time, Big Fella," Charley hooted as he and Caroline flew away. "Better view. Can't see the game very well through your leaves, and," he emphasized, "you shake your branches when you get excited, and it is difficult to hang on."

"Yaa, yaa," Clarence retorted, but was interrupted by the team introductions.

An umpire walked up to Coach Tyree and reminded him, "Rosie's will be the Visitors and bat first. When names are announced, you will stand on the line from home plate to 1st base."

Peter stood at the dugout gate leading to the field. He kicked the dirt nervously as he waited for his name to be called. *Finally,* he thought happily. *Wanted this a long time.*

"Peter Marshall, playing right field." The sound blared across the ball field into the surrounding fans, and then faded away into the forest.

"Yea-a-a-a-a! Yee-e-e-e haw-w-w-w!" yelled his teammates, and mom, Sally and Elizabeth, and Rosie's fans and, all important, his friends: Clarence, Caroline, Charley, and Maggie. Peter's grin spread ear-to-ear when he heard their bellows, hoots, and howls.

Peter was so caught up in the moment he didn't even hear the introductions of the Tigers team or the National Anthem. Then the taunts started, and Peter returned to earth. Some were directed at him and some at his Rosie's team.

"Hello-o-o-o-o Mr. Blue Jeans," a Tigers player yelled loudly, "Forget your uniform?"

Laughter and snickers followed from other Tigers.

"Nice old mitt you have there; borrow it from the museum?"

Billy Smart laughed along with his teammates, then yelled something that he knew would get to Peter, "Heard you're the best hitter in the league."

Peter had ignored the taunts until Billy's. It made him burn with anger. "Easy, Peter," Clarence bellowed across the field. "They are just trying to get under your skin. Pretend you don't hear them and head on to your team."

Peter did as Clarence advised, but he could hear the taunts every step of the way.

"Bring us that Savoy bat, and we will give you one of our cheap practice bats."

"Your bike is so old no one would want to steal it,"

Then the taunts were directed toward the Rosie's team.

"Better hope this game is short 'cause we're gonna whip your tails badly."

"What is the matter? Can't you goofs afford real uniforms?"

"Our practice uniforms are better than your game ones."

"Huddle up," Coach Tyree yelled to his Rosie's team as he glanced towards the Tigers and then back to his players, "They want you to think about something else besides the game. Think only about what you need to do so we can win." He paused for a moment, then he threw an oral jab at the Tigers to build up Rosie's confidence, "They must be afraid to play us. Now let's show them we are the best team today."

The game began. The Tigers were on defense in the field and Rosie's was batting. The first batter grounded out to shortstop, 6-3, in only two pitches, and the Tigers players continued to make fun of Rosie's blue jean uniforms. The next three batters stunned the Tigers: two base hits and Big Tommy Lassiter hit a homerun for three runs.

One of the next two batters was on base with a walk and the other struck out. The announcer called out, "Two outs and now batting, Sakine Davis."

"Time," Sakine shouted as she held up her arm and trotted to the fence where she said something to the announcer seated above in the press box.

As she returned to the batter's box, the announcer said, "Correction. Now batting for Rosie's, Chan Chan."

"Why did she have the announcer call her Chan Chan?" Coach Tyree, with a puzzled look, asked his players. None said anything, but all had grins. Peter's was ear-to-ear.

Chan Chan struck out, though, and the Tigers managed to score two runs in the first inning. Yet, for the first time all season, the Tigers, the number one ranked team, was behind.

Peter had one at bat in the first three innings. He grounded out to the defender at 2nd base, 4-3, but did hit the ball hard.

"Oh, noooo," Clarence moaned. "His time is running out."

Charley added from his perch high above the field, "And he may get just two more at bats in the game."

The score after three innings: Rosie's 3 and Tigers 2.

Both teams had to change pitchers at the end of the third inning, so a short break in the action occurred.

Clarence, Charley, Caroline, and Maggie were excited about how the game was going. "Can you believe Rosie's is leading?" Clarence bellowed his question joyously. "Tigers haven't been behind after one inning all year."

"Yeo-oow, we know!" howled Maggie excitedly doing everything she could to stay out of sight, but stay up on the game.

"Fun, fun, fun." Charley and Caroline hooted as they hopped around on the tree limb.

"Didga notice…" Clarence asked gleefully with a shake of his branches, "The nervousness building among the Tigers and fans?"

"Yes," responded Maggie, "and they're making fewer derogatory remarks about Rosie's blue jeans and tennis shoes."

"What is wrong with the Tigers?" one of the parents moaned. "Act like they're not even playing a game."

"Don't know," another Tigers parent replied.

Another Tiger fan expressed nervously, "Not like them. We are usually ten runs ahead by now. We even have Tony Spinoza on the mound, and he is the best in the league."

"Not anymore," a coach from one of the eliminated teams added.

"Tony has to come out. He pitched three innings in the first game and could only pitch three this game."

"Oh, nooo! Who is replacing him?"

"Must be Billy Smart. He just walked to the mound."

"That is right," Prissy Smart, who had overheard the comments, expressed proudly. "He is as good as Tony when he is in the groove! But..." she added a boast, "Billy throws faster."

"Lookie there," Charley squawked, "That Prissy lady must be nervous about the game. She is usually in the announcer booth, but today she is out with the other parents."

A Tigers coach was standing near the fence and overheard the parent comments. "Glad we have Billy," he said to calm their anxieties. "Their first pitcher was really good, but he had to be replaced. The good news for us is they don't have much pitching left. Their other good pitcher, Lacroy Carter, can't pitch today."

"But coach, how did they get those three runs?" an anxious Tiger parent asked. "Thought Tony was unhittable."

"Blind luck!" exclaimed the coach. He laughed as he joked, "You have heard the saying: Even a blind squirrel can find an acorn once in a while."

When no one else laughed, he continued, "Well, Tony got careless with his pitches in that first inning. Their top hitters connected, and that big guy probably closed his eyes and accidentally hit the ball out of the park for a three-run homer. Wouldn't happen again in a hundred games."

The comment calmed the Tiger team parents, and a few nodded agreement.

"Now we'll take care of business," the Tigers coach expressed confidently, "and y'all will see lots of runs."

"Batters up," the umpire yelled.

Fourth Inning, Rosie's Chan Chan was first to bat.

"Look!" Caroline hooted excitedly as she bounced up and down on the branch and pointed a wing. "Pe ... Pe..." she stammered, "Peta..." She was frustrated because she couldn't get the words out, and her erratic movements  knocked Charley off their perch on the tall pine tree. "Oops," she squawked as Charley fell towards the ground.

Charley quickly regained his balance, but his flight was low over the field back to the tree branch. "Ya gotta be more careful," he started to hoot in an angry tone, but caught himself in time, "Sweetie."

The loud noise overhead and Charley suddenly flying near the ball field mesmerized everyone for a moment. All watch the two owls. When Peter saw who it was, his eyes lit up and with a grin, he mouthed, "Love you guys."

"Love ya back," Clarence, Charley, Caroline, and Maggie bellowed, hooted, and howled.

Vicki saw the owls too and noticed Peter gestured something in their direction. ... *Can he REALLY talk with them?*

Billy Smart's pitching was on target. He struck out Chan Chan in three pitches. When he saw Peter was next to bat, he motioned to his catcher, "I'm bringing the heat."

His effort to throw extra fast caused him to lose balance and he threw wildly. The ball ricocheted off the catcher's mitt, and smacked the umpire's mask so hard it knocked him backwards and almost down.

As the catcher threw the ball back to Billy, he snickered and said in a low voice to Peter, "He is going to throw nothing but wild fast pitches to you ... Mr. Blue Jeans."

The action didn't sit well with Peter's friends, and Charley hooted angrily. "Dose guys need a peck in da nose," he said. "Wan'us ta drop a rock or sumpin on dem?"

"Yeo-oow," Maggie howled in agreement. "Do it! Do it!"

"No, hold your horses," Clarence bellowed. "I would like to do that too, but we must let Peter fight this battle."

"Ho'ses?" Caroline asked with slightly crossed eyes.

"Guess Coach Tyree's western lingo's rubbing off on me," Clarence said with a chuckle.

"Oka-doak," Maggie teased with a grin that matched.

Peter heard his friends and nodded agreement. *I want a base hit.* "Come on!" he yelled. "Throw a ball near the plate!"

Billy threw as fast as he could. Peter's swing was late, and he hit it to the right, foul, slamming the ball off the fence that protected Rosie's dugout. Coach Tyree had to dodge to avoid being hit.

"Difficult to sit still, huh?" Marilyn Davis asked as Vicki jumped up and sat, jumped up and sat with each pitch and swing.

"Yes," Vicki replied in an anxious tone and without looking at her. "I wish Peter could get this behind him." She forced a laugh as she added, "taking ten years off my life." She screamed as Peter hit the next pitch in a line drive, just right of center field. "It's a fair ball!" she yelled excitedly.

Peter watched the flight of the ball as he ran towards 1st base. *At last! A base hit!*

Clarence held his breath as he watched the action. *The boy's going to get his base hit!*

A loud gasp sounded from every well-wisher as the center fielder made a running dive and caught the ball before it hit the ground. "Oh, no!" Coach Tyree mumbled. "Tough luck."

Peter stopped abruptly, and his body bent over as his hands went up beside his head. He agonized with what he just saw. *No hit. Just a hard line drive for an out.*

> *"Don't do it, Peter. Don't give him the satisfaction."*

"Heez not movin!" Caroline hooted in a motherly concern.

"Is he paralyzed, Big Fella?" Charley asked.

"No, just in shock, like we are."

Finally Peter stood erect, and turned to retrieve his bat. Out of the corner of his eye, he caught sight of Billy on the pitcher's mound, staring in Peter's direction.

Billy snickered and raised his hand and thumb in an umpire motion, "You are out!"

He knows I have seen him, and he's taunting me to show some angry reaction.

Clarence saw the same and bellowed, "Don't do it, Peter. Don't give him the satisfaction."

"You hit it hard. You'll get one, next time," Coach Sanders said in a forced positive tone and patted Peter on the back as he walked into the dugout.

Peter looked calm on the outside, but his inside was in deep turmoil as he agonized. *My last at bat for the year!*

The Rosie's players said something positive as Peter walked by because they knew how much he wanted to get a base hit.

"Tough luck. You hit it hard. Sorry. Next time."

Peter replied to each one, "Thanks," but under his breath he mumbled, "There won't be a next time. The game will be over before I'm up again."

At the back of the dugout, he forcefully tossed his Savoy bat in the far corner as if it was the cause for what just happened and his misery.

Chan Chan nudged in beside Peter standing at the fence and whispered encouragingly, "At least you hit his pitches. I struck out."

The next batter, Larry Smith, struck out for the third out. Rosie's players grabbed their mitts, and Coach Tyree motioned to huddle up. "Tommy Lassiter is in as pitcher. Rick's at short, Jake at 1st, Phillip Edwards in at left field, John William at 3rd, Larry out to warm up. Be ready."

"Aww, coach," Terry mouthed with a grimace on his face.

"Remember? For the team," Coach Sanders said as they headed out.

Coach Tyree slowed Peter on his way to right field, and instructed quietly, "I know you are disappointed, but keep your head in the game. Our team needs your good defense."

Once the players were out of earshot, Coach Tyree whispered to Coach Sanders, "I hope we can get a few outs with Tommy. Because he throws fast, it will be a huge speed change for the Tiger batterrs if we have to bring in Larry."

"Hope we can keep his wild throws down and doesn't walk many players," Coach Sanders replied.

"If nothing else," Coach Tyree said with a snicker, "his fast wild throws will keep them jumpy in the batter's box."

"We need to keep Scrubs Johnson at catcher so not going to use him to pitch unless we absolutely have no choice."

The first Tigers batter was a lefty. He swung at Tommy's first pitch and drove it high into left field where Phillip Edwards was playing for Rosie's.

"Come on, Phillip. Make the play," Coach Tyree begged as Phillip raised his mitt up in front of his head and ran forward to catch the fly ball.

"Now we will see if our fly ball practice pays off," Coach Tyree said out of the corner of his mouth to Coach Sanders.

"Will see," Coach Sanders replied skeptically. "Hope this isn't one of Philip's groundhog day plays again."

Rick, at short stop, saw where the fly ball was headed, and took off towards left field.

"My gosh!" Coach Tyree exclaimed. "Phillip has run in too far again."

Phillip jumped in the air and backwards in a desperate attempt to catch the ball as it passed over his head, and he fell to the ground. He started to pound the ground and cry.

"Ball will roll to the fence," moaned Coach Sanders.

"Get up, Phillip," shouted Coach Tyree. "The Tiger's batter will get a homerun on an error!"

"Run, run, run!" the Tigers coach yelled and jumped up and down. "Run to 2nd base."

As the ball rolled to the fence, Rick ran passed Phillip sprawled on the ground.

The Tigers 3rd base coach jumped up and down excitedly and shouted to his runner as he waived his arm in a circle, "Come on, run to 3rd! Run to 3rd!"

Coach Tyree noticed that Rick was about to pick up the ball at the left field fence. He yelled at Rosie's 3rd baseman, "John William, get to the base! Ball coming!"

Rick let the ball fly. The runner was on the way from 2nd base. Young John William was in position. The ball was near. The runner slid, and it was going to be a split-second play.

"You're out!" shouted the umpire as he threw his arm with thumb up at the runner sprawled too late across the base.

Coaches Tyree and Sanders looked at each other with stunned expressions. After a moment, they laughed hilariously. "Do you believe what we just witnessed?" Sanders asked.

Both said at the same time while still laughing, "Pretty good coaching, don-cha think?"

Of course the Tigers' coaches, players, and parents agonized over the opportunity to score the tying run or, at least, have a runner at 2nd base.

"Terrible coaching," a Tigers parent mumbled not so quietly in an angry tone.

"A-a-a-a-men," another agreed.

Rick, on his way back to his short-stop position, helped Phillip to his feet, handed him his mitt, patted him and said, "Can't catch them all."

"Pathetic!" exclaimed a displeased Prissy Smart. "At least the top of the batting order is up and we can get some runs."

Big Tommy almost hit the next batter with his first two pitches and, on the third pitch, did just that.

"Hey, throw the pitcher out!" came loud yells from the Tigers. "That was on purpose. He is one of our best hitters."

"No, it wasn't!" Coach Tyree yelled to the umpires in a voice loud enough for the Tigers dugout. "He just lost control."

The announcer called out, "Sub-runner at 1st and one out"

After two more wild pitches to Butch Anderson, the umpire warned Rosie's coaches. "If he comes close to a batter again, pitcher is out."

Coach Sanders asked, "Time to sub in Larry Smith?"

"Yep," Coach Tyree agreed. "Rode his pitching as far as we could."

A Tigers coach reminded his players. "Don't forget. You practiced against a slow pitcher this morning, and you creamed him when you batted. You will do it again when you hit today."

Butch drilled the first pitch down the 1st base line. Big Tommy, back at 1st, stopped it, but Butch beat him to the base.

"Runners at 1st and 2nd, and one out," the announcer called out. "Billy Smart at bat and Jami Lorenzo is on deck."

Great, Coach Tyree agonized as he looked at his notes. *The two best hitters in the league, and they will swing away.* He motioned for Rick to play deep in the hole at short.

Billy hit a line drive that normally would have been a ball over the head of the short stop and to the fence, driving in both runs. Instead, Rick ran, jumped, and knocked the ball down.

"Get an out, get an out!" Coach Tyree exclaimed anxiously as Rick chose, in a split-second, to throw out the lead runner at 3rd base, because there wasn't time to go to 2nd and 1st for a double play.

"Way to go, Rick and John William," Marilyn Davis and Vicki shouted.

"Batter safe on fielder's choice," the announcer called out. "Two outs, runners at 1st and 2nd and Jami Lorenzo batting."

Larry's first pitch to Jami was in the dirt, and Scrubs Johnson accidentally kicked it allowing the two runners to move to 3rd and 2nd. Jami hit the next pitch high fly ball over 2nd. "Oh, no-o-o!" Rosie's coaches and parents groaned loudly as it looked like a definite home run.

Charley had his eye fixed on the batter, and jumped off the branch as soon as he saw the ball was headed their direction.

"It is in the trees," Coach Sanders mumbled.

"Three run homer," Coach Tyree added in a discouraged tone.

"Look out!" Clarence bellowed at Charley and Caroline. "Ball is headed your way!"

Caroline squawked loudly, "Cha'lee, do sumpin!"

Charley made a quick acrobatic turn, like when he regained his balance earlier when Caroline knocked him off the branch, and flew into the ball at an angle so it wouldn't hurt him. The contact knocked the ball down to the field, short of the fence—no home run.

"Wow!" Clarence exclaimed loudly. "Great play, Charley!"

"You are the man ... er, owl," Maggie howled in a muffled tone.

"My daahl..." Caroline was so ecstatic she couldn't squawk or cackle a thing.

Peter watched the whole thing from his position in right field and heard everything between his friends. "Charley, that was cool!" he exclaimed so loud that Lacroy Carter, playing center field, looked his way curiously.

"Time!" the umpires yelled as they huddled together.

The Tiger's coaches ran towards the umpires and pleaded, "A

homerun should be awarded. It is like when the oak tree branches in right field are hit."

Coach Tyree and Coach Sanders hurried to the umpires and Tigers Coaches, and they blurted out a counter opinion. "The league doesn't have a rule for something like this."

"Yes, it does count," insisted a Tigers coach as he stepped towards Coach Tyree in a heated gesture.

Coach Sanders eased his large body forward as Coach Tyree rebutted the comment. "No, the homerun rule includes only the tree as an exception."

Tense moments passed as the umpires huddled by themselves. Soon they announce their final decision, "Dead ball. Hitter and runners allowed two bases. Two runs score."

"At least we're ahead now," a nervous Tigers coach expressed to anyone in hearing distance.

Still each Tigers player was taking chances to score more runs. Jami, who was on 2nd, tried to steal 3rd after a pitch was thrown to the next batter. Scrubs Johnson, catching, threw Jami out for the third out. The Tigers now led Rosie's 4 to 3, though.

Billy Smart continued his good pitching in the 5th inning. The top three batters for Rosie's order batted. Two grounded out, 4-3 and 6-3, and the other struck out.

Coach Tyree subbed Larry out as pitcher. He put his arm on Jake Sander's shoulder and looked him in the face, "Pitch like your dad taught you, and let your team help get outs."

"Wow, that inning was quick," rumbled Clarence as Maggie stealthily moved to a location behind his massive trunk so she could better view the field.

"Yeah," Charley cackled. "but Rosie's players are hanging in there. Nice plays by Rick and Chan Chan on the grounders."

The announcer sounded across the ball field, "Three batters up for the Tigers and three outs. No runs. Tigers lead Rosie's 4 to 3 end of five innings." A few moments passed, and a special announcement was made. "Folks, one inning's left in the game, and all concession items are half off. Last game, so eat up, and help the league."

"Doesn't look good for Peter," Clarence whispered. "Unless there's a tie, this is the last at bat for Rosie's. He's the fifth batter, and the way Billy's pitching, Peter will never get to bat."

"Does that mean...?" Maggie started to ask.

"Yeah," Charley interrupted in a negative tone. "He won't get another chance to get a base hit." Then he turned to Caroline and squawked, "Let's join Clarence and Maggie."

"Can cha do somthin' 'bout it, y'all?" Caroline pleaded.

"Don't see a way this time, Sweetie Pie."

Peter noticed Charley and Caroline when they flew over to Clarence and Maggie. He kicked at the dirt inside the dugout. He knew his getting a base hit was on their minds too. *Great friends.*

He knew the batting order, but walked to the dugout gate and glanced at it anyway. A dejected look crossed his face. *Fifth batter. The way Billy is pitching, I won't get another chance to get my base hit.*

Billy struck out Rosie's first two batters, and a big smile was on his face as he strutted around the mound and talked it up with his teammates. "See, I told you guys we'd shut 'em out."

A Tigers coach shouted gleefully across the field, "Strike out the next one, too, and let's wrap this championship up."

"Yee-haw! Ride 'em, Tigers!" Another coach yelled just to put a burr under Coach Tyree's saddle blanket.

"Yeah, get an out. End this," a nervous parent expressed.

Billy licked his lips, and was about to take on Rosie's next batter when he noticed his mom, Prissy, motion, "Stop. I want to speak to you."

"Time," Billy yelled to the umpire. "Something is in my eye," he pretended. "Can my mom come out?"

Prissy was on the field lick-e-ty split before the umpires or Tigers coaches responded.

> ## *"Peter will bat.*
> ## *He will bat!"*

"What is she saying?" Maggie asked her friends.

"Sounds like..." Clarence started to answer but stopped. "can't make it out. Something about Peter."

"Definitely heard them mention Peter," Charley hooted. "Didja hear anythin', dear?"

Caroline moved her feathery head back and forth, "No."

Prissy left as quickly as she came. Billy mouthed to his coaches, "I'm all right," but his pitching didn't show it as he promptly walked the next two batters.

"Time," yelled a Tigers coach, who was clearly 'hot under the collar' for walking the two batters. "What are you doing? Throw the pitches we signal to you!"

"Look!" hooted Charley excitedly. "Peter will bat. He will bat! He is getting another chance to get his base hit!"

Coach Tyree gave Peter a pep talk before he batted. "Pressure is on him because he is not pitching good. You have hit his best pitches. Do it again, and bring in those runners."

Peter nodded. He also heard the excited chatter of his friends, and he grinned and waved as he walked to home plate.

"This is your time!" Charley squawked so loud everyone at the game momentarily looked his direction.

This is my time, Peter repeated as he dug his tennis shoes into the clay of the batter's box.

"Something is fishy," Clarence whispered so Peter couldn't hear. "I have a hunch that Prissy lady wanted Peter to be the last out so he will remember and agonize about it forever."

Billy decided to throw a curve ball to intimidate Peter. It bounced in the dirt, and passed the catcher to the backstop. The runners advanced to 2nd and 3rd bases.

The Tigers coaches shouted to Billy, "Stop with the fancy stuff. Blow him away and let's go home."

The next two pitches were fast balls that would have been called balls. Peter swung and hit both foul. The announcer called out the count, "One ball and two strikes."

"Come on, Peter!" Clarence, Caroline, Charley and Maggie bellowed, hooted, and howled encouragingly. "You can do it! You can do it!"

"Peter is chasing pitches," Coach Tyree mumbled under his breath. "Time," he yelled to the umpire as he motioned for Peter to come. *Gotta loosen him up.*

"Exciting game, huh, Peter?"

"Yes sir!" Peter expressed excitedly.

"All your friends, even those owls, are watching. That was really something, that owl knocking the ball down."

"Yes, sir. Awesome! My best friends."

Vicki squirmed and expressed to Marilyn Davis, "Can't sit here any longer." She was already moving, "Too nervous. Let's stand by the fence. "Maybe hear comments on the field."

Coach Tyree continued, "I want you to understand that no matter how this game turns out, they will always be your friends?"

A sad look appeared on Peter's face with that statement, and it puzzled Coach Tyree. *Oops, what's this? Did I say something wrong?*

Vicki nudged through the crowd of mostly men and coaches to the fence. *Being a woman has some advantages*, she chuckled. Then quickly her attention was to the field. *Wonder what Coach is saying to Peter?*

"Peter," Coach Tyree continued, "The Tiger's coaches are playing their team to the right. They expect you to swing away because they know how badly you want a base hit. They don't expect you to bunt, especially with two strikes. But you know, Peter, you have bunted really well in practice. A bunt right now would be a big surprise."

He paused to let Peter think about the idea, then asked the bombshell question, "Would you bunt for the team?" He paused again before he added, "I'm not going to tell you to bunt. It will be your choice. Remember this: No matter if you bunt or swing away, we will all still be friends."

As Peter returned to bat, Vicki yelled. "You can hit him." It was so loud the volume surprised her. She glanced around, and observed, *No one noticed, so she yelled again.* "You can hit him Little P." The words stunned her, and she thrust her hand quickly to her mouth. For a moment, she wondered, *Where did that come from?* But knew the answer immediately. *Peter senior's spirit! He would be proud of Little P.*

A nudge in her side interrupted her thoughts. "Couldn't stay either," Marilyn expressed.

Vicki glanced and acknowledged Marilyn's presence and looked back to the game.

"Game is getting to you, huh?"

"Yes," Vicki replied without taking eyes off the field action. With a subdued laugh, she confessed, "Never thought I would be one of those moms yelling from the bleachers!"

"Thought so. It is addictive, and it gets worse. The more you know 'bout the game, the deeper you are hooked."

Clarence rumbled a reminder to Peter, "Protect the batter box!"

Coach Tyree noticed that Peter looked at the large oak tree for a moment and nodded before stepping back into the batter's box. *What is he doing*, he wondered?

"Play ball," the umpire called out to restart the game.

Peter was set, and Billy threw the pitch.

"Can't look!" Vicki exclaimed and lowered her head.

Vicki heard a voice, "Strike three!"

"Oh, no-o-o-o-o-o," she moaned. "My poor baby struck out." Dozens of scenes flashed through Vicki's mind of how Peter anguished in not getting a hit in any of the past sixteen games. *He was so sure he was going to get one this game. How do I convince him it's okay since he did the best he could?*

"Wha-cha tawkin 'bout?" Marilyn asked as she nudged Vicki sharply in the side. "Open your eyes, honey. Watch the game."

What? Vicki wondered. *Peter's getting ready for the next pitch. What happened? I heard a "Strike three."*

Marilyn read her thoughts, "It was the Tigers coach yelling

to get Peter to swing. Ump motioned it was outside and ball two. Watch the game," she admonished Vicki again.

The Tigers coach motioned all his players to move a few more steps back and towards right field. Billy threw the pitch. It was a fast ball, right down the middle.

"Don't let this one go," Coach Tyree said under his breath. "Ump will call it a strike."

Peter bunted the ball. Everyone was surprised. The ball rolled towards 3rd base.

"Run, run!" Coach Sanders yelled excitedly at Peter.

"Run, Peter, run," Clarence bellowed loudly. Then as if the friends couldn't see he said, "Look, the 3rd baseman is back too far and Billy is the only one who might be able to get the ball in time to throw Peter out."

"Hurry, Billy, hurry!" the Tiger's coaches, players, parents, and fans screamed at the top of their lungs. "Hurry!"

Billy lunged at the ball, snatched and threw it in the same motion towards his teammate playing 1st base.

"Run, run!" Coach Tyree yelled frantically while jumping up and down and swinging his arm in a circle at the two players on 3rd and 2nd base. "Go home! Go home!"

Peter was near 1st. The ball was on its way, and one runner was going to score to tie the game if Peter was safe. If he wasn't, the game was over.

The ball hit the Tigers player's mitt a micro-second before Peter stepped on the base, but... "Look!" Charley squawked as he bobbed up and down, "The ball bounced off his mitt and it is rolling down the fence."

"Pe-ta is safe, Pe-ta is safe, and he made it to 2nd base," Caroline hooted excitedly.

"And those two runners scored!" Clarence bellowed as he shook his branches wildly. "Oops, did any humans see that?"

Rosie's players, coaches, and fans were cutting up and laughing. "We are ahead! We are ahead!"

"Way to go, Peter!" shouted Chan Chan deliriously with her teammates to him on 2nd.

Hope it was ruled as a base hit, Coach Tyree thought as he waved 'thumbs up' to Peter.

"Was that a base hit?" Vicki asked in a hopeful tone.

"Don't know," Marilyn replied, trying to hide the doubtful look on her face. "Scorekeeper will announce whether a hit or an error on the throw. But…" she added in a positive tone, "two runs scored and we are ahead no matter how it is ruled."

Peter's heart pounded in his chest as he waited.

"Hitter on by error," the announcer broke the silence. "Two runs scored. Next batter: Phillip Edwards."

Coach Tyree was elated, but he was concerned about Peter. *How is he handling being the only player in the league not to get a base hit for the season?*

"Way to go, Peter. We are so proud of you," Clarence said warmly. "You knocked in those runs for the team."

"Youw man," Charley hooted. His chest was puffed up to about twice its size. "That was some bunt."

"Peta deaah," Caroline piped in, "You shouda seen the faces of dose players 'n coaches. Evah'one was su'prised."

"Thanks, guys," Peter replied happily. "Couldn't do it without your help. We are a team, remember?"

Phillip struck out in three pitches, and now the Tigers would have their chance to score runs and win the game.

As Peter warmed up in right field, Clarence asked a serious

question, "Would you rather have a base hit or drive in the runs that may win the game?"

Peter stood silently for a moment. Suddenly an ear-to-ear grin appeared, and he took off running to his dugout.

"Peter," Clarence bellowed, "You didn't answer."

Peter yelled with a laugh back over his shoulder, "A friend would know the answer."

Coach Tyree saw Peter talking as he ran to the dugout, and asked, "You okay?"

"Yes, sirrrrr!" Peter replied with a grin on his face, "We are ahead."

"Tell me," Coach Tyree asked, "how did you know to keep from swinging at that fourth pitch the ump called ball two?"

Peter grinned, "Clarence said, 'don't swing, as he heard their coaches told their pitcher to throw a ball outside my batter's box to see if I would turn to bunt or swing away.'"

Coach Tyree stood dumbfounded and shook his head slightly as Peter walked away. *Clarence, his tree friend, told him?*

Chan Chan tossed Peter his mitt. "Nice play, but," a mischievous grin spread across her face, "don't let it go to your head."

Other players made a special effort to pat Peter on the back or say thanks in some way.

"Great hit!"

"Way to come through!"

"Gave me a heart attack."

"Your son did super," Marilyn joyfully praised Vicki. "Ya gotta be proud."

"Yes, extremely so," Vicki replied, but her thoughts were elsewhere, *Little P, your dad would be proud. Very proud.*

Rosie's players were on the field warming up for defense when suddenly, they started screaming and running about. "Watch out! Yikes! What is happening?"

Coach Tyree looked up, and saw streams of water from the new irrigation system were spraying the field. *Our players' tennis shoes will slip on a wet field. Need to get it off, pronto.* He ran towards the scorekeeper's booth and shouted, "Somebody turn that off!"

"We'll get on it," a league official replied quickly.

"What is the problem?" Vicki asked Marilyn.

"Don't know. Heard a guy say somehow the timer that switches on the outfield sprinklers suddenly came on, and the lock to the box holding the timer is jammed. They hav'ta break the lock to be able to turn the timer and water off."

"Doesn't sound good,"

"You're not kidding! The wetter the field, the more difficult it will be to run, stop, throw, and catch. It is a disadvantage to Rosie's players."

After fifteen minutes of heavy watering, the lock was broken and the irrigation was switched off.

"Look," Vicki nudged Marilyn, "Coach Tyree is talking to the officials, umpires, and Tiger's coach. He doesn't look happy."

"Who turned that sprinkler on?" Coach Tyree demanded an answer. "My team will slip on the wet grass. Has to be sabotage since the key entry to the lock was jammed."

Clarence and the friends watched as the discussion played out. "Should we tell Peter who it was?" Charley hooted.

"No," responded Clarence. "We only saw Prissy in the area. We didn't see her actually touch the sprinkler box and lock."

"Don't ca'ah," Caroline squawked angrily. "I have a feelin' sheez the one."

"Think we will finish the game?" Vicki asked.

"You betcha. Be here all night if necessary."

"You are kidding of course?" Vicki laughed skeptically.

"Absolutely not! Put it in the bank. Baseball and softball people are nuts sometimes. Outfield grass is wet, but the infield is dry except that low muddy area by 2nd base where batters slide running from 1st base to 2nd."

Marilyn pointed towards Coach Tyree and the players. "See, the team is in a huddle. Going to the field." She pointed again to Coach Sanders, "Kept his son ready to pitch."

"Kinda sweet on him, aren't you?" Vicki teased with a chuckle.

"Time for the game," Marilyn blushed as she sheepishly replied.

The Tigers' first batter hit the ball hard, but on the ground to Rick at short stop, who threw him out, 6-3. "That is one," Coach Tyree took a deep breath and yelled to the team as he held up one finger. "Be ready," he admonished them nervously.

"Uh-oh, things not so good," Maggie howled nervously after Jake put the next two batters on base by walk and hit-by-pitch.

Coach Tyree looked at Coach Sanders and asked, "What now? Keep pitching Jake, or pitch someone else? Scrubs Johnson is too tired to pitch from catching." He paused for a moment and asked, "Is there anyone else?"

"Jake is done," Coach Sanders replied, "but I have an idea. We can try Terry Smith."

"But..."

"Yes, I know. Hasn't pitched. Threw good in the bull pen, though. He pitches like his brother, Larry. What do you think?"

Coach Tyree shrugged his shoulders. "Their best hitters are up. Maybe going back to slow pitching will get them off stride."

"Terry Smith now pitching for Rosie's," blared the announcer. Then added, "Concession goodies are seventy-five percent off."

"We are in deep trouble," Marilyn expressed to Vicki.

"Why is that?"

"Terry has never pitched for us in a game before. His identical twin, Larry, yes, but not Terry."

"Doesn't sound good."

In a flash, the Tiger's coaches protested, "He has already pitched in the 4th inning. Can't pitch again."

"No! They are wrong," Coach Tyree exclaimed as he hustled to the umpire. "Larry Smith, Terry's brother, pitched earlier. They are identical twins. See," he said pointing towards the brothers.

"I can't tell 'em apart except for the numbers," the plate ump said. He looked at the Tigers' coaches and asked, "Can you?"

They shook their heads, "No."

"Pitcher stays," the ump stated, and moved to his position behind the catcher. "Play ball."

Clarence, Charley, Caroline, and Maggie bellowed, hooted, and howled with hilarious laughs. "I'm about to split a branch. Those Smith boys been changing jerseys all season." Clarence laughed so much he choked, "And no one ever caught on."

The announcer blared, "One out and runners on 1st and 2nd. Butch Anderson batting and Billy Smart is on deck."

"We can lose in one swing," Marilyn said nervously.

"How can that be?" Vicki inquired with a puzzled look.

"Three of the best hitters in the league are up," Marilyn replied.

Clarence whispered to Peter, "Don't forget. This batter is a lefty, and he hits in your direction most of the time. Be ready."

Peter waved his mitt to show he understood.

Larry, in Terry's uniform, threw his usual slow lob pitch. Butch swung too early, and hit a long, foul ball just outside the 1st base line. It ricocheted off Clarence's branches.

"Ouch!" shouted Clarence with a chuckle, pretending it hurt.

Butch hit the second pitch foul, also long and high down the 1st base line.

"Slow down your swing," the Tigers coach instructed.

Butch hit the third pitch extremely high to right field. It was going to be in play.

"Oh, no-o-o-o-o!" Coach Tyree moaned as he watched the flight of the ball. *It is in the branches or maybe over the fence. ... Either way, a homer and we lose!*

"Ye-e-e-e haw-w-w!" yelled the Tiger's coaches.

Peter tracked the ball, and moved to where he thought it would come down. *If it doesn't hit Clarence's branches, I'm ready to catch it.*

"Eas-s-s-sy, Peter." Clarence whispered. "Ease yourself under the ball like we practiced."

The ball was descending. Peter was ready. The ump was in position. Coaches, teams, and fans held their breath.

Butch watched the flight of the ball as he walked towards 1st base. He thrust his arms in the air and yelled gleefully, "Homerun derby," as he expected to receive an automatic homerun when it hit the tree.

Somehow, though, the ball miraculously missed every branch of Clarence as it came down, and hit, ker-plunk, into Peter's mitt.

"Got it!" Peter exclaimed loudly and held up the ball for everyone to see.

The ump held up his hand with thumb in the air to signal a fair catch and out, and the runners hustled back to their bases.

"He caught it! He caught it! He caught it!" Vicki screamed happily. Marilyn joined in, and they grabbed each other's hands and hopped around in a circle like five year olds.

Rosie's team and fans were delirious with joy, and the sounds of their hoopla could be heard a few blocks away in Cascades park and on the golf course across the street.

The Tigers were stunned. No homerun and no runs. The Tigers coaches rushed towards the umpires and protested. Coaches Tyree and Sanders joined the group to hear the discussion.

Every human was too occupied with the umpires and coaches to notice the merriment that occurred among Clarence, Charley, Caroline, Maggie, and Peter.

"What a catch, Peter!" Maggie howled from behind Clarence's massive trunk.

"Fab'ulus, jus fab'ulus, deaah Peta," Caroline hooted while fanning herself with a wing and dancing with Charley.

"Awwwsummm, awwsummm, awwsummm," Charley squawked as he did a square dance circle-your-partner with Caroline.

"Ah-huuummmmm," Clarence muttered to get their attention. "Don't forget the other player in that catch."

"That's right! Sorry! Please forgive!" begged the others teasingly. Even Peter chimed in, "Couldn't dunnit without ya, Big Fella."

"Okay, all is forgiven. Now go win the game."

The Tigers coaches pleaded to the umpires, "You saw the ball was going to hit into those branches, right?"

The umpire who made the "Out" call replied, "Seemed that way."

"So how could those branches suddenly move out of the way?"

"Don't know. Gust of wind."

"You're kidding!" a Tigers coach expressed heatedly, while trying to keep calm. "It would have taken a 300 mph hurricane wind to move those branches that much. Got to be something else."

Coach Tyree glanced at the tree and noticed Peter near the fence looking towards it. He shook his head gently, *Nawww, can't be. That tree can't do that! But... I think? I saw it move!*

The umpire responded in a tone of "This discussion is over." ... "There was no ricochet. The ball clearly missed hitting the tree. Two outs. ... Batter up."

The announcer blared across the field, "Runners at 1st and 2nd, two outs, Billy Smart batting, and Jami Lorenzo is on deck."

"It is now or never," a nervous Tiger's parent grumbled.

"Yeah. At least we have two good batters up," another added.

"Show them, Billy!" Prissy shouted confidently. "Get a big hit, and win this game!"

Billy swung at Larry's first pitch and hit a hot grounder down the 1st base line. Big Tommy Lassiter managed to stop the ball, but he was playing too far back to make an out.

"What happened?" Vicki asked. "Any runs?"

"Nope," replied Marilyn. "Batter safe on 1st base, and the others held up."

"Dratt!" a Tiger's coach grumbled as the two base runners were held at 3rd and 2nd.

"Wheeee," Coach Tyree mumbled, "Great stop, Big Tommy." *Would of been the game if he missed that.* "Touch any base and get the last out," he yelled encouragingly to Rosie's players.

"Bases loaded, two outs and Jami Lorenzo batting," called the announcer. He added, "Concession goodies almost a give away."

Jami let two pitches go by. One was a strike and the other a ball. He hit the third pitch in a screaming line-drive to the fence between center and right fields.

"Oh my goodness," Coach Tyree mumbled. His heart sank when he realized neither Lacroy in center field nor Peter in right field were close enough to catch the ball in the air.

"Ball game is over," Marilyn said dejectedly to Vicki.

"What? How?"

"Two will score," she said pointing to the runners.

"Oh, no-o-o-o," Vicki mumbled. *Peter will be upset.*

"Run, run," the Tigers coach at 3rd base yelled and swung his arm in a circle to instruct his runners to keep running.

Billy saw where the ball was hit, jumped up and down with joy and took off towards 2nd base while yelling, "We won! We won!" He heard the 3rd base coach yell "Run," and glanced at him just as he altered his steps to miss the slick, muddy area in front of 2nd base.

At the same time, Peter ran to where the ball would hit the fence. He slipped on the wet grass as the ball ricocheted back past him towards 2nd base. LaCroy slipped to the ground, too.

"Get up, Peter!" Clarence bellowed. "Get up. Billy missed touching 2nd base! He will be out if you can touch 2nd with the ball before he does, and those runs won't count!"

A field umpire also saw Billy step over 2nd.

"Oh, my gosh," Coach Tyree said as he saw Billy miss it too.

"Stop! Stop!" yelled the Tiger's 3rd base coach to Billy. "You missed 2nd! Go back!"

"What ya saying?" Billy hollered, but then understood. *Missed the base.* He hit the brakes, but slipped on the wet ground himself and fell as he tried to turn around.

Billy and Peter scrambled to get up. All the Tigers players, coaches, and fans were yelling for Billy, and all of Peter's were yelling for him. The one who touched 2nd first would win the game for their team.

Peter was on his feet in a flash. *Chan Chan can't get there and Lacroy's not close enough. Have to do it,* he concluded.

"Come on, Peter," Clarence mumbled. "You get only one try to pick up the ball and beat him to 2nd. Snag it on the run with your hand just like we practiced."

Billy was closer to 2nd than Peter, but he had trouble getting to his feet. *Godda get there,* flashed through his mind.

"Peter has the ball," Clarence bellowed excitedly, "But not sure he has control!"

Every human screamed, "Get to 2nd! Hurry!"

Billy slipped again, stumbled to keep his balance and finally lunged to touch the base. Peter dove with the ball stretched out. In a bang-bang play, their bodies covered the base.

"Who? Who? Who?" squawked Charley, "Who touched the base first?"

"Couldn't see," Clarence replied in an anguished tone. "I think Peter did, but not sure he kept control of the ball. Billy is safe if he didn't."

"What is the umpire saying?" Maggie asked.

"Hasn't given a signal yet," Clarence answered. "He is looking down at Peter and Billy on the ground."

No one made a sound. An eternity seemed to pass.

Finally, Peter raised the ball in the air, and the umpire signaled, "Runner is out!"

"He did it!" Clarence boomed joyfully. "Our Peter did it, and Rosies wins the championship!"

"Peta is da hero!" hooted Caroline excitedly. "Peta is our hero!"

"We won! We won!" exclaimed Marilyn as she hugged Vicki. "We won!"

"We did? How?" a confused Vicki asked. "Those two runners scored."

"Yes. No. They didn't count, and your son is a hero!"

Peter crawled out from under the pile of celebrating teammates and coaches. "I hope I can still talk to them," he mumbled

as he hurried towards the right field corner. Happiness gave way to sadness.

"Wow!" Vicki replied to Marilyn as she looked out over the pile of wildly act-ing Rosie's players and coaches on the field. Suddenly she noticed Peter headed towards the big oak tree in the corner of right field. *What is he doing? ... But, she knew.*

"Yes, Peter, you are correct. You will remember us until you cross the first base line by the player dugout," Clarence rumbled. "Charley, Caroline, and Maggie are all here."

"I just a..." tears choked Peter's words, "wanted to tell you once more how much I love you guys. I will miss you so much, and hope somehow I can remember our great times."

"Us too," Maggie replied as she stuck her wet muzzle through the fence to touch Peter's face. "How 'bout one more lick for old times?"

Peter giggled with his wet cheek, "When I see..."

Clarence interrupted, "Your team is getting ready to shake hands with the Tigers. Best hustle over there."

"Come on, guys," Coaches Tyree and Sanders said laughingly as they pulled the players from the pile. "Need to line up and con-gratulate the Tigers."

"Awe. Do we hafta, coach?" a player asked.

"Yes. It is called being good sports."

As Peter shook hands, he spotted Billy Smart at the end of the Tiger's line. Thoughts flashed through his mind. *Would he make fun of their blue jeans and tennis shoes? Would he mock his rusty bike, or how old his mitt was, or that his Savoy bat looked cheap, or I still didn't have a base hit? Nope,* Peter decided, *he is not going to ruin this moment. I'm turning back.*

Billy saw Peter turn, and he hustled into Peter's path.

Oh, nooo, Peter thought as his eyes met Billy's. *Is he wanting to duke it out?*

Billy raised his hand, and Peter started to defend himself when Billy said, "Nice game, Peter. You played good."

Peter was stunned. "You, too," he managed to say as he shook Billy's hand. "You've got a great team."

"Thanks. See ya."

"See you around," Peter replied as a big grin spread across his face. He took a step towards Rosie's dugout, but Billy stopped him with a startling question.

"Wanna be on our team next year? We are gonna be good again, and we play lots of games with other leagues in the year."

Peter was flabbergasted. *The best team in the league wants ME ... PETER MARSHALL, to play with them! Wow! Something I have wanted all my life—to play with guys who are the best. Wow!*

"Well, whata you think?" Billy asked.

"Well, uhhhhh," Peter stammered. "Uhhhh..."

Billy added, "My mom can work it out. She can arrange anything."

"Thanks," Peter replied as he thought about being around Prissy Smart all the time, "but ... I'm on a good team. Rosies are champs. Havta go. See ya in next year's championship."

Moments later, Peter's mind was on his four friends. A flood of tears streamed down his face as he stopped at the first base line. He looked down at it, and memories with them filled his mind. *I don't want to give them up!* He gazed back to the corner where Clarence and the other three friends watched his every step. Peter mouthed a big "Thank you," and folded his arms  across number 46 on his chest signaling, "I love you guys."

Clarence rustled his branches and leaves gently, Maggie howled softly, and Caroline and Charley hooted their affection in return. Peter gazed back at them for a few moments, then stepped over the ball field line, and joined the wild celebration of Rosie's miraculous victory.

[CHAPTER 38]

Geronimo's revenge!

"Whacha doin?" Chan Chan asked Peter as she stepped into the dugout to get her mitt.

"Taking the equipment to Coach's pickup," he replied as he glanced at her. "Most of the team already has gone to the picnic. Mom just left with the bucket of balls."

"I saw her. Can I help?"

"Sure. Grab the bag of helmets," Peter replied while picking up the bigger bag. He grinned and added a jab, "It is the lightest one."

Chan Chan fired a how-dare-you stare and grabbed the helmets. As they trudged towards the pickup, she purposely bumped the bag he carried a couple of times.

Vicki struggled to carry the bucket of balls. Coach Tyree saw her and said to his son, "Let us help."

"Let me take that," the coach said as he walked up and reached for the handle.

"Thanks; heavier than I realized," she replied with a sigh. "Where is the team when you need them?" she asked in jest.

"Already at the picnic. Think they are taking advantage of parents being easy on them right now."

"Probably right," she agreed with a chuckle. "Why, look at me. I'm even doing something I've not done before."

Coach Tyree smiled and asked, "Where is Peter?"

"He and Chan Chan are bringing the other bags," she replied as she nodded to the dugout.

As they trudged along, Chan Chan brought up the game. "Thanks for covering for me on that last play." She confessed after a moment, "I didn't see him miss 2nd."

"No big deal. Don't think about it. We won, right?"

"Okay, I won't think about it!"

"Hey, that is too easy. You need to fret some," Peter teased. Looking up he added, "About to catch Mom and Coach."

As they approached Vicki, Coach Tyree, and John William, Chan Chan and Peter said, "Hi."

Before any of them responded, Chan Chan thrust the bag she carried towards John William and said, "Here, rookie!" Then before he could respond, she grabbed onto the bag Peter carried and they walked on ahead.

Vicki wasn't carrying anything now so she called out to Peter, "Want me to get your bike over by Clarence?"

Peter turned and asked with a puzzled look on his face, "Who is Clarence?"

Vicki and Coach Tyree stopped in their tracks and looked at each other with bewildered expressions. After a moment, Vicki pointed towards Clarence. "The tree where you left your bike. The one just outside the corner of right field."

"Oh, you mean, Big Fella," Peter replied as he continued his walk. He hollered over his shoulder, "Thanks for reminding me. I will get it."

Vicki and Coach Tyree stopped again, looked each other in the eyes, shrugged their shoulders and raised their eyebrows communicating, "Don't ask. I don't have an answer."

"Coming back next year?" Chan Chan asked.

"Wouldn't miss it. Think we'll be good. Told that Billy Smart we'd see 'em in the championship game again."

"Think so, too," Chan Chan said as she dropped her end of the bag momentarily. "Glad you are coming back."

"Me too," Peter replied. Then he thought of the future, *Maybe I will get my base hit!*

Coach Tyree looked at John William, laughed, and motioned him to head out to their pickup, too. "ROOKIE. ... Guess ya better earn your spurs!"

Vicki laughed as the three young champions moved along ahead of them. Then she turned to face Coach Tyree and said in a serious tone, "David, the year didn't start out very well, but things really improved for Peter the last of the season. I can't say how much I appreciate your helping to make it a good year for him."

Coach Tyree didn't say a thing for a moment, then confessed. "Actually, I was the one helped. The team, you, Peter, and his imaginary friends changed my attitude and reminded me what is important."

Vicki mouthed, "Thank you," and they resumed walking.

Oops, she realized. *I just called him, "David." ... Was that a slip? ... Did he notice? ... Did I mean it?*

Coach Tyree suddenly stopped, and Vicki stopped to find out why. *She called me, "David." ... Does that mean? ...* Then he turned to face her.

Vicki blushed and smiled warmly to acknowledge she knew what he was thinking.

"Does that mean?" he asked nervously.

"Guess so," she replied with a sheepish look on her face.

"Well, Rosie's Café has a group playing blues next Friday. How 'bout picking you up at 6, we eat and listen for a while?"

Vicki hesitated before responding. "Honestly, that is a little fast for me," she confessed, "and probably evem more for my kids."

David's brow wrinkled and a sigh showed his confusion.

Vicki rescued him with a gleam in her eyes, "How about we call it an 'appointment to plan strategy for next year's team,' and I will meet you there?"

David's face brightened, "Works for me. It is a date. Er ... uh ... appointment then."

Suddenly, loud squawking and hooting from the majestic oak outside right field caused Vicki and David to look that direction. Both wondered the same thing. *Could Peter really talk to them or were they just his imaginary friends? And why did Peter call the huge tree, "Big Fella" instead of "Clarence" like before?*

"Well, we did it," Clarence expressed to Charley, Caroline, and Maggie. "We helped Peter as we hoped we could." Clarence gently shook his branches and puffed out his leaves like he was bragging. "And we did a great job, if you ask me."

"I'm sure going to miss him, though," hooted Charley.

"Me, too. Wonda'ful boy," Caroline sniffed as she snuggled into Charley's soft neck.

"Had some good laughs," Maggie howled softly with a wolfish grin. "Remember how the balls bounced off his nose in our fly ball practice? Funny. Sure enjoyed those scratches, too."

"Yeah, that was hilarious," Charley chuckled as his big round eyes blinked rapidly.

Maggie curled up in the cool of Clarence's shade, "I'm exhausted. Going to hide here 'til safe to get all those goodies the humans dropped."

Clarence's mood changed from cheerful to deep sadness, "I will never forget how that boy saved my life. ... Never forget those dragons and monsters!"

"Me, either!" squawked Charley loudly. "Thinking about that Prissy lady still makes my feathers ruffle."

"Look." Caroline hooted as she twisted her head back and forth. "There she is with her son by their dugout."

"Sure chewin' on him," Charley hooted angrily. "She lost the game for them, not him. ... Com'on, honey bunch. Have an idea."

"Whacha idea, deaah?"

"We haven't pooped since 'fore the game," Charley replied joyfully. "Follow me, and open your bomb doors."

Maggie understood, jumped to the highest root, and howled excitedly, "Gotta see this."

"Drop a big one for me," Clarence bellowed with a laugh as they flew away.

"Mom," Billy Smart interrupted Prissy, "I love you, but ya gotta back off sometime!"

Billy's revolt stunned Prissy. No one ever did that—challenge her!

"I coulda struck both those players out instead of walking them, and..." he paused to catch his breath, "and who ever turned that water on caused that mud puddle at 2nd?"

Prissy stood in shock not saying a thing, so Billy walked off to the concession stand. "Hope there is a burger left," he mumbled.

Sudden squawking and hooting sounds caused Prissy to look up and see two owls flying directly towards her.

"Bombs ready, luv?" Charley asked Caroline.

"Yes, deaah."

"Bombs awaaaaaaaaaay!" Charley hooted joyfully.

Clarence bellowed loudly across the park area, "SLIM PICKENS RIDES AGAIN! GER-RON-I-MO-O-O-O-O-O-O-O-O-O-O!"

Peter and Chan Chan arrived at the pickup, and suddenly he looked up like a sound or something caught his attention.

"Did ya hear something?" Chan Chan asked with a puzzled look.

Peter didn't answer for a moment, and continued to gaze around the ball field and forest area. After a while, he looked at Chan Chan and replied, "Must have been my imagination."

END

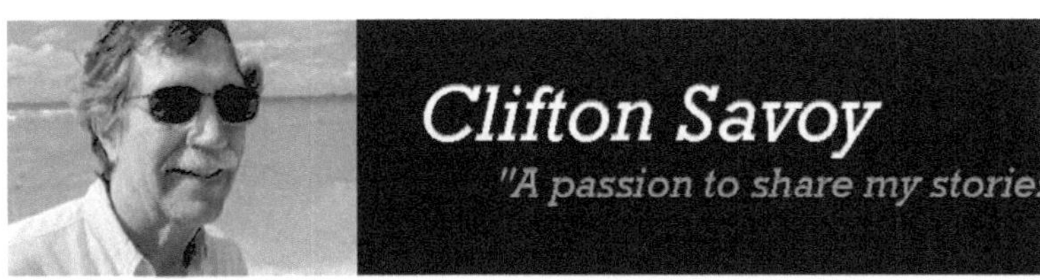

CLIFTON SAVOY IS AN AWARD-WINNING AUTHOR AND accomplished online international blogger. His writing passion is resurrecting true and unusual stories from the ashes of history. He has several published works and several 'soon-to-be-published.' His *Shades of Color* 'reveals the answer to all human conflict,' and it was a medal winner in the Florida Authors & Publishers 2023 book competition. His *Fred & Sally – The Decision* short story was a First Place winner in the Oklahoma Writers Federation 2022 Competition. *Fred & Sally* is a sci-fi romance and murder mystery, and is projected to be a three-book set.

Learn more about Clifton's published works or just join his writing blog at the link to his author website below. His Campfire Story blog is based on true events in history, and has an expanding popularity. In just ten months, it is now opened in over thirty U.S. states, including Hawaii, as well as internationally, crossing the Gulf of Mexico and both the Atlantic and Pacific Oceans. The blog is free, and you can unsubscribe any time. You can also send Clifton a comment there.

Please visit
www.CliftonSavoy.com